Christmas Comeback

Coleman Creek Christmas Book Two

Rory London

Five Hearts
PRESS

Christmas Comeback: Coleman Creek Christmas Book Two

Copyright © 2024 by Rory London

All rights reserved.

No part of this book may be used, reproduced or transmitted in any form or by any means, electronic or mechanical, including photocopying, recording, or by any information storage and retrieval systems, without prior written permission of the author, except where permitted by Law.

This book is a work of fiction. Names, characters, places, and incidents are products of the author's imagination or are used fictitiously. Any similarity to actual persons, living or dead, is coincidental and not intended by the author.

All products/brands and names/trademarks mentioned are registered trademarks of their respective holders/companies.

Print: ISBN: 979-8-9885129-2-9

Ebook ASIN: B0CNZNJXN7

Cover design by Alt 19 Creative

Editor: Jenny Sims at Editing 4 Indies

Editor: Erin McGibbon Smith at Three Black Cats Editing

Published by Five Hearts Press

*This one is for Britt. My ride or die.
The darkness keeps coming and you keep giving it the finger.
I love you always, and maybe a little more at Christmas.*

Christmas Comeback

Playlist

"Christmas Wrapping"
The Waitresses

"The Christmas Waltz"
Frank Sinatra

"Christmas in Hollis"
Run DMC

"Up on the Housetop (Ho Ho Ho)"
Gene Autry

"Mistletoe"
Justin Bieber

"It's Beginning to Look Like Christmas"
Bing Crosby

"The Christmas Song
(Chestnuts Roasting On an Open Fire)"
Andy Williams

"Like It's Christmas"
Jonas Brothers

"Do They Know It's Christmas?"
Band Aid

Chapter One

ELEVEN YEARS AGO

Will

I cupped my hands and brought them to my face, blowing over the numb skin of my palms. The gloves I'd discarded on the ground taunted me, but I couldn't work as well with them on. Frozen fingertips were a small sacrifice for the greater good of my art.

Ignoring the ice crystals attaching themselves to my eyebrows, I focused on my task, pressing my finger down on the hard plastic valve, feeling the rush of power from the aerosol can as the paint sprayed evenly across the concrete wall. Good. I'd been working on that, practicing in the gardener's shed out back where my parents never bothered me. This was the third time I'd done this. The first two times, I'd been shitty at it, leaving drips and drags. But I had my technique down now.

I worked faster to finish my piece, the cutting wind harder to ignore. It bit at me and broke my concentration—unsurprising since it was two in the morning in the middle of December. Not to mention, this part of Seattle mainly consisted of warehouses and office buildings. The little patch of brown grass where I'd dropped my gloves was lonely next to all the concrete and asphalt.

The wind blew overspray onto my black coat. I'd have to check it when I got home. If I couldn't wash it myself, I'd need to toss it and say it got lost. Josefina came in twice a week to keep house and do laundry, and she'd report it to my parents if she found my clothes covered in paint.

Riley stood ten feet away. He shook his can hard, the ball rattling around inside, sounding like a goddamn bullhorn in the quiet night. He laughed like a lunatic at whatever he'd done.

"Shhhhh!" I hissed. "Keep it down."

"Dude. Nobody's around. You need to relax." He shook his head at me but stopped shaking the can.

He was probably right. We hadn't seen anyone since we rolled up half an hour ago. A few cars had passed by, but none came close enough to spot us. Some buildings had Christmas lights shining along their rooflines—I assumed those businesses just left them on all night—but they weren't exactly spotlights.

I stepped back from the wall to survey my work.

"Billy...you corny motherfucker."

Riley came over to stand behind me. He grinned and pointed at my mini mural of a row of three Grinches. Each one was alike, except they were making different hand gestures. The first Grinch had his fingers pinched in devil horns, the second Grinch threw up the middle finger, and the third made the ASL sign for *I love you*.

"What?" I smirked. "I think it looks good."

"You know it does, asshole." His grin turned into a laugh. "But here I was thinking we were trying to be badass vandals, and instead, you're some kind of *ar-teeste*." He raised his pinky finger in salute.

Smacking his arm down, I glanced over at his tag. He'd been working on it, but it still didn't look like much to me. A bunch of triangles, basically. He'd been trying to get me to make up my own tag, but I'd drawn the line at that. I wasn't trying to be some poseur. I could convince myself doing this was okay if I called it art.

Riley had been tagging for a while. I guessed he wanted to be part of something, and I could relate. We'd both graduated from high school six months ago. He didn't have the grades for college and wasn't interested in trade school. I'd had a rough go of it the past few years and decided I needed a gap year. My parents agreed, on the condition I spend at least part of my time working. They'd tried to get me to intern at my dad's fancy financial services firm, but I was not doing that. I got a job busing tables at a steakhouse downtown. I'd met Riley there.

We'd become fast friends, united by our lack of direction, even coming from very different backgrounds. I'd grown up with money and gone to private schools my whole life, mostly a loner, with a few exceptions. He'd gotten a diploma from an online alternative high school and seemed desperate for a social life, instigating most of our hangouts. He'd been tagging on and off for years and had convinced me to come out with him a few times over the past month.

"I'm just giving you shit, man. It's good," Riley said. "But why is he doing something savage in the first two and then something schmoopy in the last one?"

"Schmoopy?" I chuckled low, still conscious of the silent street. "It's my way of saying the Grinch is very misunderstood."

He punched me in the shoulder playfully and made a gagging noise. "What'd I say? Corny as fuck."

I slugged him back, but didn't reply. I didn't care if he understood. Or if anyone did. My art was about the only thing that made sense to me. Inspiration struck how it struck, and that was the end of it. Christmas was my favorite time of year and always had been. Don't get me wrong, I wasn't going to wear some stupid reindeer sweater or join a caroling group. I just loved that it was the one time of year I knew what to expect. My parents were busy, but they always made a point of having a big family Christmas, even with just the three of us. I had held on to it year after year as a reminder that my family, while at least moderately fucked up, wasn't completely hopeless. Maybe I was a corny motherfucker.

"What do you think of mine?" Riley asked.

"It's...your tag," I said, trying not to smile.

"Asshole."

He was shoving our supplies into his backpack when a loud, unmistakable sound split the frigid air.

WOOP... WOOP... WOOP...

The red and blue lights of a police cruiser flicked in the distance, three or four blocks away. *Fuck! Had someone seen us and called the cops?*

"Get the shit, man!" All traces of the laughter in Riley's voice from a moment ago had vanished. I looked over to see him wide-eyed and frantic.

He grabbed the backpack, not even bothering with the zipper, as I picked up three loose paint cans. We ran around the corner toward Riley's car, which he'd parked two blocks away. No streetlamps shined on this area. Just one building had a few sad strings of Christmas lights above its entrance. I doubted a cop would be able to spot us if we crouched along the wall for a minute, but Riley seemed determined to get away. Tugging me toward the car, he whipped his head back and forth as though assessing the walls for threats. He practically threw me in the passenger side before rushing around the hood to drive.

Behind us, the police cruiser whizzed by.

"Dang, Riley, slow down. It's cool," I assured him as I caught my breath. "Cop drove by. Probably not looking for us."

But Riley stared through the windshield, gripping the steering wheel.

"Nah, nah," he said, gulping the air. "I don't trust it. He's trying to trick us. They always do that. I bet he's just working his way back around."

I could see the erratic beating of his pulse in his neck as he started the ignition with shaky hands. His left leg bounced against the car mat in a hurried rhythm. He scrubbed a hand over his face and squeezed his eyes shut before opening them, looking dazed.

He pulled into the deserted road, headlights off.

"Dude, you've been watching too many cop shows." With effort, I stayed calm. Reaching across the dash, I flipped the switch to turn the headlights on, grateful Riley didn't try to stop me. Ice had gathered on the windshield, so I also started the defrost, realizing with a groan that I'd left my gloves back on the little grassy area.

The car lurched as Riley took a corner too fast. I used an elbow to brace myself. He kept switching lanes unnecessarily. We hadn't been drinking, so I imagined the adrenaline pumping through his veins was making him frantic. Why couldn't he chill out and see that the threat had passed? He made several turns until we were in one of Seattle's residential neighborhoods.

In the complete opposite direction of the way back to my house.

"Where are you going, man?"

"I want to make sure that cop's not following."

"Riley, you need to come down from whatever high you're on. We're fine. No one's after us." I blew into my hands again. I was going to miss those gloves. "Maybe you should pull over and take a break. Calm the fuck down."

He still appeared to be on the verge of bursting an aneurysm. If anything proved we were not destined for the criminal life, this was it. Riley was shitting his pants at a cop car simply driving by while we'd admittedly been committing a crime, but not exactly a felony.

His breathing grew even more labored and uneven. It wasn't right, the way he couldn't get himself under control. Sweat dripped down his forehead.

I'd heard of this happening to people but never seen it up close. I vaguely recalled the mental health unit from sophomore year.

"Hey, Riley. You need to pull over. I'm pretty sure you're having a panic attack."

"Nah, dude. I'm good," he said, blinking repeatedly.

He turned again, and we were in the neighborhood's small business district. We passed a grocery store, a few restaurants, a drugstore, a dry cleaner, a coffee shop. Everything was dark except at the end of the street, where they'd converted one of the parking areas into a temporary Christmas tree lot. It still had all its lights on, offering a quick flash of illumination as we drove by.

Even though it was brief, the stab of light into the car's interior seemed to stun Riley, who threw up both arms against the momentary brightness.

Letting go of the wheel.

"Jesus Christ!" I leaned over and attempted to steer, screaming at Riley to hit the brakes.

But he pressed his foot on the gas pedal, and the car swerved violently. Thank god it was stupid o'clock in the morning because we were beyond conspicuous now. I shoved the wheel left to keep us from hitting a parked car. Then I pulled it back the other way to stop us from going onto the sidewalk.

Both our bodies slammed into the center console.

"Dammit, Riley! You need to stop! Stop!"

He nodded, finally seeming to hear me. Bringing his hands back to the wheel, he slowed the car.

We were going about ten miles an hour when a bicycle appeared out of nowhere. *A fucking bike! At this time in the morning.* It was crossing the intersection ahead of us, and I prayed Riley would see or that he'd actually stop for the stop sign.

But he didn't. I yanked the wheel as the cyclist was about to cross in front of us, maneuvering the car sideways to skirt around the back wheels. The whole thing only lasted a second, but it happened as though in slow motion. I thought we avoided hitting the bicycle, if by inches, but then I looked in the mirror and saw the cyclist go down. Hard.

"We hit that bike!"

I looked back, and it didn't appear as though the bicycle had gone far. It hadn't flown across the road or anything. More like tipped over. Still, the person on the ground didn't seem to be moving.

"Stop the fucking car!" I shouted directly in Riley's ear. "We have to go back. Have to call 911!"

Riley's eyes glazed over. He beat his fist against the steering wheel. "Shit!"

"Dammit, stop!" I screamed.

But he didn't stop. He kept rolling down the street—barely a crawl, but still moving. "Shit. Shit. Shit," he kept repeating.

I wasn't sure what came over me. I only knew I had to help that cyclist, and Riley was just...gone. There was no time for a well-thought-out plan. One moment, I decided I needed to help, and the next, I opened the car door and pitched myself onto the asphalt.

The hem of my pants caught in the doorframe for a second, causing me to exit the vehicle shoulder-first. Even going as slow as we were, the jolt of pain that ricocheted through me as I collided with the ground was like nothing I'd ever experienced.

I was scrawny, short, and hardly made of muscle, so hitting the street felt like landing on a bed of nails, even with my heavy coat. I rolled—maybe five times, maybe a million—and my head hit the asphalt repeatedly with sickening smacks.

The impact shredded half my coat right off my body, along with some of the skin on my torso. I cried out as pain sliced across my hand.

Finally, I stopped rolling, but when I tried to stand, I crumpled to the ground. One of my legs wouldn't hold me, almost like it wasn't there at all.

My breathing came in short pants as the pain took hold. I needed to move.

I stumbled into a bear crawl. Focusing on my purpose kept the agony at bay. I had to get to that bike. Had to call for help.

Relying mainly on my left hand and right leg, I dragged my useless left ankle behind me. I collapsed onto my right elbow, my right hand bloodied beyond recognition.

I struggled, inch by torturous inch, from half a block away—numb, shocked, and dizzy.

By providence, I made it to the bike, only to pull my phone out of my pocket and find it completely trashed. Crushed by my fall.

I huddled next to the cyclist. I could see now she was an older woman, probably in her sixties. She breathed evenly but remained unconscious. There didn't seem to be anything bloody other than some scratches on her face. But she didn't wake up. My mind began to cloud as the pain settled deeper into my body.

I needed to do *something* for this woman.

My hand hurt so much. Blood poured from my palm, dripping over my wrist.

Had Riley turned back around?

I needed to do something.

With my last breaths, I yelled for help like a wounded animal. Wailed my frustration that this night had gone so horribly wrong. Finally, I surrendered to the anguish, huddling next to the biker and whispering, "I'm sorry," before the blackness pulled me under completely.

Chapter Two

FIVE YEARS AGO

Maureen

The holiday season never truly began until I heard "Christmas Wrapping" by the Waitresses. Memories of the record ticking and popping every December on my mom's vinyl player had made a lasting impression. It didn't matter if it happened randomly in the car or standing in line at the grocery store. Once that song came over the speakers, the time of merry and bright had begun.

That's why I was stoked to hear the new wave classic as I got my hand stamped and walked through the grimy entryway into Musicbox's main room the Sunday after Thanksgiving.

The first band wasn't due on stage yet. I approved of the venue unapologetically playing Christmas tunes for the less-than-receptive crowd, as well as decorating for the season. A pink plastic tree stood prominently in one corner. Felt dollar store stockings hung behind the bar. A few audience members directed aggrieved looks at the speakers, rolling their eyes as "Christmas in Hollis" came on next.

Geesh. Tough crowd. I wasn't a Christmas fanatic or anything. But in this room full of concertgoers frowning at the holiday music—*it was Run DMC, for goodness' sake, not Bing Crosby*—I felt downright festive as I hummed along. Across the room, I noticed a guy with blue-black hair also nodding to the song. It was comforting to know I wasn't the only person here not drowning in ennui.

My best friend Bren and I shoved our way toward the front. A second later, the holiday playlist cut off, and the opening band started its set.

It was a triple bill tonight. Three pop-punk bands from Europe. Not my favorite type of music but not the worst option either. And beggars couldn't be choosers. I'd just gotten back from Coleman Creek that morning, still buzzing with the odd mix of happiness and guilt that followed every visit to my hometown. Bren had registered my mood the minute I'd dropped my suitcase back in our central Seattle apartment, and because she was the world's greatest roommate and friend, she'd scored us these last-minute tickets.

The bands turned out to be surprisingly decent and just what I needed. But they weren't the only thing capturing my attention. As the night wore on, my eyes kept drifting to the guy with the blue-black hair who stayed near the back of the room. The one pretending not to notice me.

At least twenty bodies stood between us, the crowd packed shoulder to sweaty shoulder in the overheated venue. Still, I felt his gaze. Each time I glanced back, he looked away quickly and resumed a blank expression, stuffing his fists into his pockets.

My interest rose as I cataloged little details. He was shorter than most of the guys in the room, close to my own height of five feet, six inches. His pale skin glowed in the crowd, stark beneath a head of dark curls. Thick lashes framed striking gray eyes, making them look as though they'd been lined. But something else was in his enigmatic features, a softness underneath.

I was intrigued. This guy might be just the thing to help me forget myself for a while. The next time I caught him staring, I attempted to hold his gaze. He tried to look away again, but I persisted, determined to bring this little dance to a head. I smiled—cheeks lifting just a fraction—enough to let him know I was open to a conversation.

He held my stare another moment before making a move in my direction. Abruptly, he stopped and shook his head. His face dropped into a scowl, and his jaw clenched. Turning away, he headed toward the back of the venue.

What the hell? I didn't think I'd read that wrong. He *had* been checking me out.

I sighed as I watched him retreat. Disappointing, but whatever. The guy was sexy, no doubt, but he had zero chance of me chasing him. Especially not tonight. Besides just returning from an exhausting trip, I had a new job starting soon, so there was plenty on my plate already.

If I wanted to hook up, there were other men here. Or I could just enjoy the music. At the least, my position near the speakers would get me out of my head for a while. With the way my ears already rang, I'd be half deaf tomorrow.

Bren returned from a mission to the bar, handing me a bottle of water.

"Where'd he go?" she shouted, doing her best to be heard over the amplifiers.

"Who?"

"The guy who's had his eyes on you all night. The short king with that killer black hair."

I shrugged. "Dunno. I got tired of waiting for him to come over, so I gave him my best *I'd be down* look, and he walked away."

"Fucker."

"It's okay. Band's good, though."

Bren and I faced the stage. Musicbox had grown famous for its acoustics—a charitable way of saying it was inexcusably loud. Despite the rainbow-colored foam plugs in my ears, my teeth still rattled with every guitar strum.

I noticed another guy a few feet away. He dipped his chin forward, eyeing me with a leer. With his muscular build, backward baseball cap, and loose-fitting Levi's under a Guinness T-shirt, he looked like he'd just wandered in from frat row. I knew this sort of obvious interest and generic handsomeness appealed to a lot of women, but unsubtle dude bro wasn't my type at all.

He stared at me. I looked away, hoping he'd get the message.

Meanwhile, Bren had been proactive about ensuring she'd have someone to go home with. I saw Chase pushing his way through the crowd halfway through the main act's first set. He and my best friend had been close since high school, and he was one of her regular booty calls, her friend-with-benefits, or whatever she labeled it this week.

I smirked at her. "Chase is here."

"What can I say?" She winked. "I needed a sure thing."

"That poor guy. You realize he'd marry you tomorrow if you'd let him, right?" It came out slightly more admonishing than I'd meant, but it was hard not to feel sorry for Chase when he looked at Bren with such clear adoration.

She had no patience for my opinion. "He's a big boy, Maureen. And I've been honest with him about where I stand. If he's willing to accept the *limited arrangement* I'm offering, that's on him."

Accurate, of course. "Is he taking you to his apartment?"

"If that's okay?"

"Sure. I can Uber back to our place on my own."

"Alright. But we'll stay with you until the end of the show, or at least until you're ready to leave. Make sure you get in the car safe and sound."

"Thanks."

Chase wrapped himself around Bren from behind like a koala, resting his chin on her head.

"I'm gonna grab a soda." I had to yell even though Bren stood right next to me. She nodded in reply, squeezing Chase's arms around her ribs.

I made my way to the bar with minimal shoving. While I waited to grab the bartender's attention, a prickle of awareness ghosted across the skin of my neck.

I glanced to my left.

Blue-black curls gleamed like the ocean at midnight. He sat on a stool across the bar, posed casually, but unable to hide the tension in his shoulders as he caught my eye. He didn't look away this time. Instead, he bit his bottom lip.

A hint of excitement traveled down my spine. My mouth turned up slightly as I peered at him through my lashes.

He gazed at me for the type of fleeting instant which felt like an eternity, all the people and noise between us fading into the background.

I took a step in his direction, and his lips flattened. He looked away quickly, shifting uncomfortably on the seat.

I huffed. What was this guy's problem? I did not have time for men who went back and forth between eye-fucking me and looking like they swallowed a lemon.

Shaking my head in annoyance, I raised an arm, aggressively trying to flag down the bartender. Screw soda. I needed a shot.

As I took the shot and slammed ten bucks down on the counter, I wasn't paying attention to anyone else at the bar. Which was how I turned around and found myself facing backward baseball cap dude.

"Hey," he said, giving me an *aw-shucks* smile.

Irritation flared. After getting mixed signals from blue-black hair guy—again—this was the last thing I wanted.

"Um, hey," I replied, twisting my hip to snake through the tight crowd.

"I'm Paul."

He moved in front of me as I tried to scoot around him. The audience was rowdy. I couldn't be sure if he'd intentionally gotten in my way or if he'd been pushed from the side.

"Um, okay," I said. I didn't want to be too friendly or give him an opening, but being outright rude probably wasn't a good idea either. Dude bro seemed harmless enough, but you never could tell.

I squared my shoulders and stood as tall as I could. "Hey, Phil, I'm going back over to hang out with my friend, okay? It's girls' night." Hopefully, he wouldn't follow my path too closely and spot Chase.

"It's Paul. And I came over to talk to you. You were checking me out before," he said, unmistakably blocking my path now.

I exhaled heavily. "I wasn't."

"Pretty sure I know when a cute girl is looking at me." He smiled again, sure he'd won me over with his amazing compliment. "I get it if you're with your friend, but can I get your number? Or maybe we could meet up later?"

Was this doofus for real? My hackles poked beneath my skin. Off-brand Ken doll must be extremely used to closing the deal if he moved this fast. Part of me itched to give him a piece of my mind for being so pushy, but I didn't want to make a big dramatic scene. Not after the week I'd had. "Um…no thanks. Listen, I'm sorry you got the wrong idea, but I just want to get back to my friend." I attempted to squeeze past him.

He sidestepped in front of me. "So you don't want to even talk to me?" He seemed genuinely perplexed, completely unfamiliar with the concept of *no*. "You won't even tell me your name?"

I glanced over and tried to grab Bren's attention. She didn't notice, completely wrapped up in Chase. I didn't think this guy would do anything to me in a room full of people, but his lack of chill was unnerving.

"Look, Paul, I'm going to need you to let me pass by. Otherwise, things are about to get very real, very fast. We're about five seconds away from my knee becoming intimately acquainted with your nutsack."

His incredulous frown deepened. "I feel like we got off on the wrong foot. Because I just want to talk. I like a feisty girl. I don't mind having to work for it."

Ugh. Seriously? "We are done here. Let me pass. Now."

"Just give me a chance—"

"She's not interested, man. What the fuck more do you need?" Suddenly, blue-black hair guy was next to me, giving the other man a glare so icy his backward baseball cap could have frozen.

"Who the fuck are you?" Paul demanded.

"I'm just someone who thinks it's messed up that asshats like you give the rest of us a bad name. This woman obviously isn't interested in your bullshit. So how about you run along and go practice your keg stands, or hit up some sorority party to find a woman who's more willing to find out how disappointing you are in bed."

I couldn't help my small giggle. Paul looked between the two of us, finally throwing his hands up. "Fuck this."

I watched him go, making sure he was well away before turning back to the man next to me. "Thank you for stepping in. But just so you know, I had that handled."

He replied with a grin, and I noticed how full and red his lips were, standing out against the paleness of his smooth-shaven face. "You absolutely did. And I'm sorry I intruded on what I'm sure would have been an epic takedown. He was just really pissing me off. Allow me to apologize on behalf of all men, especially those who are still figuring out how not to let their dicks run the show."

I barked another laugh. "Feminist, are you?"

"I like to think so." His features still showed caution, but no scowl. I was charmed. And I wanted a reason to forgive him for making the sucking-lemons face at me earlier.

When he didn't step away, my initial interest resurfaced. Heightened.

Except he'd given me whiplash all night. And I wasn't into playing games.

"I saw you before," I said. "During the warm-up act. Watching me. Then you were doing it again just now, at the bar." I leaned my elbows against the counter behind me. "You couldn't have missed me looking back at you. But you got all weird and turned away. Both times." His Adam's apple worked as he swallowed, but when he remained quiet, I continued, "I'm in the habit of being aware when people are staring at me. Call it self-preservation."

"Sorry." He dragged a palm across his face before shoving both hands in his pockets. "I...uh...did notice you." His sexy voice was lower than I expected.

His expression remained unreadable. Partially intrigued, but also...pained somehow. I grew impatient with his non-reply. "So, there we were, noticing each other—" I gripped the edge of the bar top. "Why'd you look away, then?"

He muttered, mostly to himself, "You could call that 'self-preservation,' too."

I wasn't sure I'd heard him correctly through the hum of the surrounding crowd. "Huh?"

"It's hard to explain. Tonight...I didn't really come here for...that." He bit off the word. "I sort of wanted to be alone, and I guess I was trying to stick to the plan. But after noticing you before, then watching you hand that guy his ass a minute ago, I just...had to meet you."

I still didn't know what he wanted, and I'd given him plenty of opportunities to clarify. Hot and cold didn't work for me. Too bad. With that moody, dark gaze, he was exactly my type. "Well, we've met now. I guess I'll leave you to your alone time." I pushed my elbows away from the bar. "Thanks for the assist with frat douche. Maybe I'll see you around."

His eyes widened. "Wait! I'm sorry I made it so complicated. Can we start over? Please." He stepped closer and made a throaty entreaty, "Now that we're talking, I'd like to keep doing that."

I supposed I could give him a pass for being weird at first. We all had our reasons for bad moments. As long as he didn't make *his* complications *my* complications, we could still have a good time.

Or maybe he wasn't a casual hookup type of guy? That would explain some of the odd behavior. I could respect that. He'd helped me out with Paul the garbage person, and seemed fun to talk to. I wouldn't be too disappointed if that was all we did.

"I'm cool to chill. But I won't apologize for interrupting your *me time*," I joked. "Since I offered to walk away."

"I'm glad you didn't." His heavy-lidded gaze raked over my body from the top of my head to the tips of my black calf-height boots. "Like I said, I wasn't looking...but I'm not sorry."

I smiled. "How about we start with something simple. Like, what's your name?"

"Oh, jeez." He rolled his eyes. "I know I'm rusty, but apparently, I'm also an idiot. Sorry. I'm Billy." It would have felt natural to shake hands, but his fists stayed determinedly in his pockets. I assumed he wanted to be extra gentlemanly and hands-off after the dude bro situation.

"Mo."

"Mo. Cool name. Is that short for something?"

I always used Mo with potential dates and hookups until I was certain it was safe to give my real name. A girl never could be too careful. I tsked. "Ooh, tough break for you, Billy. That's information I reserve exclusively for people I've known longer than fifteen minutes."

He laughed. The look of indecision I'd seen pass over his features earlier broke through for a moment, but he washed it away quickly.

"How about we remedy that?" he asked. "There's a twenty-four-hour diner north of here. Sophisticated place called Denny's. Can I buy you a late, late dinner? Or coffee?"

My stomach did a somersault as his question resolved into a beautiful smile. It pulled on my insides like gravity. We'd been able to speak at a normal volume for a few minutes with the band between sets, but the pounding bass started up again.

Billy evidently didn't want a speedy hookup. And I wasn't in the mood for quick and meaningless either. That wasn't the vibe between us. The smart thing to do would be to call it a night. Exchange numbers and plan for another time. But now that we were finally talking, I was reluctant for the conversation to end. And the band was performing its encore.

There was an urgency to the moment I couldn't explain or dismiss. *Dang.* I'd come here tonight trying to get out of my head after a stressful few days, and now I was considering something more than a casual hookup with someone I'd barely met. I couldn't even recall the last time I'd gone to a restaurant with a guy.

But the more I thought about it, the more I realized I wanted to. As attracted as I was to those full ruby lips of his, I was just as interested in finding out if his confidence was real or forced. I wanted to know if he truly considered himself a feminist, and who had taught him that. Did he actually like Joy Division, or was he wearing their T-shirt ironically? And what had he seen in me that made him want to stop being cautious?

"Yeah. I could eat," I said. "Although I might be too deaf to carry on a conversation." I reached up to touch the foam in my ears. "We're good as long as you're in the mood to potentially be eating french fries with me in stony silence."

"Sounds perfect."

Chapter Three

Maureen

I found Bren and filled her in on my plan. After giving Billy a hard stare and a warning that she "knew a guy" if anything happened to me, she smirked as I left with him.

The ringing in my ears turned out to be temporary and immediately improved when I exited the concert.

Billy and I strolled two blocks in easy silence to the lot where he'd parked his car. When we arrived, he opened the passenger side door to a sleek black Audi.

I blanched. "Oh, um, okay." I wasn't sure what I'd been expecting, but it hadn't been a car that would have looked at home in the VIP lot on the Microsoft campus.

He looked downward, pasting on a self-deprecating smile as I slid into the buttery soft leather seat. "It was my mom's. She handed it down to me when I got my MBA."

"Ah." Even used, it was an extravagant gift, so I guessed his family had money. I thought of the ancient Ford truck my mom had maintained for years before her illness made driving impossible.

When Billy started the engine, one of the holiday channels for his satellite radio came on. A midcentury version of "Up on the Housetop" sounded through the speakers as he backed out of his spot.

"Station okay?" he asked.

"It's good."

The car drove like a dream over the bare roads, smooth even on the steep climb up James Street. Billy had probably received the same driver's ed instruction I had—keep your hands at ten and two on the wheel—but like me, he drove with his left hand at midnight and his right resting on the console, hidden by shadows.

"You know, that's what made me notice you at first," he said, hitching his neck toward the song info on the dash screen with a picture of Gene Autry in a Santa hat. "You were mouthing along to that song, the '80s one by that girl band—was it the Go-Gos? It was cute."

"The Waitresses. One of my favorites."

"Although you and I might have been the only ones to think so," he added with a laugh.

I rolled my eyes playfully. "My mom would have labeled that crowd 'too cool for school.'"

With his dark clothes, dark hair, and even darker facial features, Billy didn't give the impression of someone who'd be into holiday songs. I also wouldn't have pegged him for an MBA. Which was silly because it wasn't like people went to clubs and concerts in their work clothes. His black jeans had holes that seemed as though they'd been earned, not bought, and a chunky silver wallet chain rested next to his hip. As much as I tried, I couldn't picture him in a button-down and slacks. Then again, his watch looked expensive. And there was this car.

After fifteen minutes of chatting about our favorite holiday songs and the Musicbox show, we pulled into the Denny's parking lot just north of Seattle, in Shoreline. Billy slid his Audi into a space between a decade-old Corolla and an ancient Subaru with red duct tape over the left brake light.

"It's funny. I've only lived in Seattle a year and a half, so I haven't explored many places yet," I told him. "But I *have* been to this Denny's a few times."

"Yearning for the soft touch of a pancake?"

"Um...what?"

"Sorry. Fun fact—Denny's has a hilarious Twitter feed. I'm a fan."

I laughed. "Seriously, I've made Bren—my guard dog you met at the concert—drive up here a few times. Seattle can be a little bougie for me since I grew up in a small town. Don't get me wrong, I love the city, and I can order an overcomplicated latte with the best of them, but if I'm choosing, I'll take sticky tables and pleather booths every time."

Billy held the door open for me as we walked in. I didn't miss his eyes scanning the large dining area thoroughly before his posture loosened.

It was after midnight, so we snagged a booth right away, but only one beleaguered server appeared to be working. Tired but friendly, she came over to grab our order, warning us it might take a while since they were short-staffed. We assured her we weren't in a hurry and ordered french fries, nachos, and a strawberry milkshake to share.

Five other booths were occupied—two folks having solo dates with their phones, one older couple sipping coffee and eating oatmeal, a table of teenagers laughing without being obnoxiously unruly, and a two-seater occupied by another couple in their twenties.

The laid-back atmosphere was exactly what I needed. The concert had effectively drawn me out of my funky headspace, but sitting here in the middle of the night, I finally relaxed.

"So, tell me more about this not-bougie place where you grew up." Billy's voice broke into my thoughts.

I smiled, running a finger along the edge of my water glass. "Coleman Creek. About five hours northeast. Far enough from I-90 that most folks never have a reason to drive through. Everyone's friendly. Not much to do. Small town as fuck, if you know what I mean." I shrugged. "But it's home. How about you?"

"How about me what?"

"Where did you grow up?"

Billy mimicked my movement with his own glass, the index finger of his left hand moving rapidly around the rim until a low whistle hung in the air. His right hand stayed in his lap. "Here. North Seattle."

"A true native." I tipped my glass at him.

"I guess. But I'm with you," he continued quickly. "I like the parts of the city that are a little less polished. It's so different now than when I was a kid. Less Nirvana, more Amazon, if that makes sense. I'm sure all places change if you live there long enough, but it's one thing to understand that intellectually and another to watch the elementary school you went to get demolished, or your favorite gyro place turned into condos. It's kind of my hobby to recreate what I remember—" He stopped abruptly, cheeks reddening. "Sorry. I don't mean to ramble."

"No, it's interesting," I said sincerely. "Sort of the reverse of my experience. When I was growing up, it annoyed me that everything seemed to stay the same, like the world was passing Coleman Creek by. Other places changed, but we didn't seem to. That's one reason I left."

"How did you know?"

I made a face. "How did I know the world was changing? Life moved slowly there, but we *did* have the Internet."

He chuckled softly. "No. I mean, how did you know you wanted to leave? Just because the pace is slower doesn't mean it's bad, right?"

There was a complex answer to his question—that a lot of my desire to leave had been driven by the intense sense of obligation I'd had in Coleman Creek. That wanting to get *out* was much more a product of not wanting to be forced to stay *in*.

"I think I was a typical teenager, eager to explore," I said, a shorter version of the truth. "I went to college at Washington State and ended up in Seattle a year after graduating."

"And is it everything you'd dreamed it would be, when you were a kid using your very-readily-available Internet?"

My brows drew together, my focus drifting to the lopsided Christmas tree in the Denny's lobby. "I've loved living in Seattle. But I keep waiting for it to feel like home."

"Don't worry. I've lived here my whole life and sometimes still feel like that." He leaned back in the booth, rolling his shoulders and keeping both hands under the table as his lips pursed into a nonchalant half grin. Sexy as hell.

"So...what were you saying about your hobby?" I asked.

"Oh. I draw. Sometimes from memory. Sometimes from life. Lots of different things, but I try to capture places that remind me of my childhood."

"Is that what you do? You're an artist?"

He released a hollow laugh. "I wish. I'm in finance. Putting that MBA to work." I detected a note of bitterness. "Drawing is something I do in my spare time."

We spent the next half hour before the food came out talking more about our childhoods and his art, about my time in college studying fashion merchandising. After some coaxing, I got him to show me pictures of his artwork on his phone. He used his left hand, keeping his right one beneath the table. I'd read somewhere that left-handed people were supposedly more creative, which tracked since I became absorbed in the stunning images as he scrolled.

Our food arrived, and we dug in. Moved on to new topics. I found out Billy worked for Wallingford Capital, one of the top money management and investment firms in the city. He was some sort of mid-level executive, having interned there throughout college. I told him about the temporary retail gigs I'd been stringing together to pay rent, and that I'd just scored a role as a buyer for an upscale boutique.

"Is that the goal, to work at a store like that?" he asked.

"I'm not sure, to be honest. I've always been interested in clothes and fashion. Not as a designer but more like a stylist. The way people decide what to put on in the morning fascinates me. How they make their outfit choices. I like the idea of helping people find things that make them feel good in their skin."

"That's cool," Billy said. "I don't think about my clothes generally. On workdays, I usually just put on whatever suit my hand touches first."

"And I would argue that is a legitimate approach if it's the one that works for you," I replied, popping a fry in my mouth. "Working high-end retail probably isn't my end goal, but I'm hoping it's a decent foot in the door."

We talked until the lights outside dimmed and cars passed by only sporadically. Whatever had drawn me to Billy at the club continued to hold my interest, even as he remained an enigma. His words and responses, while engaged, were carefully measured. It was almost unnerving how firmly he had control of himself. But then I noticed his brief intake of breath when I smiled at him, or the way his gaze lasered on my lips as I ran them across the milkshake straw.

In the three o'clock hour, we sipped coffee and struggled to keep our eyes open. Tired as I felt, I was afraid to let the night go. Billy held himself back but looked at me intently. Our connection was so potent it hung in the air like a physical thing.

He must have felt it too, because he didn't remark on my yawning, seeming to have the same desire to prolong our evening.

"At the concert, it sounded like maybe you were coming off a hard week. Tough Thanksgiving?" he asked, following up quickly with, "You don't have to tell me if you don't want to."

"It's okay." I never spoke about personal stuff to anyone except Bren, and even then, only occasionally. But since it already felt like this night existed in an alternate dimension, I took a sip from my drink. "I was home last week, in Coleman Creek, with my mom and two sisters. The four of us have always been close because my dad died when I was a kid." I paused. "Last year, Mom got sick, so the holidays have been rough."

"Oh. I'm sorry to hear that. It's bad?"

I nodded. "Parkinson's. It's affected her mind a lot more than we thought it would, so on her worst days, it's almost like she has dementia." I exhaled, circling my mug with both hands in front of me. "It's also hard because I feel guilty not being there. My younger sister Marley moved in to take care of her. Uprooted her entire life.

Left her job and even her long-term boyfriend in Portland to move back."

"You feel guilty because she did that and you didn't?"

"I mean, I'm the oldest. It feels like it should have been my job."

"Is your sister resentful?"

I snorted. "Hardly. She keeps telling me she would have moved home eventually anyway and that Portland wasn't for her. She loves Coleman Creek. Got a job teaching at the high school we all went to. Yesterday, she mentioned getting a dog for her and my mom."

He reached his hand out instinctively but pulled it back at the last moment. "I don't want to keep you from beating yourself up if that's what you want to do—we've all been there—but it sounds like maybe things worked out okay."

I tugged absently on my sleeve. "Honestly, I don't feel guilty about not being there so much as I feel guilty about not *wanting* to be there." I'd only recently been able to articulate those feelings in my mind. Especially after the conversation I'd had three days ago with my mother, the one I'd thought about the entire way back to the city. "Sorry, I guess you drove me all the way to Denny's to find out I'm kind of an asshole."

This time, he stretched his hand across the table and laid it atop mine.

I shivered at the touch, our first.

"That doesn't make you an asshole," he said. "I bet a lot of people would feel the same in your situation. The thing that matters is that you visit and you're there when she needs you. You do visit, right?"

"Of course."

"And you accept her phone calls, answer her texts?"

"Yeah."

"And if your sister was having some kind of emergency or needed help, you'd go?"

"Definitely."

"Okay, then, I think you're good. If you were an asshole, you wouldn't do those things. I mean, you can post it on Reddit if you want to find out for sure, but every response is going to be NTA."

I couldn't help the laugh that escaped, or the smile that followed. He kept his hand on mine, looking at me with hooded eyes as his thumb rubbed back and forth over my skin, across the handstamp I'd received at Musicbox. I bit my bottom lip, and his hot gaze landed on it. It was heady, breaking through his reserve. And the thrumming in my veins, coupled with admitting things I'd barely been able to tell my best friend, had my mind racing.

The air teemed with...*possibility*. Sitting and talking for hours with no sex involved—even though I was sure we both wanted to do dirty, dirty things to each other—I'd never had this before.

The server came by with the coffeepot, and the intrusion caused him to snatch his hand back. "You can't help your feelings, the guilt over not always wanting to be there. I understand. I'd feel the same if it was one of my parents."

It took me a moment, feeling the loss of his hand on mine, to re-engage. "You're close with them?"

"Close-adjacent. Kinda depends on the day."

"I bet they're proud of you being at Wallingford Capital. For your MBA."

He picked up the napkin in front of him and brought it below the table. I could tell by the way his biceps flexed, he was twisting it with his hands.

"It's a steady job. And it makes my parents happy I work there. When I was a kid, I think they worried I would pursue art as a career."

"They don't like your art?"

"Not exactly. They just think finance is more sensible. It doesn't excite me, but they're probably right."

That sucked for him. The only guidance I'd gotten from my mother in terms of my career was when she'd said, "Find something that makes you happy and do that." She'd always supported my love of clothes and accessories and had taught me to sew. I still wasn't one hundred percent certain I'd chosen correctly with fashion merchandising, but I was at least in the right ballpark.

Despite my efforts not to, I eventually felt myself fading.

"Shoot," Billy said. "I can't believe it's past four in the morning. Can I take you home?"

With our attraction clear but his behavior so hesitant, I doubted he wanted to *take me home*. Something he confirmed with his next words.

"I can drive you and make sure you get in safe."

Outside, he followed me to the passenger side of his car. I figured his plan was to open the door for me, but instead, he leaned against it, folding his arms across his chest. He tucked his hands under his armpits, the fabric of his tee stretching enticingly over his pecs. His eyes stared into mine, but when his voice came out, it shook.

"Hey, Mo, I just want to say again that, when I went to the show tonight, I wasn't thinking anything like this would happen. I wasn't expecting to meet anyone—"

"You don't need to keep telling me." I cut him off. "I already told you I wasn't looking either." Feeling bold in my fatigue, I let my eyes travel slowly up and down the length of his lithe body. "But I can't say I'm sorry."

"Jesus." Billy's posture stiffened at my perusal, his face and neck flushing in the moonlight. He sucked his lower lip into his mouth and released a heavy breath. "I know you said you're not up for anything complicated. And I get it, with everything going on with your mom and the new job—"

"It's okay. After tonight, I'm thinking a little complication might be worth it."

He ran his hands harshly over his face before resting them on the door behind his hips. The gesture was fast. But I'd seen.

He'd been hiding it all night. In his pockets. Under the table. The shadows of the console. His right hand. Just a thumb, pointer, and middle finger. Missing space where the ring and pinky fingers should be.

My gaze remained steady. He obviously didn't want me to notice, consciously or not.

He shoved his hands back in his pockets. "I need to deal with some shit," he said. "But can I text you? I want to see you again."

"Yeah. I'd like that."

I stepped forward, until only an inch or two remained between us. We stood shoulder-to-shoulder and knee-to-knee as I gazed into his gray eyes, getting an up close look at his inky lashes. I heard his soft breathing. In the chilly air, it came out in white puffs, mingled with my own in the space between us as our chests rose and fell in tandem.

He closed his eyes and exhaled, reaching his left hand up to tuck a strand of hair behind my ear. Drawing his palm down and around my neck, he squeezed delicately and leaned his face in. The faint drag of his nose along the skin of my cheek sent tiny shocks along my spine as he whispered into my ear, "I really, really want to see you again."

I dared to rock forward on my toes, all but offering my lips. His eyes opened, and I saw him swallow. But instead of kissing me, he leaned his forehead down, pressing it against mine, panting faintly.

We stood there a few moments, the temperature rising between us, until he finally dropped his hand from my neck. His arm jerked, and I realized he'd reached behind himself to open the car door for me.

I startled at the movement, then stepped away, nodding in understanding.

As we drove home, Frank Sinatra's "The Christmas Waltz" our accompaniment, I reflected on how surreal this night had been, like an altered state. Probably safer not to give in to the intensity.

At least not yet.

Chapter Four

Maureen

Waking up only hours after Billy brought me home felt like coming out of a fever dream, the *time-out-of-mind* sensation so acute I could easily convince myself last night hadn't happened. Except, brushing my hair in the mirror, my fingers drew to that place in front of my ear where he'd grazed his nose. My breath caught with the memory.

Bren was home from Chase's and eating grapes at our small kitchen table when I came out of my bedroom. She asked how my night had gone.

"Fine. We got some food, and then he brought me home." I gave a bored shrug, snapping a grape from the bunch in front of her.

Letting her think my date with Billy had been unremarkable kept me from having to answer a bunch of questions I wasn't ready to deal with. I'd been so indifferent toward romance my whole life. And now, without trying, I'd gotten a taste of the type of connection I'd always scoffed at. With a chuckle, I remembered that I'd forgotten to give Billy my real name at the end of our night. Hopefully, he'd have a laugh about that.

I went to work at the big box store I'd been at for over a year. My manager had been accommodating during my time there, so I'd given three weeks' notice, other than the few days off for Thanksgiving. It was tough waiting to start my new job, but I wanted to be professional.

As I folded merchandise and inwardly cursed the teens making a mess of the displays, my thoughts drifted. I didn't want to jinx it, but it felt like things were finally coming together for me—a career and possibly a relationship.

I waited for Billy's text.

One of my coworkers grinned at me the hundredth time I pulled my phone out to check it. I narrowed my eyes at him and made myself focus on helping customers. Never in my twenty-six years had I waited on a guy. But I was excited, dammit. Last night was *good*.

When Billy asked to text me, I'd assumed he meant as soon as possible.

But he didn't text that day.

Or the next.

I went through the motions at work, trying to ignore the lack of buzzing in my back pocket. That night, sitting next to Bren on the couch and pretending to watch the Christmas movie she'd put on, a knot began to form in my stomach.

A third day passed, still with no word.

I couldn't have read him wrong, right? I mean, he hadn't tried to sleep with me, so what would have been the point of him messing with me if that was what it was?

No. I felt positive he'd been sincere.

A few more days passed. I went through the motions of holiday shopping and decorating our little apartment. Played the third wheel at the movies with Bren and Chase. The pit in my stomach grew, but my pride kept me from reaching out to Billy first.

Finally, one week after we'd met, just before I was about to break and message him myself, he texted me.

Two words.

BILLY: I'm sorry.

What. The. Actual. Fuck.

A million thoughts ran through my head. *He was sorry? Sorry for what? Not texting? Leading me on? Our whole night? Something else?*

I waited for another text that would provide clarification, but none came.

He'd been right there with me. I hadn't hallucinated him at Musicbox. Or Denny's. Discussing his art, listening to me talk about my mom. And at the end of the night, he'd wanted to kiss me. Hell, I was sure he'd wanted to pull me into the back seat.

I'm sorry.

Apparently, I wasn't worthy of details. I waited an hour, but as the minutes ticked by, it became obvious no further messages were coming.

I thought about texting back. Insisting he explain. Ripping him a new one for playing with me. But I didn't run hot like that. When it came to someone screwing me over, I ran very, very cold.

I thought there'd been meaning behind meeting Billy, how he'd made me feel things I never had before. And, clearly, it *was* significant. Just not in the way I'd envisioned.

Whelp, lesson learned. I should have just taken backward baseball cap home for a forgettable lay and a see-ya-never.

Billy had backed away from me initially in the club, held himself in check during our conversation, told me flat-out things were complicated, and didn't go for more than a cheek graze even though our chemistry was lethal. I'd known something was off. What a stupid, stupid mistake I'd made.

Letting him in.

He could take his lame-ass *I'm sorry* and shove it.

STARTING A NEW JOB IN RETAIL less than a month before Christmas demanded my full attention. I channeled my rage at Billy into relentless focus on my work and a desire to be the best damn buyer Kolya's had ever had. For the first few months, I'd be shadowing the store's current buyer and vowed to learn everything I could. Luckily, Krissy was a lovely woman, eager to take me under her wing.

On my third day, she told me as gently as possible that I'd need to elevate my personal style to be taken seriously at work. "It's fine to be a little different, but you want people to think of you as bold, not quirky. Betsey Johnson can get away with pigtails in old age, just like Anna Wintour can wear sunglasses indoors. But until you make a name for yourself in the industry, it's important to only stand out in the best ways, at least at first."

The advice came at an excellent time. My goth-meets-thrift-store college wardrobe and makeup had grown tiresome. I'd never be a loud colors or cheerleader type, but my deep skepticism and world-weariness didn't need to manifest in an all-black wardrobe and thick eyeliner. I could keep my combat boots, as long as they were clean and polished, and pair them with sheath dresses and wide-legged slacks. Krissy advised me to lean into my boyish frame, clucking her envy that I possessed a body type that lent itself to boat necks and pleated pants. She espoused the value of tailoring and having quality staple pieces as the foundation of my wardrobe, no matter my budget.

The first two weeks on the job were a whirlwind of absorbing new information and experiences. My feet ached from being on the ladder, working on store displays. The pads on my thumbs went numb from pinpricks. I arrived home exhausted every night. Cereal became my go-to dinner.

Bren was my champion, offering to pick up the slack with the house chores so I could focus on my new gig, and she kept the pantry stocked with my favorite drinks and snacks.

I knew I was lucky to have such a supportive best friend, which was why I felt bad about retreating to my bedroom whenever Chase came over. But watching him make cow eyes at her as she fought their inevitable coupling was not something I needed to witness.

Not when I was trying to keep my mind off a particular someone.

I'd been able to put my night with Billy from my mind. Mostly. But I found it harder late in the evenings when it was quiet and dark. I couldn't pretend it didn't hurt, and more than that, it stung that Billy had gotten to me and made me feel something more than a passing attraction. Since I'd started dating as a teenager, I'd avoided that, and he'd broken me down in one night.

Thankfully, those thoughts disappeared with the sun. The mornings kept coming. Keeping busy helped me avoid thinking about Billy during the daytime.

An effective strategy.

Right up until I saw him.

I'd volunteered to do an early afternoon Starbucks run. The closest location to Kolya's was on the ground floor of a hotel in our downtown neighborhood. I ordered everyone's drinks on my app and did the five-minute walk to pick them up. As I entered, Justin Bieber's "Mistletoe" came through the lobby speakers. I paused to admire the ornamented garland near the elevator banks. Things had been so hectic I'd practically forgotten Christmas was only a few days away.

But I was here for caffeine. Not to look at decorations.

I rushed through the lobby.

A flash of blue-black hair caught my eye.

I stopped dead in my tracks.

There had to be other men in Seattle with that hair color. Hundreds of thousands of people lived in the city. But not today. Even from behind, seeing only his head and shoulders peeking out above an armchair, I knew it.

He sat at a little table along the side of the lobby, the kind used for bar seating during other times of the day. And even though Starbucks was on the opposite side of the cavernous room, I felt myself drift toward Billy. Toward disaster. Like a magnet.

I couldn't help it.

The chance to ask why. Or rail at him. I wasn't sure.

A voice in my head screamed at me for this insanity. I'd held on to my pride this long. My dignity was the only thing I had left.

I'd never messaged him. Never let him know how much he'd hurt me.

How successfully he'd played me.

But my feet would not stop moving. Driven by the part of my brain that couldn't resist, the part that couldn't stop asking, *what was the "I'm sorry" for?*

He hadn't seen me yet.

A beautiful woman with wavy blond hair and a megawatt smile sat across from him, talking and laughing elegantly. She wore cream-colored slacks with a blush-pink blouse. A gorgeous brown Birkin bag sat in the chair next to her.

The possibility existed that this woman was one of Billy's colleagues. She certainly looked like someone who could work at Wallingford Capital. But there were tells in her soft features, something in the way she occasionally touched his hand as she spoke that told me they were more than coworkers. The smart thing to do would have been to turn around and walk away. After three weeks of hardening my heart against Billy, my instinct should have been to protect myself. He still hadn't seen me, after all. No good could come from moving closer.

The woman noticed me as I approached. I imagined my expression looked determined. I felt the hardness in my eyes, but also the shakiness of my limbs. She stopped speaking as I came up along Billy's side.

He looked up, not understanding what he saw at first. Then his eyes bulged comically, and he flailed in his seat, rising without thought to a standing position.

I'd been sure, of course, but at least a part of me was still surprised. It was Billy, but also...not. More like the *American Psycho* version of him. Gone were the jeans and T-shirt and messy curls. His suit fit perfectly, cut sharp and angled to give his compact frame maximum advantage. Product held his slicked-back hair firmly against his skull. The only thing the same was the enormous, expensive watch dominating his wrist, more at home flashing in the lobby lights than under the dull fluorescents of Denny's.

"Mo?" he asked, disbelievingly, looking me up and down.

"Hey, Billy." A part of me had been dying to open with something more like, "Hey, you fucking ghosting liar," but it hadn't felt right. Still, I narrowed my eyes.

"Billy?" the blond woman questioned, staring up at us.

"Um... It's a nickname," he stuttered.

"Really?" She eyed me with interest. "I've never heard anyone call you that."

I coughed as my breath hitched.

He registered my response, quick to reassure me, "It's a nickname. For William."

"William." It sounded rotten on my tongue.

"What are you doing here?" he asked, as though I'd wandered into his living room.

"Working." I pointed at the Starbucks sign. "Coffee run."

Billy's eyes burned as he studied me. I felt certain he noted my upscale outfit, along with the taming of my hair and makeup. "It's nice to see you," he stammered, raising his left arm before catching himself and lowering it to his side. Becoming aware he'd jumped to his feet at my approach, he took a calming breath and sat back down.

"You too," I replied. Even though it wasn't nice. It was the opposite of nice, running into this *Wolf of Wall Street* version of Billy—William—in the middle of my workday. It was disconcerting and nausea-inducing. Every wrong thing about allowing myself to imagine possibilities with him came barreling to the forefront of my mind. I was a stupid fool. A terrible thing to realize, considering I'd taken so much pride in not being foolish.

Billy didn't dispel the uncomfortable air. He just stared at me.

If he thought I was going to smile and make small talk, he was sorely mistaken. I wasn't going to help him out. I waited. He owed me more words.

Finally, he darted his eyes at his companion before speaking to me. "I know I should have texted more," he began. "Except I wasn't sure—" He looked at the blond again. "I couldn't—"

Billy gulped audibly as his gaze raked over me again. His regard shone nakedly, the longing so unmistakable I couldn't excuse it as anything else. I'd been right. He wanted me. The evidence of his desire should have felt like vindication. But it didn't. It just pissed me off. Because I was more confused than ever.

He swallowed hard. "I didn't know how—"

The blond huffed exasperatedly. She was done. Done with his clumsiness. Done with him looking at me like I was his favorite flavor of ice cream.

"I'm Rosalyn," she said, tossing her hair and reaching her arm out. "William's fiancée."

Chapter Five

LAST YEAR

Will

It seemed impossible, but she'd somehow grown more beautiful in four years.

Her hair shone a rich, decadent auburn under the bright lights of the auditorium, not the honey-brown I remembered. Her sophisticated long-sleeved black dress fit like a glove, the sleek material standing out in an ocean of rainbow-hued puffy coats and holiday sweaters. As she leaned out to say hello to a woman passing by in the aisle, her movements seemed different, more subdued.

I drank in the sight greedily. Of course, I should have expected she wouldn't be in combat boots and heavy makeup like the night we'd spent together. Or flustered and rushing as she'd been that terrible day in the hotel lobby. This woman was polished and controlled. But as I watched her lips moving, unconsciously mouthing the words to the Christmas carols playing over the PA, I smiled. Definitely Mo.

No. *Maureen.*

My heart hammered into my throat. Even though I'd been ninety-nine percent sure she'd be here, I had no control over the way the reality of seeing her affected my body. I itched to go over there and explain myself. She might never forgive me, but I wanted to say my piece. Four years ago, Mo hadn't stayed one nanosecond beyond Rosalyn cattily announcing our engagement. She'd also immediately blocked my texts, so I'd never been able to talk to her.

Not that I had anything magical to offer. No tidy explanation to excuse what I'd done. I'd once messaged her a cowardly "I'm sorry." I owed her those words to her face. She might give me a knee to the groin—I'd never forget the way she handled that frat bro at the bar—but I deserved it.

Standing in the shadows near the back of the cavernous room gave me enough cover to stare somewhat blatantly. I watched as her lip sync turned into delicate chuckling at something Marley said. Even her laughter was elegant.

"Hey, man. Are you okay?" Leo came up on my left side. "You look kinda red."

"I'm fine. Just hot in here after being so cold outside."

Leo nodded but slipped a bottle of water into my hand anyway. He was a good guy, always had been.

Last week, I'd reconnected with my former best friend James at our ten-year high school reunion. Back in the day, I'd been tight with his family as well. When I'd run into James's parents and his brother Leo in the parking lot half an hour ago, we'd all been pleasantly surprised. But it made sense they'd be here to support James on his big night.

"We're still trying to hang in the back," Leo said. "I don't want the big guy to see us until after he does his thing. Don't want to make him more nervous."

I chuckled. James's nerves were probably at critical mass over what he was about to do. I still couldn't believe my old friend was planning such a public gesture.

Marley, a fellow teacher, had been James's plus-one at the reunion. As he'd faced our bullies from a decade ago, he'd drawn heavily on her silent support. Unlike him, I'd had dealings with a few of our former classmates over the years, my role at Wallingford Capital occasionally bringing me into their orbit. But I hadn't put a period on those high school days until James and I did so together last Saturday.

That night had gone so well I'd been shocked to learn he and Marley weren't a bona fide couple. Tonight, James wanted to rectify that. He'd texted a few days ago asking me to make a sign on a posterboard giving a reason I thought he and Marley were a perfect match, and then send a picture of me holding it. Apparently, his plan was to collect as many of these pictures as possible from friends and family, and then assemble the images into a slideshow to prove to Marley they were meant to be together. He'd be debuting the slideshow this evening, at the Coleman Creek High School Holiday Talent Show, while he sung in front of the standing-room-only crowd.

I felt flattered he'd asked me to take part, considering up until last weekend, we hadn't spoken in a decade. I'd left behind so much of my youth, especially after the accident, but I wanted to reclaim my friendship with James. Reflexively, I removed my right hand from my pocket and stretched out its three digits, using my opposite hand to massage the two stumps of my ring and pinky fingers.

The show began on a high note, with an older man doing an incredible rendition of "Snow." There were dancers and singers. A shy-seeming blond boy absolutely killed it on the guitar.

I imagined James would be surprised to see me. And I wouldn't have come, would have left it at sending the picture. That had been my plan, anyway.

Until I'd realized Marley's sister was Mo.

I'd started to wonder at the reunion when James had introduced me to Marley. It wasn't a rare name, but not super common either. And I'd never forgotten the name of Mo's sister. I'd never forgotten any of the things she'd told me.

So many times over the past four years, I'd thought of that night. I'd held on fiercely to the memory of those stolen moments. Dreamed of them, woke with them, vividly imagined her voice, the way she smiled and tossed her hair over her shoulder. The way she laughed at my jokes and asked about my art. I'd imagined going further than I had when I'd touched her hand or pressed our foreheads together. Played the *what-if* game in my mind until I thought I'd go crazy.

I'd used my text conversations with James to line up all the information Mo had given me four years ago. The name of the small town where he'd moved to become a teacher, Coleman Creek. I found out Marley had cared for her mother until her death just over a year ago. James and Marley had had lunch recently with Marley's older sister, who lived in Seattle and worked in fashion.

That last one seemed definitive, other than Marley's sister was named Maureen. I realized she must have given me a different name at the club, I assumed for safety reasons, since James and Marley never hinted she had a nickname. More proof that night had been surreal. Just like I wasn't Billy. Or William. I'd circled back to Will. Except Will with less darkness riding him than he'd had in high school. I hoped.

Finally, it was James's turn. The slideshow ran. He performed a horribly off-key rendering of Kelly Clarkson's "Underneath the

Tree." And in the end, hundreds of pairs of eyes teared up as he and Marley embraced.

It was a happy ending for my oldest friend. I didn't expect my own, obviously. The Christmas miracle had already happened—the insane coincidence of James's Marley being Mo's Marley. I just wanted to talk to her. Even if she hated me afterward.

As the auditorium cleared, I followed Leo and James's parents over toward the happy couple. Marley's sisters stood on the other side of her, with their backs to us, talking to a woman with a baby in each arm. I kept my gaze low, wanting to give Mo a chance to notice me before I attempted to speak to her. We drew closer, my pulse kicking into high gear.

The presence of both his family and me stunned James. He'd been grateful we'd sent the pictures but hadn't expected us to make the trip. I told him the partial truth, that I'd come because I admired what he was doing and didn't have other plans.

"What if Marley had turned me down?"

His ridiculous question helped calm my nerves. "Dude, I saw you two at our reunion. The way she showed up for you. If that's not love, I don't know what is."

He smiled. I gave Marley a quick, congratulatory hug as James's parents and brother started asking them about some of the student performers. Taking a few steps into the aisle, I drifted away from their conversation as my racing heart reminded me of my purpose. As much as I'd enjoyed reconnecting with my friend this past week, I hadn't driven three hundred miles to hide behind him and make small talk.

My heartbeat moved from my throat to become a pounding orchestra in my head. Mo stood only feet away.

Keeping my eyes downcast, I took a fortifying breath and ran my palms over my thighs a few times before stuffing them in my pockets. Yet even as nerves threatened to consume me, it was almost a relief to feel this flustered. It had been a while since I'd felt much of anything.

I lifted my gaze as Mo turned in my direction.

A brief flinch was the only immediate evidence of her surprise. Cool green eyes met mine, the pupils dilated to black pools. She gripped a large purse in front of herself, knuckles whitening. Her jaw twitched beneath slightly flared nostrils as she attempted to maintain a neutral face. For the most part, she succeeded—except as the seconds passed, she couldn't stop those stormy, searching eyes from narrowing.

Good. I'd been thinking she might pretend not to recognize me. I squared my shoulders and schooled my breathing, about to initiate conversation, when a sandy-haired ball of energy popped up in front of me, arm outstretched. "You're Will, right? James's friend from high school? I'm Miranda, Marley's sister." Her infectious smile broke through the tension in the air, and I found myself unwittingly charmed. But Mo looked concerned, glancing down as I removed my right hand from my pocket. Well, that answered that question. I'd always wondered if she'd noticed that night.

She needn't have worried. Over the years, I'd improved at managing both daily tasks and the rude stares or questions that occasionally came my way. I shook Miranda's hand and waited. There was a momentary pinch in her expression when I knew she registered my missing fingers. But it disappeared as quickly as it came.

"Yes, I'm Will. Great to meet you."

"Cool, cool." She bounced up on her heels and took her hand back, clapping it together with her other one. "Well, I really liked your slide. We heard a bit about you on the way here because Marley was telling us about going to James's reunion—"

"That's true," Mo piped in. "She was telling us all about James's friend, *Will*." Her eyes narrowed at me again, and I imagined it was only because Miranda was made of cupcakes and sunshine that she didn't pick up on the animosity in her sister's voice.

"Oh, sorry," Miranda said. "This is my other sister, Maureen."

Mo—I really needed to think of her as Maureen—stuck her arm out. "Nice to meet you." Ah, so she wasn't pretending not to know me, but we would play that game for other people.

I stared down and realized I was about to touch her for the first time in four years. I reached out with my injured hand. In my dreams, my hand was always whole. And her palm wasn't icy cold. In my dreams, when she pumped her arm up and down a few times, her eyes didn't bore into me like I disgusted her.

"Nice to meet you as well."

There was a reception happening in the room across from the auditorium. Most of the audience had made their way over there already, and James, Marley, and his family headed in that direction.

"We should catch up with them," Maureen said to her sister, grabbing Miranda's hand and moving to follow the crowd to the doorway. Away from me.

Miranda looked over her shoulder at me. "You're coming, right?"

The two of them turned toward the exit. *Damn, was that it?* Four years later and all I'd gotten was a glare, a handshake, and a dismissal. I wasn't entirely sure what I'd been expecting, but it hadn't been that. I'd thought there'd at least be some questions, loud words maybe—not one minute of introductions and bye.

Should I follow? Try to confront her? That's what I'd come here for. But dammit. If she didn't want that, did I really have the right to push? If she wanted to ignore me or pretend I didn't exist, didn't I owe it to her to let her? Shit. I really wanted the chance to explain. My phone buzzed in my pocket.

MO: Still your number?

My head whipped up to look at her across the auditorium. She still didn't glance my way but had moved away from her sisters, standing tall and collected with her phone in hand.

ME: Yes

I watched the three dots bouncing for a minute before her next message appeared. I took that time to change the name in my contacts.

MAUREEN: I need to make an appearance at the reception. You should too. Find a reason to slip away after fifteen minutes. I'll do the same and meet you at your car. I'm assuming you're in the parking lot here.
ME: Yeah. I drove.
MAUREEN: What am I looking for? A rental?
ME: Still driving the same black Audi.
MAUREEN: Of course you are.

Chapter Six

Maureen

He still drove the fifty-thousand-dollar car. Because that was who he was. William the finance bro. William sitting across from his perfect blond fiancée. William wearing an expensive watch. I guess he called himself Will now, but so what? All I knew was he wasn't Billy. Billy had never been real.

When I saw him standing in the aisle, I understood what people meant when they talked about having out-of-body experiences. Because from the moment I noticed him, my brain struggled to process that it wasn't some sort of hideous illusion. Somehow, I'd missed his contribution to the slideshow, likely because I'd been watching Marley's face the whole time. By the time we were feet apart, it felt as though I'd floated above myself. Four years later, and Will had sucked me right back into an unwanted reality, a nightmare where the *Will* Marley had mentioned a few times as being "James's super awesome friend from high school" turned out to be the *Billy/William* I'd spent nearly half a decade trying to forget.

I'd considered not saying anything, giving him the evil eye while fantasizing about throat-punching him. But in the end, I knew we needed to talk. Because it appeared as though he was going to be in my life in the supporting role of my sister's boyfriend's good friend.

This past week, I'd insisted Marley keep an open mind about James—she'd been pushing him away hard, not feeling worthy of his love. Now she finally had the happiness she'd dreamed of, and I wasn't about to taint it by informing her that James's best pal from high school was a lying douchenozzle.

Thank god I'd never told my sisters about Billy. It would have been too humiliating. The one time I'd allowed myself to catch something resembling real feelings—within a few hours of meeting someone, no less—I'd been burned in the worst way. Better they continued to think of me as an impenetrable man-eater.

I just needed Will to agree to my plan. We'd stay out of each other's way so no one would pick up on the fact we had history.

Also, we would never, ever speak of our night together. Ever.

The festive decorations and twinkling lights barely registered as I walked from the auditorium into the high school's breezeway. Nodding to some acquaintances as I entered the reception, I remained focused on the fact I had fifteen minutes to pull myself together before I needed to step out to the parking lot and face him. I stuck out from the crowd in my black dress, but no one seemed to care. My old teachers waved to me and raised cups in my direction. Former classmates introduced me to their spouses and kids. I managed a few bites of Katy Baumbeck's cinnamon maple cookies. Tasted like home.

Truthfully, I loved being back in Coleman Creek. I'd been so adamant about getting out and moving to the city, but I might be more like Marley than I'd thought. It wasn't bad living in Seattle, necessarily. I just wasn't sure the big city benefits—and there were many, especially for someone working in fashion—outweighed all the things I missed about where I'd grown up.

Running into Will seemed like a Murphy's Law type of situation in terms of timing.

The career I'd built was at a crossroads. After three years of working my way up, I'd attained the position of lead manager and buyer for Kolya's. But the high-end market was hypercompetitive, and we weren't the new, shiny store in town anymore. We'd recently hired an in-house stylist, trying to expand into the personal shopping space, but it wasn't taking off as much as the owners had hoped. There was a decent chance I'd be looking for a new job next year.

My living situation was also in flux. Bren and Chase had been dating for so long it seemed inevitable they'd move in together soon. I had an inkling my best friend would tell me she wanted to move out when our lease came up for renewal in a few months.

Everything was changing. I was on the precipice of…whatever came next. So, of course, I'd run into my loosest of loose ends. Most regrettable of regrets. Confusingest of confusions. Billy.

Will.

Slipping away from the reception proved easy enough. I still had friends in town. If my sisters noted my absence, they'd assume I was catching up with someone. Out of the corner of my eye, I saw Will with James's family saying goodbye to Marley. Luckily, they headed to a different parking area.

I crept into the darkened hallways of the high school. Once I was sure no one could see or hear me, I attempted to shake off my nerves. I took my noisy heeled boots off, pacing in my socks, back and forth across the terrazzo floor. My heart rate and breathing were finally under control, but my mind raced.

I could still picture William that last day I'd seen him. Sitting in the hotel lobby. Horrified by the sight of me. Too cowardly to speak. Until his companion uttered the terrible truth. *Fiancée.*

Stretching my arms above my head and rolling my neck a few times, I exhaled through my nose. Five more minutes until I needed to go outside.

And say, what exactly? *Why didn't you tell me you were engaged? Why did you take me out that night, be wonderful, and make me believe we had something? That you were interested? Why are you such a giant tool?*

Stopping short, I leaned my head against a cold concrete wall. No context could explain away the moment I'd stood in that lobby. Shocked and devastated and embarrassed. There was nothing to say. Nothing to know. I didn't need to ask the questions because that would imply I cared. And I didn't. Because fuck him.

I pulled my boots back on and walked out the side door, braced by the frigid December wind on my face. Fuck him and his tailored suit and his designer watch, his fancy job, and his perfect fiancée, who was probably now his perfect wife.

I got closer to the north side of the student lot, where he'd parked, enjoying the harsh sound of my heels on the pavement.

My eyes lifted to his car. Fuck him and his Audi and—

Fuck me.

Will leaned his elbows against the sleek exterior, ankles crossed casually in front of him. He glanced up, and my breath caught as his wind-tousled hair grazed his forehead. Raising an arm, he gave me a soft smile. His gray eyes shone, half-mast and hooded—*and goddamn, those lashes.* Still so thick they made his lids appear rimmed with liner. His expression so full of hope and expectation, I almost surrendered my glare. Almost.

"Hi," he began artlessly, pushing away from the vehicle as I approached.

"Hey."

"I'm glad you texted." He folded his arms over his olive-green sweater. I recognized the brand, Buck Mason. The fashion buyer in me approved. I scowled at him.

"What else could I do?" I hissed, not mincing words. "It's not like I would have chosen to see you again. Or talk to you. But you're here. So, obviously, we need to."

He nodded, and his breaths grew long and drawn. "Okay. I get it. Even so, I'm grateful. I tried to talk to you after that day in the hotel—"

"I don't want to discuss that, *Will*." Gnashing my teeth together, I leveled him with a hard stare.

His brows knitted together. "Then why—"

"I don't want to talk about that day. Or about the night we hung out."

"Okay, but—"

"I just want to make sure we're clear moving forward that four years ago didn't happen. None of it. As far as everyone else is concerned—especially Marley and James—you and I never met before tonight. Got it?" I inhaled deeply, proud I'd gotten my words out quickly and succinctly.

"Maureen, I know you're angry. And of course you have every right to be." He dropped his arms to his sides as urgency clouded his features. "But if you'll give me a minute, I'd like to tell you what was happening back then. I promise I'm not trying to make excuses. I just want to explain."

"No."

"No?"

"No. I don't need your explanations. If I wanted them, I wouldn't have blocked your number."

"But, Mo—"

"Don't fucking call me that!" I smoothed my hands over my dress as I checked around to make sure no one could hear us.

"Sorry, sorry." He held up his palms, seemingly unconcerned about his lack of fingers being prominently on display. "Maureen. I won't forget again." He cupped his hands together and blew into them. "I get what you're saying, but if you let me—"

"I already told you I don't want to hear it," I whisper-snarled. "And you don't get to clear your conscience or whatever it is you're trying to do by forcing me to listen—"

"That's not what I'm trying to—"

"Just. Stop. Nothing you can say will make it better. Nothing I need clarity on. There are no misunderstandings here. Four years ago, I found out you are an enormous prick. That's all I really need to know. I'm not interested in re-litigating the past, reliving it, or whatever it is you're trying to do here."

His face fell. He paused before speaking again. "I'm sorry. The last thing I wanted to do back then was hurt you."

I barely escaped choking on my breath. "Whoa. Hold up." My cheeks heated. It was a strange sensation, being full-up with emotion. I stepped back, crossing my hands back and forth in front of myself. "Don't put words in my mouth. I said you were a total dick. I never said you hurt me."

"Of course. Sorry." He crooked an elbow behind his head and exhaled heavily. "Look, I'm just saying I know you're right. I *was* a prick."

"Exactly. And you don't get to ask for anything now. Especially absolution."

He looked like he had another reply, but ultimately, he simply nodded before exhaling gravely and stating again, "You're right."

"Obviously." I huffed. "From now on, I only want to talk about what we're going to do in the future."

He appeared sad, but the fight had left him. "Okay."

"Great. Then you agree to pretend we just met tonight?"

"Whatever you want."

"Awesome." I stood back on my heels. "Well, then we're done here. I guess I'll see you tomorrow at Marley's house for lunch. You're leaving in the afternoon, right?"

"Uh-huh. I need to drive back tomorrow. Christmas with my parents."

"Then it shouldn't be too hard to avoid each other for a few hours. Agreed?"

"Alright."

I breathed out. It was done. We had a plan, even if he looked like a kicked puppy right now. Even if there was nothing of the slick finance bro I'd seen in the lobby that day and everything of the fascinating guy I'd met at a concert and talked to for hours in a greasy coffee shop.

I was determined to walk away quickly. Except something compelled me to look back and ask, "You came alone? Wife's not with you?"

The kicked puppy expression dissolved somewhat as he squared his shoulders and looked me in the eye. "I'm not married." My stomach flipped when he said it, my brain picturing the woman in the hotel. But I didn't want to lose my advantage. I gave a clipped nod as I turned away. He called after me, "Maureen, so you know…I've never been married."

THE NEXT DAY WAS EXCRUCIATING.

Miranda and I wanted to give Marley and James privacy, so we'd checked into the Hampton Inn last night. Separate rooms since I wouldn't have been able to handle my baby sister's Susie Sunshine personality after talking to Will. Of course, after spending another hour at the talent show reception, I'd arrived at the hotel to find Will's Audi parked there. In the morning, I hid in my room until check-out time. Will's car was gone when Miranda and I left.

Never been married.

I felt positive Rosalyn hadn't been lying about being engaged. But they hadn't gone through with it. The question of why ran through my brain on a loop. Taunting me.

Will wasn't at Marley's house when I arrived, but that didn't stop James from gushing about how his old friend had made the effort to drive to Coleman Creek for the slideshow. I had no intention of bursting James's bubble, but after reflecting on last night, I recalled Will had seemed totally unsurprised by my presence. I guessed he'd probably come because he suspected I'd be here, something easy enough to confirm.

"James?" I asked, attempting nonchalance as I sat on the counter behind him in the breakfast nook.

"Yeah?"

"Is it really so shocking Will came? I mean, from the way Marley talked about him and your reunion, it doesn't seem far-fetched he'd do you a solid."

Saying that made me grimace a little, but I needed James to spill on what he'd told Will prior to yesterday.

"I guess not." He shrugged. "It surprised me to see my parents and brother, too. They didn't have to come. I appreciate everyone making the extra effort. Especially Will, considering the two of us have only barely started reconnecting. He's a good guy."

I rolled my eyes as James looked down at his crossword puzzle. "Did Will know Miranda and I would be here?"

If James thought my non sequitur of a question odd, he didn't give any sign, and merely smiled as he answered, "I think so. Pretty sure I told him we'd have a full house because you guys were staying here until Christmas."

That settled it in my mind. I knew I'd mentioned Marley's name that night we'd talked at Denny's. And Coleman Creek. It wouldn't have been hard for Will to put two and two together.

Thirty minutes later, Will walked through the door with James's family, talking animatedly with James's brother Leo about football, again making no effort to hide his missing fingers. I thought about the way he'd shoved his hands in his pockets four years ago. Or folded them in his lap underneath the table. That discomfort seemed to have lessened since our night together, and I wasn't callous enough to begrudge his progress there.

I was, however, callous enough to spend the rest of lunch ignoring him and making sure we stayed on opposite sides of the room. We didn't speak, didn't interact. But I caught his eyes on me a few times and knew our proximity affected him as much as me.

To that point, I took advantage of the mimosa bar Miranda had set up. It wasn't typical for me to drink a lot—I had good reasons to be careful—but Will's presence loosened my usual strictness with it.

My focus fell three glasses later, huddled in the living room with my sisters. Marley's loving expression lasered in on James as he told a story, and Miranda lamented how she wanted to find someone too. Without meaning to, I revealed I once thought I'd found a special person myself, but that I'd been wrong. My sisters' mouths gaped. They'd never known me to be serious about dating anyone. Before they could launch an interrogation, I retreated into the kitchen to get some water.

Clearly, I needed to flush the mimosas from my system before I said something truly stupid.

I pushed a glass against the dispenser and watched as it filled, heart thumping from what I'd almost let slip. *Get it together, Maureen. You just need to make it an hour, and then he'll drive away.* I opened the fridge to grab a snack before deciding against it. Even though I'd only managed a few bites at lunch, I wasn't hungry. I shoved the door closed.

And came face-to-face with Will.

He'd been finishing a phone call in the adjacent laundry room, and his eyes went wide when he saw me. The galley-style kitchen of Marley's home blocked us from the view of the others. Their voices seemed a million miles away.

We stood frozen. I hadn't expected to be alone with him again. Not after last night. I watched the slow slide of his throat as he gulped. Locking eyes with me, he inched closer.

"Hi," he murmured.

The awareness of him I'd been fighting all morning became a concentrated force in the room, invading my body. I shuddered lightly as the woodsy scent of his cologne drew out the memory of his nose grazing delicately along my cheek. Horrifyingly, the water I'd just poured started slipping through my fingers. Will acted fast, reaching a hand out to steady it. I blinked as our fingers touched in the place we both held the glass.

"I've got it," he said, breaking our contact as he put the glass on the counter. "Sorry I startled you."

"You didn't." I recovered my senses, stepping back to put a foot of distance between us. "I'm just, uh, clumsy."

"No, you're not," he whispered. My breath hitched, gaze landing on his dark stubble as he scrubbed a hand roughly over his face. I cursed inwardly. Why did he have to be even hotter than he was four years ago?

I didn't plan on waiting around to find out. He sighed and moved aside as I motioned to get by him. As I passed, I asked in a low tone, "You knew I'd be here this weekend, didn't you?"

He looked up, pausing significantly before responding. "It's why I came."

"To see me?"

"To talk to you. To say the things you wouldn't let me say last night." He angled his forearms to grip the counter. "Even if you hated me, I wanted to try."

"To explain why you lied about being engaged?"

"I didn't exactly lie." I glared at him, and he held up his hands, letting out a nervous cough. "Okay, yes, to explain about that."

I thought about how I'd denied him last night. It had felt good getting that power back. Pushing my palms into my rear pockets, I straightened to my full height, meeting him chest to chest. "Can I ask you a question?"

"Of course."

"That woman—Rosalyn—was she lying when she said you were engaged?"

"No. But there's more—"

"And that night we spent together, when I poured my heart out about my mom and my life and opened myself up to you, were you engaged then?"

He glanced down at the floor.

I snorted. "There's nothing to say here, Will. I don't want to hear it."

I turned away. He spoke under his breath, stopping me. "I wanted to talk to you...to make sure you knew how much our night together meant to me. How much I think about it. Think about you. I don't want you to..."

"Don't want me to what?"

"I don't want you to regret it. Because I don't." He pushed out an unsteady breath. "And even if it makes me an asshole, I don't want you to hate me."

I frowned. "You don't get to decide that."

He winced. I studied him and thought about why I didn't want to hear any explanations for his actions. Was it really to prove I didn't care? Or was it because I feared he could somehow find the right words to make me forgive him? I couldn't risk it.

I leaned back to look through the doorway into the living room. James was in the middle of another lengthy story, and it appeared no one had noticed our absence yet.

Will would be in my life, at least on the edge of it, for the foreseeable future. And judging by my body's electric response to him, I had a lot of work to do to maintain my resolve. I couldn't allow myself to be manipulated again. I shivered as the memory of seeing him in that hotel lobby washed over me. The shock. The embarrassment.

I straightened before speaking again. "Let's do a better job of steering clear of each other."

Striding off, I didn't look back.

An hour later, Will drove away. I stayed in the house while everyone else went outside to wave goodbye.

Chapter Seven

PRESENT DAY

Will

"You can't possibly be serious about staying here." My mother gave me a pained look, running her manicured fingernail along the sill of my living room's picture window. She moved across the room to the arched entryway of the kitchen, dipping her head to glance inside before retreating quickly, as though walking into my newly renovated kitchen was equivalent to entering a particularly foul porta potty.

"Mother, you're being ridiculous." While my apartment certainly had a lot of the quirkiness and character that came from being housed in a 1920s-era building, it had been completely gutted and redone with every conceivable modern upgrade. But the narrow hallways and cage elevator had my parents convinced it was basically a slum.

"I'm not," she insisted. "Sweetheart, this move is ill-advised. What was wrong with your condo in Bellevue?"

"We've been over this. I bought that place because I thought it'd be a good investment—and it was—but it never really felt like me. This is a much better fit."

She sniffed. "Well, your father and I don't like it. Not at all. We hate having to worry about you so much."

My chest tightened as the words hit like knives—digging into old wounds. Sighing, I sought to reassure her. "I'm twenty-nine years old, Mother. I can handle myself. Pretty sure you and Father don't need to be on top of my living situation. Besides, you know full well this is a nice neighborhood."

"It's certainly...colorful," she allowed.

"C'mon. It's full of beautiful old architecture, million-dollar homes, and all the galleries, bars, and restaurants anyone can ask for. At my old place, the neighborhood died at eight o'clock every night." I walked over to kiss her on the side of her head, feeling the crunch of her hair products. "I'm staying here, so you'll need to make peace with it."

"Well, I suppose it is good for you to be in a place where you can be more social. Get out and meet people." She turned her head away and spoke to the wall. "You know, Rosalyn is still single. She asks about you sometimes—"

"Mother. No." Her posture stiffened as she adjusted her purse higher on her shoulder. It had been a few months since she'd brought up my former fiancée, to the point I'd begun to hope my parents had finally accepted my choice to end the engagement. Especially since it had been almost four years. Apparently not.

But they would need to get over it because I honestly couldn't remember the last time I'd thought about Roz. If that didn't confirm I'd made the right decision, I didn't know what would.

Recently, only one woman had been on my mind. One with a sharp wit and even sharper tongue, not to mention a wicked sense of style. I couldn't stop thinking about Maureen because, after a year of dodging one another, I'd be seeing her again in less than two weeks.

My mother brought me back to the present, laying a hand on the radiator cover. "Are you sure this is safe?" she asked. "I've heard these things can explode out of the blue."

I scoffed. "Good grief. Have you been on TikTok again? I assure you, no explosions are imminent."

"This electric panel looks old too."

"All the electrical was just redone."

"By a licensed electrician?"

"Yes." I gritted my teeth. "This is my building. Do you think I'd allow shoddy workmanship?"

"Of course not, darling. I'm just saying that charlatans are out there trying to take advantage of good people like you. Certifications can be faked."

I thought of Hank, the electrical contractor I'd hired for the building, a gruff older Gen-Xer with a reputation so sterling I'd had to wait months to get on his project list. I chuckled, imagining introducing him to my mother so she could accuse him of being a snake oil salesman.

"It's truly amazing that you allowed me to handle millions of dollars' worth of accounts at Wallingford, yet you don't think I can hire someone to rehab a building."

"That's different." She stepped over and reached for my hand. My right hand. "Your father and I were there with you at the company. And then these past few years, you've been making all these *choices*." She hushed the last word like it was dirty. "Ending things with Rosalyn. Leaving Wallingford. Establishing your company. Selling your company. This building. It all seems a little...haphazard." She ran her hand along the scars on my palms, over the taut skin where my ring and pinky finger used to be. "Sometimes it feels like you're slipping away from us. Like I don't understand you at all."

I exhaled, grasping my mother's wrist lightly to halt her examination. I'd let her and my father dictate my life for so long after the accident that they interpreted my making decisions for myself as a betrayal. They loved me, but for most of my life, that love had meant being stifled and smothered. The last time I'd attempted to rebel, I'd ended up in a medically induced coma with sixteen broken bones and minus two fingers. So I understood why they feared the worst.

Before I could reply, a knock signaled my father's arrival.

As soon as I opened the door, he barreled through, barking, "Parking is hell outside."

"Wonderful to see you too, Father. And in such a chipper mood. Happy Thanksgiving."

He hmphed. "William, when you said you wanted to spend your time on this little project, I expected a much different result. Something sleek and modern. I thought you could convert these old apartments into condos for sale. Everything looks the same as it did when you bought it."

I pinched the bridge of my nose. I wanted to remind him this project had nothing to do with him. Wallingford Capital wasn't invested, and he knew full well I had the financial capacity to do whatever I wanted. I could blow my money on a cotton candy food truck or convert an old church into a paintball venue—ideas pitched to me at my last firm—and barely feel the dent in my bank account.

"Father, I already told you that one of my goals was to maintain the integrity of the building. The architect's design kept as much of the original structure as possible, so the exterior looks the same, with some safety upgrades. But I assure you—gas, water, electrical, Wi-Fi—all the modern amenities are top-notch. Plus, we added some common areas people will love, like the rooftop garden and gym. It's the best of new and old."

When I purchased the building on a short sale as an investment property, I'd originally thought of tearing it down, but after taking stock of the beautiful hardwoods, crown molding, and plasterwork, I decided on an extensive remodel instead. It had been a labor of love, but I knew I'd made the right call. I was so thrilled with the results, I moved into one of the third-floor apartments myself.

"What's the square footage on your unit?" my father asked, frown still fixed in place.

"Twelve hundred."

"Christ. If you wanted to live in a closet, you could have moved into your bedroom back home."

My parents continued scrutinizing my living room. I'd fallen in love at first sight with its expansive view of downtown, but they recoiled as though expecting a family of rabid raccoons to burst through the walls at any moment. I tried to be patient, my habit of appeasing them long-standing, but I couldn't help getting annoyed.

"Alright, both of you, this is important to me. And I wanted you to see it now that it's done because I'm really proud. But if you're just going to dump all over it, then we can leave right now."

My father's lips flattened, and my mother looked over at him, laying a hand on his arm before responding, "We're just getting used to the idea, sweetheart. You know we only want what's best for you."

They wanted the best for me. They just had no faith in my ability to know what that was. And while I understood the reasons for their worries, I was done allowing them to dictate the terms of my existence. Done sleepwalking through my days. My penance had cost me years of my life. Suffocated my career. Kept me from my art. Turned me into a coward with Rosalyn. And Maureen.

Dammit. Why did my mind keep going to her? *Because, dummy, it's been a year since you've seen her, and now you're scared about what will happen next weekend. Especially since you've been watching those videos nonstop.*

I walked over to my parents and slung one arm over each of their shoulders in a move meant to placate them. My specialty. "Look, I really appreciate you coming to see the building now that it's done. Even if you're not enthusiastic. How about we head back to your house for dinner? I bet the caterer has it set up by now. You can fill me in on which of your business contacts will be joining us." Thanksgiving had never been much of a family holiday for my parents. It was more of a chance to network for Wallingford.

They took my words for the peace offering they were, and we headed to our separate cars. The tenants were moving in over the weekend, and having the building full of people would be nice. I'd felt awful having to buy out some leases when the remodel started, considering it took the better part of a year. But I'd offered the previous tenants the first shot at the newly remodeled apartments, and most had taken me up on it, likely because I'd agreed to do the first year of rent at the old rates. I wasn't trying to be Robin Hood or anything, but I had enough money I could afford not to be a dick.

I straightened the wreath I'd hung on the entry door on my way out.

ALMOST A WEEK LATER, I'D FULLY MOVED into my new apartment. It had been a workout getting everything to the third floor. Movers had taken care of the large furniture, but I'd done the rest myself, hefting most of the boxes up the stairs rather than trying to make dozens of elevator trips. The last item I needed to bring in was a side chair I'd had since college. My grip faltered as I carried it up the steps from the second-floor landing.

Luckily, another set of hands appeared to grab it from the side above me, preventing the green velvet piece from bouncing down the stairs.

"I gotchya." My savior walked backward as we lugged the chair to the top of the stairs, putting it down with a thud.

"Thanks," I said, wiping an arm across my brow. "I guess I've gotten a little too confident in my gym routine because I honestly thought I could manage that on my own."

"No problem." The tall man smiled and made a *come here* gesture to a woman poking her head out of the nearest doorway.

"You're Chase, right?" I asked, panting slightly with exertion. I was still getting to know all my tenants.

"Yeah. And I remember you're Will, from when I picked up the key. This is my girlfriend, Bren. We're here, 3C."

"Cool. I'm in 3F." I reached out to shake their hands. As usual, I caught the tiny flinch as they clocked my missing fingers, but they didn't stare or make it weird. "Nice to meet you. Appreciate the help with the chair. It's a favorite." My breathing steadied. "I guess I better get it out of the hallway."

I moved to pick it up when Bren stepped out in front of me. "Do I know you from somewhere?" she asked.

"Um...I don't think so." I'd felt a flicker of recognition the first time I'd met Chase, and I was experiencing the same with Bren now. But I couldn't place either of them, so I chalked it up to the power of suggestion.

She tapped on her pursed lips as her eyes moved over me. "Hmm...I could swear." More lip tapping. "Have you ever come into Mackenzie's Brewery? Four blocks over. I work there."

"No. I haven't been much of anywhere yet. I'm still getting to know the neighborhood."

"Well, when you start exploring, put Mackenzie's at the top of your list," Chase said. "The brewmaster is a wizard."

Bren scrunched her eyes at me one last time before shrugging. "Definitely a wizard. I work nights, Tuesday through Saturday. I'd love to comp you a tasting flight if you come by, seeing as how the rent here is so reasonable. We probably owe you a few beers since you're basically letting us rob you."

I laughed, considering the offer. It had been a long time since I'd attempted to make friends outside the finance world. Since reconnecting with James, I'd realized how much I wanted that.

"I have to travel this weekend, but I'll take you up on that when I get back." Smiling, I gave a slight wave before resuming my task. Even after picking up the heavy chair and walking down the hallway, I felt lighter.

By the time I packed up my car to leave for Coleman Creek a few days later, I'd officially welcomed all fourteen of my tenants. Three units remained to lease out, but that would need to wait until after the new year. Since I had the time, I was acting as property manager for now. I'd contracted with a handyman service in case quick repairs were necessary, but I didn't expect to need much of that yet, since the interiors had been gutted and everything was essentially brand new.

I'd arranged all the furniture in my apartment and even hung up some of my paintings. They'd never looked right in my condo. I also put up a Christmas tree. It was small and plastic, nothing spectacular, but I'd never been inspired to have one before. I figured I could decorate it when I got back from my trip. Heck, I might even go nuts and hang up a stocking since I finally had a fireplace that looked like a fireplace and not an oversized stainless-steel toaster oven.

My parents had stopped launching daily objections to my living situation as well, so I felt cautiously optimistic this piece of my life was coming together.

Which left me free to overthink about Maureen. Seeing her in person and not behind a computer screen. I wondered if she would consider it a violation of our agreement that I'd watched her videos. But once James told me about them, how could I resist?

Even though it might be awkward, I couldn't say I dreaded our upcoming interaction. Because in an ideal world, we'd be able to hash out what happened five years ago and move on from it. I still wanted that. Wanted to know Maureen in whatever way she'd let me.

I knew her anger was justified. I shuddered when I thought of how I'd compounded lies with self-serving silence. But I didn't believe it was sustainable, given our connection to James and Marley.

If I'd been honest with Maureen that night at Denny's, maybe things would have progressed differently. Even if we'd turned out to be incompatible, our intense spark an anomaly, I couldn't help wishing we'd had the chance to find out.

Sure, I'd been with other women since Roz and I broke up, but when it came to how comfortable I felt with someone, how intrigued, how easily the conversation flowed, how invested I felt from the jump—Maureen was still the gold standard. I'd never been so immediately, magnetically pulled toward anyone, never felt that same buzz under my skin.

I'd sensed that wild energy with her five years ago, and I'd felt a ghost of it last Christmas, when we'd been alone in her sister's kitchen. That moment we'd both touched the stupid water glass haunted me more than any of the dates I'd had recently.

I had been careful to prevent any potential run-ins with Maureen in Coleman Creek this past year. Like when I'd told James I'd attend their Fourth of July barbecue, then claimed a stomach bug once I discovered Maureen would be there. Despite my desire to be near her, I'd respected her wishes and kept my distance.

But this trip would be different. James and Marley were having an engagement party, and as we'd both be part of their wedding next summer, there was no reasonable way for Maureen and me to escape being in the same room.

I tossed two of my favorite pillows in the back of the Audi before hopping into the driver's seat. The hotel outside Coleman Creek was comfortable enough, but I was picky about pillows. I also threw in my sketch pad, some drawing pencils, and my travel easel. My muse didn't appear easily, but I was always hopeful.

I'd parked in the loading zone in front of my building. As I was about to pull out, I realized I'd left my charger on the kitchen counter. I opened my door without checking the side mirror—a bonehead move I usually avoided—and narrowly missed clipping a bicycle speeding past.

"Watch it, asshole!" the man screamed as he swung wide into the street to avoid hitting my car door. After rounding the hood, he reached his arm back and flipped me the bird. "Fucking dick!" he shouted for good measure.

"Sorry," I mumbled into the air. My body trembled as the near-miss registered.

The sharp knife of adrenaline bit into my veins.

If I'd opened my door one second later, that guy would have been laid out on the street.

I slunk into my seat, slamming the door shut and leaning my head against my hands on the steering wheel. *The cyclist. I almost hit a cyclist. I was usually so careful. So conscious. Ever since...* My heart hammered, and a steady whooshing sound in my ears made me dizzy. The feeling of drowning, of being pulled under and surrounded by the thickening air, overwhelmed me. *It's okay... He's not on the ground... You're not on the ground... It's okay.*

A *tap, tap, tap* against the glass broke into my consciousness.

"Hey, man, you alright?" Chase made a motion for me to lower the window, which I did.

My heart still thumped a million miles an hour, but I wrangled my breathing into something resembling normal. "I'm fine. Just a little shaken up. I almost hit that guy on the bike."

"Yeah, I saw from the steps. But that wasn't all on you. That dude was way too close to begin with, considering the loading zone, plus he could have gone one block over where there's an actual dedicated bike lane."

"Still, though. I didn't look." My heart rate began to level.

"I wouldn't worry about it. Happens to all of us. He got to call you an 'asshole' and a 'dick' loud enough to wake the neighbors, plus flip you off. I'd say you're even."

I released a mirthless chuckle. Chase was right. An almost-accident wasn't the same as something terrible happening. And one thing I'd learned as I'd wrested my life from my parents' vise grip was not all risks could be mitigated.

I'd probably always have a mild panic attack whenever a moving bicycle got too close to my car. The sensation of asphalt beneath my thighs as the street literally ripped the skin from my body would stay with me forever. But did that mean I should never drive? I looked up at the building. I felt proud of something I'd worked at for the first time in a long time. My risk to take.

Chase continued making small talk as the adrenaline worked its way out of my system. I went to my apartment and grabbed my charger before getting back in the Audi. Carefully checking for cyclists, skateboarders, pedestrians, delivery drivers, door-to-door salespeople, stray dogs, and tumbleweeds, I pulled into the street.

I set off for James and Marley's engagement party, thinking about taking another risk.

Chapter Eight

Maureen

"Oscar, watch Bambi do it, okay? C'mon, Bambi. Shake." James's labradoodle obediently lifted his paw and let me tug it up and down a few times. I rewarded him with a candy cane–shaped treat from the side table.

"Okay, Oscar. Now you. Shake." Marley's Labrador looked at me curiously and angled his head to the side, tongue lolling out lazily. "Shake," I implored. He tilted his head in the other direction and used his hind leg to itch the back of his neck. I sighed. "I think your dog is broken," I called to my sister in the kitchen.

One of the best parts about staying with Marley and James was their two dogs, both of whom fell into the "loveable but dopey" category, although James's had a few more tricks.

I stretched lazily on the green tufted couch. I'd been here for over a month with no imminent plans to depart. Crashing with my big-hearted sister had done a lot to soothe the restlessness I hadn't realized I'd been feeling.

Kolya's had shuttered at the end of summer, and I became unemployed. Although I'd felt like a failure at first, that sensation quickly evolved into relief. I'd known for a while I was unhappy. Managing and buying for a high-end boutique—working in elite fashion—didn't spark my passion. I'd learned a ton and would always be grateful for the opportunity, but I didn't want to build an unsatisfying career in fashion merchandising just because those were the words on my college diploma. I was only thirty-one years old, too young to give up on the idea of being genuinely fulfilled by my work.

Regrouping in Coleman Creek had proved to be a wise decision. Especially this time of year. My hometown always showed well during the holidays. The corny displays in business windows and over-the-top lawn decorations lifted my spirits in the way only familiar things could.

The season had also exploded inside the house. Marley and James had three enormous trees—two upstairs, one downstairs—covered in ornaments, and photographs from Christmases past lined every spare inch of the bookshelves. My eyes caught on one picture, probably twenty years old, of my sisters and me in matching reindeer pajamas. I hadn't taken any of our older family photos when I moved to Seattle, so I loved unlocking these memories.

"Do you want sour cream on top or on the side?" Marley appeared in the kitchen archway.

"On top is fine."

I stretched out my fingers and closed one tab on my laptop. No more work today.

I'd taken a flexible remote position handling insurance claims. I'd been working since age sixteen, had done everything from cashier to landscaper to cater waiter to process server, and I'd accepted this job more to feel like a productive member of society than to pay the bills. Thanks to my mom's inheritance and

Marley buying Miranda and me out of our childhood home, my finances were stable. While I figured out my next career step, claims processing kept me busy and put a little extra money in my pocket.

Of course, Marley and James wouldn't let me use that money to pay rent, so I compromised by keeping their fridge fully stocked. I'd also bought new linens and end tables for the guest room and paid a company to clean up the backyard for their engagement party. They'd been particularly grateful for that last one—school activities kept them extremely busy this time of year, sending hedge trimming and leaf blowing to the bottom of their priority list.

I knew they were glad to have me, but it hadn't all been smooth sailing.

I'd messed up last week when I came home with a Christmas tree bought fresh from the Coleman Creek High School lot.

Seeing the noble fir propped up against the garage door, Marley lamented, "But I wanted to go tree shopping with James."

Whoops. I'd unknowingly thrown a wrench into my sister's plans to couple-bond with her fiancé. In my defense, it hadn't occurred to me that getting a Christmas tree could be some big, romantic production. It was simply one of those necessary holiday chores—they didn't have a tree yet, so I bought a tree. Done and done. I hadn't realized something so perfunctory could be an *experience*.

Except the moment that thought crossed my mind, it hadn't rung true. Our mother had raised us on these types of rituals. There had been plenty of Christmases during my childhood where Marley, Miranda, and I darted around the lot, playing hide-and-seek while our mom wandered around, trying to find the perfect tree. I'd just forgotten.

"But didn't you say you and James wanted two trees?" I'd asked, her sad face making me feel like crap.

"Yes." She sniffed.

"Well, I only got one, so you two can still go pick out the other one together."

Some of the tension left her features as she walked closer to the tree I'd purchased. "Hmm. That makes sense. It would be easier if we only had to tie one to the car." She lifted a branch. "And this one is very pretty, nice and full."

"Seriously, Marls. I'm sorry I didn't ask first, but I appreciate you letting me buy one. Bren and I used to just put up a little fake tree. Lugging this monster to my car and getting needles in my hair trying to strap it down really made me feel like I'm home for the holidays."

She'd cracked a smile, unable to stay grumpy for long. "I guess I can't argue with that." Her face lit with mischief. "Maybe I can talk James into getting a third tree—you know, since we're having the party?"

"Why not?"

The next day, she and James had gone together to pick out the second tree. And the third.

Teasing my sister reminded me how much lighter I was in Coleman Creek. Bren had moved in with Chase at the same time I'd lost my job, keeping me from renewing the lease on our apartment. Coming home to figure out my next move had felt like surrendering at first, but now I was grateful.

I'd been reconnecting with my past in more ways than one.

Hovering my finger over the touchpad, I hesitated a fraction before opening another tab on my screen.

My earnest face from four years ago stared back at me. Sitting on a park bench as people strolled by in the background, I spoke directly to the camera. At the time, I hadn't learned about angles or lighting. A severe shadow cut across my cheek, and the microphone picked up tons of ambient noise, muffling my voice. My hair, which I'd been dying auburn the past few years, shone in its natural honey-brown shade.

A sense of surrealness surrounded me as I contemplated my YouTube channel, a pet project I'd started a few months after I began at Kolya's but had neglected recently.

I browsed through the oldest clips, mentally reminiscing.

The videos could not be described as cohesive. The only thing unifying them was that I wanted all my content to be positive. Plenty of fashion channels critiqued looks and trends. Many of my Kolya's colleagues had been dedicated to those. Watching them stress about the dos and don'ts of fashion culture inspired me to make my channel a respite from all that pressure. I'd shown my face and identified myself vaguely as someone who worked in fashion merchandising but had used my middle name to separate YouTube me from Kolya's me. At its peak, *Fashion Vibes with Francesca* only had around three thousand subscribers, but it made me happy.

In the first months, I'd mostly commented on fashion I saw in the real world. The video of me in the park was an example—I'd aimed my camera at folks walking along the nearby trail, captured a variety of outfits, and later edited it together, narrating on the general theme of *all the fun, unique athletic wear looks I saw at Green Lake*. It was juvenile, and honestly a little boring, but its sincerity counterbalanced the artifice of Kolya's.

At the store, I'd been very careful to toe the line and not rock the boat—to agree with the owner, the designers, and my peers when it came to choices about what to stock and how to present merchandise. For the store to remain viable, it had to stay ahead of the curve. I understood and supported that concept because I truly wanted its success. Kolya's' commitment to supporting new, upcoming designers also provided motivation. But the relentless dogma around being on trend had been a prison for my creative soul.

I'd always used fashion as a way of communicating with others. Maureen—Francesca—on the park bench smiled widely in a casual, colorful outfit. Accessible. In my work life, I'd veered dramatic and sleek. But both were still me.

Dress-up had been my favorite activity as a child. I'd enthusiastically investigated the contents of my mom's closet, trying on jewelry and tottering around in her one pair of high heels as she looked on indulgently. And while I didn't have many memories of my dad, I recalled putting on a fashion show in our living room as he cheered and clapped around a newborn Miranda.

In my teenage years, I'd leaned into an angstier, rocker style, and my go-to as an adult was usually a softened-up version of that. But some mornings, I woke up feeling country, or I'd dress formally for no reason. I'd mix interesting jewelry and vintage pieces in my wardrobe with thrift store finds and treasures from the bargain bin at Walmart. I rarely dressed "down" in the traditional sense, and I wore light makeup to the gym, but I had a healthy respect for those who kept their wardrobe entirely casual. The full spectrum of style preferences had always intrigued me, even as my own evolved.

What I liked best about clothing was how it could make the wearer feel a certain way. I was much less concerned with what fashion said about wealth, status, or how adept one was at *dressing for body type*.

But those things had been important to Kolya's customers. And if dressing to signify a healthy bank account made someone feel confident, who was I to yuck their yum?

So, I'd played along. But, ultimately, helping rich people dress like rich people kind of sucked.

Enter my YouTube channel.

I laughed out loud as I pulled up another of my earliest pieces, done after I started offering styling advice in some of the videos. In it, I'd captured different folks on the street wearing overalls. I'd spliced those images with me speaking over visuals of an online article declaring no one over the age of five should wear overalls. I listened to four-years-ago me:

"*Overalls as fashion suicide? I say nope to that. Look at how happy and comfortable these people are*"—cut to an older lady wearing overalls tending to her front lawn, two teenagers wearing overalls with one side undone at the bus stop, a woman walking her dog in enormous pregnancy overalls—"*how could anything be wrong with cozy and comfortable? That being said, if you're interested in elevating your overalls look, I have a few suggestions—*" This was the part where I showed my face, wearing a pair of dark red overalls. By the time I'd made this video, I'd purchased a ring light and a better camera setup for my home, so it was easier to film myself standing and showcasing outfits properly. I modeled the overalls with a blue-striped tee and denim coat with a trucker hat. For the second look, I'd rolled up the bottoms and paired them with chunky bright-white sneakers and a white tank top, floppy hat optional. "*These are just suggestions. If neither of these ideas works for you, no problem. Tell me in the comments how you rock your overalls. And remember, when it comes to fashion, you do you!*"

I put my fist to my mouth at that last line. Total cringe. For the first year, I'd tried to end every video with that catchphrase, but over time, as the topics became more varied, it stopped making sense.

Oscar put his nose on my knee as Marley came in, brandishing a tray of nachos. "Whatchya looking at?"

"My old YouTube videos."

"Francesca?" Marley grinned. "I miss her."

"Yeah? 'Cuz I was thinking I could start working on some new content."

"Oooh. That's a great idea."

Marley sat down, and we watched a few more videos.

I pulled up the clip I'd made of her last Christmas, where she modeled her holiday sweater collection and talked about wearing things that belonged to our mom. That video was part of a series where people told stories about clothes they kept for sentimental reasons. In one, Bren talked about the rose gold bracelet that had belonged to her great-grandmother, who wore it while marching for women's suffrage. In another, I'd filmed Chase hitting at the batting cages. He spoke about the cleats he'd hung onto from his *"epically awesome"* high school baseball days—even though they *"pretty much smell like butt now."*

Some of those videos were random folks telling me about their outfits. Over time, I'd simply gone out in public to film anyone willing to talk to me.

One playlist had clips of me showing people pictures on my iPad of the latest fashions and getting their thoughts. *Would You Try the No-Pants Trend?* had the most views. Every euphemism for female private parts could be found in the comments section—unsurprisingly united in favor of wearing bottoms—although I called foul on "lady sandwich." Sorry @juliasnotyourmom68.

The videos where I offered styling advice, like with the overalls, comprised another playlist. I'd made a point to feature people of all ages, genders, ethnicities, and body types. Marley's ugly sweater video appeared in both the *Sentimental Fashion* playlist and the *Holiday Fashion* playlist, which I pulled up.

"You should add to that one," Marley suggested. "While you're in town." She dipped a chip into the salsa and chewed it before continuing. "There's no place like Coleman Creek at Christmas. I bet Francesca's followers would be interested."

She wasn't wrong. One of the most charming things about my hometown during the holidays was just how not-charming it was. Nothing curated. Nothing matched. Main Street was a mishmash of different colored lights. Some stores painted their windows, while some hung banners or did picture box displays. From the Hawaiian-shirted Santa outside the bowling alley to the twenty penguin plushies lining the window of a family dentist, local flavor abounded. Everyone knew the stories. The Hawaiian shirt had belonged to the original bowling alley owner, a beloved former mayor who'd started many of the city-sponsored holiday activities before passing away a decade ago. The penguins had been gifts sent to Dr. Mendelsohn's young daughter the year she had to spend Christmas in the hospital battling cancer. Our town would never look picture-perfect, but no one seemed to mind. There was plenty of interesting content to be found.

"Do you think Mrs. Allen would do a video talking about how she's kept the same style over all her years of teaching?" It was still odd to me that the teacher my sisters and I all adored in high school was now one of Marley's colleagues. "I love that she rocks that early '80s midi skirt and turtleneck combo. Plus, it'd be great to feature more older people."

Marley chuckled. "I bet she'd be flattered if you asked her. Just leave out the part about her being 'older.'"

"Will do." I used a chip to scoop up a stray dollop of sour cream before taking a bite. "Dang, Marley. Why are these so good?"

She grinned. "Mom's trick, remember? Sprinkle the chips with taco seasoning and lime and pop them in the oven for five minutes before taking them out and piling on the good stuff."

Oh, right. Our mom had done that. Another thing I'd forgotten.

Oscar came up to me, rubbed against my calves, then rested his chin on my thigh. I gave him a candy cane treat.

Then I clicked open another video as ideas started taking root in my brain.

Chapter Nine

Will

I took my time driving to Coleman Creek, traveling on some back roads through King and Snohomish County before finally joining Highway 2. Going slower and not having to deal with freeway traffic helped calm my nerves, which were still slightly frayed from almost clipping that cyclist in front of my building.

My determination to set things right with Maureen was another story. There was no getting relaxed about that. I'd just have to jump in and give it my best shot.

Two hours into my trip, I pulled off the road to grab lunch. A diner off the highway had an enormous sign advertising the "World's Best Pancakes." Sounded good to me.

The restaurant looked like something out of a movie. Vinyl booths lined a wall of windows painted with Santa in his sleigh being pulled by eight reindeer. A paper chain made of cut-up children's menus circled a giant tree in the corner. Glass enclosures perched on the countertop showcased desserts, and an old-fashioned reader board behind the counter listed twenty varieties of pancakes. After ordering a five-pancake sampler of chocolate chip, banana, blueberry, maple walnut, and pineapple coconut, I tucked into a booth.

Thankfully, even though this place looked vintage, the Wi-Fi was solid. As I waited for my food, I popped in my earbuds and pulled out my phone.

Watching Maureen's videos strengthened my resolve to find a better status quo with her. I'd watched everything at least twice. From the moment James had inadvertently mentioned her channel last spring, I'd become a little addicted. How could I resist? Seeing her on my computer or phone screen as Francesca was like getting a window into the woman I'd met at Musicbox.

I found her oldest clips most interesting. Besides the fact Maureen's hair was still the golden-brown color she'd had when we met, her on-screen personality was so much the Mo I remembered—a total badass with a great sense of humor. I couldn't help but catch my breath at how she sometimes stammered and mishandled the camera, giving the screen a wink and a self-deprecating smile once she'd righted things. It reminded me that the icy, elegant woman who'd stared me down last Christmas wasn't all of who she was.

I watched a video from four-and-a-half years ago when Maureen commented on the practicality of rain boots and another where she interviewed a man speaking about his extensive sneaker collection. In one from three years ago—hair dyed auburn—she'd covered a pop-up fashion show at a local college and provided great commentary on why it was important to have body diversity among the models.

"Body diversity" was a phrase I'd only learned since combing through her channel, along with things like "capsule wardrobe," "ready-to-wear," and "boho." I'd also learned I had a few suits in my wardrobe that were "bespoke," and I should appreciate what a privilege that was. *Duly noted, Francesca.*

I'd never cared much about clothes. As an artist, I could appreciate style aesthetics, but my regard ended there. Yet Francesca seemed determined to find something for everyone to enjoy on her channel, including those indifferent to fashion, by never taking herself too seriously. Even in the more straightforward videos discussing trends and offering advice, there was always an undertone of being *in on the joke*, of reminding viewers never to take getting dressed so seriously that it made them feel like they had to be or think a certain way. Her channel had a definite agenda—positivity for every style.

Whether it was a video where she and women on the street dissected the wearability of peplum styles—"peplum" being another word I'd never heard prior to Francesca—or one where she made styling suggestions for the fall line at Old Navy, none of her channel was tailored for folks interested in high-end fashion. I guessed she got enough of that in her day job.

This woman laughing on my screen was fascinating.

I couldn't take my eyes off her.

I'd spent the past five years untangling myself from the life I fell into after my accident. Maureen had spent it working, making these videos, probably dating around—although I knew from some stealthy conversing with Marley that she was single and currently between jobs.

We were both different people now. And I wanted more of Maureen. More smiles. More laughter. More of the warm person hiding behind the hard woman I'd encountered a year ago. With every video I watched, every nugget of information I gleaned from Marley or James, I wanted to keep peeling back the layers.

I only hoped she'd be willing.

I'D JUST GOTTEN UP TO LEAVE the diner when a call came through on my phone. Rosalyn's name flashed on my screen. I wondered what she wanted. She worked for my parents, so we still had the occasional run-in at Wallingford, although our contact had grown less frequent since I left the company. But I had enough on my mind right now without adding my former fiancée to the mix. She could leave a voicemail.

The phone buzzed again as I reached my car. A text this time.

ROZ: PICK UP!

Three seconds later, the phone rang again. She'd never been this insistent before, so I figured it must be important.

I hit the green button. "Hey, Roz."

"You need to call Wicklein! Talk him down!" I held the phone away from my ear as Rosalyn's biting tone came through the line.

"Hello to you too."

"Don't patronize me, William." I could practically hear her gnashing her teeth. "We don't need to bother with chatty small talk. I didn't call to make nice. I need you to call Wicklein and make sure he's okay. He hasn't returned my calls in a month."

I heaved a sigh, knowing it galled her to ask me for anything. Even though I'd helped her out with more than a few business matters since we'd split, I didn't want to make our situation more acrimonious.

"What's going on?"

"Same as this summer. He likes you. Only you. I've explained to him you're not at Wallingford anymore, but he refuses to acknowledge it, keeps saying you must be available to help since it's your parents' company. I've tried to make him understand. Your mother and father have tried. He keeps insisting you handle his account."

Bryan Wicklein was one of my first clients. Over the years, even when I'd transferred from asset management to capital investments, I'd maintained my position as his point of contact. His account was a priority. It had seemed prudent for me to stick with him.

By the time I left Wallingford almost two years ago, I'd been down to a handful of long-standing clients—all of whom I'd transferred to Rosalyn. Everyone else wished me well, but Wicklein had been threatening to take his business elsewhere ever since.

"He won't admit it, but he doesn't want a woman handling his account," Roz said with disdain.

I frowned. "He doesn't need to admit it. We all know that's the reason. Even if he never says the quiet part out loud." I tugged at my hair. "Can you transfer him over to Benjamin, if he's going to be a problem?"

"I mean I *can*." Rosalyn stretched out the last word. "But I don't want to. I want to show your parents how valuable I am to the team."

"They know how valuable you are, Roz. Everyone does."

She exhaled audibly. "Do they really, William?" Her voice tightened, and I knew she was shaking her head, pinching the bridge of her nose. I'd seen her do it a thousand times. "Do they? Or do they just feel sorry for me because I'm the woman their son dumped—"

"Roz—"

"No, save it. I know we've been over it a hundred times." She cleared her throat. "But you don't realize what it's like, William. With our old coworkers. Do they really know? That I'm here because I'm valuable? And not for some *other* reason? You left. You're not here to worry about what they say behind their cubicles or at happy hour."

I sucked in a breath. She was correct. We'd rehashed our split ad nauseam. When I'd finally broken it off for good, just over a year after meeting Maureen, Rosalyn had been incredulous. The first few weeks, she assumed I would "come to my senses," and when that didn't happen, she spent the next four months alternating between yelling, accusing me of leading her on, with entreaties to give us another chance. I felt certain her motivation was fear of falling out of favor with my parents, not undying love for me.

We just didn't fit, no matter how much my mother and father liked her. She didn't care about my art, or my wish to find creative investments for the company, didn't enjoy going to the concerts and festivals I thrived on. We never conversed about anything other than work. She never laughed. But for months, I'd allowed her to rail at me. Because I'd earned it. Because Rosalyn hadn't been wrong when she'd accused me of going through the motions in our relationship. One night with Maureen had shown me what I'd been missing.

I'd questioned initially why Rosalyn stayed at Wallingford Capital, but ultimately, I agreed that her career shouldn't have to suffer because we broke up. She was a senior VP, on track to lead the company one day. The situation was awkward, but my parents wouldn't have kept on any employee out of guilt. She was there because she was extremely competent. I also knew her coworkers respected the hell out of her.

Still, I understood her concerns about office gossip. Our breakup had been a huge blow to her ego, and she'd never conceded that our lives would have been a million times worse if we'd actually gotten married. She would have gone through with it and started a whole life with me just to save face.

"Look, Rosalyn. I don't think you realize how much people admire you, especially my parents. I'm sure everyone at Wallingford feels the same, and I doubt they're talking about our breakup since it's old new—"

"William, just stop. Christ. I didn't call for a pep talk. You don't need to pretend to care anymore. I know it's bullshit."

Damn. We'd had our share of arguments, but I hated it had come to this.

"Roz, I'm really sorry—"

"Can you just call Wicklein? Please. Tell him I know what I'm doing, that my pretty little female head can still process all those big, scary number wumbers."

I stared down at my phone. "Yeah, I'll call him on Monday."

She hung up without a goodbye, and I put a reminder in my phone to make the call Monday morning. I thought the company could withstand the financial blow if Wicklein walked, but I sympathized with Roz's need to have a win. It must have killed her to call me, and I'd honor that.

On Monday. This weekend I had a party to go to.

Chapter Ten

Maureen

I closed out of YouTube so I could focus on wedding stuff with my sister. The dogs retreated to their blanket underneath the Christmas tree when it became apparent we would not be sharing our nachos.

Marley and I perused a stack of vintage bridal magazines given to her by Mrs. Allen—she of the midi skirts and turtlenecks. We'd been looking at dresses all week. I opened my browser to wedding websites, in case I needed to steer Marley away from the '80s puff sleeves dominating the ancient copy of *Bride* she had open in her lap.

"Do you think you'll bring a date to the wedding?" Marley pretended to ask casually. She'd been low-key harping on my lack of love life since I'd come home.

"This again? C'mon, Marls. The wedding is in June. Pretty sure I can scrounge someone up if you insist on me bringing a plus-one. But I don't think we need to worry about it six months in advance."

Thinking about dates reminded me of the best one I'd ever been on, which led to thinking about a certain someone I'd been trying very hard not to think about.

Marley made a face as she thumbed all the way past some 1987 advice on *How to Satisfy Your Man on the Wedding Night*.

"I'm not trying to start anything, Maureen. All I'm saying is you could put yourself out there more. If you wanted to."

I stared at her. "I'm fine taking a break from the dating scene. Besides, who am I gonna go out with in Coleman Creek? Coach Hurley still single?" I laughed, picturing the gym teacher at Marley's school, a sweet guy notorious for his football coach shorts and too-tight ringer tees.

"How about Kasen? You guys have been getting along better lately."

"What!? Eww, gross." I made a gagging motion at the mention of Marley's ex-boyfriend. "That's basically incest, since you guys were together so long. Are you that desperate to pair me up?"

"Exaggerate much?" She huffed. "We broke up a lifetime ago and I'd like to see him smile. He always looks so sad these days."

Marley and Kasen had had a terrible breakup shortly after college. They didn't speak for years afterward, but since he moved back to Coleman Creek last December, they'd formed a solid friendship. I marveled at how she'd opened herself up to love with James, even after Kasen hurt her. Marley was a romantic, like our mom had been—our mom who spent two decades mourning her husband.

"Well, I'm sorry Kasen's sad, but that doesn't mean I want to date him. I'm okay being single. My priority is figuring out my next career move. And a living situation. Unless you want me crashing at your place indefinitely?"

Marley studied me intently. "Sometimes it sounds like you're considering not going back to Seattle."

Her statement was more of a question, but not one I had an answer to yet.

"Haha," I replied lamely.

She sighed. "You know you're welcome to stay as long as you need to. And, as far as dating goes, I guess I'm just so happy with James, I want that happiness for you, too. It was you who convinced me to take a chance and give him a real shot. And you were right."

"That's because it was obvious James is completely in love with you. The only thing I've ever looked at that way is a really good burrito."

She laughed but kept a one-track mind. "What about Oliver? He can't make it to the party because of work, but he'll be at the wedding."

"James's friend Oliver? The one who owns the bar?"

"Uh-huh."

I huffed. "We had dinner with him the last time you guys visited Seattle. There was absolutely no chemistry. Nothing there."

"Fine." She paused. "Leo?"

"James's brother? Jesus. Again with the incest. Hard pass. Besides, Miranda would probably kill me since they're besties."

Marley nodded. "They are pretty tight these days. But honestly, you're so stubborn." Popping a loose jalapeño in her mouth, she tried again. "Well, then, what about Will? He'll be here for the party."

She'd directed her eyes down at a magazine and missed me tensing up at Will's name. I'd worked so hard this past year to play it cool, not to act weird when anyone mentioned him. I was trying to ignore the fact we would be in the same room tomorrow.

"Will and I don't really click either." I kept my voice even. "Seriously...Please. No more. I don't need a matchmaker." Before Marley could open her mouth to argue, I changed the subject. "How about you let me worry about my relationship status and you worry about deciding what kind of dress you want to get married in. We have to figure out if you're going to order something online and have it tailored or if we need to go into Seattle for a shopping trip." I angled my computer to show her an online retailer specializing in gently used vintage wedding dresses.

We continued looking through the magazines and websites while my head remained filled with unwanted thoughts about Will. As my own harsher edges had dulled over the past year, so had some of my animosity toward him. I could no longer pretend he was an asshole or a narcissist who'd gotten off on hurting me. James and Marley had shown me too much evidence to the contrary.

Part of me wanted to let him give his full explanation—the same part that wanted to find out why he'd never gotten married.

But another side of me resented his continued presence in my life. That side felt like shutting him down gave me the upper hand.

Because even though some of my anger had faded, there was no getting around the fact Will had devastated me. He had no idea how severely.

Maybe it wouldn't have been as bad if it had ended with him ignoring me after our night together. I'd had other dates ghost me before and since, never after a night as amazing as that one, but still. It would have hurt, and I'd have been pissed, but I would have gotten over it eventually.

Except it hadn't ended that way.

It had ended in the hotel lobby, weeks later. That feeling of being blindsided remained in my subconscious. It sometimes popped into my brain for no reason, or sat in the pit of my stomach, as life's worst moments had a nasty habit of doing. Sure, there had been sadder days in my life—my dad dying, and the first time my mom's illness was so bad she didn't recognize me. There had been other embarrassing moments—ripping my pants open during gym class in fifth grade, or Toby Kindman asking me to prom and then taking back the offer in front of the cafeteria when Greta Thornson said she'd go with him.

But that moment of finding out Billy had a fiancée felt like a lead pipe being thrust against my back, brutal in a way nothing else ever had been. That kind of moment lived with you. Lived in you.

I'd watched my mom become a shell of herself after my dad died. Held Bren's hand when she'd miscarried the baby of a boyfriend who couldn't get to the hospital because he was busy fucking some other girl. Listened to Marley cry over Kasen when she thought no one could hear her. I knew better than to let myself get tripped up by infatuation.

The realization I'd let it happen anyway had been a gut punch I wasn't prepared to handle. To say I'd managed it poorly would be a colossal understatement.

That day, I never picked up the order from Starbucks. Never went back to work. Never said a word to anyone as I turned and walked out of the hotel on autopilot.

The lead pipe to the back feeling had intensified as the minutes passed, Billy's betrayal an assault. My ears rang with Rosalyn's declaration she was his fiancée.

Somehow, I made it home. The first thing I saw was the bottle of champagne my mom sent me when I got the job at Kolya's. I started drinking. I rarely drank, but that day I could easily justify it, since getting the shit kicked out of me by a man was also unprecedented. After the champagne, I took care of all the beer we had in the fridge. Then the liquor stash Bren kept above the sink. I hadn't intentionally tried to harm myself—at least I didn't think so—I'd only been trying to go numb and get out of my head somehow. I had no memory of throwing an empty bottle against the living room wall and smashing it, of getting three huge gashes in my calf. No recollection of blacking out.

I'd woken up the following morning in the hospital, recovering from alcohol poisoning, with six stitches in my right leg. The first thing I saw was Bren hunched in a chair next to me. I was too embarrassed to come clean about Billy. I gave her a bullshit story about new job jitters and not knowing my limit. It was only by the grace of my very kind supervisor I didn't lose my position at Kolya's and my fashion career didn't get snuffed out in its first month.

I'd felt disgusted with myself for how I allowed a man to get under my skin. Having control of the situation now meant everything.

Will might think he had a way to explain his actions to me, but I had better reasons not to let him try. I'd built my defenses back up. No one had come close to me since then. I might be a little softer than I was a year ago, but I wasn't stupid. I wasn't about to let him in again.

A SHORT WHILE LATER, Katy Baumbeck came over to help set up for the engagement party, brushing some sort of orangey powder off her shirt as she shuffled through the door.

"Sorry," she said. "Braxton got into a gross ancient bronzer my ex-mother-in-law gave me. I didn't notice until I drove halfway here that I hadn't wiped it all off."

"No worries. Although I would have guessed Doritos," Marley teased, reaching out to swipe across Katy's shoulder. "Lucky for you, I've relaxed the formal dress code for tonight."

I got up to take Katy's coat and give her a quick hug. We'd all grown up with her since she'd been in Miranda's year in school. Now she worked as a server at The Landslide, Coleman Creek's best pub, and she and Marley were close friends. They'd become even tighter since last year, when Katy's husband, Mike, suddenly left her and their two children. I didn't have all the details. I only knew he'd been gone for months prior to their split, helping his parents. He'd come home last Christmas and asked Katy for a divorce, saying he'd fallen in love with a nurse in Phoenix.

The town had immediately rallied around her, helping with meals, babysitting, and anything else she needed. Her ex paid enough child support and alimony that Katy didn't have to worry about losing their home or starving. But even with support, it wasn't easy. Every time I'd seen her recently, she looked exhausted. Yet another instance of how someone's *love of their life* turned out to be a total nightmare.

Katy sat with us as we perused the magazines, tittering over the outdated styles. It quickly became clear why she and Marley were BFFs. Even with all the setbacks life had thrown at her, Katy still brimmed with genuine happiness for my sister and James.

"Maureen, you have such amazing style." Katy sighed as she watched me get up to grab more treats for Oscar and Bambi.

Among Kolya's crowd, I might have wondered if that statement was passive aggressive. But I knew Katy was sincere as she complimented my wide-legged evergreen pants, fitted and high-waisted around my middle with sailor-style button detailing, and boat-necked cashmere sweater in a green so deep it appeared almost black.

"It's sweet of you to say that. You're looking pretty stellar yourself." She blushed at my words, but I wasn't just being polite. Katy absolutely rocked the plaid flannel and beat-up Wranglers look. With her glossy dark ponytail, all she needed was a cowboy hat and a few hours to sleep off the fatigue in her eyes, and she'd be ready to shoot a country music album cover or star in a truck commercial. Anytime I'd attempted a version of the denim and plaid combo, I'd come across looking like a defeated scarecrow.

I also couldn't have pulled off Marley's outfit. She had on a Rudolph sweater with holly leaf print leggings. I never felt comfortable wearing anything kitschy, but my sister looked adorable and completely at ease in her own skin—exactly the way everyone should feel in their clothes.

That's why I'd started making my videos. They helped me feel creative, but I also wanted to give viewers permission to have fun, be themselves, and understand fashion didn't need to be planned or defined to count as "style."

"Hey Katy, did Marley ever tell you I have a YouTube channel?"

She laughed. "Of course! Like she'd keep that a secret when she could brag about her big sister instead. I've seen all of Francesca's videos. Cool stuff. I especially liked the one about the 'No-Pants Trend.'"

Marley winked at me. I felt my cheeks flush, pleased she liked my videos enough to force her friends to watch them.

"'No-Pants' is a classic," I agreed, giggling when Katy mouthed *lady sandwich*. "Anyway, I'm thinking of going back to it while I'm in Coleman Creek. Maybe you'd be willing to do a piece with me?"

Katy ran an arm across her brow. "Like you want to interview me for your channel?"

"Uh-huh."

"But why? I don't really have a style."

"First, everyone has a style. Even if it's by default. Second, I bet we could find some looks in your closet folks could draw inspiration from. Or you can just tell me about your approach to getting dressed as a single working mom. Or even how your style has changed. Or what your favorite trend is. I'm pretty flexible with topics. I'm just looking to interview some Coleman Creek folks. Give my channel a little hometown spice."

"Well, I don't think I'm particularly spicy, but I guess doing a video might be fun. I've seen enough of them to know you never embarrass people."

"Maureen—I mean Francesca—would never let you down," Marley chimed in. "I'm glad I did the one last year with my mom's sweaters. It's like having a little time capsule."

"I think viewers would be into it," I said to Katy. "You're basically the epitome of small town mom chic."

She huffed good-naturedly, leaning back against the couch. "Is that a thing?"

"It should be," Marley said. "Because Maureen is right. You always look great, which is pretty darn special considering all the hours you put in at The Landslide, plus taking care of two rambunctious kiddos."

"Pretty sure you mispronounced 'demons.'" Katy joked. "Braxton spilled his milk on my laptop yesterday, and that was after Rosie decided to poop in the sink instead of the toilet."

I cackled, but Marley's eyes went dreamy. "I can't wait until I'm a mom."

"Really?" Katy raised an eyebrow. "Horror stories make you want kids? Well, if that's the case, just wait until I loan you my handwritten copies of *The Vomit Diaries* or *Inappropriate Things My Toddler Said in Public.*"

"Did you just make those up?" I asked.

"Sure did."

"Nice." I reached over to give Katy a fist bump.

Marley snorted. "It's fine. Make all the jokes. Nothing will scare me off. I've been imagining me and James with our babies since the minute we got together."

I put my arm around my sister's shoulder. "We're just teasing, Marls. Real talk—I'm excited to be Auntie Maureen." I kissed the top of her head as I remembered the reason for Katy's visit. "I guess we should put down these magazines and start doing some actual prep for this party."

"Just put me to work," Katy said.

The house was already completely decked out for the season, but we still needed to hang a banner above the back door slider and fifty strands of twinkle lights around the patio and backyard.

While we worked, Marley and Katy threw out ideas for videos I could do in Coleman Creek.

"Karaoke Night at The Landslide would be great for funny content," Katy said. "Especially this time of year when it's all holiday songs."

"Maybe you could talk to the kids at the high school if their parents are okay with it," Marley offered. "Interview them about how determined they seem about bringing back the '90s."

Katy nodded her head before suggesting, "You could shoot at the carnival next weekend."

"Oh my gosh, that's a great idea. I can't believe it wasn't my first thought," Marley enthused. "Everyone will be out having fun, and it's so festive. Although the fashion will probably be limited to heavy coats and beanies."

I hadn't been to the Coleman Creek Holiday Hoopla in a decade, but it had been a big part of my childhood, a tradition for most residents. Put on by the city and the local Rotary Club, there were dozens of booths for crafts, food, and carnival games. There was a Ferris wheel and a merry-go-round. The wooden structures holding up the tents were always decorated for the season, in a wide range of themes celebrating Christmas, Hannukah, the Solstice, the town's Scandinavian heritage, Kwanzaa, Boxing Day, and New Year's, along with more vague themes like snowflakes and fireplaces. And while my sister was correct that most carnival-goers would be bundled up, maybe that just meant it was time to have a peacoat vs. puffer coat debate in one of my videos.

"I think the carnival would be a great place to film," I said enthusiastically.

The rental company arrived a minute later, dropping off ten enormous outdoor space heaters.

It took all three of us to lug them into position in the backyard. We also prepped as much food as we could, knowing many of the guests would bring dishes of their own, even though the party hadn't been labeled as a potluck.

We laughed a lot. Gossiped about our friends and neighbors. And in the end, Marley's house looked beautiful, her indoor trees and garland picture-perfect, the backyard a winter fairyland of lights. Even with my nerves about tomorrow—*I'd been doing so good all day not thinking about him*—and my career uncertainty, having creative energy again brought joy.

I hadn't thought of myself as creative or joyful in five years. It was scary, the prospect of softening, but there was no way to stop it. Not in Coleman Creek, and definitely not at Christmastime.

I just needed to make sure I stayed tough enough to face Will tomorrow.

Chapter Eleven

Will

Sleep was elusive last night. My guilt-inducing conversation with Roz played on a loop in my mind, and every time I closed my eyes, my brain unleashed the mental image of nearly hitting that cyclist yesterday. The resulting fatigue left me feeling extra anxious about seeing Maureen, which is how I found myself parked half a block away from James and Marley's house, fingers clenched on the steering wheel, trying to psych myself up to go inside.

My energetic optimism from the previous week seemed to have vanished, the cold from the freezing temperatures outside seeping under my skin. I watched as people made their way up the home's front walkway, periodically using my hand to smear a peephole in the fogged windshield of my Audi to get a better view. Some faces were familiar. I'd visited James in Coleman Creek half a dozen times since the talent show last year, and he'd made a point of introducing me to his friends.

I saw Travis Bloxham arrive with his wife Vivienne and their four kids. Travis was a fellow teacher of James's and a solid dude. Like me, he would be a groomsman in the wedding. James and Marley were adamant that this engagement party be casual, low-key and child-friendly, which is why it began at three p.m., and why most of the guests I'd observed had been wearing some version of jeans and sweaters, usually holiday-themed. Marley's sister Miranda appeared to be on door duty, welcoming everyone with the manic enthusiasm of Cinderella waving atop a Disneyland parade float.

Maureen was nowhere in sight, but I knew she had to be here. On the drive from Seattle, I'd thought more about the choices I'd made with her—both five years ago and last December—and ultimately decided that, while I owed it to her to respect her wishes not to rehash the past, it might be okay to push her *just a little bit* when it came to how we could interact moving forward.

That buzz I'd gotten from being around Maureen, that hum of possibility—I wanted it again, even if all it evolved into was tolerance. We needed to get to a place where I wasn't stressing out in my car fighting nausea just because she was nearby.

I released the steering wheel and rubbed the three fingers of my right hand, flexing out the stiffness from the cold. I'd recovered from disaster before. That day in the lobby hadn't been the end of me and Maureen. Fate had a different plan. And if she was here, and I was here, I had to believe we could make things better between the two of us.

With one more fortifying breath, I exited the car. We hadn't gotten snow in Seattle yet, but there were three inches on the ground here and I nearly slipped on the sidewalk. James had shoveled and salted, but I'd made a precarious choice with my shoes. Vegan leather monk strap loafers. Understated, but high quality. On some level, I was trying to impress Maureen. I'd seen her give me the once-over last time and assumed noticing other people's fashion choices was a side effect of being in her line of work. Still, I had no desire to stick out or telegraph my *city boy* status, so I'd kept the rest of my outfit simple—dark wash Levi's and a cranberry sweater.

Miranda hugged me so effusively when I got to the door that I feared she might leap into my arms. She didn't, but after receiving her full octopus welcome, I felt some of the tension leave me.

"Will! It's so great to see you again." She looked past my shoulder in case anyone else was coming up the walkway. Satisfied there were no stragglers, she pulled me inside and shut the door. "It's been since the end of summer, right?"

"Early September." I'd come out to visit James after finalizing the sale of my company and crossed paths with Miranda for a few days before she'd flown back to school.

"Of course." She took my coat and hung it nearby. "Well, it's nice you could make it. I'm always down to listen to any embarrassing stories you may have about my soon-to-be brother-in-law. Need to have that ammunition in my back pocket, for future family dinners and such." She chuckled and made finger guns, which she blew over and holstered in her front pockets. "And I'm excited to hear all about what you've been up to. James mentioned something about you renovating a building. That's cool." Points to Miranda for remembering those details and genuinely caring. That was why it had been easy to pick up my friendship with James this past year—he was good people, and so was his new family.

"I think you've heard all my best stories, but if anything new comes to mind, you'll be the first to know." I surreptitiously scanned the space for Maureen. Dozens of people crowded into the open living room, but there were also partygoers outside under a massive covered patio. The snow had been shoveled to the side of the yard, and outdoor space heaters made the chilly temperature palatable.

"I'll hold you to that," Miranda replied. "I'm going to go see about rounding up the glasses. This party is casual like the bride and groom wanted, but we're still going to do a champagne toast around six."

"Sounds good. I'll find James and let him know I'm here."

She headed off, and I took a few breaths before doing one more perusal of the main room. Where was Maureen?

I couldn't find her in the backyard, but I located James and Marley sitting at one of the tables. They'd rented a dozen for the occasion, and every seat was filled. When James saw me, he jumped up clumsily and made his way over, arms outstretched.

"Hey man, sooooooo glad you made it!" His eyes sparkled and I surmised that, while he wasn't quite drunk, he was definitely feeling good.

"Nothing could have kept me away." No need to mention how long it had taken me to get out of the car. I eyed the patio. Still no Maureen.

He stumbled into my right shoulder. "Whoops. Sorry. I've had a few."

"You don't say?" I grinned.

He looked sheepish. I pulled my arm away, massaging the scars on my palm reflexively. "Oh shit! Did I hurt you?" James waved his hand toward my wrist. I'd told him a little about my accident, not all the details, but enough so he didn't need to pretend he didn't notice my missing fingers.

"Nah. I've told you it doesn't hurt. I'm just a little stiff from the cold, the way anyone might be."

His relief was evident. "Oh, good." He threw an arm around my shoulders and directed me toward the tables. "Hey, everyone." He spoke to whoever was listening. Half-drunk James was funny.

"This is my buddy Will, from high school. He's gonna be a groomsman."

A few people sent waves and smiles my way before returning to their conversations.

"I'm so fuckin' happy." James lolled his head on top of mine, easy to do since he had six inches on me. "Oh...whoops. Marley doesn't curse, so I'm try'na stop...I'm so *fudging* happy."

Marley stood with a laugh and disengaged James's arm from my shoulder, slipping hers around his thick waist. "Alright, big guy. How about we switch out that beer for a few glasses of water?"

James leaned his bearded head down to kiss her on the temple. "I love you so much. I can't wait to get married."

She tipped up her face to kiss him back. "I know, baby. I fudging love you too." She glanced at me. "Great to see you, Will. And don't mind this lug nut. He's sentimental. There's nothing like having all our friends and family here, especially around the holidays."

"Am I the last to arrive?" I asked.

"You know, I think you are, other than James's parents couldn't make it since they both came down with the flu. His brother is here, though."

"Okay. I'll make sure to find Leo and say hello. And, uh, what about your sisters? I saw Miranda."

"Yeah. Miranda got in late last night. She's been trying to make up for not being here for the party set up yesterday by helping this afternoon—and by *helping*, I mean playing hostess on steroids." Marley huffed playfully. "Maureen's around here somewhere, too."

Nice to receive confirmation Maureen was 'somewhere,' but she certainly wasn't in the backyard. And she hadn't been in the living room.

Marley and James sat down, bottles of water in hand. Most of the outside guests were looking at the side of the house, where a projector displayed photos of the happy couple onto the cream-colored siding. I gave James an upnod—which he sloppily returned—before heading back into the house.

My gut told me Maureen and I were playing opposing games. I searched for her. She hid from me.

From speaking with James, I knew Maureen was temporarily living there, so I guessed she was in her room. It seemed impolite to wander to that side of the house, since none of the other guests had, but after a while the strain of not being able to locate her outweighed my need to be polite. I allowed myself a few steps toward the bedrooms.

As I neared the cracked-open door of the guest room, it wasn't Maureen's voice I heard. It was the squeaky, high-toned voice of a child, then peals of laughter. A deeper, full-throated sound I recognized followed those giggles. Maureen's laugh.

Pinning myself against the hallway wall, I listened for a moment, preparing to knock.

"Mo-reen, I wanna try the shiny purple one!" A squeal of delight followed the sound of things being shuffled around.

"That scarf is perfect, Scarlett," Maureen said. "You look very chic."

"Huh? Cheek? That doesn't make sense, Mo-reen."

"She's saying you look like a butt." A young boy's voice came from a corner of the room. "That you look like butt cheeks."

"I did not say that!" Maureen protested, an edge of laughter in her tone. "Connor, that's not a nice joke. You know full well I said your sister looks chic, as in beautiful and fashionable."

"Yeah," the sister stated indignantly. "I'm beautiful and *cheek*. You're the buttface!"

"Alright, you two. Enough." This time, Maureen didn't stop herself from a small laugh, and I couldn't catch myself before also letting out a chuckle, immediately clamping my hand over my mouth. I crossed my fingers that she hadn't heard it.

No such luck.

"Hello?" Maureen called. "Is someone out there?"

I knocked softly on the door a few times before gently pushing it open. Maureen sat on the bed next to the girl. Her mouth fell open in an *O* when she saw me.

"Sorry," I said. "I was walking by and couldn't help overhearing."

"Who are you?" The boy, probably eight or nine years old, walked over from beside the bed and spoke without looking me in the eye.

"I'm Will. An old friend of James's. And Maureen's."

Maureen inhaled loudly. But since she didn't dispute my words, the kids seemed satisfied.

"I'm Scarlett," the little girl, maybe six or seven, said brightly. "Mo-reen was giving my brother a break from the party. Connor is au...autistic. He's okay, but he needs lots of breaks when it's loud and stuff." She looked at her brother and smiled, giving him a thumbs-up. I noticed James's dog Bambi was also in the room, resting his head gently against the boy's thigh.

Maureen gazed at the girl with fondness. "Scarlett, do you want to know a secret?"

"What?"

"I'm glad you guys came to my room with me. I needed a break myself. We all need them sometimes."

"Of course we do, silly," Scarlett agreed. Turning back to me, she added, "Mo-reen's letting us look at her box of ax...ax...axetories."

"Accessories," Connor corrected his sister kindly, apparently not truly believing she was a butt cheek. "I like the bracelets."

Scarves, hats, pins, and other jewelry covered every surface in the room. Maureen got up and murmured to me quietly so the kids couldn't hear, "They fight, but Scarlett is very protective of her big brother. When the party started getting crowded, he told his parents he needed a breather, and she insisted on accompanying him."

"Oh. That was nice of her." I glanced around. "And they ended up here...with you?"

Maureen arched an eyebrow. "These are two of Travis and Vivienne's kids. Have you met James and Marley's friends, the Bloxhams?"

"Oh, uh, yeah. Them, but not their kids yet." In all the times I'd pictured running into Maureen for the first time in a year, I'd never considered a scenario where I'd catch her *babysitting*.

"His parents seemed to be enjoying themselves when Connor asked for some space, so I volunteered to take him in here. With four kids, they don't get much chance to relax."

"Of course."

Above the children's line of sight, Maureen gave me a questioning stare, the husky laughter I'd heard moments ago entirely gone.

I missed it immediately.

Looking at what Connor held, I grasped for something to say. Anything. "Why do you have a tiara in your accessory box?"

She exhaled. "I have lots of interesting things, Will. Goodies from photo shoots." She kept glaring at me. I knew what I wanted to say to her. I'd been thinking about it for days. But I couldn't force the words from my mouth. Finally, Maureen interjected into the silence, too low for Scarlett and Connor to hear, "What are you doing here, Will?"

"At the party?" I mumbled.

"At the door to my room."

I took a deep breath. *Get it together, idiot. Time to put it out there.*

"I was looking for you."

Her stare could have cut glass. "That wasn't our agreement."

"That's why I was looking for you." I gazed back at her, straightening my shoulders.

"Why?"

"I want to renegotiate."

Chapter Twelve

Maureen

I want to renegotiate.

The words reverberated in my head, churned in my belly.

I want to renegotiate.

Will stared, waiting for my response.

If I'd had any doubt whether he still affected me, it dissolved the moment he stepped into my doorway, all rugged appeal with refined edges. Ruddy winter cheeks. V-neck sweater stretching tautly across his lithe chest, hints of chest hair peeking out. Gray eyes blazing behind thick lashes. I itched to run my palm along the dark five o'clock shadow sprouting along his face and neck.

Luckily, I was a pro at maintaining my composure. And a neutral expression.

We stepped into the hallway, ensuring the kids were out of earshot while still keeping an eye on them. Voices rose from the living room fifty feet away. His breath tickled the skin of my jaw as he stepped close and whispered, "We've avoided each other for a year." He inhaled before sighing breathily. "Maureen, it's not working."

I squeezed my eyes shut for a second. That voice. Holy fuck. *Hello, Billy from Musicbox. Billy from Denny's.* The wispy hairs on the back of my neck stood at attention. I swallowed roughly. "What do you mean, 'it's not working?'"

He peered at me. "I've steered clear of you since last Christmas, like you asked me to. But I can't stop thinking about... There's still this...tension...between us—" He pulled back as a woman came into the hallway to use the bathroom. After she'd gone in and shut the door, not paying us any mind, he continued, "Not knowing whether I'm going to see you when I see James hasn't made it better."

His deep voice vibrated in my ear and, alarmingly, heated my blood. I understood his sentiment. Knowing he was out there on the edge of my life this past year, I'd worried I might run into him any time I visited my sister. I hadn't been able to simply leave him in the past.

However, whether we needed to amend our agreement to reduce the "tension," my immediate concern was getting control over my unwanted reaction to him. Leaning away, I rested my hip against the hallway wall. "I won't deny it's been strange." I folded my arms across my chest. "Knowing I might see you unexpectedly. Kind of like waiting for a jack-in-the-box to pop."

His eyes lowered, focusing on my neck. My pulse beat so rapidly I imagined he could see it.

He opened his mouth to reply, but we were interrupted by Vivienne, coming to collect her two youngest children. Unaware of the loaded conversation she'd interrupted, she gave Will a quick hug hello before turning to me.

"How'd they do?" she asked, reaching over to pet the dog.

I cleared my throat and took another step away from Will. "Great. We've been having a mini fashion show."

She grinned at the sight of her kids sprawled out on my bed. "Sounds fun. Thanks again."

"Anytime."

"Mama, I really like these bracelets." Connor raised his arm to show the jeweled circles of all different shapes and sizes he'd layered up to his elbow.

"Those are very pretty, sweetheart," his mom said. "Maybe we can buy you some bracelets next time we go to the store."

He glanced down at his arm. In a small voice, he asked, "Like these?"

"Whatever ones you like. I'm sure Scarlett will help you decide."

Scarlett grinned and rubbed her brother's hand. "We'll find cheek ones."

The little girl giggled at her own joke, but her brother's face remained serious. "Will you write that on my calendar?" he questioned his mother.

"Of course I will."

Vivienne turned her attention back to me and Will, shaking her head and gesturing to Connor. "It's an adventure every day with this one. He doesn't mind having fifteen bracelets clanking on his arm, but if he so much as touches a microfiber towel, it's sensory overload." She laughed at Scarlett trying to fit even more bracelets on her brother as Bambi carefully observed. "But I couldn't ask for better kids."

"They're sweethearts," I agreed, squeezing Vivienne on the shoulder. "I hope you'll let them hang out with me more while I'm staying here. In fact, I'd be happy to take all four kids sometime, so you and Trav could grab a date night."

"I'll never say no to that," Vivienne said, eventually herding her offspring back toward the living room.

Will stayed behind. I understood he wanted to continue our conversation, but I felt too unmoored. "I know we have to talk, but I can't yet," I stated firmly. "You kind of brought up the whole *renegotiating* thing out of the blue. I need some time to get my thoughts together."

Before he could say anything, I moved back into my room and closed the door behind me. Turning around, I slumped heavily against it and sank to the floor, gathering my knees in my arms. I felt the lurch of him resting his fist on the opposite side before his footsteps eventually retreated down the hall.

I busied myself putting my accessory collection away. After carefully separating the jewelry and folding the scarves, I fell on my bed, hugging a pillow. I'd channeled my inner badass last year when I saw Will and could surely do so again. I wasn't ready to be soft with him. But the way his whispering in my ear sent shivers down my spine showed he could get to me if I allowed it.

My phone buzzing interrupted my thoughts.

WILL: I've been told that I snore.

Huh? Was that a mistake? Had he been randomly texting someone about his sleeping habits while I'd been stressing out in my bedroom? What the hell? I paused before typing the only possible reply.

ME: ???

He was ready for me, his response instantaneous.

WILL: I snore. Also, I'm terrible about sticking to a workout schedule. It makes me self-conscious of my calves. I'm basically a human cricket with tiny stick legs.

ME: ???

WILL: I can't cook anything properly. I can produce burned grilled cheese and maybe some watery scrambled eggs on a good day, but it's usually takeout or microwave meals for me.

I couldn't help it. I smiled.

ME: What is this Will?

WILL: I'm not trying to deny your need to process. I just want to take the edge off. Maybe give us a light start to talking. Staying away isn't good. It's making me build things up in my head. I'm guessing it's the same for you. If you know the stupid, mundane bad stuff about me, maybe it will help.

I stared at my screen. The three dots appeared and disappeared a few times before his next message came through.

WILL: Marley and James are getting married. You're going to know me whether you want to or not.

And that was the core. Staying away from him, worrying about seeing him, had only amplified our situation. Made the inevitable interactions loom larger.

I clutched my phone to my chest. I wanted to keep hating him. He didn't even know the full reason. Didn't know I'd drunk myself stupid over him. Didn't know my mouth had tasted like cotton balls for months afterward. Didn't know I'd never had a second date with anyone after that night—just as I'd never had a second date with him. Hate was easy.

Letting my guard down was hard.

But here we were. He was part of my life. And no amount of pretending or avoiding would change that.

ME: Okay
WILL: Okay?
ME: Let's renegotiate
WILL: *smiley face emoji*
WILL: Just let me know when you are ready to talk. Hopefully soon. *fingers crossed emoji*
ME: Will?
WILL: Yeah?
ME: Sometimes I go four or five days without flossing.

TEN MINUTES LATER, I FOUND MYSELF in the kitchen waiting for Will to join me. I hadn't wanted to invite him to my bedroom. Too intimate. I figured we'd be able to snatch a few moments alone since most of the partygoers had made their way outside, eager to sample the buffet set out along the patio's edge.

A small window in the laundry room allowed some visibility to the backyard.

The food tables held a mix of favorites we'd ordered from local restaurants, along with the potluck items guests insisted on bringing. The twinkle lights Katy and I had wrapped around the outdoor heaters and greenery sparkled merrily. We'd also hung large glass ball ornaments from the patio cover, designating a section for dancing. An Ed Sheeran ballad played over the sound system, tempting a dozen couples to the makeshift dance floor. There were soft clinks as plates filled and glasses tipped together in celebration. A magical, soft glow overlaid the scene as the sun set, moonlight bouncing off the snow piled against the fence.

Yet the cheerful conversation and laughter floating into the kitchen took a back seat to the humming in my brain. I couldn't stop thinking about Will. I wanted to be okay with him. But did that mean I had to pretend he'd never burned me?

Not a chance.

I paced between the countertops. I supposed I could be slightly less hostile when we were around one another. It seemed wise to have less volatility between us. By the time Will arrived, I'd resigned myself to the necessity of doing just that.

He tapped lightly on the archway to alert me to his presence. "Hey, Maureen." Although he kept his hands in his pockets, his eyes flashed. "Thanks for agreeing to talk."

I stopped pacing. "You mean *renegotiate*?"

He grinned, its warmth reaching his entire face. "Yeah." A nervous chuckle worked its way from his throat. "So, uh, here we are...again." He spoke quietly, and I recalled our close moment in the kitchen last year. "I know we weren't ready to have a talk like this last Christmas, but I'm hoping we can get to a better place now."

He was so guileless. Considerate. I resented it even as I acknowledged the truth. Good thing I'd worked out how I felt before he'd come in. Being near him threatened to short-circuit my brain.

It wasn't only because of what happened five years ago. I also struggled to reconcile those memories with everything else I knew about Will.

I had learned quite a bit about him from Marley and James over the past twelve months. Stories about how he'd been good to James in high school, the lone rich kid willing to be friends with the scholarship student. How he'd stood with James at their reunion last year, helping him face their former bullies.

And there were things I'd seen for myself. Will had respected my request to keep his distance—I knew he'd intentionally made sure we didn't see each other on the Fourth of July. When James's parents' house in Seattle flooded last spring, Will let James and Marley stay at his condo for three weeks so they could be nearby to provide support. He'd picked Miranda up at the airport once when Marley got stuck in traffic and I was out of town. With time, it had only grown more undeniable that Will was just as much the personable, kind man I'd met at Musicbox as he was the villain who'd lied to me about having a fiancée.

Not to mention, I continued to find him criminally attractive. All that tousled dark hair surrounding a glass-cut jaw, on top of a strong, wiry physique. And goddamn, could he dress. His jeans fit like a glove, his trendy faux crocodile loafers a perfect complement.

He rolled his shoulders and pulled a hand from one pocket to pull on the neck of his sweater. Another self-conscious bit of laughter escaped him before he said, "I'm not sure how to start."

Propping myself against the counter, I remained as far away as possible while still in range to have a hushed conversation. "Maybe we start with what exactly you want to renegotiate." I exhaled and rushed out, "I think I can commit to being nicer to you."

Will raised an eyebrow. "Nicer?" He drew out the two syllables into about fourteen.

I nodded faintly as I regarded him, unfolding my arms to rest my elbows behind me. "Yeah, dum-dum—*nicer*. You know, less snappy."

"Ah, I see. Well, I guess being called 'dum-dum' isn't too *snappy*. It's certainly better than worrying you're about to google how to dispose of a body." He grinned. "Although, I'm kind of fond of your don't-fuck-with-me attitude."

I pinched my lips together to stop a smile from forming. "You are, huh?"

"You know I am, Maureen." His tone sobered. "That night at the bar, when you took down that frat bro, it drew me—"

"Alright." I interrupted. "Like I said, I can be nicer. But it's all contingent on keeping that part of our original deal intact. We don't talk about that night. As long as you stay quiet about our history, I'm good."

"Sorry. I shouldn't have brought up... Anyway, thank you. This is exactly what I was hoping for."

"Really?"

"Course." He reached up to brush a curl off his forehead. "I don't want to worry about being with James and Marley and needing to avoid you, or having to stay away from events. My friendship with James is important to me, and I want to be in his life without pissing off his future sister-in-law."

Standing in the same spot we'd been in last Christmas, I acknowledged to myself that I didn't feel the rage I'd felt then. I'd probably always be angry with Will on some level, and I'd live with the sting of that humiliating day in the hotel lobby until I died, but there was no escaping that getting to know Will through Marley's and James's eyes had softened me toward him.

"We're okay," I said, voice quivering only slightly, and I extended my arm to shake on it.

He took my palm in his, and I felt the evidence of his missing fingers. I wondered vaguely if we'd ever get to a place where he'd tell me what happened. But as he held my hand, I stopped noticing the scars and became fixated instead on looking down at his thumb as it pressed against mine.

The noise from the party sounded miles away. For stretched-out seconds, I allowed myself to acknowledge it, my response to his touch. The heat in my core. The flutters in my stomach. I'd forgotten how good it could feel to be affected by someone. Even this complicated man I had such a torturous history with.

As the pad of his thumb grazed along my skin, burning with each pass, I felt that empty well within me, the one only he had ever filled. And I must have let his touch linger too long, because a second later, I heard Will's rough swallow. I looked up and saw the exact moment he registered the evidence in my eyes.

The evidence of something he hadn't expected to see.

Desire.

"Oh my god," he blurted.

Shit! I snatched my hand back quickly and gazed down, but not before I registered his astonishment.

"Maureen?" Will clasped his fingers together behind his head, wearing a stunned expression of both elation and disbelief. "Wow... Okay. I never thought—"

I struggled to hear him, still processing how I'd responded to his touch. *He had to know that didn't mean anything, right?* "Huh?"

"Not to take a mile when I'm grateful for the inches...but..." He released a deep, steadying breath, leaning away as though preparing to take a punch. "If there's a chance—"

His stammering tore me from my thoughts. I raised my face, eyes narrowing swiftly.

"You don't have to say yes," he continued hurriedly, Adam's apple working as he gulped. "I know you've already given me more than I deserve. And I hadn't planned to say this, but I'm just going to put it out there. If you're ever willing, I'd love to get to know you again. Spend some time together."

My jaw dropped. *What?* This was way beyond taking a mile. I'd just told him I could maybe stand to be a little nicer to him. And now he was asking for...what exactly?

Spend some time together. The fuck?

So what if I'd had a teensy weensy, itty bitty, so-slight-you-could-barely-notice-it reaction to his touch?

My head swam. Why did I always feel like this around him? Never able to get the upper hand. Just as I was about to give him an epic set-down, Leo came into the kitchen, my sister Miranda following.

Thankfully, they seemed oblivious to the heavy air in the room.

"We can finish this later," I said to Will, casually enough Leo and my sister probably thought they'd caught us discussing the weather or our Netflix queues.

"It's almost time to have cake and do the champagne toast," Miranda said excitedly. "You two will help us get it all ready, right?"

Leo was only marginally more measured when he added, "I brought the cake from Seattle. I think the happy couple will love it." He snapped his fingers and made wide eyes at Miranda. "I didn't bring any candles. Is that okay? For an engagement party? It's not like a birthday, is it?"

"I think you're good, Leo-Bear. No candles required."

"Leo-Bear?" Will smirked at his friend's brother.

"I dunno." Leo slung a long, muscled arm around Miranda's shoulders, his massive Viking-like stature making her appear even more spritely. "She started calling me that a while back, and now it's just this thing we do. Isn't that right, Miranda-Panda?"

"That still makes no sense," she retorted, smiling up at him. I'd gotten used to their friendship over the past year, but I guessed Will had never seen it up close. Miranda and Leo met last Christmas at the talent show and had become fast friends, getting together in Seattle whenever Miranda flew in or out—Leo lived south of the airport in Tacoma—and I knew they texted regularly, too. It tracked since Leo was marginally less effusive, but they were both giant, combustible balls of sunshine.

Miranda pointed at a box on top of the fridge. "There are plastic flute glasses in there for the champagne toast. I thought it would be more special than using plain plastic cups. And I wanted to do something nice for Marley since I'll be stuck at school from after Christmas until basically the wedding day."

Leo patted her on the back. "Don't worry, Mir. Marley knows you love her no matter what. She understands school is important. Especially since you're finally graduating," he added with a snicker.

"What are you studying?" Will asked Miranda. "I don't think I've ever asked."

"Business. I'm finishing my MBA." Will couldn't disguise his surprise. "I know, I know." Miranda laughed. "Everyone thinks since I like to travel and do outdoor things, and I'm so—let's say peppy—I must be an airhead. Or at least something other than a business major. But I love numbers and problem-solving."

I leaned over and kissed my sister on the top of her head. "She's getting her degree in bits and pieces because she can't turn down the chance to go hiking in Guatemala or rafting in Wyoming. She even spent a month last year volunteering to build houses in Mexico." I couldn't help the pride in my voice.

"It's awesome," Leo said. "Miranda has the best stories." He winked at her. "I love doing construction and working with my hands, especially when I can be outside. But I've never been anywhere interesting. Unless you count Disneyland."

"I love Disneyland." Miranda booped him on the nose.

Good lord. Being around these two was going to give me a toothache. While James would officially be our brother-in-law, we'd certainly be getting a two-fer with Leo. He was the brother Miranda always wanted. Or maybe he was more like the pet dog she used to beg our mom for and never got.

I glanced at Will. I couldn't believe he'd dared suggest we *spend some time together.*

He looked back and gave me a small, tentative smile. I scowled at him. To my astonishment, his smile remained.

Although he tried to hide it.

Chapter Thirteen

Will

I couldn't believe I'd been so bold. I certainly hadn't planned it. But then I'd seen that look in her eyes. The unmistakable heat.

I'd driven all the way from Seattle hoping to negotiate a cleaner truce, to come away feeling like I could be James's friend without always having to find out Maureen's whereabouts. I'd wanted the buzz of being in her vicinity, hungry to take whatever scraps she was willing to offer. Forgiveness had seemed like a lofty, impossible prospect.

But that was before I touched her hand.

What was that saying—something about missing all the shots you didn't take? The moment presented itself, so I had to try. It remained to be seen if my gamble would backfire spectacularly, but at least Maureen hadn't punched me in the nuts. Even though I felt sure she was fuming behind her unreadable expression.

As angered as she'd been by my audacity, I couldn't help but think how she brought out the best in me. I'd felt more alive tonight, igniting first the desire and then the fire in her eyes, than I'd ever been during any of my *big* moments with Rosalyn—first date, moving in together, getting engaged. Nothing with my former fiancée had lit me up the way even the barest moments with Maureen did.

Leo walked between us into the laundry room and through the door connecting to the garage. "The cake's in the second fridge out here. Along with about a million bottles of champagne."

"Don't exaggerate, Leo-Bear," Miranda said. "It's only two dozen. I had to make sure there was enough for everyone."

"Hey, this is good stuff." Maureen examined the labels on the bottles. "How did you afford this?"

"I know a guy." Miranda shrugged, uncharacteristically not offering further details.

"You know a dipshit," Leo muttered under his breath as he carried in the enormous cake. I wanted to laugh but kept my face placid since I didn't think he'd meant for me to hear his words. Leo obviously knew something about Miranda's "guy." I didn't allow myself too much curiosity. I had my own Davis sister to worry about.

Miranda pulled the plastic flute glasses out of the box as Leo set his burden on the stovetop. The cake had three layers, red-and-green-striped buttercream with wreath accents. Every sweet-smelling inch was beautiful, but the large spun sugar snow globe atop the cake stole the show. Inside it, two figures danced next to a Christmas tree. The baker had done an amazing job making the figures look remarkably like James and Marley.

Maureen laid a hand on her chest as she breathed out, "Oh, Leo. It's beautiful. Marley is going to love it."

"James too," I piped in, thinking about what a softy my old friend was, especially with his bride-to-be. I chuckled, hoping he'd sobered up a bit from earlier in the afternoon so he could appreciate this masterpiece of a confection.

"I certainly hope so," Leo said. "Going over the mountain pass and driving on the freeway with it made me so nervous. I must have set a record for most times getting flipped off in a five-hour drive."

Miranda examined the cake. "I'm sorry you had to take a few middle fingers for the team, but you did a good thing here. They'll never forget this. Look here." She spun the cake around and pointed at the CONGRATULATIONS MARLEY AND JAMES written on the bottom layer, flanked by two dogs in Christmas bow ties and Santa hats, modeled after Oscar and Bambi. "The details on this are insane."

All four of us took out our phones and began snapping pics. It was a shame this cake needed to be eaten. I hoped it tasted as good as it looked.

"Can you take the cake outside so everyone can see it while Maureen and I get the champagne into glasses?" Miranda asked Leo. "There's an empty table to set it on near the buffet."

Carrying the cake in from the garage had been easy enough, but the path from the kitchen to the patio was a gauntlet filled with Christmas decorations, errant folding chairs, and tipsy party guests. "I'll walk in front of you and make sure no one accidentally dips a finger in the frosting," I said to Leo.

"Thanks, man."

We made it through the living room, briefly waylaid by two middle-aged guests who insisted on *oohing* and *aahing* over the cake, and out onto the patio. I thought we had a clear shot to the table when a guest unexpectedly leaned back in his chair just as we walked behind him.

Several partygoers' mouths dropped open in horror as Leo stumbled and took an awkward step sideways to avoid falling. Luckily, he managed to go down onto one knee as I turned around to help steady him, and we stabilized the circular aluminum dessert base about six inches above the ground.

The cake wobbled precariously, and for a moment, it seemed like the snow globe topper might tumble right off, but with a flick of my finger, I held it in place as we leveled the base. Leo's knee and ankle remained at an awkward angle as two guests stepped forward to take the cake from us, depositing it safely on the table.

Breathing a sigh of relief, I rose and reached out a hand to Leo.

"Whew," he said. "That could have been a disaster."

"Could have been doesn't count," I said, laughing away the stress from our near miss.

Behind us, Miranda and Maureen stood at the patio door carrying trays of glasses.

"Well, that was exciting," Maureen said dryly as she began distributing the champagne.

"I can't believe how close that came to total catastrophe," Miranda whispered without her usual good humor, emitting an anxious breath. "Sheesh."

"No bigs, Panda. I had it all along." Leo winked at her.

Maureen took charge, giving her sister's shoulder a squeeze. "Will, can you and Leo pour more champagne in the kitchen while we pass these out? We uncorked all the bottles, so it shouldn't take too long for everyone to have something in hand. There's apple juice for the kids, but still put it in the fancy cups for funsies."

Leo and I poured as quickly as the bubbles allowed. Miranda and Maureen returned five minutes later to grab round two, including the apple juices. With so many guests making the patio a tight squeeze, it was necessary to take the glasses out rather than fill them at the tables. From the laundry room window, I saw Marley and James admiring the cake, looking teary-eyed. Big, sentimental babies. I loved them both so much.

"Okay, I think this is it." Miranda came in for the last of the drinks, slightly manic. "Then we can start the toasts and cut the cake."

"You need to chill, little sis," Maureen said. "We'll get them out there soon enough. Relax."

"I just want it to be perfect."

"Don't worry. This is Marley we're talking about. She uses fast food napkins as tissues and feeds Oscar store-brand dog food. She's not fussy. Why are you so worked up?"

"Sorry," Miranda said. "Tired, I guess." Leo looked at her with concern, and I again had the feeling he knew something her sisters didn't. Whatever was going on, she was lucky to have him in her corner.

I wanted to be that person for Maureen. If she ever stopped scowling at me. "Let me help you get the last flutes on the trays," I offered.

Maureen took one tray and delivered glasses to guests on the outer edges of the patio. Leo and I brought out the last few apple juices. Miranda carried champagne to the head table on the second tray, where Marley and James had re-seated themselves after ogling the cake. Travis, Vivienne, and their kids were also there, along with Katy Baumbeck, a woman who'd been introduced to me earlier as a member of Marley's bridal party, and her two toddlers.

From beside the dance floor, I watched Katy attempt to wrangle her children into their seats. They wiggled and resisted, wearing identical stubborn expressions.

"No!" the smaller of the two kids shouted. "No! No! No!" He picked up his apple juice and flung it across the empty dance floor—directly in Miranda's path. The assembled guests gasped. Miranda stumbled, glasses clanking as her tray wobbled.

A collective sigh of relief rippled through the crowd as she righted herself.

But then the toddler burst into tears at the loss of the drink he'd tantrum-tossed. He shoved his body away from his mother's hold. Miranda had dodged the hurled glass, but she couldn't elude the tiny body leaping across the patio in front of her. She tripped over her own feet to avoid running into him.

And launched the tray out of her hands.

"Nononononono!" Miranda cried, reaching out futilely to stop the inevitable.

Partygoers watched in slow motion as the champagne went flying, glasses tipping mid-flight, soaking the glittery runner as they landed sideways on the table, rolling onto the ground.

Everyone seated at the head table jumped up, splashed with various amounts of liquid. Marley appeared to have taken the brunt of it, her entire torso soaked.

"Eeeeeeeeeeehhhhhh!" Connor's piercing screech cut the air like a blade, drowning out the Christmas standard blaring over the speaker. He slapped at his clothing. "Wet! Wet! Wet!" He looked at his parents beseechingly, face flushing crimson. "Get it off! Get it off! Get it off!" Scarlett burst into tears at her brother's reaction, less so at the wet spots blooming across her own jacket.

Mild pandemonium ensued as every guest somehow manifested napkins and began passing them to the head table. Maureen got on top of the situation quickly, directing Leo into the kitchen for paper towels and clean dish rags.

Katy scooped up her son. The young mother wore an understandably chagrined expression while the tiny boy seemed to sense the part he'd played in the chaos. He buried his face in his mom's chest, along with his sibling, and began to cry, their wails eclipsing Connor's.

Maureen cleared a path for Travis and Vivienne to take Connor and Scarlett into her bedroom to give them a quiet place to regroup. "Don't worry, I've got an eye on the older two," Maureen assured them, although the tweens still sitting at the table seemed mercifully unaffected. "There are fresh towels in the linen closet by the bathroom," she added.

Vivienne nodded gratefully. "Don't worry. We always travel with spare clothes, and we'll get him calmed down quick enough. His behavioral therapy has been working wonders with these types of situations, and once he's dry, I'm sure he'll be alright."

"All good. Whatever you need."

Katy managed to calm her children before peering glumly at Marley. "I'm really sorry, Marls. He's been so defiant lately." Her voice wavered.

"Hey, don't even worry about it," Marley said, dabbing her sweater with a dishrag. "I know you're doing your best, and don't forget, I'm a teacher. I understand better than most how kids can be unpredictable."

Marley patted Katy's arm. I helped James and a few other folks clear the table while Leo picked up the plastic flutes scattered across the ground. Maureen stood waiting with a fresh tablecloth.

While soaking up the last of the mess from the concrete patio, I noticed Miranda standing listlessly near a potted Christmas tree, eyes downcast. I tapped Maureen on the shoulder and gestured toward her youngest sister.

"Miranda, are you alright?" Maureen asked as we both walked over.

"I'm okay." Miranda sniffed. "I can't believe I dropped the tray."

"You didn't drop it on purpose," I reassured her, encouraged by Maureen's approving glance. "I saw it all happen. That kid ran in front of you. What else were you supposed to do? It was an accident."

"Well, it feels like my fault," Miranda insisted. "And now the party is ruined."

"What?" Marley joined our discussion. "Nothing is ruined. Like Will said, it was an accident. We're going to let everyone get cleaned up a bit, and then it'll be right back to toasts and cutting the cake."

Leo returned from the kitchen, carrying more glasses and two bottles of champagne. "Don't worry, Miranda. We still have enough for everyone." He stood tall and used his booming voice to announce, "We hope you enjoyed the excitement, folks. Just give us a few minutes to get dry and re-pour, and we'll be right back to the party. I didn't drive that beautiful cake all the way from Seattle for nothing. We're going to eat that sucker, and it's gonna be worth the wait!" He chuckled.

His affable declaration put the crowd at ease, and the low hum of conversation and laughter resumed. The guests politely avoided drinking from their flutes, waiting for the formal champagne toast.

"See that," Leo said to Miranda. "All taken care of." She still looked somewhat doubtful, but as she straightened her shoulders and smiled, her natural optimism pushed to the surface.

"Great," Marley said, clapping her hands together. "I'm going to my room real fast to switch out this Santa sweater for a different Santa sweater. Back in a jiffy." She leaned over to say something in James's ear, giving him a peck on the cheek before retreating.

"Exactly how many Santa sweaters does your sister have?" I whispered to Maureen.

"Trust me, you don't want to know." She grinned, and I watched as she intently scanned the room, determining that everything had been handled as well as could be. I admired the quiet way she'd taken control of the situation. Although her temper ran a little hot, and her words could be as sharp as an ax, her actions were always decidedly cool. She handled business, that was for sure. Maureen shocked me from my thoughts by reaching down to squeeze my hand for an electric beat before letting go. "Thanks for helping, Will."

"Thanks for letting me."

Chapter Fourteen

Maureen

By eight o'clock, the party was winding down. Guests still danced and picked at their plates, but the atmosphere remained decidedly low-key. The outdoor space heaters were no joke. Even with the December air and snow piled along the edges of the backyard, most folks had discarded scarves, hats, gloves, and even coats.

James danced with Mrs. Allen. I walked over to where the bride-to-be watched the scene fondly.

"Do you think she's okay?" Marley asked me after a moment, pointing subtly toward our little sister. Miranda sat on a bench near the slider, her head resting against Leo's shoulder. He swung his arm around and pulled her against his side, giving her a chaste kiss on the forehead.

"I think she's fine. Looks like Leo's taking care of her."

"You think something's going on there?" Marley's gaze turned inquisitive. "More than just future in-laws type of stuff?"

"Maybe," I conceded. "But probably they're just good friends. They are a lot alike."

"True."

We watched Leo coax Miranda into a smile as he waved an arm to the guests at large—apparently reminding her again that the snafu with the glasses hadn't been a big deal, that the toasts and cake-cutting had eventually gone off without further incident.

I sighed softly under my breath. Thinking of the toasts brought Will's to mind. I couldn't get it out of my head in the hour since he'd said the words.

"Congratulations to my good friend James and the love of his life, Marley. It might have taken them a while to admit they're perfect for one another, but now that they have, I'm sure they'll have a lifetime of joy. Sometimes, the happiest destinations are at the end of the roughest roads. Cheers!"

It didn't take a genius to figure out his words had been at least partially directed at me, even if no one else realized it.

Leo pulled Miranda onto the dance floor. She giggled as they executed a very uncoordinated head-bopping movement to the beat of "Do They Know It's Christmas?" It was odd how Miranda had been so hard on herself earlier. She wasn't normally high-strung. Something seemed to have changed over the past few months.

"What about you?" Marley's voice pierced the night air.

"Hmm?" I replied absently, my attention still focused on the dancing.

"I saw you talking to Will earlier. Looked like you were getting along." She elbowed me playfully.

My heart rate increased even as my tone stayed even. "Obviously, we were talking. He's a groomsman. I'm a bridesmaid. We have shit to discuss."

I turned my head away, unable to stop a small half smile from forming as I pictured Will and I having heated debates about flower arrangements and wedding favors.

"I hate when you call yourself a bridesmaid," Marley said. "You're more like a second-in-command maid of honor."

I barked a laugh. "That's not a thing, Marls. But don't worry, I'm totally fine letting Miranda have the glory of holding your flowers."

Marley laughed and picked at some lint on her sweater. After a few minutes, she returned to what was apparently her new favorite topic. "So...how do you like Will?"

I huffed irritably. "Still on this? What do you mean 'how do I like him'? He's James's friend. He's fine."

"Like, he's fine, or he's *fiiiiiiiine*?" Marley waggled her brows.

"Jesus. Are you Oscar with his bone? He's plain old fine. And I told you yesterday to stop playing matchmaker." I shook my ponytail behind my shoulder. "He's your good friend, not mine. To me, he's just a dude I make small talk with sometimes because we have mutuals." *Was she buying this steaming pile of horseshit?*

Marley went back to picking at her lint. "I'm just saying, if you got to know him better, you'd probably like him. You have a lot in common."

Oh, sis, if you only knew.

I needed to get Marley off this topic, and the best way to do that meant bringing up the one subject I knew would distract her.

"So, I noticed Kasen didn't make it here tonight?"

Marley frowned at the mention of her ex. "Yeah. He's supportive and everything, and we're trying to be friends. But I get how it might be a little much for him to come to something like this."

"Maybe he'll come to the wedding," I said. I couldn't help feeling sorry for Kasen. He'd been like family when he dated my sister, and I hoped he'd find his own happy ending.

"Maybe," Marley mused. "I'd like that."

We hummed softly with the Christmas tunes playing over the speaker, waving as more of the guests departed. There hadn't been an end time on the invitation because Coleman Creek didn't operate like that. Fingers crossed, the stragglers would clear out by midnight.

Will sat at one of the round tables with Travis, Vivienne, and their kids. They all held playing cards, engaged in an intense game of Go Fish. I watched Will offer Connor a fist bump, stopping about an inch short of actually touching the boy's hand, respecting his sensory issues. Seeing Connor's wide smile in return made my heart stutter.

When Will caught my gaze on them, his eyes softened. He gestured to Scarlett. The table was too far away for me to hear him, so he mouthed exaggeratedly, "She's kicking my ass."

I shook my head, grinning.

"Marley?" I asked.

"Yeah?"

"What did you mean when you said Will and I have a lot in common?"

She sat up triumphantly. "I knew it! You're interested in him."

I glowered at her. "I promise you I'm not. Just curious."

"If you say so. But since you asked, I've gotten to spend more time with Will over the past year, and you're just very similar in your approach to things. Like how it's obvious why Miranda and Leo are friends. And how James and I are sort of evenly matched. Will's creative, like you, and he's witty, always with the sarcastic comebacks. He doesn't suffer fools. But then he can also be really sweet and take care of people, like he did for James at the reunion. Or like he's doing for the Bloxhams right now."

The air swirled in my lungs. She was describing the Will I'd gotten to know five years ago over endless hours of coffee and carbs. *Billy.* Would my curiosity to find out how that man had turned into Rosalyn's fiancé, *William,* eventually outweigh my instinct for self-preservation? Should I take him up on his suggestion to spend some time together? To Marley, this was all straightforward, but to me, the Will she described still felt like an enigma. I knew there was much more to him than she had ever seen.

"Maybe we're a bit alike," I conceded, since my sister expected a reply.

"More than a little."

I scooted closer to her. "Do you know what happened to his hand? His, uh, fingers?"

Marley's features tightened. "No. I only know he had an accident. I don't know when or what it was. He once told James he never goes bike riding, so maybe it has something to do with that. Whatever happened, he's so adept with only the three fingers, I never notice."

"Same."

JAMES CAME OVER TO PULL MARLEY to the dance floor. With both my sisters occupied, I figured I could slip away and start cleaning up inside.

I found Vivienne in the kitchen, wrapping some of the food and getting the first load of dishes started.

"Didn't I just see you outside?" I asked.

"I was, but Travis and the kids were doing fine without me. Katy was in here a minute ago, but she needed to get her babies home, so I volunteered to keep the process moving along so she wouldn't feel bad."

I pulled on an apron and tied it behind my waist. "I'd love to get everything done without Marley having to lift a finger."

"Agreed."

We worked side by side for a while, hand-washing plates and organizing the casserole dishes neighbors would come by to pick up over the next few days. Vivienne monitored her family through the laundry room window.

"Will has been great with the kids tonight," she remarked. "Especially considering he hasn't met them before. Connor never takes to new adults like this. And when Scarlett got squirmy during the toasts, Will found one of James's puzzle books and spent half an hour with her doing Christmas word searches."

Ugh. I needed fewer people telling me what a great guy Will was. It messed with my head.

As did Will walking into the kitchen twenty minutes later, looking chivalrous and adorable with a sleeping Scarlett in his arms. "Out like a light," he whispered to Vivienne. "Travis said to tell you he's rounding up the other three to get them into the car, but he's fine if you want to stay."

Vivienne ran a gentle finger along Scarlett's cheek. "Honestly, I'm beat too." She turned to me. "You okay if I take off?"

"No problem. We're almost done here, anyway."

She tsked cheerfully. "Well, I know that's not true, but I appreciate you saying it."

Vivienne reached to take her daughter from Will. Scarlett barely stirred, flopping across her mother's shoulder like a sack of potatoes.

"Don't worry about the rest of the mess," Will said. "I can help Maureen." He looked over to see if I would object, but I nodded my head at him. There were still a lot of dishes, and I'd need to tackle the patio once the guests departed.

"Be careful outside," I warned Vivienne. "It's really slippery, especially now that the sun's fully gone."

After the Bloxhams departed, I handed Will a heavy dutch oven. "Here you go. Have fun scraping off the last of Mr. Lemon's tuna noodle casserole." He pulled up his sleeves and made a show of wrinkling his nose but didn't complain as he stood over the sink and began scrubbing.

We worked for a few minutes in silence. I stood next to him while he washed and I dried.

"So here we are again in the kitchen." Will spoke lightly, but I heard the edge in it.

"Hmm."

"It seems like we're doing okay, you know, being normal around each other."

"Uh-huh."

The sounds from the party melted into the background. I sucked in my lower lip and tried not to notice his forearms flexing as he worked. Tried not to think of how endearing it had been to see him playing Go Fish with Connor. "Normal" wasn't the word I'd use to describe the way I felt around him.

Will's breath made waves in the steam rising from the hot water. Placing the sponge on the counter ledge, he turned off the tap and ran an arm across his damp forehead. He wiped his hands on a dish towel.

"Maureen—"

Our hips brushed as he turned to face me.

I flinched at the contact.

"Listen, Will. It's cool that we've made some progress here—" Twisting to look at him, I moved a finger back and forth between us like a seesaw. "Except you need to remember that, like, twenty-four hours ago, I seriously still hated you."

He nodded thoughtfully. "But you don't hate me now?"

Slowly, I exhaled, speaking with more confidence than I felt. "I'm...conflicted. But one thing I'm sure of is I don't have the capacity to put a label on this right now, other than 'not hate.' My career is in limbo, if you hadn't noticed. Plus, the holidays. And not having a permanent place to live. So please don't add to my load by saying anything else about wanting to *spend some time together*, alright?"

Will winced. "I'm not trying to push you. I promise." He blew out his own loud breath. "You can do what you want with it... Do nothing with it. I just needed to put it out there—" He gazed at me intently, our chests inches apart. "Make sure you...had the information."

He paused, the silence deafening.

My breath hitched as hooded gray eyes bored into mine.

His nostrils flared. Other than that, he didn't move. Warmth radiated from him, the walls of the kitchen our cocoon. I blinked slowly, understanding the next play was mine. He wouldn't take it from me. Not this time. I knew what I needed to do.

Get away. Protect yourself.

I took a small, infinitesimal step...

Toward Will.

My eyes drifted to the tick of his pulse beating a visible symphony in his throat. He swallowed.

Finally, cautiously, his hand crawled through the air near the side of my face.

When I didn't flinch or pull away, he grew braver. He pinched my ponytail between the thumb and pointer of his right hand, giving me a close-up view of his missing fingers. As his palm trailed back down my cheek, just barely touching—the contact couldn't even be called a graze—I had to close my eyes against the tidal wave of sensation. I shouldn't want this, yet my body said otherwise.

"It's okay," he said hoarsely. "I know it's kind of gross."

Huh? My hazy brain required a few seconds to sort out his words. What was gross?

He started to pull his hand away.

Wait. Did he think I'd closed my eyes because of his fingers? I forced my lids open and peered at him through my lashes. I saw the dart of insecurity in his expression.

"Oh no, Will. Never that," I whispered. Instinctively, I reached up and put my hand on the outside of his, pushing his palm back against my face. With purpose. I turned my nose to press into the center of it, feeling its heat even as I registered the jagged silvery scar tissue. "You're beautiful."

My words were quiet, but their effect was immediate. His features clouded as he scraped his thumb along mine, mimicking our actions from earlier tonight. He moved his hands to lace his fingers behind my head. With our near-equal heights, the action brought us face-to-face. I stared into his tender gaze. The raw desire I saw reflected there forced caution to the back of my mind. I licked my lips, and my palms drifted to his lean hips.

He inhaled sharply, resting his forehead against mine. "Goddamn, Maureen. Tell me this means you want to start over."

The distinct sound of a boot sole squeaking against the hardwoods reverberated like a cannon shot.

"Oh shit! Sorry, guys. I didn't mean to, uh, interrupt." The abrupt sentiment came from Leo, standing slack-jawed on the edge of the kitchen, carving himself into the moment with the subtlety of a chainsaw.

Will and I jerked back from one another.

Oh my god. What had Leo just caught us doing?

"You're not interrupting." Will recovered faster than me. "Maureen and I were just talking." He looked pointedly at the other man. "And I'd really appreciate it if you didn't mention this to anyone else."

"No problem." Leo put his hands up and walked backward out of the kitchen. "I never saw a thing."

My body trembled as Will and I found ourselves alone again. Jesus. What if that had been Miranda who'd caught us? Or Marley? While I trusted Leo not to say anything, his seeing me with my arms around Will made the situation real. Made my weakness for Will real. I wasn't ready.

"Don't worry. He won't say anything." Will squeezed my shoulder reassuringly. "Now, where were we?"

"Nowhere, Will. We were absolutely nowhere."

I untied my apron, threw it on the counter, and ran out of the kitchen.

Chapter Fifteen

Will

Maureen opened the front door and flew outside. I grabbed my coat from near the front entrance and raced after her.

Her fists tightened into balls at her sides as she stomped down the front stairs, muttering incoherently. She paused when I shouted into the chilly night air. "Maureen!" I caught up with her on the front walkway, compelled to take a step back when she turned and directed her wild eyes at me. In a quieter tone, I asked, "What happened back there?"

She unclenched her palms and placed her hands on her hips, glancing up at the sky before speaking. "When I said I could be nicer to you, I meant I wanted us to co-exist. I didn't mean I wanted…"

She trailed off, looking somehow both angry and resigned. When she didn't pick up the thread after ten achingly silent seconds, I prompted, "That you wanted…?"

The white-gray mist of her harsh breaths hung in the air. "That I wanted… Shit!" She pushed one fist into the other, shaking her head as she regarded the frozen ground. "I don't know! I'm not ready to forgive you... And you touching me back there—it's too confusing right now. Too much."

I reeled back. When she'd called me beautiful and pushed my hand to her face, it lit me up inside. I honestly thought we'd been working our way somewhere. But whatever I'd seen in her eyes, she was afraid of it.

"I'm sorry," I said. "Truly. I thought we were having kind of a moment."

A car honking blared in the distance, causing us both to startle.

"We were having a moment. There's no point in pretending otherwise." Sighing, she dropped her arms to her sides. "I'll admit you make me...feel things." Softly, she murmured, "I wish you didn't."

Even with the disclaimer that she didn't want to want me, her words gave me hope—because she was acknowledging something between us. But I'd also upset her again. Fuck.

She shivered, and I pulled off my coat. I held it at the end of my arm like a white flag, keeping a foot of distance between us. She hesitated a moment before taking it from my grip and throwing it over her shoulders.

Selfishly, I wanted to ask what she'd been thinking when she pressed her nose to my scarred palm. But of course, I'd never do that. Not when she'd already given me more than she'd intended to. I settled on, "I feel things for you too, Maureen."

Our gazes locked. She nodded resignedly. "I know you do."

Naturally, she knew. I hadn't been subtle tonight.

Maureen coughed delicately and squared her shoulders, drawing my coat tightly across her torso to fight the frigid night. "Will, these feelings we're having...I...I don't want them. When you touched me, it was like I turned into a puddle of goo. Like all the promises I'd made myself, all the resolve just vanished." She touched all the fingers of her right hand together before stretching them out quickly. "Poof."

Her troubled eyes sparkled as a bloom of pink invaded her cheeks. My eyes lasered on her lower lip as she chewed it. Even rejecting me, she was magnetic. I longed to pull her into my arms, to show her she didn't need to be afraid. Instead, I blew air into my cupped palms and struggled for the right words. "Maureen, I know I hurt you. You'll never know how sorry I am." I dragged a hand across my neck, resting it in the mouth of my sweater. Unashamedly, I pleaded, "But does that have to mean we ignore this amazing connection between us forever? Why should we take it for granted when it's so...rare?"

Spending a night with Maureen five years ago had been like striking a match. Afterward, I'd begun to want other things too. Art. Choices. Challenges. Conflict. Everything I'd lost since the accident. Standing in front of her magnified the impulse tenfold.

Feeling that deeply for someone. How was this a bad thing?

But she shook her head.

My eyes landed on the house next door. The lawn hummed with the noise of motors maintaining four different blow-up Santas. Twinkle lights dancing in the snow seemed to taunt me.

Maureen softened, not immune to my frustration. "I'm not sure I can make you understand, Will. But I'll try. The bottom line is, I don't want to be that woman again, the one who loses herself in a man. I don't like feeling that way, not being in control."

"Okay. But that happens to all of us, right? There are times you just have to let go and take a chance. Some things are worth it."

Her eyes flared. "And sometimes, not being in control means being completely and utterly out of control. Inviting disaster." She released a humorless laugh. "And what happened between us... That was a disaster of *epic* proportions."

I recoiled.

"I don't believe that." My hushed voice resounded in the stillness. "I can't. Maybe I felt it more strongly than you did, but that night we had was fucking great. I know everything went to shit, but it was amazing—"

"Until it was fucking horrible!" she snapped, one hand still clenching my coat together as the other waved animatedly up and down. "My whole life I never missed a beat—handling my shit, being there for my family, trying to carve out a future. I was a boss bitch. And then I met you, and all that went out the window. All because you made me *feel things*."

"And I'll never stop being sorry for hurting you."

"No! Not hurt. You humiliated me. Hu-mil-i-a-ted. What happened that day in the lobby turned me into the worst version of myself."

I felt the weight of her words wash over me. Clearly, more was going on than just what happened between us. I wasn't sure if I should say "sorry" again. It might piss her off more. I shoved a hand through my hair and tugged on the ends, grateful for the sting.

At my non-reply, she huffed. "I know what you're thinking."

The cold started seeping under my skin. I stuffed my hands in my pockets. "What am I thinking?"

"That you've apologized repeatedly, and where has it gotten us?"

She'd read my mind. "If I thought it would help move us past it, I'd apologize a million more times. If you want me to, just say the word."

Maureen stepped closer to me, a surprise. In a low voice, she stated, "I almost died, Will."

My brows drew together. "What?"

"After that day in the lobby, I almost died."

"What?... Died? What do you mean?"

"Do you really want to know? Because I'm still not interested in your excuses for why you lied back then, so it seems only fair to offer you an out from hearing about that day from my perspective."

"Tell me."

She squeezed her eyes shut for a second and pulled my jacket tight around her torso again before speaking.

"To your point, we connected that night. In a way I hadn't with anyone else. Ever. When you didn't text, I was upset with myself for letting you in. I'd been careful never to get so involved with anyone that they could get to me like that. It stung that you dismantled all those defenses in one night. I'd seen it happen to other women, and it was almost a shock to recognize it in myself. It pissed me off. You need to understand that all I could think at the time—when you didn't text me other than the world's lamest 'I'm sorry'—was that you had totally played me, that you had somehow tricked me into believing you'd felt something for me. I felt disgusted with myself because I'd allowed that to happen. So, I was already in a pretty dark place. Then I got blindsided by you and *your fiancée* in that hotel lobby. A sick, out-of-body experience, a hammer to the gut. The immediate self-loathing was…unmanageable."

Her words upended a picture I'd had in my mind for five years. That day. Maureen had coolly shaken Rosalyn's offered hand, added, "Nice to see you again," in my direction, and walked away. To my eyes, she'd appeared perfectly collected.

Maureen paused before releasing a slow, deliberate breath. Near enough I felt it on my chin. She continued, "I went home. Couldn't drag myself back to the office, didn't even call my boss. My best friend—my roommate—wasn't there. I'd never told her the truth about you, which was weird since we talk about everything, but being hung up over a guy was unfamiliar territory, and I hadn't known what to do with it.

"She found me in the morning. I'd spent the night drinking anything I could get my hands on and passed out in a puddle of my own vomit. Got a nasty cut on my leg, too. Later, the doctor said I'd gotten lucky passing out on my side. I could have choked if I'd been on my back. But the truly crazy part is, when I woke up, I still didn't tell my best friend why I'd gone on such a bender. I made up something about work stress and not realizing how much I'd had...blah...blah...blah." Maureen made a derisive sound. "I didn't even tell my mom or sisters about going to the hospital.

"And that's what I'm trying to make you understand, Will. I'm not interested in revisiting that day. Or changing the way I perceive it. The memory of what happened has kept me from forming any new attachments. It's kept me sane. Safe."

My heartbeat increased steadily as she spoke, realizing the full consequences of my actions. How she had processed the aftermath of meeting me.

Not only a man she'd made an instant connection with but also the cause of a near-death experience.

Her hesitance made much more sense to me now. But after the glimmer of hope she'd given me today, I no longer believed our past was something we couldn't come back from.

I inhaled heavily. "You said before you felt like I'd tricked you into feeling things. Back then."

She side-eyed me. "That's right."

"So, I just want to say that I intend to convince you that you're wrong about me. About us and what we can be. I'm not manipulating you. I'm saying it plainly."

"Saying what?"

"That I'm going to keep showing you who I am. Get to know you better, as much as you'll let me. I'm not the monster you've built up in your head. I'm the man who just spent a half hour washing dishes with you. The one who snores and is bad at pouring champagne. You're right that I did a terrible thing. I had reasons—" At her tight expression, I held my palms open. "I know, I know, you don't want to hear them. But I don't think we should stop exploring this thing between us because you're afraid to give up control. Were you planning on just being alone your whole life and never being in a relationship?"

"It doesn't matter because that's not what's happening here." She pursed her lips in a sexy little pout, cocking her hip.

"Isn't it?" I challenged, raising my eyebrows.

"No. Even if a time came when I allowed myself to feel things for someone, do you honestly think I'd let it happen with the man who humiliated me the way you did? Wouldn't it be smarter to let my guard down with literally any other person? How big of a chump should I be?"

Her stubbornness was maddening, but then again, it was kind of glorious. It was one of the things that had drawn me to her initially—she could be sweet but also totally fierce. "Look, Maureen, I get where you're coming from. But ten minutes ago, you admitted that you feel things for me. You may not like it, but here we are. Sometimes we don't decide."

She snorted. "You mean like it's fate? The universe calls the shots? I don't believe in that shit."

I smiled wryly. "Honestly, neither do I. I'm just stating facts. And the fact is, I never felt with anyone the way I did with you five years ago. I think the same is true for you. A year ago, when I saw you in the auditorium, I felt it again. Just deep in me. You spark something. And the more I learn about you, even now, seeing how you are with your sisters, or Vivienne's kids, just listening to you laugh, I'm greedy for more. It's impossible not to want you."

She pursed her lips. "Well, that's too bad. Just because you want something doesn't make it right, doesn't make it good for you. If I drank strawberry shakes from Five Guys as much as I wanted, I'd have diabetes. If I told off annoying customers at work as often as they deserved, I'd have been unemployed a lot sooner. Our gut instincts don't always serve us well."

Her words sounded decisive, but I saw the conflict in her stormy green eyes as she glared at me—an unmistakable hint of challenge lighting her features.

I could work with that.

I braved a step toward her. When she didn't retreat, I ventured, "You sure about that?"

"Yes." Her nostrils flared.

"You don't even want to try to work out whatever this is between us? Explore things?"

"No."

I inched closer. "Maybe pick up where we left off five years ago after talking all night?"

"No."

"Or last year, when you shivered after I touched your fingers?"

"No."

"How about fifteen minutes ago, when you put your arms around me in the kitchen before running away?"

"No." It was the barest whisper.

I was practically on top of her now. My electrified brain wondered if I was pushing too hard, too fast, but the thumping of my heart dulled my restraint. I felt her proximity everywhere, arousal coursing through my veins. Even though it was freezing, I was a furnace, burning from my scalp to my toes to the tip of my very interested cock. It made me bold in the way I'd only ever been with her.

I angled in so we stood cheek to cheek and breathed into her ear. "Liar."

I leaned my head back, anticipating her expression of fury—satisfied as it materialized instantly. Even as I felt bad for raising her ire, I couldn't help reveling in the fire between us. Her passion was manifesting as anger now, but it was there. I could be patient. But I was done pretending the explosive pull didn't exist.

She stepped back and practically spat, "Dream on, Will. We may be in a better place now. And I may accept you're a part of my life—a tiny, inconsequential part—but you don't get to tell me how I feel. And you don't get to flip my world upside down. Again."

With that, she shrugged her shoulders dramatically out of my coat. Steeling her expression, she balled it up and smashed it roughly against my chest, turning away in a graceful, defiant huff.

It would have been a magnificent exit, a parting shot worthy of an Academy Award. Except for the not insignificant detail that the ground outside was frozen and slippery. And I'd worn very insensible shoes.

I barely had a moment to admire the brilliant flush of her cheeks before her face crumpled. Before she realized she might have shoved me a smidge too hard. The last thing I heard was her calling out my name. Then pain. Searing—not unfamiliar—pain. And after the pain, blackness.

Chapter Sixteen

Maureen

The waiting room in Coleman Creek's small hospital at two a.m. smelled of freshly mopped linoleum and decorative cinnamon-scented pine cones. Blue lights lit up a plastic tree decorated with mini stethoscope ornaments. Paper snowflakes taped to the walls gave off distinct elementary school energy, as opposed to a place where doctors could walk in any minute to deliver bad news.

Please let there be no bad news.

I shivered, still shaken even though it had been hours since Will's fall. It felt like everything had happened in slow motion.

Will's head hitting the pavement, thudding like he'd dropped a bowling ball.

Terrifying minutes where he lay deathly still, not moving or responding to my voice.

Me dropping to my knees next to him, screaming and calling out for help.

Marley and James running outside with looks of horror on their faces.

Will regaining consciousness, able to feel his arms and legs and wiggle his toes, but unable to say how many fingers Marley held up.

James—having recently received first aid training as a volunteer firefighter—giving the all clear for me to take Will to the hospital in my car since it would be quicker than an ambulance.

During the drive to the emergency room, Will stayed awake but yammered like a deranged encyclopedia-slash-personal-diary most of the way, his head lolling against the side window as he rambled.

"Did you know they established the Secret Service to fight counterfeiting, not protect the president? For my fifteenth birthday, my parents took me to the restaurant on top of the Space Needle. I'd never been there before even though I lived in Seattle my whole life. Crazy, huh? If there are seventy-five people in a room, there's a ninety-nine percent chance two of them have the same birthday. Did you know Bob Ross once helped a color-blind viewer by doing an episode where he only used gray paint? Isn't art amazing? You're so interesting and funny and pretty and cool. I like you so much, Maureen. I really wish you liked me..."

When we arrived, they'd taken Will to be seen right away. Marley and James came fifteen minutes later—party guests had trapped their cars—and we sat down in the green vinyl chairs to wait for news.

I fished three quarters from my wallet that had probably been there since the Obama administration and got a Twix from the vending machine. It took actual coins, no credit card tapper in sight, not to mention the candy cost less than a buck. Thankfully, old-school, reasonably-priced vending didn't mean Coleman Creek wasn't modern where it needed to be. There was a helicopter pad on the roof, and the doctor reassured us that if Will needed to be seen at a larger trauma center in Spokane, they could get him there rapidly.

"It wasn't your fault," Marley leaned over to tell me for the dozenth time, as though she'd heard my thoughts.

"How do you know?" I snapped. "I shoved him, and he fell. That pretty much makes it my fault."

"It was an accident."

I scoffed and swallowed down a dry bite of my candy.

James interjected, "You didn't mean for him to fall, right? Hence—accident."

I didn't reply. We'd been having this same circular conversation for hours. The nurse had come out twice to let us know they were running tests. Luckily, Will had been cognizant enough when he arrived to tell the staff to consider us family. He consented to them speaking freely with us about his condition.

Marley asked James if he had a number for Will's parents, but James didn't. It would be simple enough to track them down if need be, but I wasn't convinced Will would want them to know. I recalled him telling me the night we'd met that he had a tricky relationship with his family. James didn't have much insight, saying he'd only met Will's parents a few times when they were kids.

"What were you and Will talking about before he fell?" Marley's voice interrupted my thoughts.

"Nothing important. I went outside to get some fresh air, and he followed me because I didn't have a coat. He gave me his. When I decided to come back inside, I took off the coat and handed it to him, but I must have passed it back too hard because he slid and hit the ground."

"But you were out there a while before that," Marley persisted.

"Just chatting about nothing."

Marley's lips flattened. She'd seen the tears streaming down my face when I'd kneeled next to Will. She didn't push further, but I knew it was time to come clean. I didn't have a lot of faith in Leo's ability to keep what he'd seen from Miranda. And my need to confide in someone felt more important than saving face. Marley wouldn't judge me.

Although she might judge Will. And hadn't that been my other reason for keeping quiet? I didn't want to drive a wedge between my sister and James's oldest friend.

There was a lot to consider, after five years of staying mum. Especially with Will lying in a hospital bed. Having tests run. After I'd hurt him. Even if it had been an accident.

I needed to focus on something else, just for a minute.

"Did you check in with Miranda?" I asked Marley.

"Yeah. She just texted that everyone's finally gone home."

Miranda and Leo had stayed back. Unsurprisingly, many guests had lingered to make sure the house and patio got cleaned up. No one wanted Marley and James's engagement party to end with them coming back to a gigantic mess after spending hours in the ER.

Finally, Dr. McNulty came out holding a clipboard. We'd met her earlier when she told us Will was awake and talking, but that they were going to do a CT scan since he was most certainly concussed.

"I have good news," the doctor said. "Mr. Yardley is going to be fine. Other than a concussion and some light bruising on his hip, we don't see any signs of other major injuries. However, with his medical history, we want to be extremely careful with how we proceed."

Medical history? I had no idea what she meant, and by the looks on Marley's and James's faces, neither did they. My mind went to Will's hand.

The doctor apparently thought we knew much more than we did. She continued blithely, "Due to his previous concussion, and because he was in a coma for so long, we want to monitor his recovery. It's possible his trauma could manifest differently. Or later than we'd usually expect. In cases of brain injury, it's hard to know or make predictions. Also, the bruising on his hip would certainly be considered minor and manageable in another person, but because he has so many metal pins in his leg, there's the possibility his pain levels will persist and need to be managed in a different way."

Brain injury? Coma? Metal pins?
What the hell?

Marley and James also tensed, but the three of us kept nodding. God forbid any of us appear confused and make the doctor stop talking.

"We'd like to keep him overnight for observation, so you three should probably head home and come back during regular visiting hours or even in the afternoon because he'll probably want to sleep for a while."

James shook the doctor's hand. "Thanks so much, Dr. McNulty. We appreciate everything you've done for our friend."

"Of course," she replied. "Frankly, this could have been a lot worse. A Christmas angel was surely on his side. I've seen plenty of falls on the ice result in catastrophic injury." I winced at the reminder I could have seriously hurt Will.

"Can we see him before we go?" James asked.

"Sure. But one at a time, and just for a few minutes. Mr. Yardley told the nurse he'd like to see Ms. Davis first." James gave his fiancée a questioning glance as the doctor looked down at her chart. "Sorry. There's a note here to make sure I say he's requesting to see Ms. *Maureen* Davis."

James's inquisitive stare flew from Marley to me.

"I'm sure he just wants to reassure Maureen that he knows it was an accident," Marley said, raising her eyebrows so I understood I was on borrowed time. She *would* be getting the whole story from me, and soon.

"Oh right, that makes sense," James said.

I followed Dr. McNulty back into the small ICU area. There wasn't much privacy. Heavy curtains separated the beds, although the only other patient I saw was an elderly woman who appeared to be sleeping.

Will's eyes remained closed as I sat on the small stool beside his bed. Nearby monitors beeped rhythmically.

"Hi," I whispered, not wanting to wake him if he slept.

Slowly, Will's eyes fluttered open. He turned and gave me a lopsided grin. "Hi, yourself." His words slurred. He raised his left arm and waved toward the IV bag. "Good drugs."

I snorted. "You don't say?"

He reached through the bed rail to put his right hand on my knee.

"Hey." His grin widened.

"Hey."

Knitting his brows, he flopped his head in a hazy shake. "Not you," he said. *Huh?* I felt the ridges of the scars on his palm through my pants as he rubbed circles on my thigh. "Tonight. The ice. Not your fault." *Oh.* I doubted he'd have been so bold without the *good drugs* as he continued, "You know, right? Not your fault." He closed his eyes and exhaled thickly. "My fault. My...talking. Pushing. So sorry. Keep screwing up...with you."

I moved my hand over his. I laced our thumbs, index, and middle fingers. My ring and pinky fingers curled over the stubs of his, and I squeezed, drawing his attention. He peered at me apprehensively. "No, Will. I told you." Raising his hand to my lips, I kissed the back of it.

"Thank you," he whispered.

"You're not screwing up with me. And it's not all your fault. We just burn hot, I think, when we're together. This thing we're trying to get past...it's a lot. And when you're feeling better, we should actually talk about it. And you can tell me your story. All of it."

I'd realized over long hours in the waiting room that I'd allowed my fears and resentments to fuel me for too long. I didn't want to be that brittle live wire anymore. It wasn't me.

"I'd like that," Will said, appearing more focused than when I'd come in.

After a few minutes, his eyes drifted shut and my gaze fell to our hands. I traced my pointer finger along his scars. They crisscrossed across his palm and the back of his hand like a pineapple. When he didn't stir, I continued my exploration over his ring finger. About an inch remained, up to the first knuckle. The pinky had been severed entirely, a small mound of scar tissue the only sign it had ever been there. "What happened, Will?" I spoke quietly. A question to myself.

"Accident." Will surprised me by responding. He took a deep, slow breath, eyes remaining closed. "I'll tell you when I tell you...everything."

I nodded even though he couldn't see. "Sorry I got so upset I knocked you down."

"Not your fault," he mumbled, his hand slipping from mine as fatigue claimed him.

"When we're back at the house, we'll talk. I don't want to be mad at you anymore."

I wasn't sure if he heard those last words as his breathing grew steady and even. Watching him asleep in the hospital bed reminded me of those bleak seconds on the sidewalk when he'd been unconscious. I'd known in that instant I'd been fooling myself about not wanting to hash things out with Will.

Because I finally understood that he'd lost something five years ago, too. He'd lost the possibility of us, just as I had.

Will had never once tried to minimize his lie or his other actions, and he never once told me I was blowing things out of proportion or that I didn't have the right to feel the way I did. He'd never done anything other than continue to tell me how sorry he was, to humble himself and ask for my forgiveness, to let me know he'd wait for it, even as I insisted it would never come. To show me in every possible way he thought I was worth fighting for.

I returned to the waiting area. Even though Will slept, James wanted to see him before we left. "I can give him a fist bump while he's resting," James said. "I'll feel better if I see him with my own eyes."

I smiled at the sweet man who would soon be my brother-in-law.

After James disappeared into the ICU, Marley asked, "Did Will say anything? Before he fell asleep?"

"Yeah. You were right. He wanted to tell me it wasn't my fault."

She made a humming noise. "That's it?"

"C'mon, Marls." I slumped in the chair next to her. "You know that's not it. But I'm not ready to tell you yet."

She patted my wrist. "Maureen, you don't owe me your secrets. But you're my big sister, and I love you. Whenever you want to talk, I'm here." Her cheek ticked. "You know, when I was giving you heck about bringing a date to the wedding, I honestly had no clue about any of this. I wouldn't have teased you if I'd known the situation was...complicated."

"Don't worry about it. How about we table the conversation for tonight? I'm dead on my feet."

"Same," Marley said, tipping her head onto my shoulder and yawning.

A minute later, I snuck out from under her arm, needing to stretch the tension from my legs. I paced, and eventually found myself in front of another vending machine, deciding to complement my Twix with a seventy-five-cent Diet Coke. Drinking a soda at three a.m. wasn't an issue. Years of working odd hours at Kolya's translated to caffeine not affecting me.

Now that I'd spoken to Will, I felt more relaxed, able to focus on something other than worrying about him. And I had the perfect task to distract myself.

Pulling out my phone, I opened the camera app to the video setting and grabbed some quick footage of the empty hospital waiting room, being careful to avoid filming staff or anyone who might wander by.

Talking to Marley and Katy yesterday solidified my plan to make some fresh content for *Fashion Vibes with Francesca* and capture the spirit of Coleman Creek. A holiday tour of small-town America might not be totally in line with a fashion-oriented YouTube channel, but I didn't care. Almost anything could be connected to the concept of style, and maybe viewers would be interested in finding out exactly where Francesca's vibe had come from.

I knew this meant my worlds colliding, likely my identity unmasked, but with Kolya's in my rearview, it was time for Francesca and Maureen to be the same person.

I filmed the vending machine, the paper snowflakes, the Christmas tree, the months-old *People* magazines, and a low table with photocopied coloring sheets and half-broken crayons. The linoleum and chairs in the main waiting area looked newer, but the wall behind the reception desk still had wood paneling, unchanged since my childhood.

The welcome bite of crisp December air hit me when I stepped outside. Continuing to avoid filming people, I captured both a wide shot and a close-up of the hospital signage. Then I panned across the roof and the icicle lights circling the ambulance bay. It would make useful b-roll.

A gust of wind whipped against my cheeks, and I tugged my beanie over my ears to make sure it didn't fly away. But even with the chill, I felt more settled than I had in a while. I was making videos again. Will and I were finally ready to clear the air. I almost laughed. I wouldn't, not with him lying in a hospital bed. But some sort of switch had flipped during this long night.

The past few years, Bren had harped on my lack of a personal life. She'd told me constantly I needed to "unclench." I hadn't understood.

But now, I knew what my best friend had been driving at. Because I could feel myself opening up. To new possibilities.

Opening up, not unraveling.

Chapter Seventeen

Will

I'd felt okay at the hospital. Okay during check-out. Okay during the long ride to James and Marley's house. I'd even felt okay during the walk from Maureen's car to the guest room, though that short distance had seemed like a marathon.

But now that I was here, propped up against a million pillows, I was too dizzy to even lift a water glass to my mouth. I felt wrecked. The medications were wearing off.

Dr. McNulty cautioned me this would happen. She'd even offered me an extra few days of painkillers to get through the worst of it. But I declined. I'd faced the nausea, vertigo, and dizziness that came from a concussion before. In my mind, the pain was better than the feeling of helplessness that came with being totally out of it.

I felt a straw touch my lips. "Just a few sips at a time today," Marley said, leaning down next to the bed. "Doctor's orders."

"I know the drill. Not my first rodeo," I said, hearing James's intake of breath across the room. I knew the doctors had given them the barest details of my medical history, and I needed to fill in the blanks. But not now. What I needed to do now was concentrate on not throwing up.

"Let Marley Mother Hen you, Will. She'll be unbearable otherwise," Maureen spoke up from the doorway.

My cheek rose slightly as I released the straw. Speaking slowly and concisely—damn, I hated the side effect of having to search for my words—I asked, "Are you planning on huh-huh-huh..." *Fuck!* "Hovering...for the next five days?" I'd been diagnosed with a relatively mild concussion, but they were being extra careful because of my history. The doctors planned to do another scan on Friday to compare it to the one they'd taken after my fall to make sure they hadn't missed anything.

"Of course." This time, it was James speaking unapologetically. "We're going to Florence Nightingale your ass so hard you won't know what hit you."

I smiled, wanting to laugh or at least say thanks, but I couldn't because if I opened my mouth, vomit might come out.

James's phone buzzed, and he stepped out to take the call.

"Maybe we should leave so Will can rest," Maureen said to Marley. "He might be more up for talking after a nap."

I dipped my chin as best I could and hoped she knew I was grateful. I had so much to say. But my forehead was throbbing. Full-blown metal concert going on in there. Maybe I should have taken the prescription for the harder drugs? No. I needed clarity for these conversations.

I wanted to talk with all three of them about my accident so they could understand why the doctors were being cautious. And then, of course, Maureen and I had *things* to discuss. She said she was ready to hear what happened five years ago, and I wanted to tell her before she changed her mind.

My thoughts grew muddled. Vaguely, I heard commotion coming from the kitchen and the living room. The distinct sound of James lumbering around his bedroom. Marley and Maureen speaking rapidly. Even the dogs were barking. Something was happening. But my stupid head. I tried to fight it. Tried to concentrate on the raised voices and the sound of James's car tearing out of the driveway, the crack of tires on the icy road. But sleep pulled me under.

WHEN I WOKE UP, I COULD HEAR MARLEY and Maureen speaking quietly somewhere outside the bedroom. My foggy brain couldn't distinguish between their voices, and I only picked up snippets of the conversation.

"...I'll just stay... Whose responsibility is it then... James said it's bad... Heard from Dr. McNulty... We should wait and ask Will... About three hours... You know you'll have to tell me eventually... Not sure about the timing..."

They walked farther away, and I couldn't hear any more. Not that it mattered, because my awareness faded again.

When I woke a second time, Maureen was in my room, perched against the dresser and looking at a tablet. She had it set in dark mode with the screen faced away from me, so there wasn't much light, but she still powered it off quickly once she noticed my eyes were open.

"Hey," I rasped.

"Will." She breathed out and smiled. "I was wondering if I should wake you again. We've been doing it every two hours like the doctor said to, but you keep going right back under."

With some difficulty, I tilted my head toward the window to see the sun had set. "What… time?"

"Just past seven. You were awake for a few minutes when we brought you home from the hospital, but you've been sleeping ever since."

I felt so groggy. I tried to lift myself, but the pain in my head had me immediately falling back against the pillow.

Maureen jumped over and put a hand out, like she was going to make sure I stayed down. "C'mon, Will. None of that. The doctor was clear. Rest and stay still as much as possible. At least today and maybe tomorrow. If you need to get up, like to use the bathroom, you have to take it slow, and one of us needs to be nearby to make sure you're okay."

"Cool. I'm…toddler."

"I mean, if you're going to pout like one." She raised an eyebrow. "But otherwise, you're just a lucky man recovering from a head injury, which could have been much, much worse." She leaned down to touch my shoulder as though reassuring herself I wasn't going to move. "The doctor said you should feel a lot better tomorrow and over the next few days. The good news is, you're stuck in Coleman Creek. No way you'll be cleared for driving for at least a week."

I'd guessed as much. Good thing I didn't have a company to run anymore. But I'd need to figure out something to tell my parents. No way could they find out I'd had another concussion. They'd flip.

God, my head was pounding. It hurt so bad, simply breathing caused pain, and I felt so nauseous, I was practically about to…no, wait... I was definitely going to... I waved my fingers at the trash can, and Maureen got the hint just in time to put it under my chin as I retched into it. Not much came up, and it made me feel worse rather than better, but stopping it hadn't been an option.

When I finished heaving, Maureen had a cool washcloth ready for me. With effort, I swiped it across my mouth and face. The motion had my head spinning, but I forced myself back against the pillows and didn't need the trash can again.

"I know you...want me now." I attempted to deadpan.

"Meh. I went to college," Maureen replied, nonplussed. "I've seen worse. At least you have a better excuse than being dared to drink a twelve-pack to win the last bag of Doritos."

She got up and disappeared for a moment, taking the garbage can with her. When she came back, she put it next to the bed. "I cleaned it out and put an air freshener under the liner, so it won't smell like a dive bar bathroom. It's here if you need it."

"Thanks." I kept my head immobile, which helped. I could speak at a low volume, though it still made me slightly dizzy, my own voice ringing in my ears.

Maureen sat down on the edge of the bed, careful not to jostle the mattress. "This okay?"

"Good."

"One of us has been checking on you every half hour or so. But now that you're up, I can give you some privacy if you'd prefer."

"No." A powerful sensation of something akin to panic gripped me. "Stay." Even in my pain haze, with the aftertaste of bile in my mouth, I wanted her nearby.

"Okay," she murmured. "Let me know if my voice bothers you. I know you can't watch TV or use any screens yet. I have the lamp dimmed, but I can turn that off too if you want."

"No. I'm good. You can...talk to me." I crept my hand across the bedspread until one finger touched her hip. "Please."

"Alright. I know there's so much to say between us, but the big stuff should wait until you feel better. James and Marley and I are obviously curious about the things the doctors assumed we knew, about your previous injuries." She peered down at me. "I'm guessing some stuff happened to you after you and James lost touch but before I met you?"

"It wasn't...wasn't—" I closed my eyes. *Dammit!* When I'd woken from my coma eleven years ago, it had been like this. I could hear what I wanted to say in my head, but everything came out garbled. At least this time wasn't as bad as all that. "Wasn't secret. I would...have said. To James. Just never mannered. No. *Mattered*. Never mattered. I got...better."

Maureen nodded. "We can talk about it later." She picked up a glass with a straw in it from the nightstand. "Do you want to try some water, or do you think that will send you nosediving back into the trash can?" She held the straw to my lips. I took a small sip without feeling like it would come right back up. Progress. "If you need to use the bathroom, James will be back in a little while. But I can help if it's urgent?"

"No. All...good for now." Small mercies. I wasn't sure I'd be able to withstand the indignity of Maureen having to lower me onto the toilet or, god forbid, pull my dick out for me. "James...gone?"

"Oh, yeah," she said, still hushing her voice. "While you were sleeping, you missed all the excitement. Because apparently this weekend can't be crazy enough. The building in the lot next to The Landslide caught fire. It's been vacant, so I guess it took a while before anyone noticed and called it in. James volunteers with the fire department, so he went out on the call. He was super excited. It's his first one."

"Cool for him. Bad for...building."

"Yep. Double-edged dagger for sure. He worried about leaving you, but Marley told him we can manage one invalid perfectly well on our own. Also, you're going to be staying in this room for the next week, and you have zero chance of Marley taking no for an answer on that. And I suppose I'll also be your nurse since Marley and James work tomorrow."

Maureen was going to take care of me? "You...okay...when that. No. *With* that?"

"Of course. It's at least partly my fault you got hurt." She put up her hand to stop any protest I might make. "I know you don't think so, but it's how I feel. It'll make me feel better to help."

"Okay," I murmured.

"It's going to be different between us. You realize that, don't you? We're going to talk, and it's going to be different. I meant what I said. I don't want to be mad anymore."

My lips twitched in what passed for a smile. Even that tiny move hurt. "Maybe...this...worth it then," I said.

She rolled her eyes, not touching that. "Honestly, Will, you look so pale. The doctor said you turned her down for the stronger meds. Are you sure you don't want me to call her back, get you a different prescription? You don't need to be in pain like this."

"No. You'll understand...when I tell you...my accident."

Maureen reached out and gripped my scarred hand in reply. I lay there, mesmerized, as she threaded our fingers together in what I was beginning to think of as her signature move.

Rosalyn had always been careful not to grab my injured hand. I assumed my former fiancée thought she was being sensitive, like the way you didn't point out someone's receding hairline or a big mole on their face. She never seemed to realize that being polite was for the rest of the world. When you love someone, it's a different assignment. The person with the receding hairline or the mole—they wanted to know the person they loved saw the supposed flaw—saw it and loved them anyway. With Rosalyn, for two years, I never knew.

In the span of only a few days, I felt completely reassured Maureen didn't care about my missing fingers. My scars. The sensation of her wrapping her warm palm around the reminders of the worst day of my life was the affirmation I'd needed for eleven years.

WHEN I WOKE UP THE THIRD TIME, James sat on a folding chair by my bedside. His large frame took up all the space in the tiny room. He had one leg crossed crookedly over the other, and his bearded face stared down at a crossword puzzle book in his lap, lit by a small penlight in the darkness.

He noticed me stir. "You're awake."

"Yeah." My voice shook, but I felt a lot less dizzy compared to a few hours ago.

"Good thing. I was about to wake you since it's been a while since the last time. Are you feeling better?"

"Headache is a bitch, but my thoughts are clearer." Words were coming easier. Thank god for that. The last time, it had taken months for full cognition to return.

I figured it must be the middle of the night, judging by the pitch-black outside.

James's next words confirmed it. "I pulled the night shift with you, bud. I wanted to. Because I'm so wired. I got to go out on a fire call tonight. Did I mention I volunteer with the department? It was mostly over by the time our truck got there, but I still came home totally amped. I knew I'd never sleep, so I sent the ladies to bed. I don't think Maureen ever went to sleep last night. Except now that you're up and don't need to be woken again until six, I might try to catch a few Zzz's."

James's babbling sounded like music to my ears. I loved this guy so much. I wished we hadn't missed out on a decade of knowing one another. And it might have been the lingering drugs in my system, but my next thought was *why not tell him?*

"James, I'm glad you're here. Glad...we're friends."

He froze momentarily before smiling. "Me too." But then, he pinched his chin and added, "Although I figure maybe I haven't been as good of a friend to you as I ought to have been."

"What are you talking about? You've been a...great friend."

"I dunno. When we met again after such a long time, at the reunion, I was so impressed with the way you took down our old bullies. And you're always so relaxed and cool, quick with the commentary. I guess I just assumed everything with you was good. Easy." He blew out a deep breath, and I turned my head to see him better. His eyes were teary. "All night I kept thinking about how we haven't talked much about what happened with you after high school. I know you said you had an accident—and that's why you have a bum hand—but I don't know the details. And I never asked more questions because I figured you just seem so collected. Like maybe there's nothing to know. And why pick at scabs? But I should have. All the stuff the doctor said—I didn't know any of it. This whole year, we've been talking and texting constantly. Except I've been focused on myself. First at the reunion. Then Marley. The engagement. But maybe I should have asked." He paused again, longer this time. "So, I'm asking now. Will, my friend, are you okay?"

Feeling tears in my own eyes, I gathered my breath. I knew the words would be tough, and it felt important to get them right. "James, you are the...best friend I could have hoped for. There were...bad things after high school. Not all, but some. But I'm good now. I promise. This past year has been the best yet." I thought of my apartment building. Being part of James's wedding. Maureen. "Everything keeps...getting better."

"Thank you for saying that."

"Don't...thank me yet. 'Cuz I'm gonna need you to help me pee."

He laughed and reached out to assist me. It was slow going, but I managed to hook my legs over the side of the bed and stand without falling, being careful of my bruised hip, even though the room spun immediately. James walked me to the hall bathroom and sat me down on the toilet, stepping out while I did my business. When he brought me back to bed, I leaned back and realized the gold velveteen pillows were familiar.

Understanding dawned. "You brought my things?" I asked.

"Oh, um, yeah. I hope you don't mind. We found the key card to your hotel room, and Marley went over to grab your stuff since you're due to check out tomorrow anyway. She said to tell you thanks for being neat and tidy, which made her job easy. Maureen said to tell you it's super high-maintenance to bring your own pillows to a hotel, and she reserves the right to make fun of you about it until the day you die."

I snorted. "I can live with that."

"I'll bet," James said, eyeing me carefully. "You wanna tell me what's going on there? Because my fiancée is going to get it out of her sister soon."

"Not yet, okay? Not until I talk to Maureen."

"Understood." James gathered up his puzzle book. "I'm gonna go lie down for a few. I have six classes to teach tomorrow, and I should get a nap if I can. Glad you're feeling better." He backed out of the room.

I fell asleep on my high-maintenance pillows, knowing I'd feel like hell tomorrow, but I smiled because Maureen would be the one staying with me.

Chapter Eighteen

Maureen

Leo and Miranda left Monday morning to head back to Seattle. Leo needed to get home for work, and Miranda wanted to spend some time with friends during her winter break. They'd both be back in Coleman Creek by Christmas Eve, along with James's parents. As they gathered their things and drove off in Leo's gigantic work truck, they appeared to be in some sort of silent standoff. I didn't know what was going on with my youngest sister, but since she was an adult, I decided not to worry about it.

With Marley and James busy molding young minds at Coleman Creek High, I took on Will duty. He'd likely sleep most of the day. Not as much as yesterday, but a lot. It had been scary how much he'd slept and how out of it he'd been when he was awake, but James said he'd seemed more like himself when they spoke during the night.

My plan for today was to do some editing. I hoped to post a new Francesca video this week, just to get back in the habit of it.

Yesterday, I'd gotten an unexpected opportunity when Katy let me come over and film her. Marley had taken over as Will's nurse after James went out on his call. The building that caught fire was next door to The Landslide. Out of caution, the restaurant closed for the day, so the manager sent Katy home. Since her parents had taken her kids to Spokane to go holiday shopping, she'd ended up with a rare free afternoon.

It surprised me she wanted to spend that precious time filming with me, but she'd explained, "We're never going to get another chance like this, and I want to do it before I lose my nerve."

We'd talked options, and eventually focused on Katy telling my camera about her approach to getting dressed for days spent with tiny humans and rowdy customers. A lot of her thought process revolved around ease of movement, and absolutely nothing could need ironing or, heaven forbid, dry-cleaning. I filmed her closet and did some styling with her, using her own clothing and preferences to put together outfits she hadn't thought of.

She'd also spoken about her husband leaving, starting over, and how some days were better than others. This led to an interesting monologue about how her divorce had affected her style, which I knew would lend some gravitas to the piece.

If she let me use it.

I hoped to plug the clips into my editing software and get a rough cut done today. I wanted to send it over to Katy and make sure she was okay with me including the more serious bits. If she wasn't comfortable, I'd cut them. It would still be a fun piece without the heavy stuff.

By eleven o'clock, I'd finished my first full edit. I'd also bought Christmas gifts for Bren, Chase, and my sisters online, plus eaten two pieces of leftover cake for breakfast. I couldn't help but think how different my Monday mornings had been when I'd worked at Kolya's.

Close to noon, a groan came from the third bedroom. Opening the door, I found Will hunched over the bedframe, one foot planted on the floor, the other still straight along the edge of the mattress. He'd used one arm to prop himself into a seated position.

I kneeled next to him, and he immediately put a hand on my shoulder to brace his frame, emitting a pained grunt.

"Sorry, Will. I didn't realize you were up. Can I get you something? You probably shouldn't be trying to stand without help yet."

His face pinched as he choked out, "I need—" He tried to swing his bruised leg over as though he meant to roll out of the bed. A bead of sweat dripped down his neck, and he pressed a hand to his stomach.

I understood. "Let me help you walk to the bathroom."

He nodded gratefully, and I assisted him in rising to a standing position and hobbling to the bathroom. Leaning on the counter and using the towel bars for support, he was able to handle the rest of the process himself, so I waited in the hallway to give him privacy. Afterward, I helped him back to bed.

"Thank you," he said, leaning back on his gold velvet pillows.

"How are you feeling?"

"Like I just got run over by a dump truck while Metallica mixed a new album inside my skull. But that's an improvement from yesterday. I think the worst is over."

"Good." I sat down next to him on the bed. The room was small, with only a bed, nightstand, and dresser. There was a folding chair in the corner James had brought in last night, but I preferred being closer to Will. I needed to keep reassuring myself he was okay. "The doctors said the timeline on your recovery would be unpredictable. That the main thing is you make progress every day."

"I'm dizzy, but my mind is much clearer. And my words." He flexed his fingers on top of the bedspread, taking a measured breath before speaking. "We'll be able to talk, really talk, soon." He stretched out a hand and touched my hip like he'd done last night. That small touch had my synapses firing.

I popped up from the mattress.

"There will be time for talking," I said, clapping my hands together at my waist. "But for now, can I bring you something to eat?"

"Actually—" He crooked his elbow and tilted his head toward his armpit, sniffing. "I'm a little self-conscious about how ripe I am. Do you think you can help me use the shower?"

Based on my reaction to the tip of his finger on my skin, helping him shower seemed like dangerous territory. Then again, he smelled objectively foul, a combination of hospital, stale sweat, and the flowery detergent Marley used on the bedsheets.

I laughed.

"What?" Will asked, smiling softly. "My funkiness amuses you?"

I shook my head. "No. It's more the fact I'm sitting here *smelling* you. I'm probably loopy from the past few days—" Righting myself, I met his gaze. "Like, how did we get here? I mean, I've only been around you, what, maybe five days in my entire life. But somehow…somehow, we're—" I waved my hand indiscriminately, searching for the right word, before finally settling on, "We're *us*."

He sat up straighter, wincing with the effort. "Maureen, let's be real. Even if it's only five—and I actually think it's more like seven, depending on how you're counting—" He grinned wryly. "However many it is, they've been some pretty memorable days, right?" He closed his eyes and opened them slowly before continuing in a serious tone, "And ever since I met you, even when you haven't been there, you've always kind of *been there*, you know?"

As he kept his gaze locked on mine, I dipped my chin in acknowledgment.

During the four years we didn't communicate, I'd still thought about him. Inadvertent, unwanted thoughts sprang up randomly, from nowhere, to remind me how deep the pain had cut, how something so beautiful had ended so cruelly. The depth of my instant connection to him had been the unmet benchmark of every man I met after. And then this past year, knowing he'd be part of my life again, my mind could not settle on one way to feel. I only knew no one had ever gotten under my skin like Will.

We'd been in it. He and I. Since the minute we'd locked eyes at the concert.

"What did you have in mind for your shower?" I asked, changing the subject. Fear and arousal thrummed at the prospect of assisting with the intimate task.

He cleared his throat, eyeing the doorway as though contemplating the distance. "I was okay before, using the bathroom, so I'm pretty sure I can do most of it myself as long as I take it slow."

"I wish the hall bathroom had a tub. It might be easier. Would you rather use the one in Marley and James's room?"

He thought for a moment. "No. I think I can do it quick. But can you stay close, just in case?"

"Of course."

The air in the bedroom suddenly seemed way too warm. I needed to approach this clinically, like any good nurse would. That would stop me from thinking about how we were alone together in this house. Stop me from admitting how attractive I still found him. Stop me from picturing him naked in the shower, with water running over that strong, sinewy body—

Nope. Nada. Not gonna go there. Totally professional and detached Nurse Maureen, reporting for duty.

"Can you help me get my clothes off? I'd shower in my boxers, but I really need to, uh..."

Totally. Fucking. Professional.

I could do this. Cold and clinical. I raised an eyebrow. "Wash your ass? Scrub your balls? I get it. I'm not a pearl-clutcher, Will."

He chuckled even as his cheeks flushed. "God forbid I forget what a complete and total boss you are. Alright, if we get most of my clothes off here, and you start the shower for me, I can kick off my underwear in the bathroom and get in. If I lean against the tiles, I bet I'll be okay."

I hesitated. "Will, I'm not sure about this. That all sounds very...slippery. Maybe we should wait for James. Or I could give you a sponge bath in bed. That's a thing, right?"

He grimaced. "You're not giving me a sponge bath, Maureen. I can do this. I've been sick before, so I'm pretty good at gauging my abilities. If it really bugs you, we can wait, but I'm not nauseous like yesterday or having vertigo. Just mildly dizzy and weak. Besides, you'll be there if there's an emergency, right?"

"And you promise to call out if you need help? You won't be stubborn about it?"

"I promise."

"I'm going to put a folding chair in the shower so you can at least sit."

"That's a good idea. Thanks."

I took the chair into the bathroom and started the water. At first, I worried the wobbly plastic would slide all over the stall, but the shower bottom had a sandy, grippy finish that kept it in place. I put a few towels on the toilet and some washcloths near the chair. I found the bottles of soap and shampoo and unsnapped the plastic lids. Not knowing if Will would be able to put on fresh boxers or wrap a towel around himself after washing, I grabbed my robe from the back of the door, placing it on the counter so he'd have some post-shower options.

When I got back to the bedroom, Will had managed to remove the loose sweatpants he'd been wearing, as well as push the bedspread and sheets to the bottom of the bed. He was struggling to pull his T-shirt off over his head.

"Here, let me help you with that." I kneeled on the mattress to grasp the bottom of his shirt, being careful not to jostle him, restraining myself from taking a more careful inventory of the very prominent dick print evident in his black boxer briefs.

Totally. Fucking. Professional.

I lifted the shirt over his head and tossed it on top of the dresser. He slumped back against the pillows and closed his eyes.

"Are you sure you're up to this?" I asked, swallowing hard as his heavy breaths highlighted the slight definition of his abs. I couldn't help but notice the smattering of coal-dark hair across his pecs, trailing down his stomach and disappearing into his waistband.

"Eyes up here," he teased. I looked up quickly, caught. My face heated as he grinned.

But I wasn't about to apologize. I'd been low-key imagining what he looked like without his clothes on for five years. I could admit it. "What? Your body is...nice. I'm only human, Will."

At the huskiness in my voice, he moved a hand over his groin, hiding the evidence of his thickening cock. "Christ, Maureen. Don't look at me like that. Not when my head is spinning, and I can't do anything about it."

"Pffff. You wish."

He laughed.

Sitting on the bed next to him, I guided his arm over my shoulder. "Now, let's get you in the shower before all the hot water is gone."

I helped him walk down the hall and into the bathroom, his mostly naked body pressed firmly against me. The steam from the shower had already fogged the mirror and turned the small space into a sauna.

Will slipped out from under me and leaned against the vanity with both hands. "I've got it from here. Thank you."

I nodded, still wary, but I stepped back and let him shut the door. "Don't lock it," I said. "Just in case."

"Alright." Ten seconds later, I heard the clack of the curtain rings sliding along the shower rod and a thumping sound I assumed to be Will sinking into the chair.

While he showered, I quickly changed the sheets on his bed, figuring he'd appreciate fresh ones. I was slipping the elastic of the last corner under the mattress when I heard a muffled cry.

"*Maureen.*"

My chest tightened, and I dashed into the hallway.

"Will!" I shouted through the closed door of the bathroom. I shifted on my heels, waiting for his reply. When none came, I knocked, still with no answer. I grasped the handle. "I'm coming in."

The steam hit like a force field, the thick air stifling. Through the cloudy white of the snowman shower curtain, I could make out the shape of him, thankfully still seated in the chair. Had he fainted?

"Maureen," his voice croaked. *Thank god!* "I'm sorry. I just ran out of energy." He labored to get the words out. "I thought I was managing, but then, it was like my battery died. I worried I was going to fall out of the chair."

"It's okay. We'll get you sorted." Damn, it was hot. The foggy mirror dripped with condensation. I felt the ends of my ponytail plastered to the back of my neck as I hurried to shuck off the denim button-down I wore over my tank top. "What can I do, Will? How can I help?"

"I just need to... Can you help me...finish?"

"Finish." I said the word with no inflection, but my mind immediately went somewhere inappropriate. My jaw ticked. Maybe it was because I hadn't slept properly in days, but seriously—a smoking-hot man, naked in the shower, was asking me to help him "finish."

Maureen, what is wrong with you? Will is in distress here. I blinked away my naughty thoughts, but the momentary mental lapse into levity allowed me to gain my equilibrium despite the temperature of the room. And my blood.

Will continued, unaware. "I was able to wash my body, but I ran out of steam washing my hair. It's still full of shampoo. But every time I try to rinse it, this wave of dizziness hits, and I just can't. That movement of raising my arms above my head... It's gonna make me throw up."

"Are you okay if I open the shower curtain? I don't think I can help you without actually, you know, seeing you."

"Yeah."

I pulled back the curtain to find Will slumping in the chair. Foamy suds covered his blue-black hair, though it looked like he'd slicked the strands back to keep the soap from his eyes.

He'd also thrown a washcloth over his lap.

Keeping my eyes determinedly northward, I contemplated my options, eventually deciding it would be easier if I rinsed his hair using water from the sink. It would have been a tight squeeze for me to hop into the shower stall with him, not to mention I would either have to get naked or soak my clothes to do so. I reached out to grab the water handle as I told him my plan.

Once I'd turned off the shower, and with the door to the hallway open, the steam cleared quickly. I found a clean cup in the cabinet and turned the sink on lukewarm. Will tilted his head back. Minutes ticked by as I poured cup after cup of water over his silky curls.

His eyes stayed closed, and it was impossible not to look at him as I went about my task. The water sluiced over his tight body, down the long line of his exposed neck, across the indents of his collarbone and chest, pooling around the washcloth in his lap. I watched, hypnotized, as soap bubbles traveled and popped over the wiry dark hair covering his thighs.

An angry purple bruise covered most of his right hip, its edges already fading to a greenish-yellow. It reminded me of the doctor's revelation that Will had metal pins in his leg, and upon examining his left side, I could make out the faint line of a surgery scar across his thigh extending to above his knee.

I developed a rhythm of filling the cup from the tap, bringing it over to pour wherever soap remained. Head. Shoulders. Chest. Thighs. The scrap of fabric in his lap. Carefully. To make each cup count. Still, his eyes stayed closed, those heavy lashes commanding my attention as I worked above him. Two days' worth of stubble shadowed his jaw. Back and forth, I pivoted from the wet floor of the stall to the bathroom tiles, resulting in the occasional unintentional brush of my breasts against the crown of his skull.

He sank into my ministrations, shoulders relaxing, humming in contentment as I raked my hands through his hair, coaxing the last bits of shampoo away. His reaction prompted me to massage my fingers against his scalp. At the deeper touch, a small sigh escaped him, and the washcloth over his cock twitched.

His eyes opened quickly.

"Sorry," he said, both hands coming down over his groin.

"Don't worry about it." Turning my back to him, I released my own uneven breath. I filled another cup of water, running it over his neck. "I think all the shampoo's out now."

"Thanks."

"Let me help you back to bed."

Without preamble, I placed one of the large towels I'd brought in earlier over his lap. I coaxed him to use my shoulder for leverage to gain a standing position. Once he stood, I bunched the ends of the towel together at his lower back—getting a split-second view of the two perfectly round mini-basketballs that comprised his ass—before bringing the gathered ends around for him to hold in front of himself.

"There," I said. "You're showered and covered up. I think that's good enough for now, and you can deal with getting dressed once your energy levels are back up."

He looked deathly pale already. He slung an arm over my shoulders just before his left leg buckled. We almost fell together—I barely stopped us—and I glared at his hands when I realized he'd placed a priority on holding the towel together as opposed to reaching out to brace himself. "I don't want to give you a show you didn't ask for," he offered by way of explanation.

"Don't worry about being modest." I huffed. "Just don't fall. James and Marley would kill me if something happened to you on my watch."

"You're only helping me for them, huh?"

"I suppose there are other reasons." I leaned back to make an exaggerated show of checking out his butt.

He barked a laugh.

In the bedroom, I sat him down on the edge of the bed before drying off his hair and the rest of his body with a fresh towel. He watched with hooded eyes as I ran the soft cotton over his head and neck, then along his arms. I kneeled in front of him to dry off his knees, calves, and feet, pushing up slightly against the towel he still had wrapped around his waist.

After I finished, I pulled back the clean top sheet.

"In you go," I ordered. "Drop your towel around your waist on the floor. I'll close my eyes to protect your virtue."

I heard a rustling before Will said, "Okay." When I turned around, he was lying against the pillows, the sheet covering him to mid-chest.

Gingerly, I lowered myself to the mattress edge. "Whelp, that was way more exciting than it needed to be."

"Sorry I overestimated my abilities."

"S'okay. At least we got it done." I handed him his sweatpants. "I bet you'll be able to slip these on in a few minutes, once your next wind comes. No one here is gonna blink if you go commando."

He chuckled. "James told me you and Marley grabbed my suitcase from the hotel. Thanks for doing that. I have fresh underwear in there, but yeah, I think I'll wait a few minutes before I move again, if that's okay."

"Fine by me. Whatever you need."

I got up and rolled my neck from side to side, working out the kinks from three days of sleeping poorly, stretching my arms and fingers in an arch above my head. At the motion, Will sucked in a sharp breath. His intense gaze met mine. I glanced down to find my tank top completely soaked, the curve of my breasts and the pebbled state of my nipples entirely on display.

His eyes burned.

"I'm going to heat some soup for you," I said, and got the hell out of there.

Chapter Nineteen

Will

I flopped my head against the pillow as Maureen shut the door behind her.

Jesus Christ. That shower. Even with dizziness bordering on nausea, my body tense and strung out, head aching a hundred times worse than any hangover, I was rock hard.

Maureen's hands—undressing me, washing me, rubbing my arms and legs—had me struggling for control. I could not stop picturing that confident sway of her hips. The way she'd taken control. Not to mention the outline of her breasts in her soaking wet tank top. When she'd given me that scalp massage, I'd almost blown right there.

And the attraction wasn't all sexual. I could tell it pleased her to comfort me, to make me feel better after I struggled to do something as basic as showering.

I'd desired her two days ago when she'd been furious, expression blazing at me. But her kindness? It made me want to lie down at her feet.

Last week, I'd been determined to get to a new normal with Maureen. To take whatever she'd give me, just to have that buzz of being near her. I never dreamed it would lead me here.

To a moment when she blatantly checked out my ass.

This was it. This was where I wanted to be. Every day since my accident, I'd been waiting to experience this certainty in my decision-making, to feel this strongly about something. Anything.

Sleep came for me again. But I surrendered this time, knowing it would be okay. Even if I had to wait a little longer. For the first time in eleven years, I found myself planning for a life beyond the recovery stage.

When I woke up, the fogginess in my head had lifted further, and I no longer felt as dizzy.

I glanced at the nightstand and saw my phone, face down, plugged in. Someone must have rescued it for me. Picking it up hesitantly, I turned it over, pleased to discover I could stand to look at it. On the home screen, I saw the reminder to call Wicklein to plead Rosalyn's case. Damn. There was no way I could talk to him today. Besides the fact concussion-induced nonsense could escape my mouth at any time, a quick check of the window confirmed the sun had set. I checked the time. Five thirty.

I heard the TV in the living room. *Monday Night Football*, so I figured I could do a voice-to-text without alerting anyone. It took a few tries, but I finally got it to translate correctly.

ME: Hey, Roz. Sorry but I couldn't call Wicklein today. I've got some things going on that make this week tough. I'll call him next Monday.

I used another voice command to put the reminder in my phone. My CT scan was scheduled for Friday, and I hoped to get back to Seattle by Sunday night. The thought of driving such a long distance made me want to hurl, but I'd figure it out somehow. Assuming I made it back to my apartment, I could call Wicklein the following morning.

My phone rattled in my hand.

ROZ: You're an asshole. You couldn't do this one thing for me? Lucky for you I found out Wicklein is on vacation. So next week is better anyway. But don't forget.
ME: I won't.

She didn't reply. I contemplated our exchange, knowing her anger was valid. But I couldn't explain to Roz what was going on because I couldn't risk her telling my mother and father. If my parents knew I'd gotten a concussion, they'd freak out and make a huge deal of it. Probably insist on coming. Then we would have a massive argument, and they'd try to convince me to go back to Seattle and see a team of specialists or something. I'd like to avoid that fight. They'd only recently loosened up somewhat. I didn't want to backtrack.

The TV volume lowered. James, Marley, and Maureen spoke amiably in the living room. They were discussing some sort of holiday carnival.

Maureen appeared in the doorway five minutes later.

"Oh, good. You're up. I was just coming to wake you." I registered that she was perfectly put together again, her close-fitting denim top buttoned back in place, her ponytail sleek and unmussed.

"Did you tell James and Marley about our adventure today?"

"Uh, no. I mentioned I helped you shower. Luckily, they didn't ask for details."

I laughed and inwardly assessed my head again, finding my thoughts clear. I'd fallen asleep knowing exactly what I wanted and woken up even more certain. Time to press forward.

"Do you think James and Marley are up for talking now? I'd like to tell you all about my accident, if you want to hear."

Her lips flattened. "You just woke up. Are you sure?"

James and Marley must have heard us. They appeared a moment later, Oscar and Bambi thumping along after them.

"There's no rush to talk," Marley said, sidling past her sister into the room, James behind her. "Of course we want to know, Will. But only if you're up for it. And only if you want to tell us." They leaned against the wall closest to me in the tiny bedroom. Maureen folded her arms and hung back in the doorway.

"Thanks for that, Marley," I said. "But I'd really like to get this out." I took a deep breath—nerves churning in my stomach—and launched into the story I'd never told in full to anyone.

"It started eleven years ago," I began, fisting my hands on the bedspread. "James probably had the right idea, going away to college after all the shit we dealt with in high school. But for me, after years of feeling like other kids' punching bag, I couldn't let all that anger go. I acted out. Lots of bad decisions... One night, I was with my friend Riley, and things went way too far."

The three of them listened attentively as I relayed the details. Spray painting the wall. The cop. Riley's erratic driving. The cyclist going down. My split-second decision to bail out of a moving car.

The decision that put me in a coma, cost me two fingers, and bought me years of rehab.

The decision that probably saved my life.

"Until the day I die, I'll wonder if Riley had a legit panic attack or if he was just scared out of his mind. But I'll never know because he wrapped his car around a tree four blocks away."

Maureen flinched, and Marley released a gasp, bringing her hand to her mouth.

"He died?" James asked quietly.

"Instantly."

"And the lady on the bike?"

"A few cuts and bruises, and she got knocked out for a minute, but overall, she was okay. The car never touched her. The drag of it going by just startled her, so she fell over. My parents had to unleash their lawyers to keep it mostly out of the news since our family is pretty well known in some circles, and they paid the biker a small fortune to settle things quietly. I'm not sure exactly what else they did. All I know is, I was in a coma for six weeks, and when I woke up, everything had been handled."

"Six weeks!" Marley exclaimed. "Your parents must have been out of their minds."

"They were, but not because they were afraid I wouldn't wake up. It was a medically induced coma. I broke sixteen bones, one of my legs was shattered, and the other wasn't much better. My hand was basically reduced to pulp, all the skin shredded like hamburger meat. I lost the two fingers—" I raised my right hand up to wiggle it. "And I was lucky not to lose more. My hand was nearly severed across the palm. And this was all besides the biggest concern—that

I'd taken a terrible blow to the head. By the time I got to the hospital, I'd completely lost consciousness. They put me under, and I went into surgery right away to relieve the pressure in my brain. According to my parents, it was touch and go for three days, and I even flatlined once on the table. While I was in the coma, I had multiple surgeries. Pins in my leg, skin grafts. I still have a little soft spot where they had to remove a piece of my skull.

"But what my parents were truly scared of was what might happen once the doctors brought me out of it. They spent those six weeks wondering if I would be the son they remembered. Would I have brain function? According to my mother, the doctors had been confident I wouldn't be in a vegetative state, but they weren't sure how severe the cognitive damage would be. Or how long-lasting."

I relayed my disjointed recollection of waking up with aphasia, losing my words, unable to always speak coherently. How I couldn't walk on my own for months. Countless hours spent working with speech therapists, occupational therapists, and physical therapists. Days and weeks with minimal progress, where my mother and father waited with haunted eyes, terrified my recovery had stalled.

"My parents had enough money to afford the specialists and legal help I needed. Besides making me square with the bike lady, they also fought for my right to start college with an aide. As my reading and writing skills returned, I needed less help, but they were there every step of the way, trying to make sure this wouldn't be the end of my life." *Although they'd eventually over-corrected.*

"I can't believe you went through all that and I didn't know." James shook his head, genuinely upset with himself.

"It's okay, bud. There's nothing you could have done, anyway, other than feel sorry for me." I smiled at him. "And believe me when I say you're lucky you weren't there for the years after when I had to figure out how to use my hand again. Who knew your pinky and ring fingers could be so important? All these things we take for granted—holding a steering wheel, going to the bathroom, putting on clothes—I had to relearn it all, especially with the injury being to my dominant side. Honestly, you dodged a bullet not having to watch me use a fork those first few months." I chuckled.

"I guess it's good you can laugh about it now." Maureen came into the room, scooting past her sister to sit on the mattress next to me. She grabbed my scarred hand and clasped it between her own. "But I'm trying to wrap my mind around how awful it must have been to require doctors to put you in a coma."

Marley and James glanced pointedly at where Maureen held my hand, but she didn't seem to care.

Finally, James said, "It makes a lot more sense now why the doctors here were so concerned, even though they said your concussion was relatively minor. Thank god you could tell them your history. We wouldn't have known."

Frowning, I thought of the superficial friendships I'd made during the years after my accident, the business acquaintances and people I ran into at fundraisers. None of them knew the story. They'd all seen my hand, all pretended not to notice.

Accepting that level of isolation was a side effect of my accident. I hadn't been able to make friends in college since no one wanted to be friends with the weird dude who needed a personal health aide with him in class until junior year. I'd shut down, gotten good at being alone, being assisted, needing less, demanding nothing.

Until, one day, something woke me up. Someone, rather. Made me want more. I ran my thumb along Maureen's hand.

"I'm glad you know now, James," I said. "Glad you all do. I'm thankful for your friendship, and that you're letting me stay here."

"Of course! You're always welcome, even when you're not recovering from an injury." Marley patted my calf. "You're family."

I smiled as my eyelids grew heavy again, even as my mind felt remarkably unburdened. But I hadn't completely fallen asleep when I heard Maureen whisper next to me.

"That's right. You're family."

Her lips ghosted over my forehead.

I SLEPT THROUGH THE EVENING and into the early morning.

Around five a.m., I felt completely lucid for the first time since my fall. With effort, I propped myself up against the pillows. Maureen must have heard me thumping against the wall because she came in to check on me.

"Sorry I disturbed you," I said, trying not to ogle her in her silky tank top and pajama pants.

"No problem. I'm a light sleeper. Do you need anything?"

"My duffel?"

"It's in my room," she answered. "Since yours is so cramped. I can bring it in if you want. Did you want different pajamas or something?"

"I was hoping I could use my drawing stuff. I don't think I'm up for playing on my phone or watching TV yet, but something analog sounds doable."

"Sure. I noticed your sketch pads yesterday when I grabbed your boxers. I didn't peek, but I really, really wanted to."

"They're nothing special." I shrugged. "Just basic stuff. Mostly street scenes. I've been drawing more lately, but inspiration doesn't always strike."

"I'd still like to see, but since it's ass o'clock in the morning, I'm going to go back to bed for an hour or two first if that's okay. You'll be alright?"

"Uh-huh. It's nice to think clearly. I don't mind waiting for the rest of the house to wake up."

Maureen left and returned with my sketch pads and pencils, depositing them on the nightstand. She yawned and nodded, shoulders sagging as she backed sleepily out of the room. After she left, I hobbled to the bathroom. It felt good to do it myself—although I still peed sitting down as a precaution—but it was mildly disappointing there was no more excuse for Maureen to help me in the shower again.

I returned to the bedroom, and Bambi met me in the doorway. Once I'd gotten back under the covers and positioned myself against the wall, he laid down next to me on the bed, placing his snout on my knee. Not to be outdone, Oscar arrived a minute later with his favorite Elf on the Shelf stuffy in his mouth, tossing it onto the pillow like an offering.

"Thanks, boy," I said, scratching between his ears.

I started sketching, attempting to capture the coziness of my surroundings. A two-foot fake Christmas tree with silver garland sat on the dresser, a recent addition that hadn't been there yesterday. The soft glow of the tree's tiny lights added a touch of holiday cheer.

At seven thirty, James and Marley came in briefly to say hello before heading to work, coaxing the dogs out to the backyard. Since Oscar snored like a buzz saw and Bambi farted like he'd just eaten chili with a Brussels sprout chaser, it didn't pain me to see them go.

Maureen showed up five minutes later, holding colorful mugs shaped like Christmas presents in each hand. Steam swirled up and faded into the cool morning air, the spicy aroma of tea filling the room.

I gestured toward the little tree.

"Marley insisted," Maureen said. "A bit of Christmas in your room. To keep your spirits up."

"The sweaters she wears every day aren't enough?"

Maureen laughed good-naturedly. "You haven't seen anything yet. She and James have matching holiday pajamas. Footie ones."

I could easily picture it. "And you? Any adult onesies with candy canes or snowflakes you'll be modeling for me?"

She made a face before asking, "Are you up for some chai?"

"I think so. I don't feel nauseous anymore. Just need to get my strength back."

"How do you take it?"

"Plain."

She set the mugs down on the nightstand, then sat in the chair as I passed her one of my sketchbooks. I stayed seated on the bed, propped up with pillows against the headboard. "You can look. Honestly, the ones I did in the past few hours are probably the best. I meant it when I said inspiration doesn't come easily, but this morning it has."

She took the pad from me and opened it, studying each drawing carefully before turning to the next page. "That's like me and my vid—" she started, before stopping herself. "Me in Coleman Creek. I feel the creative flow here, too."

"Were you about to say videos?" I grinned. "I know all about *Fashion Vibes*."

Her mouth dropped. "You do?"

"James spilled the beans by accident a few months ago."

She put the sketchbook down and reached for her mug. Blew over the top of it. "Which clips did you watch?" she asked.

I hesitated as my cheeks heated. "Um...all of them."

"All?" Her eyes went wide.

"Maureen, you wouldn't speak to me. You wouldn't even let us be in the same room together. I wanted the piece I could have."

Inhaling slowly, she placed her mug on the dresser next to the tree. She ran her hands back and forth over her thighs. "Well, what did you think?"

"Honestly?"

"Of course."

"Seeing you as Francesca reminded me why everything that happened between us five years ago matters. Who you are. Why neither of us can let it go." I reached out and pulled her chair closer to the edge of the mattress. "It reminded me how much I like you."

Maureen hmphed. "You realize I've murdered you a thousand times in my head. Not to mention all the things I've said to you out loud."

A rough laugh escaped me. "I remember. You swore you'd never forgive me."

"And I meant it."

"But you don't anymore?"

"No," she whispered.

I paused, drawing out a thoughtful breath before continuing, "For a few years after my accident, to anyone looking, I would have seemed okay. But inside, I raged at the world. I swore to myself I'd never draw again, never make any kind of art."

She glanced down at my sketch pad, open to a beautiful rendering of Bambi's sleeping face on my thigh. "What a waste that would have been, to hold on to that anger."

"A terrible waste." I ran my ragged palm along her knee.

"Terrible." She hinted at a smile.

"Can we talk now? Really talk?"

"I think we'd better."

Chapter Twenty

Will

Maureen sat up taller and folded her hands primly on her lap. "Okay, I'm ready. Tell me."

I coughed dramatically, straightening my spine against the headboard. "After all this time, you finally want to hear?"

"Are you planning to make this difficult?" Her voice teased as she shifted in her seat. "It's not like whatever your big reveal is won't be a total letdown anyway." She raised her hand to her mouth and yawned exaggeratedly.

"Ouch." I laughed. "Bored already? Maybe I shouldn't bother then."

"Seriously—" She slapped me lightly on the arm. "You've been begging me for a year to let you *have your say*." Her fingers crunched into air quotes. "Now I'm ready to listen, and you want to play around?"

"I enjoy playing with you. It's been my favorite activity the past few days." My mind immediately went to the shower, and I assumed hers did as well since her neck flushed and a swallow worked its way down her throat.

As much as I wanted to explain things to her, I didn't want our conversation to be how it would have been if we'd had it months ago. Or even three days ago. A somber mood didn't feel right for this discussion. Not anymore.

I kept playing.

Clapping my hands in front of me, I blew out a breath. "Are you certain you're ready to hear? I just want to make doubly sure—"

"Will—"

"I mean, you've been so adamant." I couldn't stop myself from grinning.

She huffed. "Just tell me, jackass."

"So, so adamant." I cleared my throat again and inhaled deeply, practically hyperventilating.

"I swear to god, if you take one more big, dramatic breath without actually telling me anything, I'm gonna hurt you."

"But, Maureen...the *suspense*."

"You know, I bet recently concussed people are much easier to smother." She grabbed a small decorative pillow near the foot of the bed. It had a picture of Will Ferrell's face as Buddy the Elf on it.

"Alright, alright." I held my hands up. "But it's going to take a minute to get the whole thing out, so you need to promise to listen to all of it before you attack me with the goose down."

"Pretty sure it's cotton batting, but I'll do my best." Maureen smiled, but her white-knuckling of the pillow said something different.

I turned my head to face her directly.

"There's part of it that has to do with everything leading up to my accident and its aftermath—the stuff I told you and James and Marley yesterday—but truthfully, I barely scratched the surface.

Between the two of us, I want to say all of it. I want you to understand."

The last traces of levity left her face. "Okay."

"It's probably easiest if I start by expanding on what you already know. Putting things in context. Starting with how it was for me in high school."

"You mean how you and James struggled?"

"We were bullied, Maureen. That's the right word. I know it might seem strange now that you know us as grown adults, but you have to picture me as the short, skinny, kinda-goth, kinda-emo teenager I was. It just didn't fly at Seattle Elite. James wrestled with being the shy, chubby kid, but I was always the mouthy little punk who defended us both."

She chuckled. "Yeah, James told us about some of the shit you pulled. Like when you knew one of the jock kids was copying off you, you deliberately bombed a test so he would too."

"Oh man, I forgot about that one." The memory came back to me, and I stifled a laugh. "I think the reason I fought back more than James is that I had a different relationship with our classmates. You remember I told you I worked at Wallingford Capital? Well, it's actually my family's company. My grandfather founded it. So I knew those rich kids my whole life. Our parents did business together, golfed at the same clubs, attended charity functions. You can guess the rest. James didn't show up until freshman year, and his family was different. Working class."

"At least you had him for high school."

"You have no idea. It made those days a little better. But at home, it was still tough."

"Tough?"

"You could probably imagine I wasn't the kid my parents had envisioned for themselves. They never had a second child, and I grew up feeling like a constant disappointment. Not athletic, or brainy, or social. When I was little, they took me with them to all their events and tried to make playmates out of their friends' and colleagues' children, but eventually, they gave up. I embarrassed them."

Maureen startled. "They said that?"

"No. Not outright. I felt it, though. To give them their due, they tried. This time of year always reminds me. They were away a lot while I was growing up, but always made time for Christmas. It's one reason I like the season so much. But even the rest of the year, when I had nannies and later housekeepers, they called and talked to me a lot. Asked how I was doing. I never doubted they loved me, even though I knew they were...*confused* by me. When it became clear I wouldn't be a country club brat, they gave me art supplies and video games and tried to make me happy. I'm pretty sure they knew what was going on at school—that the kids their friends bragged about made my life a living hell—but they didn't know how to help.

"Every month or two, one of them would come into my room with some great new idea. 'Why don't you try the debate club, William? That could be fun' or 'Eloise Murphy told me her daughter still needs a date to prom.' My father offered to pay for private coaches so I could 'consider joining lacrosse.' They refused to see I would have sucked at debate. I could barely keep my grades up as it was. Eloise's daughter—Adelyn—would have died laughing if I asked her to a dance."

"And lacrosse?"

I waved my hands a little. "Um...yay sportsball?"

She giggled before covering it with a cough, taking a sip of her tea. "It must have been rough, having them keep pushing you to try things they knew you weren't into. I'm glad my mom supported my purple hair and kept me stocked with fashion magazines."

"I bet you looked cute with purple hair." I smiled, picturing it.

"That's what I mean by wanting to put it in context. I told you yesterday I'd been acting out before my accident. But it wasn't just that I was being rebellious. I was in pain. For years, I felt like a shit person. A disappointment. An embarrassment. My parents didn't know what to do with me. And not that I needed them to compliment me on my art—although that would have been nice—it was just this empty feeling that came from knowing the people who loved me most in the world didn't really like me."

"Oh, Will—" She slid off the chair to sit next to me on the mattress. I scooted against the wall to put a few inches of space between our sides.

"After graduation, I told my parents I wanted to take a gap year, that I needed a break. I thought I could reinvent myself and figure out what came next. I focused on my art and spent my days busing tables, dismissing my parents' offer of a cushy internship at Wallingford. At my job, I met Riley. I started calling myself Billy, as though a fresh name could help me be a different version of myself. A version I could like, even if my parents never would. I'd hit a *fuck everything and everyone* stage."

Maureen looked at me. "You were Billy when I met you."

I shook my head sadly. "No. I was William when I met you. I stopped being Billy when I lost my fingers." Splaying the digits of my right hand on the bedspread, I invited her gaze to linger on them. "On the road, there was a piece of glass. Sliced them right off." I shuddered, thinking about the pain I'd felt then, the only real pain from that night I could remember. "Somehow, I had enough adrenaline coursing through my system to stay conscious for a few minutes, enough to crawl to the fallen bike. I've been told the noises coming out of me didn't sound human. Woke up the neighborhood. One witness told police he would never forget the sounds I made before I passed out, as long as he lived."

Maureen smiled wanly. She ran her fingers along my scars. "Now I can't stop picturing you making, like, wolf howls or something."

I choked out a laugh. "When I woke up from the coma, I kept waiting for my parents to show me those disappointed faces they'd perfected during my childhood. But they never did. On the night before I left the hospital, they came into my room and sat down next to me. They told me how much they loved me, and how worried they were something truly bad was going to happen to me. Not just with the accident, but because of the choices I'd been making beforehand. They seemed petrified."

"I'm sure they were. I used to get scared whenever Marley or Miranda had a cold. I can't even fathom worrying about brain damage."

"Exactly. Which is why something flipped in me that day. Being Billy, the free-flowing artist, hadn't served me any better than being Will, the angry high schooler. I was so tired, and I felt like I owed my parents so much, that I surrendered to the idea of doing things their way. I figured I should stop fighting it and just be William, the finance robot. It wasn't like the alternative made *me* happy, so at least with that, I could make *them* happy.

"For a long time, I lived as the William my parents wanted me to be. Convinced myself that going through the motions of a life was the same thing as living one. I went to college, graduated early, got my MBA, and started working at Wallingford. I began dating Rosalyn, who also worked there. She was someone my parents wholeheartedly approved of."

Maureen squirmed at the mention of Roz, and I put my hand on her leg.

"I was never in love with her. I was sleepwalking through my existence at that point. In a way, it was unfair to her, but deep down, I think she knew, and the way I functioned worked for her. It was steady. It was good for business. Where it all went sideways was when my parents started hinting about marriage. Rosalyn lives to please them and started pushing for it. Not because we had an undying love for each other. More like she wanted to bring our partnership to its inevitable next level."

Maureen settled back against the headboard, although her expression remained tight.

I squeezed her thigh reassuringly before continuing, "Another important piece of context is that, through those years, I also went to therapy. At first, it was just physical rehabilitation and occupational therapy, but eventually, my physical therapist convinced me to see a psychotherapist about my mental trauma from the accident, about how numb I'd grown. I was waking up to what my life had become, realizing that I didn't want to live for my parents, no matter how grateful I was for what they'd done for me. I didn't owe them all my choices.

"One day, five years ago, Rosalyn and I had another fight about marriage. I'd been putting it off for months since she'd initially brought it up, and she basically demanded an engagement. She accused me of stringing her along, not being a good son, being indecisive—basically whatever buttons she could think of to get me to feel guilty and see things her way. I knew I needed to break up with her, but I didn't want to do it in the middle of this huge argument. So, I told her we'd talk about it the next day. I needed some fresh air, so I took a walk..." I gave Maureen a meaningful look, knowing she'd make the connection.

"And ended up at Musicbox," she finished.

I nodded. "I wish I could say I had a legitimate reason for ghosting you after our night together, that me being engaged was a misunderstanding. But I don't want to lie. On the night we met, I was in a serious relationship with Rosalyn, and most of the world knew me as William, an executive at Wallingford Capital."

Letting that information sit in the air for a minute, I watched as Maureen exhaled, sending the hair framing her face sideways. "Okay." Her voice caught.

"I was standing by myself, and then you were there, laughing with your friend and lip-synching to the Christmas music. Seeing you—" I closed my eyes, remembering the way I'd felt at that moment. "It was like the universe opened a crack and let in colors I forgot existed. I tried to fight it, tried walking away, but I know you felt it too—that lightning bolt. And then when you took down that guy who tried to pull you at the bar, I couldn't deny myself the chance to meet you. It was selfish, and I should have been honest about my situation, but I didn't want the dream to end. I decided to give myself one night to be the person I might have become without the accident. For once, I was Billy, someone artistic and funny, hanging out with a girl I was insanely attracted to, who looked at me like she wanted to eat me, but didn't put up with my shit when I threw out mixed signals. Until that night, I'd forgotten what it was like to feel a spark inside. And I know I fucked it all up afterward. But that doesn't mean meeting you didn't change everything."

Her face remained unreadable, and I willed her to understand.

"Maureen, it was the best night of my life. You must know that. And when I left you in the early morning, I honestly felt so sure I could make a change. That Roz and I were over. When I said I'd text you, I meant it."

"Then why didn't you?" She clenched her fists before folding her arms across her chest. "All you did was send me a pathetic 'I'm sorry' way too late."

"And I'll never be able to explain how ashamed I am for doing that."

"Then why did you do it?"

I gulped the thick air. There was no way to make the next part sound good enough to excuse my actions, but it was the truth I had to offer. "When I came in to work the next day, I got the shock of my life when my parents came up to congratulate me on my engagement to Rosalyn. It took me a minute to figure it out, but I realized Rosalyn must have told them we'd gotten engaged the night before. I don't think she intentionally lied. Throughout our relationship, our disagreements ended with her getting her way, because I rarely cared enough to argue. I honestly believe she interpreted me giving up on our fight that night as agreeing to the engagement, and I never got a chance to speak to her before she told my mother and father. That morning, for the first time, I got the unqualified look of approval from my parents I'd been waiting for my entire life. It was surreal, standing in the center of the office with them and all my coworkers offering their congratulations.

"I'd spent my entire childhood trying to please my parents. I'd been weak and complacent for so long, and I couldn't change my entire mindset overnight. As powerful as meeting you was, it still took some time to shake myself out of it. I didn't necessarily mean the 'I'm sorry' as an ending. I was spinning. My parents were so happy. So *approving*. For days, all I could do was revel in it.

"After Roz and I ran into you at the hotel, my head finally dislodged from my ass. I realized what my behavior cost me. It was devastating, knowing I'd destroyed the one thing I would have chosen for myself."

I paused as my voice grew steely. "By that point, my parents had gotten used to me taking all their advice. Pulling myself out from under their thumb wasn't easy, but I eventually ended my engagement. I walked away from Wallingford. I began making art again. This past year, I renovated an apartment building. It took time, but it's like I finally recovered from my accident.

"I'm fully aware that the way I treated you, humiliated you"—I cringed—"was unforgivable, but I hope you know how much you changed me, how meeting you started me on a different path."

She eyed me neutrally. "You want to know something? Before you told me this, I had pushed to the back of my mind how much you hurt me. It was easy to do that because of how intense everything has been these past few days."

Damn. Had I just totally shot myself in the foot? Except I'd had no choice but to be honest. There would be no way to move forward without settling this. Otherwise, it would always be there, waiting to strike.

"Is this why you didn't want us to call your parents and tell them you're here?" She surprised me with the question.

"Yeah. They worry still. They would assume my life is about to be totally derailed because I slipped on some ice. As you can guess, they were pissed when I left Wallingford and broke my engagement. But it's been a while since that all went down, and they can see I'm a fully functional adult now, even without their careful guidance. We've called a truce these past few years. They're back to disapproving of most of what I do, but they seem to accept I'm in control."

She let her arms fall to her sides, turning her face toward me. "Do they still call you William?"

I raised my eyes at her perceptiveness. "They do."

A powerful sigh escaped her. "Why is it that even when you're being as honest and transparent with me as you've ever been, you're somehow more complicated than ever?"

"Special talent."

Maureen's lip quirked. She reached to twine her hand with mine, resting them between us. "And how do you feel about everything now? Do you feel you're on the correct path? As Will the apartment owner and maybe artist?"

"I hope so. But being true to myself doesn't mean a lot if no one sees, right? If no one cares or likes you for who you are. I want someone to look at me and know me, and for me to feel like I'm enough for them."

"I think everyone wants that." She lifted our laced fingers to my chest, both of us feeling the rapid beat of my heart. "No matter what happens between us, you are enough. Billy or William or Will. You're enough."

"Thank you," I rasped. "It means everything to hear you say that."

"Because of our history?"

"Because you're the person who was with me on the best day of my life...and my most shameful." I swallowed. "You know me better than anyone."

Chapter Twenty-One

Maureen

I left Will on his own after our talk. I needed to be alone with my thoughts. He came out of the bedroom to grab a snack and use the bathroom, but other than that, he gave me space.

In the quiet house, I heard the scratch of his pencil moving against sketch paper throughout the day.

Forgiving him wasn't a question anymore. Even before he'd explained, I'd made my peace with our history. Now that I'd heard the whole story, I felt even more sure. Until this week, I'd only been able to picture my pain, the result of his actions on my life. But he'd suffered too.

What I didn't know was how I wanted to move forward.

Did we simply forget about the past? Give in to our attraction? After everything we'd been through, did I want to start going on dates with Will, pretend we were in the *getting to know you* phase of our relationship?

I didn't know his favorite color or his middle name. He'd never had the chance to tell me how he liked his eggs cooked or whether he was a good swimmer.

You know me better than anyone.

But I knew some things. Big things. Little things. From our night together, our hours of conversation. How many favorite bands we had in common. That we were both night owls. I knew he'd almost gotten a dragon tattoo on his twenty-first birthday, and that he had a touch aversion to packaging peanuts. That he put a ton of hot sauce on his fries.

Five years ago, we'd been so comfortable, as though we'd started in the middle. Now, he'd given me his secrets. His trust. I'd never forget the way he teared up over how I caressed his scarred fingers.

Immediate intensity between us would be a given. *What did I want from Will?*

Marley and James returned home from work just as I popped a pan of enchiladas into the oven. Bambi and Oscar sat nearby, ready to catch anything that might fall on the floor.

"How's Will been?" Marley asked me after peeking into his room to find him napping.

"Much better. I haven't needed to help him with much. He used the bathroom on his own and has been drawing. Very limited screens, though, and he'll probably need another few days staying mostly in bed."

James hummed. "Has he been sleeping all day?"

"No. That's improved a lot. Pretty sure this is the first nap he's taken. Unless he cat-napped and I missed it."

"Fingers crossed, that means good news for his CT scan," Marley said. "He'll hopefully be back to himself by then."

"True. But I still doubt he'll feel up to driving a ton this weekend." James gave Oscar and Bambi candy cane dog treats. "And I know he wants to get home. We'll need to figure something out."

"I'm sure we will," I said. "Now, why don't you guys go amuse yourselves and let me keep working on dinner." James waggled his brows at Marley, and I made a face at him. "Sheesh, brother-in-law. Get your mind out of the gutter. I meant, like, amuse yourself playing Scrabble or something."

Half an hour later, James was downstairs in the rec room working on a jigsaw puzzle. Marley brought in the mail. She lovingly opened the many holiday cards before attaching each one to the fridge with a Christmas tree magnet.

"You're sure Will was okay today?" she asked, placing a picture of Katy and her kids in Santa hats on the freezer.

"Uh-huh."

"And did you two...talk?"

"That's a loaded question, but yeah." She gave me a curious look, so I added, "And it was way overdue."

"I figured." She pushed off the fridge to stand next to me near the counter. "You want to tell me what's going on there? Or are we still acting like Will is just a friend of your future brother-in-law who you barely know?"

I sighed. It would be nice to have someone else's opinion, and there was no one I trusted more than Marley.

Leaving out some details—*ahem, our little scene in the shower*—I spent twenty minutes giving her the story, starting with what happened five years ago and ending with the basics of what Will told me earlier today.

"Wow," Marley said once I'd finished. "I knew there was something, but I had no idea you were going to tell me you met him five years ago. That's wild."

Out of curiosity, I asked, "What did you think I would say?"

"I don't know. Maybe that he made a move on you last Christmas or that you'd run into him in Seattle. But that you've known him for that long never occurred to me." She shook her head and pinched the bridge of her nose. "You really almost died?"

"It's why I don't drink very often."

"Other than last year...when you ran into Will."

"Yes, but that was an anomaly, and if we're being fair, it wasn't even that bad—like, a minor hangover doesn't exactly compare to hospitalization."

"I can't believe you were in the hospital, and I didn't know."

"You didn't know because I didn't want you to. It was Christmas, and Mom was really sick. You had enough on your plate. Plus, I was embarrassed."

"I don't understand what you thought you had to be embarrassed about. I mean, he's the one who lied about being involved with someone. You did nothing wrong."

"I appreciate the defense, Marls, but think about it. You know me. I pride myself on being independent. Not to mention highly capable." I nudged her with my elbow as I pointed at myself. "Major older child syndrome, right here."

"On an intellectual level, I get it. But on a personal level, it's tough knowing you hid something so important from me."

"You know I've had boyfriends. It's not like I've been a nun. But Will was an exception. He's the only person I ever cared about enough to get hurt by. All my usual plays went out the window—including telling you everything."

Marley paused. "But it's good that you fell for someone, right? To know it's possible. Even if it ended badly. It's not like you were planning on being alone forever?"

"Honestly, I can't say." I tugged on the oversized sleeves of my sweater. "Recently, I've wondered if watching what happened with Mom messed me up."

"Mom? What?"

"You and Miranda were too young to remember, but I was six when Dad died, so I have memories of them together. For you two, it's all theoretical, a story—they had this great love, and Mom lived happily on her memories for the rest of her days. But I remember the other side."

Marley threw down the dish towel she'd been twisting and turned to face me, her expression solemn. "You never talk about this."

There was a reason I didn't speak about that time. The last thing I wanted to do was taint my sister's memories. But I owed it to her to be honest.

"I remember Mom crying herself to sleep at night. She had to pick up the pieces and move on while still raising us. I was too little to understand it, but looking back, I can see she was afraid. It took her a long time to rejoin the land of the living. I can remember being seven, eight, nine years old, and helping her with dinner, laundry, or putting Miranda to bed at night.

"She was a wonderful mom, but those first years after Dad died were awful. She seemed committed to making sure you two were okay, but with me, it was almost like she knew she couldn't fully hide it, so she just gave in and let me help her. Don't get me wrong—I'm not complaining. I think any sane person would have been as hurt and nonfunctional as Mom was. But now, as a thirty-one-year-old, I can see the effects of it on my life. Seeing her staring out the window for hours, barely moving, never laughing, and smiling the way I remembered from when Dad was alive. It stuck with me."

Marley scrubbed a hand over her face. "I honestly don't remember Dad at all. There are fragments, flashes of memory, but that's it."

"He was an amazing guy. And he loved Mom to pieces. I'm glad I have the memories I do. But in a way, I lost something different than you guys did. And it made me a very protective big sister." I shoved her playfully on the shoulder.

Marley pursed her lips thoughtfully. "That's why you went to college close and took your time to graduate."

"I didn't want to be a burden financially, and I wanted to be within driving distance, in case you needed me. But I was so ready to get out of here. And Mom supported me. She never pressured me to stay or do anything other than live my life."

"You put that on yourself."

"Helping take care of you guys was something I could do. Something practical, handling logistics. It helped me deal. Getting emotional—that was Mom's thing."

Marley scoffed. "Big sis, just because you're brilliant at shoving all those pesky *feelings* down doesn't mean they're not there. I know you're more closed off than me or Miranda, but you'll never convince me you don't have a big heart."

"Thanks." I smiled. "I'm glad Mom lived long enough to see me get my degree and move to Seattle, to start working at Kolya's."

"She was proud."

"I know. She never stopped telling me." I exhaled a weighted breath. "On Thanksgiving five years ago, a few days before I met Will, Mom pulled me into her bedroom to talk. I think she knew her decline was escalating. She wanted to make sure I knew how sorry she was that she'd relied on me so much when I was young. I'm glad I got the chance to tell her I didn't resent her for any of it. As much as it might have made me gun-shy when it comes to relationships, it also made me resilient and confident in myself. I told her she had nothing to be sorry for, and I'll never forget the look of relief on her face."

"It's a good thing you had that conversation when you did. No way would she have been able to have it the next year. She was too far gone."

I fingered the ring on my index finger, one of the many I'd inherited from my mom. Marley got our mom's extensive holiday sweater collection, but she and Miranda were happy to let me have the contents of Mom's jewelry case.

Marley eyed me as I fidgeted. "You really think that's why you've never had a real boyfriend? Because of watching Mom lose Dad?"

"She was never the same after he died, even though she was still young. But she didn't date. Kept her same job at the factory. Her entire identity was raising us and being a model citizen of Coleman Creek."

"What's so wrong about that?"

"Absolutely nothing. I just knew I didn't want it. I figured to avoid Mom's pain, I needed to be the opposite of her. Be on my own. Live in a big city. Have a fancy job. Like, if I lived my life differently, I could have a happier outcome."

Marley slumped back against the counter, her frown deep. "You don't think Mom was happy?"

"I think she had pockets of happiness. She loved being our mom. But she wasn't the same person after Dad died. The mother I remembered from before never came back. She died with him."

My sister flinched, like my words were a physical blow. "God, that's so sad. I never thought of it that way. Never felt that."

"Good. I think Mom would be glad to hear you say that. Because she dedicated every day of her life after Dad died to making sure we never did."

"I miss her so much."

"Me too." I slung an arm over Marley's shoulders and kissed the side of her head.

"I'm pretty sure if she was here, she'd remind you that you're not her. You can have a relationship and love Coleman Creek and still not be her."

"I wouldn't mind being the best parts of her."

"Do you remember last year when you told me I needed to give James a chance?" Marley side-eyed me.

"Of course."

"How come you want that for me but not for yourself?"

I'd been thinking about that all day. "I'm not sure that's the case anymore," I stammered.

"I won't tell you to give Will a chance, or that he's the one, or anything like that. Truthfully, I'm sort of inclined to pinch him for what he did to you back then. But you should give yourself a shot to find love. With Will or someone else. Don't assume you're better off alone. That's dumb."

Marley dropped an imaginary mic and strode out of the kitchen. She headed downstairs—I assumed to relay our conversation to James.

I pulled the enchiladas from the oven, almost dropping the casserole dish when the thin potholders couldn't take the heat. Speaking with Marley about our mom and dad was unexpected. It had been so long since I'd thought about any of that.

Will stirred in the third bedroom. I'd talk to him soon but still wasn't quite ready. I needed some more time alone with my thoughts, and at least two enchiladas first.

James assumed sickbed duty the rest of the night. He and Will played cards in Will's room after dinner while Marley graded papers and I sat at the dining room table putting the finishing touches on the video I'd made of Katy. I'd included a lot of the more serious material about her divorce and starting over because I knew viewers would connect with it. I just hoped she'd give me the green light to post.

Marley and James went to bed earlier than usual. We were all tired after three days of worrying about Will. After emailing Katy a link to the video, I tried falling asleep as well. But after an hour of tossing and turning, I gave up and decided to watch TV in the living room.

I saw light from underneath Will's closed door as I walked past. The bluish hue told me he was watching something on his computer since the room didn't have a TV. He'd been able to start looking at screens again although he still needed to take frequent breaks.

What if he'd fallen asleep with the computer on? That wouldn't be good for his recovery.

I knocked softly on the door. "Will?"

No answer. Shoot. I didn't want to wake him if he'd drifted off. He still had a low-grade headache and needed a lot of rest. But leaving the laptop on seemed like a bad idea, too.

I rapped on the door with slightly more force. Again, no reply. Okay, I could just go in quickly and close his screen. No bigs. I turned the knob and cracked the door.

"...I'm gonna give it a shot because I always want to keep an open mind about the latest trends—" Was that...? Yep. It was me, my voice. Or rather, Francesca's. *"Alright, I'm going to do a light application. I'm pretty sure this won't work for me, but you never know, right? And besides, it's fun to play."* A moment passed where only the background music could be heard. I recognized the clip and knew exactly what was happening on screen. I was staring into the camera, trying on the dark shade of burgundy lipstick that was popular a few years ago. *"No, um, just no."* The me on Will's computer screen broke into hysterical laughter. *"This looks terrible."* More giggles, and I remembered wiping away the lipstick enthusiastically. *"Alright, maybe this will work on some folks, but I thought I looked like a vampire who just had a snack. But remember—if you love it, wear it. Absolutely. Personally, I'll stick to my pale pink and nude shades, maybe a berry stain if I'm feeling frisky. What do you think of the dark burgundy lip trend? Tell me in the comments below."*

I listened to myself laughing through the computer speakers. Finally daring to peek my head around, I found Will staring at the screen with a big, goofy grin on his face. At the sound of the door opening, he looked up. Totally nonplussed at being caught, he pointed at the screen and said, "This is one of my favorites."

Venturing farther into the room, I shut the door behind me. Marley and James might be heavy sleepers, but Oscar and Bambi would come begging for midnight treats if they heard us. I sat on the mattress next to Will. He appeared to have changed into a fresh white tee, the thin cotton doing little to hide the definition of his torso and the impression of taut nipples beneath the material. Absently, I wondered if he wore sweats or just boxers. I couldn't tell with the bedspread rucked up to his waist.

He scooted against the wall to give me extra room. I leaned back on one of his gold pillows, sitting on top of the blanket.

"You've really watched all my videos?"

"Yep."

"Why?"

He snapped the laptop closed and reached across me to place it on the nightstand. The sound echoed, reminding me how alone we were. "I already told you. At first, it was curiosity, but then it was just good to...see you like that. Laughing." He shifted, sitting up so we rested next to one another, legs flush. "You avoided me today. After our talk."

With the computer closed, only silvery moonlight lit the room. I relaxed against Will's shoulder.

A flash of memory assailed me. I'd felt this way with him before. A sense of perfect gravity, the night protecting us. Like we were the only two people in the world.

It hadn't been true then. It wasn't true now.

"I needed time to think." I paused before sighing. "Being around you and all that floppy dark hair and pretty eyes is too distracting."

He laughed softly, hesitating momentarily before throwing his right arm around my shoulders. "This okay?"

"Yeah." I breathed into his neck.

"I'm just reveling in the fact that you're not actively angry with me anymore," he said. "Having you near me like this, it's..." His Adam's apple bobbed.

"It's good." I ran my fingers along his scars, and he emitted a low groan.

"I love that it doesn't bother you." He sucked in his bottom lip, letting me trace the raised lines on his palm for a few loaded seconds before asking, "Did it help you? Having time to think?"

"Yeah. I also talked to my sister and gave her the basic rundown of what's up with us."

"All of it?"

"Just the bullet points, but yes."

"Does she hate me now?" He attempted a light tone, but there was genuine fear behind it.

"I mean, she reserves the right to stab you if you ever hurt me like that again, but I think she's taking her cues from me. And she can see I've moved on from it."

He considered my words as our hands continued to caress. "That's a relief. I'd like to stay on Marley's good side. And not just because of James."

I nodded. "She's a solid one to have in your corner, that's for sure. Hashing it out with her helped, but that doesn't mean I have it all figured out yet."

"You're here now. I'll take the W."

I exhaled into the darkened room. "Honestly, Will, in a way, it would have been easier if you had told me you'd had temporary amnesia, or that there'd been an accident that kept you from texting me after our night together. Or that maybe some nefarious character blackmailed you into lying to me. Something other than normal human fallibility." I squeezed my eyes shut as I thought of how hurt I'd been in that hotel lobby. "Tell me—in those weeks after we met at Musicbox and before you ran into me again, were you trying to figure out a way to get out of your engagement, or were you trying to make yourself come around to the idea of marrying Rosalyn?"

His lips flattened. "It's hard to say. But when it comes down to it, I truly believe I would have ended the engagement eventually. One thing I know for sure is that, from the moment I saw you in the lobby, it became a hundred percent certain I'd never marry Roz."

"That's what I'm still processing. I believe you. We both got hurt by your actions. I've known for a while you're not some slimy fuckboy who set out intending to harm me."

After talking with Marley, I realized most of the pain I carried from five years ago had to do with feeling embarrassed over the idea I'd been played, that I'd allowed myself to give in to my emotions and promptly gotten burned. But the truth was, I hadn't been the weak one. That had been Will. He'd been weak, not standing up for himself and what he wanted. Now that I saw the truth, I could let go of the unfounded shame.

It finally felt as though the past was in the past, thoroughly examined and given a proper burial.

In the here and now, I was left with my connection to Will, my desire for him. While knowing he felt the same.

What was stopping us from jumping into something?

I touched the side of my forehead to his. "I need you to keep being direct and honest, Will."

"Of course."

He shivered as my mouth whispered against his ear. "What exactly do you want from me?"

A low sound left his throat.

"That's like a thousand questions in one," he began. "But I think you know." He placed his warm palm on my thigh. "I want you. I think—no, I know—something is there. Something amazing."

Even though I'd known that was what he would say, the force of his words still hit me hard. My pulse drummed rapidly as he turned to gaze at me in the moonlight. The gold flecks in his gray eyes shimmered as his pupils blew wide. His lips were an inch away. I stared, mesmerized, as the tip of his tongue darted out to wet them. It would be so easy to lean forward and—

The buzzing of Will's phone on the nightstand saved me from...whatever was about to happen. I pulled my head back.

Wait. It was past midnight. Who was texting him in the middle of the night?

He removed his arm from my shoulders, flipped his phone over, and frowned.

"Everything okay?"

Will exhaled loudly. "Yeah. It's just Rosalyn. She needs my help with something."

I tensed and pushed his hand off my leg. Rosalyn, as in former fiancée Rosalyn? They still texted? In all our talking today, Will had left that little nugget of information out.

He clued in to my reaction. "Oh shit! I promise I wasn't keeping it from you or anything. She still works at Wallingford Capital. She wants me to help with one of my old accounts. Her text is just a link to a shared drive with some files. And she's a workaholic. I doubt she even realizes she's texting so late."

I felt that knowledge in the pit of my stomach. Rosalyn worked for his family's company. I wondered how often they spoke. How often they saw one another. "Does she know where you are?" I asked.

"No. My parents knew I was coming to James's party over the weekend, but no one knows I'm still here. Like I said, I don't want them to find out about this new concussion."

My brain recalled the annoyed look on Rosalyn's face five years ago when she'd stuck out her manicured hand and introduced herself to me. It brought another question to mind.

"That day, what did you tell her—your fiancée—about me?"

Will had the good grace to look abashed. "After you left the hotel lobby, she asked me who you were, and I told her you were an acquaintance I'd known in college."

"Did you ever tell her the truth, later on?"

"No. I thought about it. But when I finally broke it off, the first question she asked was if there was someone else. I didn't want to tell her about our night because my breaking up with her wasn't about that. But she wouldn't have seen it that way."

"That makes sense," I concluded carefully.

But understanding his decision-making helped me gain clarity about my earlier reluctance.

It was obvious the aftereffects of Will's accident were ongoing, even if they'd improved over the past few years. Him feeling uncomfortable telling his parents about this new concussion—the result of a legitimate accident and not carelessness—proved that. Not to mention Rosalyn still had a significant foothold in his world, working for Wallingford. And even though he said he hadn't kept that information from me intentionally, it felt like something he should have mentioned earlier.

Will and I had already proven we had the power to hurt one another deeply. And so many of the same pain-causers from five years ago were still part of his life.

This. This was what made me hesitate to jump into something with him.

He wanted to explore something between us. But neither of us could afford to behave recklessly.

Yet I couldn't imagine denying ourselves forever. I felt the heat of him pressed next to my side on the bed, responding to every little touch between us. Each breath an invitation. It would be so easy to let that instinct carry me, to reach over and straddle him, to move my hips back and forth over him until he'd been coaxed to full hardness, to tug down his sweatpants and wrap my hand around his cock. I squeezed my thighs together, wanting it.

Luckily, his concussion recovery protocol kept the urge at bay. But that wouldn't always be the case. My body wanted to taste, to cash the check Will wrote five years ago.

I needed to get ahold of myself. To think rationally. I needed to be somewhere other than cuddled in bed next to him.

"It's late, and I'm finally feeling sleepy." I pulled myself up hastily and stood on the floor, leaning down to kiss Will on the head. "Good night."

A look of confusion passed over his features, but he didn't try to stop me. Just as I was closing the door, he called out, "Maureen?"

"Hmm?"

"I meant what I said. We could have something amazing."

I looked at the hopeful raise of his eyebrows, his face glowing in the moonlight reflecting off his tee. But I couldn't give him the words he wanted.

Dipping my chin in a quick nod, I shut the door behind me.

Maybe we could have something amazing.

Or, maybe, my heart would break all over again—and this time, I wouldn't be coming back from it.

Chapter Twenty-Two

Will

I thought Maureen might pull another disappearing act after our middle of the night conversation, but she popped her head into my room soon after Marley and James left for work.

"Need anything?" she asked.

"Thanks, but no. I think I'm good to get up and start moving around more today. I showered and dressed before everyone got up."

She gave me a once-over, registering my jeans and UW sweatshirt.

"Do you need me to do any laundry for you? Since I know you didn't plan on staying this long."

"I can do it. I'll give it a shot this afternoon."

"Do you want tea or maybe something to eat?"

I smiled at her hovering. "Maureen, the only thing I want from you is your company, if you can spare it."

After a moment's hesitation, she glanced quickly at the folding chair before sitting gingerly on the mattress, not quite touching me. A sketch pad rested on my knees. "Working on something?" she asked.

"Another portrait of Oscar." I opened the book and showed her the half-done pencil drawing.

Maureen made an *aw* sound. "He's pretty cute, especially when he shows his bottom teeth like that."

"True." I flipped to another page, where I'd done ten quick sketches of the little tree in my room. There was also a full-size drawing of Marley and James's snow globe cake.

"Did you give them an engagement present yet? Because if you haven't, this would be a good one."

I'd gifted them a fancy blender but I put a reminder in my phone to have the drawing framed for them as well.

Maureen watched me make the note. "You're a good friend."

"I'm trying."

She sat up straighter. "Speaking of friends, I have something I wouldn't mind getting your opinion on?"

"Sure."

I knew what I wanted from Maureen, but I'd gotten the impression she wasn't ready to go there yet. I figured these overtures were her way of testing the waters. To see how we fit. At least I hoped so.

She left the room and returned a moment later with her laptop, sitting back down on the bed next to me, brushing my arm against her own.

"This is a piece I completed over the past few days, between worrying about your head." She lightly tapped her knuckles against my skull. "It's my first Francesca video post-Kolya's and the first in Coleman Creek. I'm hoping to do more if this one works. It's of Katy Baumbeck."

"The woman with the toddlers?"

Maureen snort-laughed. "Yes. And the fact you remember her that way is kind of why I made it. She gave me her approval to post, but now I'm second-guessing myself. It's super different from everything else I've done."

"Well, now you have to show me," I said. "I'm sure it's great."

She took a deep breath, balancing the laptop between us atop our thighs. I took a chance and tentatively slipped my arm around her shoulders as she hit play on the queued-up video. She leaned into me.

The piece started simply enough, like other videos Maureen had made where she'd gone into someone's closet and asked them about their style, showing outfits to the camera. There was an intro segment where Francesca told the audience about her hometown, introducing Katy as a local single mom with two small children. B-roll showed the modest ranch-style home Katy lived in. Francesca's voiceover narrated, *"It's a miracle anything stays neat when there are tiny humans around. I don't have kids myself, but sometimes I wonder if there's a secret parent manual that gets handed out when you have your first child saying it's a requirement to have a play kitchen and a big tub of Mega Blocks in your living room."* The camera panned in on said items before Katy came into the shot to add, *"It's a rule to have a copy of 'The Very Hungry Caterpillar' and a stack of wooden puzzles which immediately lose one piece."*

The cuts highlighted Maureen's editing skills. She'd obviously tailored her later narration to the quip Katy made during the original filming.

The focus shifted to the home's main bedroom, where Katy modeled her favorite casual outfits and Francesca offered suggestions for how she could change things up if she ever got the urge. Then Francesca coaxed Katy to try on some dresses in the back of her closet.

"Do you think you'll feel like wearing more of your dresses and nicer clothes once the kids are a little older?" Francesca asked.

"Maybe. But it's only recently I've started even considering my fashion again."

"What do you mean?"

Katy sat on the bed, and Francesca was out of the shot.

"Well, I'm fine sharing with your viewers that I'm recently divorced. Not to be too blunt about it, but my husband left me for another woman. I don't think he did it because he's a terrible guy or anything. It's complicated. Sometimes bad things just happen, and you have to keep putting one foot in front of the other." Katy spoke to Francesca off to the side, so she wasn't looking directly at the camera. Still, her words were powerful. "Have you ever heard of 'The Five Stages of Grief'? Well, I feel like my fashion choices since my split have been like the 'Five Stages of What to Do When the Man You Thought You'd Spend the Rest of Your Life with Leaves You for Another Woman.'" Francesca could be heard huffing, but she didn't interrupt as Katy found her stride and continued, "*Stage One was basically I could barely get out of bed and lived in my pajamas. Stage Two was when showering and leaving the house felt like an accomplishment. All my energy was for taking care of the kids. Pretty sure I still mainly wore pajamas, but I was clean and brushing my hair at least. Stage Three was after I got through the worst of my pain and anger. I was back to living my life, but being a newly single mom required serious streamlining. I developed a uniform and stuck to it. Jeans and a sweatshirt every day. Usually in dark colors so I didn't have to worry about stain management. Stage Four was when I felt a little more like I had a handle on things. I added in a few sweaters and some button-downs. I'd been doing* all messy buns, but occasionally, I got wild and did a ponytail." She made an up-and-down motion over her outfit, a fitted red button-down and dark jeans.

There was a lull. Katy looked placid, and Francesca came around into the shot with her. On screen, both women reached to sip from wineglasses that had been out of camera range.

"*Was there a fifth stage?*" Francesca asked. "*Like with the grief?*"

"*Oh, yes.*" Katy glanced coyly at the camera. "*Stage Five is where I'm a kick-ass single mom who's finally confident enough to let a fashion vlogger convince me to put on some dresses I haven't bothered with since my divorce. I'm getting up and facing the days with some sense of hope. And humor. To be clear, I'm not judging anyone who wears pajamas to the grocery store or has a uniform, but for me, I think wanting to mix it up means I'm healing.*"

"*Well,*" Francesca began, turning to face Katy, "*I can't imagine a better note to end on. Other than I want to make sure you know, no matter what you wear, you are one hot mama!*" She took a sip of wine before looking at the camera and adding, "*I hope all my viewers enjoyed this fashion adventure. Thanks again to Katy. And to all the moms out there—be easy on yourself. I hope you're doing well, especially if it's pajama day. Sending lots of love.*"

The shot faded to black with a "like and subscribe" note. Maureen looked at me with a question in her eyes.

"It's great," I said. "Pitch-perfect. I agree it's different, more therapy than fashion maybe, but it fits with the aesthetic you've created for the channel, and it has the humor viewers expect."

She ran a finger across the top of the screen. "Thanks."

"I mean it. It's okay for you to grow. You don't want the channel to get stale. You've been evolving the whole time, from the first year to now, so maybe this is the next step in that."

"That's kind of what Katy said. She gave me the best compliment when she told me she wants to show it to her kids someday."

"If she said that, then you have to post it."

"I'm doing it," Maureen said, bringing her fingers to the keyboard. She added a caption, then clicked to begin the upload. Once the video went live, she added the link to her channel's social media pages before closing the laptop and putting it aside. "I'm going to stay off for a while. Let it simmer."

"Smart idea. Should we distract you?" I tightened the arm I still had wrapped around her shoulders. The gesture was meant to be friendly and affirming, but she looked pointedly at where my hand squeezed her upper arm. "I wasn't suggesting anything *untoward*." I grinned.

She smiled back, and I swore the whole room got brighter.

"What could we do?" she asked. "I'm not sure what you're feeling up to."

I unwound my arm from behind her and pointed at a stack of board games piled on the floor. "James brought me those yesterday."

"You want to play board games?" Her tone sounded as though I'd suggested we clean hair from the shower drain.

"We could. But board games aren't really my thing." Relief crossed her features. "Actually," I said, "I was kind of hoping to do something Christmas-y. Being stuck in this room so long, I've practically forgotten it's December. Other than the tree Marley put in here."

"Hmm—" Maureen tapped a finger to her lips and eyed me. "You seem recovered enough to switch your home base for the day from the bed to the living room. No one could miss the holiday explosion there."

"Sounds good."

"We can make cookies. That's pretty Christmas-y. And it'll keep my mind off Katy's video. I'm guessing you're not up for standing and moving around the kitchen yet, but you could help decorate them. Nothing screams *holidays* like messing up the frosting trying to put little eye dots on a gingerbread man."

"Sign me up."

HALF AN HOUR LATER, I SAT CURLED UP on the couch next to the dogs. Bing Crosby crooned on the vinyl player next to a beautiful seven-foot Christmas tree. The flames in the fireplace crackled and popped like a movie effect—burning actual wood from a tree as opposed to gas controlled by a knob in the wall. Maureen flitted around the kitchen, humming along to the music. I watched as she pulled out a tray of cookies from the oven, inhaled their spicy scent, and bumped the door closed with her hip.

Between batches, she came into the living room to keep me company.

"We should wait an hour to decorate them, just to be on the safe side," she said, shooing the dogs into the backyard and sitting down next to me, offering a naked cookie to taste test.

I took a bite. "Mmm. Gingerbread's not usually a favorite of mine, but this is great."

"Something my mom taught me—always use the good molasses. It makes a difference." Maureen smiled sadly, and I knew she was thinking about her mother. I squeezed her knee.

Last year, when I'd been in town for the talent show, Marley and Miranda had spoken often about their mother. Maureen stayed mostly silent while her sisters told family stories. Certainly, some of her reticence was due to my unexpected and unwelcome presence. But I also understood her better now. Although her emotions were quiet, they were no less intense. Including her grief.

She didn't need to be loud for me to hear her.

"It's okay," she said. "It's good to remember."

I kept the warmth of my hand on her thigh. "Truly, these cookies are excellent, but I'm not sure the four of us can eat the ten dozen you've made."

She rose to her feet as the oven dinged. "Actually, these are for the Holiday Hoopla on Saturday. James and Marley are working a shift at the Coleman Creek High booth. There's a bake sale."

I'd heard the three of them discussing the carnival and hoped I'd feel up to attending. I took another bite. "You might want to make a few dozen more because these babies are gonna go quick."

Once the cookies cooled, the plan was for me to work alongside Maureen to decorate them. She disinfected the coffee table and set up everything on top of it, so I wouldn't need to move from the couch after washing my hands.

Fifteen minutes in, I regretted all the life choices that had resulted in me having zero kitchen skills.

Maureen used a "fine-tipped piping bag"—she'd told me its name after I asked about the "fancy ziplock"—to draw little vests and boots on her cookie men. A few wore sunglasses, and one had on a perfectly symmetrical pair of plaid pants.

Meanwhile, mine looked like an uncoordinated elephant had tried its hand at decorating. They were sugary monsters—uneven slashes for eyes, mouths like jagged football lacings, mysterious drips everywhere. Like crime scene photos recreated with cookies.

Occupied with her own work, Maureen didn't notice mine until I'd already mangled eight defenseless gingerbread men. She couldn't hide her flinch when she looked over.

"Those are…very nice, Will."

Her face remained placid for all of three seconds before her shoulders began to shake.

"I'm sorry," she said, attempting to cough away her reaction. Then she peered at my cookies again, and a cackle escaped.

"Hey!" I tried and failed not to laugh. "They're not that bad."

Good thing Bambi and Oscar were in the backyard since I was sure they'd be bark-giggling, or whatever it was dogs did when their humans embarrassed themselves.

Maureen pointed at my tray. "He looks like if Gollum was a pirate… That one's definitely going to murder all the other cookies in the jar… Oh my god, did you draw a penis on that cookie?"

"It's a button! My hand slipped!"

"Sure."

"Glad I could amuse you so much." I grinned. "I'm choosing to embrace this."

"You should. It takes talent to be this bad, especially considering you're an amazing artist."

Inwardly, I glowed, not just at our playful back-and-forth, but at the casual way she referred to me as an artist. No one ever did that. Also because she hadn't mentioned my fingers, either when asking for my help or while teasing me about my efforts.

"I'll tell you what," Maureen said. "We'll keep these beauties you made for home consumption, and I can finish the public-facing cookies myself. Even if you can't help, I like having the company while I work." With that, she picked up the Gollum pirate and bit his head off, winking at me.

"I'm happy to be your hype man," I said.

She gave me a funny look. "Same."

OVER THE NEXT HOUR, SHE FINISHED the cookies while we chatted. I occasionally helped her out by doing non-baked-goods-destroying tasks such as filling piping bags. As evening approached, I caught her glancing nervously toward her still-closed laptop. I knew it was killing her not to check if there'd been any response to the new video.

"What do you see yourself doing in the future?" I asked. "Full-time vlogger?"

Maureen shook her head wistfully. "I love doing my videos." She leaned over a cookie to pipe some red icing. "But I doubt I'll ever be able to monetize the channel enough to make a living. I've been toying with the idea of running some sort of consignment or thrift shop. Maybe offering low-cost styling online."

It was the type of creative investment I'd supported at Yardhouse, the company I founded after leaving Wallingford.

Maureen spoke as though she'd given the idea serious consideration. "I figure if I combine a storefront with an online sales platform—something I learned a lot about at Kolya's—I could make it work."

"It's an awesome idea." I forced myself not to sound overeager. "You know, I have an MBA I'm not putting to use right now. I'd be happy to help you develop a business plan or talk through logistics."

I knew how reluctant she was to lean on others. That was why her answer surprised me.

"Really? It's overwhelming, thinking of where to start, but I'd love to bounce my plans off someone who can rein me in. I know if I mentioned this to Marley, she'd just be completely gung-ho and useless in helping me throw out bad ideas and narrow things down."

"I admire Marley's positive energy," I said. "When I established my firm, I allowed a lot of unvetted pitches. I had the privilege of time and money, so I indulged that whim to be eccentric. At Wallingford Capital, they never encouraged us to be creative with our investments. Only safe risks. At Yardhouse, I heard some of the wildest ideas you can imagine."

"Like what?"

"Well, one guy pitched a nightclub for teenagers, and the big draw would be a VIP section."

"VIP teens?" She scrunched her face.

I chuckled. "We also had a lady who wanted a nail salon for dogs—no grooming or bathing, just like, colored nails for dogs." Maureen licked a bit of frosting off her thumb before releasing a giggle. "The bottom line is, if someone who worked at a store like Kolya's and already had a built-in audience on YouTube, came to me with the idea to run any sort of fashion-centered business, I wouldn't consider it too much of a risk. I could probably even help you find the start-up capital if you want me to."

She gave me a half smile. "I appreciate you not just offering to fund it."

"I'm helpful. Not an idiot. Obviously, I'd be willing to do whatever you needed. But I already pissed you off enough intervening with that guy at the bar five years ago. I'm not going to insert myself into the middle of your dream."

"As it turns out, I have plenty of capital. My mom's inheritance, plus my own savings and the money from selling my part of the house to Marley. Not only can I afford to start the business, I can afford to fail at it, or at least take my time growing it."

"You can succeed with the right plan and setup. I'm sure of it."

Maureen grew quiet, finishing the last of the cookies. Eventually, she said, "You know, listening to you yesterday helped put some things into perspective for me."

My brows drew together. "How so?"

"When you were talking about after your accident, you said you played the part of William so well you basically lost yourself. In Seattle, I assumed the role of an untouchable fashionista. Especially once I got the job at Kolya's. Then what happened between us cemented the idea that it was better to be hard. Icy."

I shifted, but she pulled close to me, folding her knees underneath herself on the cushion and leaning them against my hip. "No. I wasn't saying that to make you feel bad. I meant it when I said I'm over it. And truthfully, it would have happened whether or not I'd met you."

She leaned up against my side and laid her head on my shoulder, the lavender scent of her hair invading my nose. "I like how I feel here. I like this in-the-middle version of me. Living in the city helped me be better in Coleman Creek, if that makes sense. Seattle Maureen had selective amnesia. I forgot about my mom's recipes and about enjoying all the Christmas traditions we used to have. I became one version of myself and pushed the rest down. Not that I regret it. If I had allowed myself to think of everything that felt *wrong* in Seattle, if I'd paid attention to that, I wouldn't have been able to establish myself. And I would have wondered my whole life if I hadn't at least tried something like Kolya's. Sort of like trying on outfits. But with my career."

I took a chance and reached for her hand. She looked surprised for a moment, then placed them together in her lap. Her head on my shoulder felt like the best kind of burden. Grounding me.

"Figuring out you're not on the track you want to be on isn't easy," I said.

"No." She hummed, absently brushing along my palm with her thumb. "And you'd know all about that, wouldn't you, from when you left your family's company?"

"Mm-hmm." I put my other hand on her knee, twisting to face her. Colorful lights from the tree reflected in her irises. "Do you know what I wish I had when I made that decision?"

She shook her head. "What?"

"I would have loved to have someone there to tell me I was doing the right thing and that it was okay for me to follow my heart."

Angling her face until we were almost nose-to-nose, she said, "I'm sorry you didn't have anyone in your corner for so long."

The knee that she'd pressed into my hip trembled slightly. My hand moved upward from her leg to cup her cheek. "I want to be that for you, Maureen. If you'll let me. I want to be the one cheering you on when you do all the amazing things I know you're going to."

"That sounds...good." Her heated breath landed on my face.

The weight of the past five years anchored my body. My fingers ghosted along her soft jaw. I'd waited so long to touch her like this, and now the moment was here, heavier than I could have possibly imagined.

I brushed my thumb over her cheek. "Can I kiss you?"

She gazed into my eyes, and hers shone bright. After a few agonizing seconds, she nodded.

As the air grew thicker, my heart beat a wild staccato. I held her stare, halfway believing this was a dream. When I finally brought my mouth to hers, she tasted like spice and honey, like she'd snuck a few cookies. With one swipe of my tongue across the seam of her lips, she opened for me.

I shuddered, deepening the kiss, feeling her palm against my back as she rubbed a line between my shoulder blades. Her other hand slid up my chest, where she explored boldly, the soft pads of her fingertips dragging heat over the thin material of my T-shirt. She circled my nipples into stiff peaks beneath the thin cotton before clenching it in her fist and pulling me closer.

The kiss was intense in the way only hard-earned kisses could be. The low hum of the vinyl player, the lingering scent of the gingerbread, the shimmery glow from the Christmas trees—everything fell away as all my senses devoured the feeling of her mouth on mine.

Suddenly, nothing was enough for either of us.

She groaned and swung her leg over my lap to straddle my hips. I felt the heat of her center through her leggings as my hands moved to grasp her ass cheeks. My hard cock twitched as she bucked against me. Once. Twice. Three times. Until I worried I might come in my pants.

I pulled my head back quickly, breathless. We stared at one another before my eyes fell to the pulse beating in her throat. Her grip on my shirt slowly eased.

Pressing the heel of my hand against my aching erection, I panted rapidly, laboring to gain my senses, feeling the pounding of my heartbeat in my veins. A sensation of dizziness threatened.

Maureen drew her fingers to her mouth. "Oh my gosh, Will. I'm so sorry. I forgot you're still recovering. Are you okay?" She reached out to place a palm on my forehead as though that would tell her anything. "You feel hot."

I laughed, holding on to her hips as I got myself under control. "Of course I'm hot. My dream girl is sitting on my lap next to a fire. I just hope I'm not hallucinating."

She angled her torso forward and buried her head in my neck. I felt her warm breath tease my sensitive skin for a few minutes as we stayed close. I ran gentle hands back and forth over her thighs.

"Dream girl," she finally mumbled into my shirt before pushing off and standing. "You seem okay."

"I am." I released a long exhale. "Promise."

"Still probably a good idea to pump the brakes."

"Probably."

Maureen looked down at me, shaking her head. "That was some kiss, Will."

I knew she wasn't ready to talk about what it meant yet, and I was okay with that. We had time.

"That's an understatement," I said. "And unless you want me to pull you right back into my lap again, we'd better switch gears immediately." My dick finally deflated, and my breathing settled into something resembling normal.

Maureen seemed grateful for the—albeit abrupt—subject change, as I knew she would be. "Got something in mind?"

"How about you open your computer so we can see how much everyone loved your latest Francesca video?"

Chapter Twenty-Three

Maureen

The Holiday Hoopla looked exactly the way I remembered. Six blocks along Main Street had been closed to traffic with every light pole and mailbox lit up along the way. There were booths and games. Cider, hot chocolate, and treats for sale. A candy cane–patterned tent for the children's coloring contest. Kitschy homemade items on display. Even though the aesthetics were slightly different—crocheted tablet covers for sale instead of potholders—the charm remained intact.

The city's official holiday tree stood proudly in the center of it all. I remembered gazing up at it as a small child. The giant star on top was the same one they'd used since my mom was a little girl. Music could be heard from all directions, with bands set up on either side of the main event area and roving groups of carolers throughout. I glanced over at the churro cart and had a momentary flash of memory—my father and I sharing the hot, sugary treat as I bounced on his shoulders.

There was a different sort of joy in attending the Hoopla as an adult, appreciating the innocence and tradition of it all.

Not to mention how happy I was to have Will by my side. Watching him experience the Hoopla for the first time was almost as gratifying as my nostalgia.

It had been an interesting four days since we'd shared that toe-curling make-out session on the couch. We hadn't talked yet about what should come next for us, and we hadn't kissed again. But something had changed. There were stolen brushes of his fingertips along my arm in the kitchen and lingering glances in the hallway as we said good night. Even now, he walked alongside me with his body pressed close, occasionally settling his hand on my back.

We'd both been eager to spend time together outside Marley and James's house. As Will improved, their home felt claustrophobic. I'd spent the past few days blushing whenever I sat on the couch, remembering that kiss.

Besides getting some fresh air with Will, my other goal tonight was to film material for *Fashion Vibes*.

I kept lifting my phone to hit *record*. Whatever this footage became, I knew it wouldn't be my usual fashion-centric content.

It would probably be like Katy's video, which had garnered more views and comments in three days than any other on my channel. Much as I'd suspected, people connected with her story, not just her relatability but also her optimism. Other than a few creepy comments from guys offering to pick up where her husband left off—Katy's awesome response had been, "the Internet's gonna Internet"—no one blinked an eye at the tone shift in my content, so it was clear shaking things up and following my instincts had been the right call.

I waved to old friends as I passed by, stopping to speak to a few and introduce Will. We slowly made our way toward Marley and James, working their shift at the high school booth.

As we walked, Will had me laughing with fun stories about his Christmases growing up. Apparently, his parents loved to celebrate but filled their home with breakable decorations. What he remembered most from being a young child was getting to pop the green bubble wrap his mom handed him as she unboxed the expensive baubles. He also recalled one of the Wallingford Capital office parties he'd attended in middle school, where he'd watched in shock as his straitlaced parents got tipsy and performed a karaoke rendition of "Baby, It's Cold Outside."

It really was too bad Will didn't feel like he could be honest with his mom and dad about this latest concussion. Their family dynamic seemed to have evolved into him hiding large parts of himself from them while they mistrusted his decision-making out of habit. But clearly, there was love on both sides.

"You know," he said, "it's nice being able to talk about those memories." He reached out his gloved hand and squeezed mine. "But I'm also glad to be here making new ones." He waved his other arm around at the lights and ribbons decorating the streetlamps. "This is definitely a Christmas I'll remember."

"Hopefully for something other than falling on the ice."

"Hopefully for more than that." He laughed and held my hand tighter.

His second CT scan had been clear, the doctor okaying him to come to the carnival. He'd been moving around on his own with only a few very minor dizzy spells the past few days.

That meant Will needed to get back to reality soon. Reality being Seattle. Yesterday, we decided I would drive both of us back in his car since a long solo drive was a no-go for him so soon after his fall. The plan was for me to come back with Leo and Miranda in time for Christmas.

I'd agreed to those logistics with a very specific motivation no one else knew yet. It was the reason I was fine leaving my car at Marley's house and being in Seattle for the next ten days.

I wanted to talk to Bren and tie up loose ends in the city because I'd decided to move back to Coleman Creek. Permanently.

Will and I rolled up to the high school booth. It was the biggest, comprised of several tables in two large U-formations. Different games benefited various student clubs and the athletic boosters, along with baked goods and holiday craft sales to support the PTSA.

James sat behind the section for the school clubs. He'd talked my ear off over Thanksgiving about how much he loved being the faculty adviser for the gamer groups.

Marley stood admonishing one of the teens handling the nearby student council table. His badge said *Senior Class Vice President* in graffiti-like font.

"Fel, you need to redo it. You're lucky I'm giving you another chance instead of just failing you outright."

"Ah, c'mon, Ms. Davis. It's an English class. We're supposed to express ourselves. And I was *expressing* exactly how I feel about this time of year."

Marley released an exasperated breath. "Fel, there are limits in my classroom. And one of them is you don't put an expletive in the title of your essay. Not unless you want a big red F."

"Alright, alright. What if I called it 'The Boy Who Gave Zero *Ducks* About Christmas'?"

I cleared my throat as Marley's eyes widened, and James intervened. "That's enough, Fel." He directed a meaningful look at the teen, fighting a smile himself. "Do better."

The boy gave James a playful shrug before nodding.

As Will, James, and Marley chatted about which bake sale items looked the best, I strained to eavesdrop on the conversation at the student council table. That kid—Fel—sat with his friends, complaining about the carnival. They threw out words in derisive tones. *Lame. Corny. Boring.* Most stared at their phones, oblivious to the booth-goers.

They didn't understand yet. But they would. Someday.

Behind another table, a blond-haired teen looked at the ground while playing Christmas songs on an acoustic guitar. Vaguely, I recalled him from the talent show the year prior.

Will and I stood and listened.

"That's Daniel," Marley whispered to us. "James says he sees a lot of himself in him." She gave us a meaningful glance, which I interpreted to mean Daniel had been bullied. "This year has been much better, though."

James paused whatever he'd been doing as an older couple arrived at the booth. "Mr. Bailey!"

The white-haired gentleman of the pair frowned at James's effusive waving. "Now, now, Mr. Wymack. There's no need to kick up a fuss."

"We didn't know you were coming," Marley said, beaming at the couple.

"Well, I wanted to bring my bride here, where I spent so many years." At this, the man brought his companion forward to shake James's and Marley's hands. "This is Ellen. My love, this is Ms. Davis and Mr. Wymack."

After they said hello, James turned to introduce me and Will to the couple. "This is Fred Bailey and his wife Ellen. Fred's the teacher who retired so I could have a permanent place at the school."

"That's not exactly true," Mr. Bailey corrected. "I took an early retirement so I could spend my golden years with the love of my life, who I'd been foolishly apart from for far too long. Helping Mr. Wymack was merely a byproduct of that decision."

James looked at the older man fondly. "Of course. That's exactly how it happened."

"Though I am slightly concerned about what's become of the students in my absence," Mr. Bailey continued. "I overheard two of them heatedly discussing 'bags of beans' and 'sovereign glue.' I swear the kids will never stop coming up with ridiculous code words for drugs." He said it with a straight face, but there was a twinkle in his eye.

"Must be kids from the D&D Club." Will chortled.

"That's right." James grinned. "Don't let Mr. Bailey fool you into thinking he's old and stodgy. He's sent us postcards from three continents in the past year, plus pictures hiking in Japan and ziplining in Costa Rica."

"The ocean was lovely there," Ellen said wistfully. "So blue."

"My Ellen was the most beautiful woman on the beach," Mr. Bailey asserted. "For now, we are in town through the holidays, and we'll be back in the summer for your wedding."

"Good," Marley said. "If it didn't work with your schedule, we'd have had to cancel the whole thing."

Mr. Bailey's lip twitched.

I pulled out my phone and asked the older couple to do a quick interview about their travels and being in Coleman Creek for the holidays. Then I did a few Q&As with folks nearby. The sound quality would be terrible, but I'd learned some tricks over the years. I also had a mic attachment, which helped. If worse came to worst, I could always use subtitles.

Mr. Bailey and his wife talked about wishing they hadn't waited so long to be together. Daniel didn't want to talk on camera, but he let me film him playing the guitar while he tried not to glare. Fel and the other student council kids gleefully told me how they couldn't wait to leave Coleman Creek after graduation. But they also spoke excitedly about the upcoming holiday talent show—agreeing no one could top last year, when Mr. Wymack declared his love for Ms. Davis—and they were eager to check out the rest of the carnival once their shift ended.

As Will and I walked away to explore some of the other booths, I held on to him with one arm while keeping my phone ready to capture more footage.

"I remember feeling exactly like Fel and his friends," I said. "Thinking all this small-town stuff was dumb and wanting nothing more than to get out. Living here these past few months has really put that all in perspective."

"You do seem to love it." Will gazed around thoughtfully. "Although, to be fair, when we spent that night together in Seattle, you seemed at home there, too. You were in your element at Musicbox, and from everything you've said, you fit in at Kolya's."

"Fair. But it's like we talked about the other day. With personas. It's not that I don't like the city. It's that I have to work harder there. In Coleman Creek, I never feel like I'm putting on a show. I'm just me."

"Will you be okay when you go back to Seattle? Or is that even still the plan?"

I loved that his question allowed for the possibility I might not return to Seattle—Will seemed to be the only person in my life who didn't take it as a given. I needed to tell him I'd decided to move back home, but this wasn't the time or the place for that discussion. Bren ought to be the first person I told, considering that, until a few months ago, I'd lived with her for a decade. Besides that, I wanted a few more days to sit with the decision solo, to conquer the small part of me which still viewed returning to Coleman Creek as an admission of defeat.

I replied with a partial answer.

"This whole time I've been thinking crashing with Marley was a stopover for me, a chance to regroup. But maybe what I need is to start over entirely, not just reset. I have a life in Seattle. All my business contacts are there. I have friends, including a best friend I'm used to seeing every day. Leaving all that would be huge."

"I understand. When I left my family company and founded Yardhouse, I realized almost immediately I hadn't gone far enough. Staying in the finance world had been safe, but it wasn't where I wanted to be."

"Do you think your future is in renovating apartment buildings?"

He shook his head. "No. I'm not sure I'd do it again, even though I loved the process. I don't know what's next, but I enjoy managing the apartments better than anything I've done before."

Will laced our fingers together and sighed contentedly. That's when I noticed Kasen twenty feet away, walking alone.

"Kasen—Hey!" I called out.

He glanced over, and I saw the *I'm trying to figure a way out of this, but I can't* expression pass over his face before he waved back.

I knew Marley worried about her ex, worried she'd hurt him deeply when he'd asked to get back together last year, and she'd told him about James. I hoped Kasen could see everything had worked out for the best.

But I guessed knowing that didn't automatically make things easier. And Kasen had been like family to me for the eight years he'd dated my sister. I wanted good things for him.

"Hi, Maureen." Kasen offered me a stilted hug.

"Let me introduce you to Will. He's a friend of James's."

The two men shook hands, and Will's expression revealed he knew exactly who Kasen was. It made sense that James had told his friend about Marley's former long-term boyfriend.

"Hey, man," Will said.

They dropped their arms. Not knowing how else to fill the ensuing silence, I asked Kasen, "How have you been? Still doing the graphic design thing?"

"Yeah. It's been going pretty good, I guess." He stuffed his hands in his pockets. "I'm glad I struck out on my own a few years ago."

"Nothing like being your own boss," Will piped in. "No worries about having to work for a dipshit."

Kasen's posture relaxed a bit in the face of Will's easy charm. "Amen."

A second later, something pushed hard against me, and I got shoved into Will from the side.

"What the—" I looked down to find a tiny, three-year-old human tornado hugging my lower leg.

Katy appeared a few seconds later, calling out as she ran after her daughter, "Rosie! For Pete's sake. Can you please, for all that is good in this world, take it easy!"

Turning to me with an apologetic glance, Katy hoisted her son Braxton onto her hip. "I am so sorry, Maureen. I promised her a hot chocolate, and she assumed that meant we were getting hot chocolate right this instant and raced off."

"No harm done," I assured her.

She kneeled in front of her daughter. "Please apologize to Maureen."

Rosie looked at me and back at Katy. Her face screwed up. I braced myself.

"I...don't...wanna!" the little girl wailed, shaking her head aggressively, loosening her pigtails. "Can't make me!"

I realized how necessary the jeans and flannel button-downs truly were to Katy's sanity. She looked ready to keel over. Even with her parents and the whole town supporting her, single parenthood was still a struggle.

Just when it appeared Katy might join her daughter in a crying jag, Kasen reached out to pull the boy from her side.

"Come on, little man," he said gently, clearly familiar with the toddler. "How about we go look at the pretty tree while your mom gets things sorted with your sister?"

Braxton stuck three fingers in his mouth and extended his other arm eagerly toward Kasen.

"That was nice of him," I said.

"Yeah," Katy agreed, running a soothing hand along Rosie's back as the girl sobbed into her chest. "Kasen's been coming into The Landslide a lot lately, and I've had to bring the kids in for my shifts when no one can take them. He always invites them over to color at his table, or sometimes he'll read to them. Last week, he taught Rosie how to play tic-tac-toe."

"He comes in alone?" I asked, looking over at where Kasen had lifted Braxton onto his shoulders to get a closer look at the decorations. Will stood near them, offering Katy and me some privacy.

"Sometimes he's with his parents. Occasionally, a friend. I don't want to make it sound pathetic or anything. He's not the only bachelor in town who prefers the cooking at The Landslide."

"Good point."

"And I'll take all the help I can get." Katy exhaled heavily.

After a few minutes, Rosie calmed down, and the men found their way back to us. Will pulled off his gloves and shook them.

"What happened?" I asked.

"I grabbed the post by the tree before I realized it was soaking wet." He sniffed. "Luckily, it appears to be spilled cider and not something more...questionable."

Braxton giggled as Will crossed his eyes.

"Katy, do you want me to walk with you and the kids to the hot chocolate booth?" Kasen asked. "I'm supposed to meet my mom and dad there anyway."

"That would be a lifesaver. Thanks."

Suddenly, Rosie looked up from her mother's shoulder and asked Will in a groggy voice, "Does it hurt?"

Will wore a *huh* expression for a moment until he registered the little girl peering at his hand.

"Rosie!" Katy's face reddened, but Will quickly offered reassurance.

"It's alright." He held out his scarred palm to Rosie. "It doesn't hurt anymore. See?" He ran the fingers of his left hand roughly over the right, poking and prodding at the raised tissue. "I had an accident a long time ago, but it's all better now, even though my hand looks a little different from most people's." He made a fist before flexing and stretching his fingers. "It's okay if you want to touch it. Sometimes it's less scary that way."

I doubted many three-year-olds would take him up on that offer, but Rosie was a baller. She reached out and traced the lines across his palm with her stubby pointer. Then she pushed against the stump of his pinky. Not to be outdone, Braxton wiggled for Kasen to lean him over so he could run his tiny finger over Will's as well.

"This is okay," Rosie declared. "It doesn't look very nice, but it's okay."

Will nodded seriously. "That's what I tell myself."

Satisfied, Rosie turned to me. "Sorry I pushed."

"It's alright. I know you were excited and didn't mean to. It makes me feel better you said sorry, though."

"Come on, baby." Katy seemed shocked by Rosie's apology. "Let's go get the hot chocolate."

"With Sen?"

"Yeah. I'm coming," Kasen said with a smile.

Once they were out of earshot, I patted Will's shoulder. "That was impressive."

"Meh. I've gotten used to people staring. And kids are always no BS, aren't they?"

"They absolutely are." I laughed, thinking of the pieces in my jewelry box Connor and Scarlett had called *hideous*. "C'mon. We should go check out the other vendor booths. Grab a peppermint cream donut. I remember them being amazing. You probably shouldn't do the Ferris wheel with your concussion, but I'd like to get some footage of it for b-roll."

We turned to walk in the other direction and ran into Marley and James, their volunteer shift complete. Marley caught sight of Kasen, Katy, and the kids drinking hot chocolate and looked from them to me and back again, raising her eyebrows.

"Don't get any ideas," I mouthed.

She shrugged and smiled.

Chapter Twenty-Four

Will

I'd never been to anything like the Holiday Hoopla. Maureen and I walked the length of the event, which extended from the business district to the town's main park. Intermittently, we held hands, but mostly she needed hers to hold the phone steady as she filmed everything she saw.

We stopped to get donuts and hot chocolate. We played a beanbag toss game to benefit the Rotary Club and entered a raffle to support the local Little League. Several bands played along the park's long walking trail, and a group dressed in Victorian garb strolled past us singing Christmas carols. There was a Ferris wheel and a merry-go-round, and a hay bale maze decorated with lights in the shape of stars. The PTSA for the elementary school had a craft booth set up, and kids laughed as they used Mod Podge and tissue paper to make colorful mason jar candle holders.

Underneath the streetlamps, connected by lit tinsel garland, tables displayed handmade ornaments and crafts for sale. The pace of movement along the trails and sidewalks remained glacial, not only because the last of the snow on the ground was melting but because people kept stopping to wish their neighbors happy holidays.

Maureen paused often to chat with carnival-goers—some she seemed to know well and others she didn't—pulling out the little mic attachment from her purse to interview anyone willing to speak on camera. She asked about their style, the holidays, fashion, Coleman Creek, and whatever else seemed natural.

I enjoyed watching her work and taking part in the festive atmosphere.

I hoped that was what I was, too—a part of it. Not just on the periphery. Not just in Maureen's life because of happenstance. If I hadn't fallen, I would have been back in Seattle by now, and I doubted we'd have gotten as far as we had this past week. But however I'd arrived here, it was exactly where I wanted to be.

My thoughts kept going back to what Katy's very wise three-year-old had said.

It doesn't look very nice, but it's okay.

The story of Maureen and me hadn't been very nice so far. Not neat, or clear, or calm. From the beginning, there had been heat, mutual attraction, and admiration. A rare level of connection. But there had also been lies and half-truths, cowardice and pain. Years of silence. Anger and misunderstanding. Penance. Grace.

So much intensity between us. Yet now—there was this.

Fingers entwined. Our relationship as scarred as my hand. It would never look entirely nice, but it was okay.

"Hey, Will?" Maureen's voice broke into my thoughts.

"Hmm?"

"Do you mind if I take a solo ride on the Ferris wheel? You shouldn't risk it because of your head, but I'd love to get some fun shots from the top if I can."

"No problem. I'll go back to the park and check out the bands. You can catch up with me there."

"Just don't get too close to the instruments, okay? That wouldn't be good for you either."

I grinned at how she couldn't stop playing nurse. "I'll be fine. The lights and the sounds have been okay so far, although I wouldn't mind taking a break on one of those benches."

She bit her lip.

"Go!" I encouraged her. "I'll be fine."

"Okay. But I'm just gonna take one quick ride and then I'll be back."

"Take your time."

I watched as she strode off before turning toward the park. Not too far from the entrance, I saw the blond-haired teen from the high school booth quietly strumming his guitar on a bench.

I pulled up next to him, remembering Marley's intel that he'd had a tough time the year before. "Daniel, right?" His fingers fell from the strings as he furrowed his brow at me. I hurried to reassure him I wasn't a weirdo. "We met a few hours ago at the Coleman Creek High booth. I'm Will, James's—uh, Mr. Wymack's—friend."

He dipped his chin. "Hey."

"Your playing is really good."

"Thanks." He looked at the ground.

Stilted silence hung in the air. The last thing I wanted to do was make him uncomfortable, but before I could walk away and leave him to his playing, a group of young women came along the path. As they passed, one of them stopped short.

"Oh my gosh! Daniel! Hey!" She came over to us. "I'm so happy to see you!" The girl, who looked around eighteen, gave Daniel a megawatt smile. She bent down to hug him tightly, careful not to crush his guitar. "I just got into town, and I was going to message you," she gushed. "I want to make sure we hang out before I go back to school."

Daniel's cheeks flushed. He awkwardly patted her back before she pulled away. One of the other girls called out in an annoyed voice, "Come on, Nan! We were supposed to be at the big tree ten minutes ago."

"Oh, shoot." The young woman—Nan—reached out to squeeze Daniel on the shoulder. "I'll send you a snap. Can't wait to catch up." She rushed off after her friends, waving cheerfully and shouting, "Bye!" over her shoulder.

I watched Daniel's eyes as they followed her, staring until she was out of sight. He looked like he'd been hit by a truck.

"She seems nice." I gestured to the bench next to him, and he shrugged. I sat down. "Friend of yours?"

"I guess. She went away to college a few months ago."

"Does she know you like her?" He jerked his head to face me, blushing furiously, and I immediately regretted my words. "I'm sorry, Daniel. I didn't mean to blurt that out. It's none of my business."

His eyes flashed for a moment before he sighed in defeat. "Is it that obvious?"

"Hey, you don't need to be embarrassed," I said, holding up my hands. "And you don't need to talk if you don't want to. I just had to sit down because I'm recovering from an accident, and I wanted to get off my feet for a minute."

Daniel traced his fingers over the frets of his guitar. Even though I'd had more bravado at his age, I could see myself in him. The red face. The lack of true confidence. I wished when I'd been sixteen, I'd had someone to tell me it was fine to be awkward and artsy and imperfect.

"I'm probably not as good at talking to students as Mr. Wymack or Ms. Davis," I told him, "but just so you know—from my perspective as an outsider, based on what I just saw—Nan seems to like you too."

He slumped against the bench. "She only thinks of me as a friend. Her *much younger* friend."

"Well, that may be true now, but I wouldn't worry about it. You have lots of time. You're what, a sophomore?"

"Junior."

"And she just started college, which means she's only two years older. That's nothing. Plus, that gap will feel even smaller in the future."

"It doesn't feel like nothing. She acts like I'm her little brother or something," he grumbled.

"Just wait. Trust me." I pointed at Maureen, now visible in the distance, chatting with folks outside the park entrance. "See that woman?"

"Ms. Davis's sister?"

"Yep. She's two years older than me."

Daniel volleyed his eyes to Maureen again and then back at me. "Are you telling me that because you like her?"

I nodded. "I figure you might appreciate knowing someone else is in the same boat. I like Maureen, but I'm not exactly sure what will happen next. Kind of like with you and Nan."

He appeared thoughtful for a moment, repositioning his guitar to face me. "Does she like you back?"

"I'm fairly certain she does, but I think it's hard for her to trust her feelings. And I don't want to push. So right now, I mostly just try to be around her as much as she'll let me."

Daniel gazed into the distance before asking, "Why can't she trust her feelings?"

"It's not something I can discuss with a sixteen-year-old." I rolled my shoulders. "How about we go back to talking about you and Nan?"

He sidestepped my attempt at redirection. "It might be alright to push, just a bit, to at least make sure she knows how you feel."

I glanced over at Maureen, looking like some sort of Christmas fairy bathed in the silvery glow of the twinkle lights. Daniel made a decent point. Even if Maureen wasn't ready to make firm plans or call us a couple yet, she deserved to know I was all in.

"Daniel, has anyone ever told you that you're a genius?" I joked.

He grinned shyly. "You could do something epic. Like last year, when Mr. Wymack made that embarrassing slideshow presentation for Ms. Davis at the talent show."

I laughed. "No. She doesn't like big scenes. If I did something like that, it would be like saying I don't know her at all."

He pursed his lips, drumming his fingers against his thigh. "You know what you should do?"

"What?"

"You should buy her the best Christmas present ever."

Hmm. I hadn't thought about getting her a gift. But of course I should. It certainly couldn't hurt.

I chuckled again as Daniel began putting his guitar into its case. "Got any gift ideas, oh wise teenager?"

"They were selling some fun crocheted tablet holders by the donut booth." Daniel's expression stayed so blank that I wasn't sure he was messing with me until he cracked up. What a cool kid.

I spoke low as Maureen drew closer to our bench. "Daniel, thank you. I'm going to take your advice."

I reached out my hand, and he shook it, seeming not to notice the missing fingers. "No problem, um, Mr.—"

"Call me Will."

"Will."

"And Daniel? Something tells me one day Nan will wake up and notice what a great guy you are."

He gave me a skeptical smile. "Uh-huh. Well, I'm just gonna try to be around her as much as she'll let me." He slid off the bench with his guitar. "See ya." He headed off toward the park entrance.

"What were you talking about with Daniel?" Maureen asked as she sat down next to me. "I got some great footage of him earlier."

"Nothing much. Mainly Christmas shopping."

WHEN I WOKE UP THE FOLLOWING MORNING, I found Maureen sitting at the kitchen table on her laptop, humming along to Andy Williams on the vinyl player. We'd made a plan to leave Coleman Creek no later than ten so we wouldn't get stuck driving over the mountain pass in the dark.

"You're up early," I said.

"I got inspired after the carnival. I worked on the piece a little last night and then got up this morning to finish."

"You finished?"

"Like I said, the muse just hit me."

"Can I see?"

Maureen hesitated briefly before turning the computer in my direction. "I guess it doesn't make sense not to show you if I'm planning to put it out into the world."

"I'm sure it's great."

She hit the play button.

A soft piano version of "It's Beginning to Look Like Christmas" played in the background, and images Maureen had filmed around town filled the screen. Clearly, she'd been capturing the footage for a while, as some clips were taken in the daytime. The big town Christmas tree loomed large in the shot before the camera panned back onto Main Street, highlighting the decorated storefronts and sidewalks. A succession of still photos followed. The Hawaiian-shirted Santa outside the bowling alley, the handmade snowflakes in the hospital waiting room, the tree lot at the high school. Sped-up video of the carnival booths from last night followed, then a driver's-eye view through some residential neighborhoods decked out for the holidays. On top of all of it was Francesca's voiceover.

"It's the holiday season in Coleman Creek, my hometown. You've already met my friend Katy, and since so many of you liked that video, I thought I'd show you a little more from my non-fashion life... I've been back in town for a few months now, getting excited to celebrate the holidays, and it's got me thinking a lot about 'Fashion Vibes with Francesca.' When I started this channel, my day job was in high-end fashion. And while that was exciting, and I met so many amazing people, it didn't entirely feel like me because it didn't allow me much opportunity to explore my belief that fashion is for everyone. That's why this channel was born. If you want to see me demonstrate how to make the latest trends accessible for lots of people or show you what outfits regular folks are wearing around Seattle, please check out my backlog of videos."

The footage slowed to real time, and the shots became images of people at the carnival—laughing, drinking hot chocolate, playing games, browsing the craft booths, and smiling at one another. If I hadn't been there myself, I might have imagined it was staged.

The distinct small-town energy and everyone looking so relaxed and happy.

Francesca's voice continued, *"I'm proud of all the fashion-focused videos I've done, but this isn't that. It's Christmastime, and I'm feeling sentimental, so this is a love letter to my hometown. I left this place thinking I'd never want to come back. I didn't think there was a place for my love of fashion in Coleman Creek. But what is fashion other than simply the clothes we put on?*

"My friend Katy was brave talking about her divorce. Now I want to be brave, too. Clothes are the way we express ourselves to others, but they can also be the way we put up walls, a way we hide. If you watched Katy's video, then you also know fashion can be a way we heal."

The video cut to Maureen's face. She sat on the bed in her room at Marley's, Oscar and Bambi resting their heads on her thighs. Since she wore the same clothes she'd had on yesterday and the video was taken at night, she must have filmed it after the carnival, after the rest of us had gone to sleep.

"This has been an interesting December for me," she said. *"I realized that I'm healing too. I'm still getting over my mom passing away a few years ago, and I'm coming to terms with the fact high fashion isn't for me. I was using my job to maintain a hard exterior, to hold myself back from others. And it was okay for me to do that because I'd been hurt.*

"One thing I loved about fashion, even when I was little, was that it gave me a chance to express myself. To wear colorful scarves or put on a ton of bracelets—what every toddler does when given access to a jewelry box. Over time, I lost that magic, that whimsy. My concerns became taking care of everyone else and pleasing others. I'm sure a lot of you can relate.

"*Moving to a big city and working at a high-end boutique was what I needed at the time. Because I still felt most comfortable hiding from the world. But now I need something else, and it took the magic of Coleman Creek at Christmas to show me. Now, let me show you.*"

The video went back to the carnival, to some interviews she'd done. As expected, the sound quality wasn't great, so there were subtitles.

First, she interviewed Fel and his friends in the high school booth. There was b-roll footage of the kids helping customers buy bake sale items and messing around with one another. Over this, Francesca narrated, "*These teens are just like I was in high school. Loud, opinionated, and eager to get the heck out of Coleman Creek.*

"*So, I want to ask you guys lots of things, but first I have to ask about fashion. Is there anything you can tell me about the way kids dress in Coleman Creek?*"

"*Um,*" Fel said, looking back and forth to his friends, all of whom were cracking up. "*That's kind of a weird question. I mean, it's mostly just hoodies and sweats or whatever, I guess. I don't really think about my clothes.*" He shrugged his shoulders as one of his buddies smacked his head.

"*I think that's most people's approach,*" Francesca replied. "*I've found while doing these videos that there aren't a ton of people out there who plan their outfits. When I've talked to teenagers in Seattle, they say the same thing.*"

"*Then why do you ask?*"

"*Just to warm people up. If I know we're going to start out a little awkward, there's nowhere to go but up.*"

A red-headed boy with metal braces flicked Fel's arm. "*Funny. That's Fel's approach to talking to girls.*"

Fel slugged him lightly. "*Shut up, douchenugget. It's not like you're any better.*"

The kids laughed.

"*Well, there are some clothes I think about,*" one of the other boys, a big linebacker-type with a black beanie, chimed in. "*Like, if I know I have a game, I have to make sure my uniform's clean—*"

"*Oh!*" a girl in the back piped up. "*There's also, like, prom and Spring Fling and stuff. My mom always takes me to the mall in Spokane when we have a formal.*"

"*Deadass,*" Fel said. "*I had to get a suit for a dance. I wanted to get something different, like blue, but my mom made me get dark gray because she said I'd be able to use it for more things. Like funerals.*"

"*Your mom said that?*" Francesca laughed off camera.

"*Yeah. She's really practical.*"

"*My mom was the same,*" Francesca said. I doubted the kids registered the catch in Maureen's voice, but I heard it.

The same girl who had mentioned shopping in Spokane spoke up. "*I can't wait until I'm an adult and can buy whatever I want.*"

"*Do you think you'll live somewhere other than Coleman Creek?*" Francesca asked.

"*Oh, for sure.*"

"*Definitely.*"

"*Absolutely.*"

"*I'm leaving as soon as I can.*"

All the teens chimed in. Francesca gave them a moment to high five one another before walking away and filming herself selfie-style, close to the camera so it could pick up her words.

"*I was just like those kids. I wanted to leave so badly. And I guess I had to do it—just like they'll have to—in order to appreciate what I had here.*" She pointed the lens back at the kids, clustered around one another, talking and sipping hot chocolate. "*They'll always remember growing up here. Sitting in this booth. Complaining about how things are boring or corny. But they're excited about the holiday* dance and the talent show. Someday they'll appreciate how everyone in town cared about their futures. No one can be a nameless face in the crowd here because the crowd's too small. That used to bother me, but now I realize it makes me feel safe. Loved. It feels like home."

The video continued to other interviews. And there was no escaping her instinct to focus on the clothes. She complimented folks on their jackets and beanies, and voiceover Francesca asked her audience to post in the comments whether they were "*team peacoat or team puffer coat.*"

Maureen couldn't be overly sentimental for too long, either. She had to stop and have fun, take a breather with a joke. I'd learned that about her these past few days—Maureen wore her heart behind well-timed quips.

Near the Ferris wheel, Francesca caught up with Travis and Vivienne with all four of their children. The couple spoke of how much they loved celebrating Christmas with a house full of children, and how blessed they were to have presents under the tree. The older kids mentioned sledding and holiday shopping. Scarlett held up the candleholder she'd made at the craft booth. Connor—who had noise-canceling headphones over his ears—looked directly into the camera and said, "*It's an okay carnival. But the hot chocolate this year was not as good as last year. Pretty terrible, actually. The tree is better, though.*"

Francesca laughed, and a montage of other neighbors played.

"*I'm excited for Christmas karaoke at The Landslide.*"

"*We're going to Grandma's house for turkey and mac 'n' cheese!*"

"*I like the way they play old Christmas movies at the bowling alley.*"

"*The Holiday Hoopla feels old-fashioned. I love that it's the same for my kids now as it was for me growing up.*"

"We always bring cookies to the hospital and the police department on Christmas Eve."

"I like all the penguins at my dentist's office."

"Did you see that Mr. Bailey came back? And he's married? Like, I can't believe someone married him."

I was mildly surprised Maureen left in that last one, but from what I'd gathered after meeting Mr. Bailey, he'd appreciate the humor.

At the end of the video, we were back with Francesca on the bed with the dogs.

"I hope you enjoyed this brief tour of my hometown. Maybe it's not as cute as the little Christmas towns you see in the movies, but there's something special about it. Or perhaps that's just how everyone feels about the place they grew up. I hope so. I hope you all have places that make you feel like this.

"I found safety in big city anonymity. When no one knows you, there's no one to hurt you. No one to fail in front of. But that kind of security made me lonely. And since this is a fashion vlog, let me tell you I wore the hell out of that loneliness. Wore it like a suit of armor. Absolutely slayed in it. But much like the leather fringe skirt I wore in middle school, it doesn't fit me anymore. In this town, I don't need to hide away. And no one else needs me to, either.

"I hope you all find a reason to heal this season, to feel fulfilled and loved. My holiday wish for everyone is that you can find the things that help you be bold.

"So, whether you've got on a peacoat or a puffer coat, I hope you're wearing a persona that feels comfortable and authentic for you. Thank you so much for letting me show you Coleman Creek. I hope you love it as much as I do."

Francesca gave a wave to the camera, and there was one last shot of the dogs in Santa hats underneath the Christmas tree before the video faded to black and the "like and subscribe" prompt appeared.

Maureen shut the laptop and turned to me expectantly.

"It's fantastic," I said honestly. "I mean, it's not new or earth-shattering or anything like that, but somehow, it's fresh. And it should be corny, but instead, it feels...relatable. It's hard to be cynical after watching that."

"That's kind of how I felt at first when I finished. I thought it was too sweet, like eating an entire batch of cookies. But that's because I'm so used to having a side of negative with anything good. Except there's no way to make this dark. Even the teens wanting to leave, Connor being unenthusiastic about the hot chocolate, dissing Mr. Bailey—" She smiled. "Somehow it all comes out optimistic."

"Because it's real," I said. "And people are going to love it. At least the ones who don't have cold, dead hearts."

"From your lips. But I'm going to make, like, five very basic fashion-focused videos in a row after this one. I'm done opening my veins to other people for a while. It doesn't come easily."

"I know." I bumped her shoulder with mine. "And you're ready for any troll-like comments that come?"

"Like Katy said, 'the Internet's gonna Internet.'"

I laughed. "That's true. The haters can fuck off."

"All the way off," she agreed, uploading the video. "And maybe there'll be some non-haters who like it. Regardless, I needed to make it. For me. And for you."

That got my attention. "Me?"

"Yes. Obviously, Francesca's viewers don't need to know our situation. But when I said I was healing, one thing I was referring to was forgiving you and getting over that anger." She peered up at me with big eyes. "And when I said I was done throwing up walls, wanting to be my authentic self... Well, I guess you can consider that an invitation."

My breath caught in my throat until I dared ask, "An invitation to what?"

She twined her five fingers with my three. "Into my life, Will. Behind my armor." In a small voice, she added, "Please don't make me regret it."

I hugged her fiercely to me. "I won't."

It was a promise I intended to keep. But watching the video, seeing how far she'd come in dealing with the remnants of her past, made me realize I had some loose threads of my own to tie up.

Suddenly, I knew what to get Maureen for Christmas.

Chapter Twenty-Five

Maureen

I drove Will back to Seattle in his car. His head felt better, but I declined his offer to take a shift. The sleek black Audi handled like a dream. When the Christmas station came blasting through the speakers as soon as I turned the key, it reminded me of our night five years ago.

For the first time, the memory was happy and not painful. It had been a magical moment, even if everything had gone to shit afterward.

We planned for me to drop Will off at his place and then catch a rideshare to Bren's apartment. After I broke the news to my best friend that I'd decided to move home, I'd be ready to have a serious talk with Will about our future. Hopefully, he'd be ready to navigate some distance.

What we said to one another this morning had been a beginning, but there were a lot of variables to consider. Things had been great in Coleman Creek, where we laughed about gingerbread men and strolled through the Holiday Hoopla. But how would our fragile bond fare here, in the epicenter of Will's life?

In the place where he'd had his accident.

Where the parents he couldn't fully communicate with lived.

Where he still saw his ex-fiancée.

As though the universe heard my questions, when I drove the Audi from the arterial into Will's neighborhood, I got another stark reminder that his past would always mark him.

Making a right turn, I jerked the wheel as I nearly collided with a cyclist going in the wrong direction. The woman pushed her bike pedals mindlessly as she came around the corner, weaving in and out of the lanes, oblivious to the fact three cars had to swerve to avoid her.

I cursed hotly under my breath as I hit the brakes, but I stopped myself from shouting out the window. The guy in the Toyota behind me was less restrained, laying on the horn and waving his middle finger at the bike as he yelled obscenities. The cyclist continued unaffected, likely only aware of whatever came through her earbuds.

"That was close," I whooshed out, pulling over to the curb to get my bearings.

I glanced at Will, whose face had gone white. His breaths came in short puffs as he gripped the seat belt across his chest.

"Are you okay?" I asked, reaching over to put a light hand on his shoulder.

He opened his eyes and nodded. After a moment, he spoke with a shaky voice, "Yeah, I'm okay. My accident. I just get that way with bikes on the road, you know?"

"I'm sorry... Maybe it'll cheer you up to know that I hate bike riding. Don't own one."

Will shook his head, releasing a brittle guffaw. "You think I'd be used to it by now. There are so many bikes in Seattle. But I guess it's always going to mess me up a touch when something like that happens."

"Understandable." I moved my hand to rub up and down his arm. "That's the thing about bad memories. They fade and change like any scar. Sometimes you notice them less..."

"But they're still there." He sighed heavily.

And sometimes you notice them more. My fingers drifted down to touch the small scar on my right leg from where I'd gotten stitches the night of my alcohol poisoning.

With an okay from Will, I started the car again. A minute later, I pulled up in front of a beautiful old apartment building in one of Seattle's more established neighborhoods. It looked a bit out of place, surrounded by newer condos, but I preferred its homey feel to the modern steel boxes on either side.

"You remodeled this?" I asked.

"Um, no. I paid people to remodel it." Will laughed. "But I worked closely with the architect to make sure it came out the way I wanted. It probably would have been more profitable to start from scratch—I certainly could have fit more units in that way—but maintaining the character of the building was important to me."

"Well, kudos. It's lovely."

"Did you want to come up?" The question felt loaded even though we'd been acting like a couple for the past few days. "It can just be for coffee or a soda," he said quickly. "No pressure."

"I'll come up for one cup of coffee or Diet Coke if you have it," I said. "But then I've got to get going. Bren is expecting me."

"Bren?"

"My best friend." Will's forehead scrunched. "What's wrong?" I asked.

"Nothing. You mentioned staying with your friend but hadn't said the name before. I feel like I've heard it recently and can't place it. Weird." His brows drew together.

We walked up an ornate marble staircase to Will's third-floor apartment. He took his bags and gold pillows into the bedroom while I looked around the main living space. The prewar, shotgun-style layout had hardwoods and rounded archways above the doors. The galley kitchen was small by new build standards, but it had been opened so one half-wall functioned as more of an island. There were also brand-new stainless-steel appliances.

I noticed a small plastic Christmas tree in the corner. It made me smile, remembering the one Marley had put in his room at her house.

As Will poured soda into glasses in the kitchen, I unlocked my phone to get the rideshare squared away. In the app, I punched in the address for Bren's apartment. *Uh...*

"Hey, what's the address of this place?" I'd never gotten it since he'd just directed me to his building from the passenger seat.

He answered, and I laughed.

"What?"

"I think my best friend lives in this building."

He snapped his fingers. "That's it! That's where I've heard that name before. Bren. Her boyfriend is Chase, right?"

"Yep."

"That's crazy. That's why they looked so familiar to me—they were in your videos. And at Musicbox. I just hadn't put it all together. They actually live on this floor."

I texted Bren to let her know where I was. "That is so strange. What a small world."

Will grinned as he brought the sodas over, placing them on a side table. "Or the world just wants to keep reminding us we're supposed to know each other." We stood side by side and looked out his large picture window at the streetscape below, string lights brightening windows in the apartments across from his, pedestrians bundled up and carrying packages. He raised an arm and ran his fingers through my hair. "You're growing out the auburn?"

"Yeah. No more dye. Letting the natural brown come back."

"I like it," he said, dropping his hand to graze his fingers along my neck. "And I like that fate keeps throwing us together."

"You do, huh?" I put my hand over his, pressing it against my skin.

"Mm-hmm." I watched his throat work as he swallowed. "And I really like that I'm recovered from my concussion now and can resume all...usual activities."

Hesitating only a second before leaning harder into his touch, I felt my heart race. "Is that right? And what sort of *usual activities* were you thinking of resuming?"

He whispered directly in my ear, "Well, there's this one thing I haven't done in a really long time because I haven't found a single person I wanted to do it with."

I hummed in amusement. "Oh?"

"Yes." He leaned in, pupils blown. His breath ghosted against my mouth as he continued, "It usually starts like this..."

Will turned and crushed his lips to mine, hungry and consuming. His arms wound around my torso, cementing our chests together. He tasted like the minty gum he'd been chewing in the car. I relaxed into the kiss, allowing him to seal us together in a slow, savoring way that made me feel cherished—as though after five years, we finally had all the time in the world.

I didn't know exactly what tomorrow held in store for us and even though I had lingering doubts about the loose ends of his past, I knew what I wanted right now. And he wanted it, too.

His hands moved lower to cup my ass, and I ground against him, thrilled at the sensation of his erection pushing against my hip. My mind recalled the scrap of fabric covering him in the shower, not to mention the bulge I'd straddled on Marley's couch. I had a suspicion this short king would prove more than adequate in the downstairs department.

Gently, I pulled my lips from his. "Your bedroom?" I rasped.

He stared heatedly into my eyes before grabbing my hand and tugging me toward the hallway.

Three sharp, loud knocks sounded on the door.

Will groaned.

"It's probably Bren coming to collect me," I said.

He pushed at the hardness tenting his pants and nodded. "It's okay. We've waited this long."

"True." I smiled as he gave me a forehead kiss and turned to the door.

Bren and Chase stood on the other side. She immediately came into the room and wrapped me in a tight hug, talking a mile a minute. "Yay! I can't believe you're finally back. Super weird coincidence you know Will." I'd only told her he was James's friend. It didn't seem like she remembered him from five years ago. "I'm so glad you came home before Christmas. I figured you'd stay in Coleman Creek until after the new year."

My expression remained neutral, knowing I'd made the right call in waiting to tell her about my move face-to-face.

"Well, thanks for putting up with me until Christmas Eve," I said, unwinding her octopus arms from my waist. "Except I gotta say, it feels like a downgrade to go from being roommates to crashing on your couch."

"Shut your face, woman. We were never just roommates. We're best friends, and nothing has changed. Also, there's this weird little hidey hole in our apartment we've set up like a second bedroom. It'll have your name on it until you find a new place."

"Oh right," Will piped in. "Some apartments had mechanical units hiding behind walls that literally went to nothing. This building is so old there were a bunch of surprises like that the contractor found. On the plus side, he also uncovered original hardwoods in most of the interiors and terrazzo in the lobby we were able to save."

"Are you sure you don't want to keep restoring apartment buildings as a career?" I asked. "You seem to love it."

"Maybe one day, but I'm good for now. I want to work on my art for a while."

"Where is your suitcase, Maureen?" Chase asked. "I can carry it to our place."

I pointed at where I'd dropped my bag in the entryway. Every atom in my body wanted to go back to kissing Will, but the moment had effectively passed.

Knowing I'd be giving Bren the whole story soon, I stepped into his arms. Leaning close to his ear, I murmured, "We're not done. I'll text you soon."

I felt the ripple of awareness go through him as the phrase "text you soon" reverberated between us. Five years after the first time. Except now he'd be waiting for me.

He pulled back and bore into me with his gaze. "Soon."

BACK IN BREN'S APARTMENT—magnificent in the quirky way only older apartments could be—she and Chase listened as I relayed my history with Will.

"I knew I recognized him from somewhere!" she exclaimed. "That fucking night at Musicbox. Man, that makes me feel so much better. It's been driving me crazy." She ran her hands through her light brown locks. "But what a dick move not to tell you he was engaged. Even if he didn't know at the time, even if he just thought that Rosalyn chick was his girlfriend, he still should have said."

"Word," Chase agreed.

"I should have known something was up when you landed in the hospital. That whole thing about it being a mistake or nerves about your new job was total bullshit," Bren continued, now pacing.

"You never would have gotten it out of me. I was too embarrassed, too caught up in proving I was the type of girl who would never let a man get under her skin."

Bren frowned. "You were never that girl, though. Not really. And I've known you since college. You could have told me the truth."

"No, Bren, I couldn't have. I wasn't being honest with myself then, let alone with you." I sat down on the couch, watching her move back and forth across the carpet. Chase stayed thoughtfully quiet, his usual mode, listening as I told them, "When I met Will, I was coming off a tough conversation with my mom, where she admitted some mistakes she made when I was a kid.

"Looking back, I think the reason my mom talked to me wasn't because she wanted to ask my forgiveness. It was because she saw the kind of person I was becoming. She wanted to warn me not to keep holding everyone at arm's length. The problem was, right after that, I met Will and got burned. It made me double down. But even if the lesson took so long to learn, I'm glad she told me. Because I still hear her in my head. And I know the fact I'm finally making good decisions now is because she's still in me. Imperfections and all."

Bren stopped pacing. "And Will is a good decision?"

"I think so." I pulled her down to sit next to me, both of us flopping back against the cushions.

"Are you saying you see a future with this guy?"

"It's murky, but yes."

"Why murky?"

"Because what do you do once you've let someone in? I've never done it before." I exhaled. "Also, Will and I are going to have some challenges."

"Like what?"

"Oh, Bren." I offered a sad smile.

THE FOLLOWING MORNING, BREN REMAINED shocked by my plan to move back to Coleman Creek.

After I'd broken the news, we spent the night catching up and watching cheesy 2000s rom-coms in front of the Christmas tree. I'd missed her the past few months. It was nice having someone to talk to who appreciated the story of me giving Will a shower.

"Alright, I give you my permission to go forth and figure out if he's worth it," my best friend declared. "Especially since it's been more than a year since you've gotten laid."

After a breakfast of cereal and toast while we finished hanging the last of the ornaments, she sat on the couch scrolling through her phone, passing time until her shift at the bar.

"Oh my god!" she yelled suddenly as her hand flew to her mouth.

I paused in my task of sorting clothes for either donating or bringing to Coleman Creek. "What?"

She shoved her phone in my face. "Look! Stone Caseman just recommended your video on his social media."

It took me a minute to process. "Stone Caseman? That jackass who got famous doing crazy stunts on the Internet?"

"Yes. That jackass with *three million* followers. And since he got cast in a movie with Naomi Butler, his numbers have gotten even more huge. And he told them to watch your video!"

Bren stopped on a reel and hit the play button. Stone appeared on screen, looking high and happy, speaking in a slow, slurred voice, like a generic-brand surfer. *"Yo. My people. I need you all to check out this clip from this chick I found online. You know how sometimes you're just sort of awake at three in the morning and start going down the YouTube rabbit hole? Well, I was feeling some kind of way about Christmas lately—mainly that I haven't had much time to celebrate because I have this movie coming up later—and, yo, it's gonna be a banger so don't forget to catch* Panic in First Class *when it opens next year—Anyway, I found this cool video of this girl talking about her hometown at Christmas, real small-town shit, so I was expecting, like, you know, snow and lights and grandmas in rockers sitting next to candles—and it's kind of like that—but then, it's also, like, a normal little town, you know, not a postcard. And there are teenagers who are mad at the world, and this little kid who hates hot chocolate, and another kid who plays the guitar like a master but keeps giving the camera fuckin' lewks—like, this shit is raw, man. So real. Anyway, if you want to see a little bit of—"* He looked off to the side as though talking to someone, nodding before turning back to face the camera. *"If you want a little bit of, like, Christmas in America shit, you should check this out. It's dope."*

He'd attached the link to the Coleman Creek video. I clicked over to my channel to discover it had over two hundred thousand views.

"Two hundred thousand!" Bren exclaimed, confirming what my disbelieving eyes saw. "That's insane."

"Do I dare look at the comments?"

"Don't worry. I already checked. There are a few awful ones, of course, but mostly, everyone is positive. A lot of them had the same reaction I did."

"You never told me you watched it. What did you think?"

"Of course I watched it. Duh. You're my best friend. I made Chase watch too. Mostly, I just kept asking myself why it was so interesting when it was just regular people talking. That should be boring, right?"

"No. I think it's kind of the same as people watching videos of kids napping with their dogs or organizing their cupboards. The best kind of Internet is the kind that reminds you we're all in this together."

"I'm pretty sure the best kind of Internet is the kind that shows you what Henry Cavill looks like without his shirt on, but sure, making your plates stack up nice is a close second."

"Fucking Cavill!" Chase shouted from the back room.

"Love you!" Bren shouted back, winking at me.

I had no idea how a dipshit like Stone Caseman had stumbled upon my video, but I wasn't going to look a gift horse in the mouth. I felt even better when I saw the viewer counts ticking up on my other videos, as though the world had discovered *Fashion Vibes with Francesca* at the perfect time.

The same time I'd truly discovered who Francesca was for myself.

JUST BEFORE NOON, BREN AND CHASE left for work. Finally alone, I pulled out my phone to text Will. He beat me to it.

WILL: FYI, I never claimed to have any chill. I'm just sitting at home taking it easy. That was literally my entire plan for the day. Come by and keep me company.
WILL: I'm sure we can find something to keep us occupied.
WILL: Some usual activities for me to resume.
ME: I'll be over in a little while.

I hopped in the shower and prettied myself up a bit, excited to finally tell Will about my move.

And I wouldn't mind getting an up close tour of his bedroom.

Half an hour later, wearing my best-fitting jeans and a body-hugging plum cashmere sweater with my mother's silver holiday wreath brooch, I knocked on Will's door.

It opened on a confident swing.

But it wasn't Will on the other side.

I blinked, needing to check I hadn't entered some alternate dimension. I pushed my heel into the floor beneath my feet and saw the vintage light fixture above me. All real.

Too real.

Even though five years had passed, I'd have known the woman standing in front of me anywhere. Same blond hair. Same fake smile.

"Yes?" Rosalyn asked, and I realized she didn't recognize me. That tracked. My hair was different. And of course, Will had never told her that the woman they'd run into in the hotel lobby five years ago was important to him. Someone she should remember.

"Is Will here?" I asked, keeping my voice level.

She looked over her shoulder. I glanced down and noticed she wore Will's sweatpants. I'd gotten familiar with them last week and knew he owned several pairs. Her T-shirt was a men's crew neck. In Will's size.

A lump formed in my throat as a heaviness invaded my head, spreading to my fingertips.

"He just hopped in the shower," she said. "Are you a tenant? I can give him a message."

Her hair looked like she'd just come through a wind tunnel.

"Um, no. No message. I'll catch him later, I guess."

"Okay." She shut the door in my face.

What. The. Hell? In slow motion, I made my way back to Bren's apartment. Why was Rosalyn at Will's apartment, looking so completely comfortable? Like she had every right to be there? The part of me that had been with him the past week knew there had to be an explanation. There had to be. No one was that good of an actor.

But even if there was a reason his ex-fiancée stood in his living room dressed in his clothes with messy hair while he showered—jeez, that sounded way worse when I laid it out like that in my head—it was the jolt I needed to remind me we would never move forward until he dealt with the hangovers from his past. Rosalyn in his life. Keeping secrets from his parents. Standing up to all of them.

Yesterday! He'd told me only yesterday that he'd protect my heart, that I wouldn't regret opening up to him. Yet here I was, already with a lump in my throat, blindsided.

Five years later. Same shit, different day.

I went back to my donation piles.

I needed to finish sorting out what would be coming home with me.

Chapter Twenty-Six

Will

"Why are you wearing my clothes?" I came out of the shower to find Roz sitting on my couch, scrolling through something on her phone.

Her eyes narrowed. "You may have caught most of the spill, but that doesn't mean the spots on my dress were going to wash themselves out. I found these in the drawer in your room. I'll have them cleaned and sent back to you later this week." She gestured to where her soaked dress hung over a barstool. "I rubbed out most of the stains in the sink, but you need to have club soda around the house for stuff like this."

My hackles rose at the way Rosalyn thought she could still boss me around. And dig in my dresser drawers, apparently. "I'll keep it in mind."

"Are you going to call now?"

"Actually, Roz, I've been thinking about it, and I don't think I should call Wicklein for you."

"The fuck! Why not?"

"Because it's not right that I keep jumping in with you, or with Wallingford. I want to make a clean break from the company. I need to."

She made a derisive noise. "You're never going to break completely, William. That's ridiculous. It's your parents' company."

"I realize that. But I shouldn't be having contact with clients. I can draw that line. You should call Wicklein. I'm sure you can use all your charm to keep him in your portfolio yourself."

"My charm?" She raised an eyebrow.

"Fine then. Your business acumen." I sat down across from her. "At the end of the day, if he won't accept you as his rep, I can't keep coming in to make him stay. No matter how lucrative his account is. If he's going to be this way, eventually you're going to have to say, 'fuck him.'"

"Easy for you to say. You don't have skin in the game anymore. Not really."

"Trust me. It hasn't been easy to break away from the company."

She snorted. "Trust you? Yeah, I'll get right on that."

I hoped Rosalyn grasped my underlying point—that I didn't want a reason for us to be in each other's lives anymore. We weren't enemies, but we also weren't friends. I wouldn't mind getting to a place where we waved at parties or made small talk at fundraising events. But I didn't want to create intentional opportunities for contact. I was serious about getting things right with Maureen. And that meant eliminating complications that might give her a reason not to be with me.

I couldn't undo the past, but I'd committed to taking the reins of my life fully in hand, making choices that best served my own goals.

First up, setting firmer boundaries with my ex.

Rosalyn had knocked on my door unexpectedly this morning, carrying a tray with two coffees. Her excuse was to make sure I followed through on my promise to call Wicklein today. She sniffed at the size of my apartment and gave me stink-eye about wearing pajamas so close to noon. When I'd asked her to please call or text before showing up, she lost her shit, calling me an asshole and slamming the drinks down on the counter. One of them fell out of the tray and spilled twenty ounces of molten brown lava into my lap. The other bounced twice before tipping sideways, spraying her dress and somehow launching a stream of coffee into her tightly coiled hair.

"Jesus Christ!" I'd screamed and jumped up, the hot liquid perilously close to my package. Racing to my bathroom, I shed my soaked pants and henley, getting into the shower to spray my lower half with cool water and soap off the sticky mess.

I came out to discover Roz had pilfered clothes from my room. She'd also taken her hair down and run water through the section doused by her latte.

And now, she was back to telling me off because I didn't want to call Wicklein for her.

"You know, you're being a real dick, William. You could just do this for me."

"I could, but I'm not going to. I'm happy to go over any of the notes I left you on his account, though, if you want to talk strategy. But that's a onetime offer."

"Oh, gee, fuck you very much for your fucking scraps of help." She stood. "You can save it. Thanks for nothing."

"Rosalyn, for what it's worth, I'm sorry my decision makes you angry. I promise I'm not doing it to piss you off."

She scoffed. "Could have fooled me." Her eyes darted around and landed on the plastic Christmas tree in the corner. "I guess you're really doing this, huh? This is you? Mr. Roper. Handling your tenants. Fixing squeaky floorboards. Wasting your MBA."

I sighed. "I'm sorry again, Roz. It doesn't need to be ugly."

She continued like she hadn't heard me. "When you were in the shower, one of them came by, and I thought, 'This is William's life now—sorry, *Will*—He's gone from managing millions of dollars to being on call when someone's toilet needs plunging.'" She shook her head.

"If you knew me before my accident, you might understand better." I stretched out my scarred fingers exaggeratedly, anticipating her averted gaze. She didn't disappoint me.

"Well, if anything, I believe I've come around to your way of thinking," she said, crooking one hand against her hip. "It's a good thing we didn't get married."

I hmphed. Then my brain caught up to what she'd said. "Did you say someone came by earlier when I was in the shower? A clogged toilet?"

"Yeah. Not specifically about the toilet. She said she'd catch you later. Didn't want to leave a message."

A low pit formed in my stomach. "What did she look like?"

Rosalyn frowned. "Good-looking. About our age. Reddish hair, but the roots were growing out."

Shit! "Rosalyn, you need to leave right now."

"What?"

"Landlord tenant emergency."

She sputtered as I grabbed her wet dress and shoved it in her hands, along with her purse, pushing her gently but firmly toward the door. "Goodbye, Roz. I'm confident you can figure it out with Wicklein."

"Thanks for nothing, William." Exhaling, she gathered her things with dignity and walked into the hall. Turning around, she shot me an appraising look that morphed into an expression of grudging respect. "When did you get a backbone?"

"The minute I realized what not having one would cost me."

I raced down the hall to Bren and Chase's apartment, knocking sharply.

Maureen opened the door, stepping back to invite me in. "I figured you'd show up soon enough."

If I'd had any doubt she recognized the woman in my apartment as the woman she'd met five years ago, the look on her face quickly resolved it.

"That wasn't what it looked like," I rushed out. "Rosalyn came by with no warning, then she spilled scalding coffee in my lap, and since I wanted to keep my testicles intact, I had to jump in the shower."

Maureen shut the door behind me with a soft click. "Let me guess—while you were in the shower rinsing off, she helped herself to spare clothes from your room."

I huffed. "Yeah. I told her it was an overstep, but she's a bit of a bulldozer. She came by to try to get me to do something for the business—for Wallingford—and got pissed when I told her no."

Maureen appeared thoughtful. "I figured it was something like that."

"You did?"

"I'm not dense, Will. We were halfway to your bedroom last night. I know you didn't suddenly decide to chuck it all to invite your ex-fiancée over for a quickie."

I let out a relieved breath. "God. I panicked for a moment that this would be history repeating itself, you finding me with Rosalyn—even though this time it was completely innocent—and I'd have to go five more years without kissing you."

I stepped forward to touch her face, but she backed away.

"The thing is, Will. It's still history repeating itself, isn't it?"

"What?" I dropped my hand.

"It's still this person lurking in the background of your life, ready to spring up at any time to get between us... For Christ's sake, Will. We haven't been home twenty-four hours and she's *showing up at your door? Digging through your clothes?* Sure, it's not as bad as you lying to me, or me going to the hospital with alcohol poisoning, but the pattern hasn't changed." She folded her arms across her chest. "You're just not ready to break away from other people's expectations. Or set real boundaries."

"That's not true, Mau—" I began, but she put up her hand.

"Will, I don't want to make it sound like I'm judging you. I'm just saying, I've finally reached a good place in my life where I've figured out who I am and what I want my future to look like. It took me a long time to let go of what I thought I wanted, of what I was doing for myself versus what other people expected." She dropped her arms, and her voice grew soft. "It's okay if you're not there yet."

I scrubbed a hand across my jaw, exhaling deeply. "I am there, Maureen."

She shook her head. "No. I think it's reasonable that when I'm interested in a guy, there is a zero percent chance his ex-girlfriend is going to be in his apartment—wearing his clothes—opening the door when I come over. I'm not afraid to admit that I want you, Will. You. And I get that everyone comes with baggage, but you need to deal with yours before you ask me to deal with it, too. You say that I'm important to you, that you want to be with me—"

"I do!"

"Really? Then how come you never told anyone about me?"

"That's not fair, Maureen. I didn't know the last week was going to happen. I didn't know we'd have a chance to be together."

"You didn't fight for me five years ago."

"And it's the biggest regret of my life! But I couldn't. My head was still so messed up."

"I understand that. But what you don't seem to realize is… You still can't. It's more important to you to avoid confronting your ex, or your parents for that matter, than it is to make sure I feel secure. It's only been days since I've forgiven you. And that makes this *thing* between us"—she moved her finger back and forth between our chests—"very fragile. But you don't seem too concerned with protecting it."

She looked at me, and I saw she believed it. That she wasn't a priority in my life. I needed to make her understand I would burn it all down, everything I had, just to take this chance with her.

I stepped closer, and this time, she didn't back away. "You're wrong, Maureen. What you said about Rosalyn, about my parents, might have been true a few weeks ago, but it's not true now. And I'm not going to let you push me away over a misunderstanding."

"I'm not pushing you away. I'm just being hon—"

"You are. You're pushing so hard it's practically a bench press. I know you're scared. You saw Rosalyn in my apartment, and it took you right back to that hotel lobby. And you're trying to make it mean something it doesn't."

"I'm not." Her voice sounded small. I prayed that meant she was considering my words.

Leaning closer, I snaked an arm around her waist. "I'm sorry seeing Rosalyn upset you. But you already knew it wasn't what it looked like. Your heart already knew. And I told her it could never happen again, that I wouldn't be helping her with Wallingford and she couldn't show up at my door anymore." I reached up to run my fingers through her hair. "You're my priority, Maureen. And I'm sorry I didn't give you that five years ago. That I didn't have it in me back then to tell everyone to fuck off so I could be with the most amazing girl I'd ever met. I'm sorry I'm half a decade late in putting you first, but that's exactly what I'm doing."

I moved my hand back down her neck and pressed in until our noses were just inches apart. "Whatever you need me to do, I'll do it. I'll tell Rosalyn I'll never see her again. I'll call my parents right now and tell them about the concussion. Even if it sends them into a tailspin about my *choices*, I'll do it because I'm ready to do whatever it takes to be with you. You're wrong that I'm not ready. I'm so ready to be with you. I want it more than I've ever wanted anything."

She leaned against the arms I'd enveloped her with, pressing her palms to my chest. A slow gulp worked its way down her throat.

We stood surrounded by the heavy silence left in the wake of my words. A million different emotions seemed to invade her features at once, and I could only guess at the thoughts in her head.

I knew Maureen was scared. She had every right to be.

But eventually, the fear in her eyes changed to something else. Something hot and determined. Her posture eased. She slid her hands up over my shoulders and twined them behind my neck, placing a soft, exploratory kiss on my lips.

After a moment that lasted a decade, she whispered, "I believe you."

I released a strangled breath. "Thank god."

Her thumbs electrified the sensitive skin of my neck. She trailed her lips from my mouth to my jaw, making me shudder. "Will?"

"Mmm...?"

"Show me how much you want me."

I froze briefly in her arms before tilting my head back to meet her eyes. "Now?"

"Now."

Chapter Twenty-Seven

Maureen

I believed him.

That was the crazy part. After everything he'd put me through, every false start and years of misunderstandings, I believed him.

There was no preamble. Will grabbed my hand and tugged me out of Bren's living room, leading me wordlessly down the hall to his apartment and straight to his bedroom door.

"You're sure?" he asked.

I nodded, stepping over the threshold.

A bed frame, dresser, and nightstand in matching maple wood took up most of the space in the modest room, books and art supplies mingling haphazardly on the flat surfaces. Familiar gold pillows rested on top of an olive-green bedspread. On the floor, a small plastic tree with multicolored lights sat proudly, a twin to the one in the living room. Dark blue curtains blocked the cloudy sun from outside—the tree's twinkling lights provided most of the illumination.

Somehow, the humbleness of the room elevated the hugeness of the moment.

Will pulled me to him as we stood next to his bed. "We can take it slow. Like I said, whatever you need." He placed a steadying kiss on the apple of my cheek. "We've waited a long time for—"

"For us," I finished his thought.

"Exactly."

"You're positive your head's okay?" I asked, brushing my knuckles along his crown.

"I mean, my big one is. The little one could use some attention." He pumped his eyebrows.

I cracked up. "That was bad."

"Maybe so, but it's true." Levity turned quickly to urgency as he wrapped his fingers around my wrist and moved my hand to the bulge in his sweats. Through the material, I felt the heat of him stir beneath me. He closed his eyes and exhaled, sucking in his bottom lip.

The press of my hand grew firmer. More assured. I rubbed over the soft cotton before trailing my fingers up to pull at his waistband. As our lips met in a fiery kiss, I pushed his pants down over the erection straining his underwear. Keeping us melded together, he helped me tug down his bottoms before kicking them away. His small black boxer briefs did nothing to hide his excitement.

We detached for a moment so he could pull his shirt over his head, and I did the same with my sweater, standing before him in jeans and a lacy black bra.

He reached out to run his fingers reverently down my arm before leaning in to kiss me again.

His tongue delved into my mouth, bold and searching, and I welcomed it like a starving person. The way he made me feel in his arms was everything. Like he couldn't get enough. As his demanding tongue tangled with mine, his fingertips grazed the top of my jeans. He released the button with a pop before pinching the zipper between his thumb and pointer finger, lowering it slowly.

Within moments, he'd removed the rest of my clothes and his own. All the while, we never stopped kissing. Will's kiss was an intoxicating contradiction—tender and, at the same time, relentless. His obvious need drove each press of his lips, every swipe of his tongue. It consumed me wholly.

We stood. Our bodies slotted together perfectly. He ground his erection against my center. Even though Will wasn't a tall man, he had a decent-sized cock, thick and dark pink, and my instinct at seeing it slap back against his stomach was to lower to my knees in front of him.

He sensed my movement and reached out to stop me, grasping me lightly by the elbows. "I'm already close, and I...I'd like to be inside you. If you're okay with that."

I nodded, rising, relishing the erotic intensity of being eye level with him as he stared hungrily at me.

"*Oomph.*" Without warning, Will showed surprising strength as he picked me up in a bridal carry and placed me gently on the mattress.

Nestling my head on one of the soft gold pillows, I reached for him.

But he didn't lay down.

My arm dropped as Will remained standing at the foot of the bed. He stared at me.

I'd thought his kiss all-consuming, but it paled compared to the feral, worshipful glint in his eyes as he raked his gaze over my naked body. Anticipation churned in my stomach.

Finally, he placed a knee on the edge of the mattress.

The bed dipped as he crawled upward like a stalking tiger, pale skin glowing in the dim room.

He pressed his mouth to my ankle. He kissed each of my calves and the backs of my knees, running his soft lips against the responsive skin there. I shivered as he worked his way up my thighs, kissing almost to my center—but not quite.

He continued up my body, languidly, hovering on all fours, straddling my hips as he leaned in to ghost his lips along my stomach. Propped on my elbows, I watched him move up my torso. The tree lights cast circles across my chest. Will kissed the colored dots one by one while keeping his eyes locked with mine.

He reached my breasts and sucked one into his mouth. I cried out.

"Wow. Sorry. It just...feels good."

His grin turned wicked. "Maureen, I'm the landlord here, so you can go ahead and be as noisy as you want. I won't be issuing any warnings." He took the other breast into his mouth, sucking hard as I arched up and flung my head back against the pillows, using both hands to dig into his hair and hold him to me.

I moaned as I felt the first brush of his fingers at my center.

It was his right hand, and I knew it was a big deal for him to be touching me so intimately with it.

His middle finger breached me, filling me on the inside while his thumb and index fingers circled my clit. My orgasm came suddenly—forcefully—and when it happened, I grabbed his wrist to press his hand firmly against me, both of us uncaring of his scars as I ground out the last of my pleasure against his palm.

He leaned down to kiss me softly.

As I recovered, sated but aching to feel him inside me, he reached across my body to grab a condom from the nightstand. He held it up. "Still okay?"

I nodded eagerly. "C'mere."

Once sheathed, he wasted no time entering my wet and willing body. The sensation of him sliding home electrified my veins like a completed circuit. My hammering pulse beat out my thoughts. *Now. Finally. At last.*

Will rocked his hips, his intense gaze demanding my own. He reached between us to circle my clit again. It took a few minutes, and I could tell he held himself back with some difficulty, but eventually, I got there, coming hard as I shuddered and bucked against him. A second later, he groaned, and I felt the warm tide of his release as he filled the condom.

"Goddamn," he said, rolling to the side. He deftly took off the condom and tied it up, tossing it into a small garbage can. "That was amazing."

Laying my head on his chest, I reached for his hand and joined our fingers together, rubbing my thumb across his scars.

"I almost don't want to ask because I don't want you to stop," Will whispered. "But why do you do that? Touch my messed-up hand so much?"

"Because I can tell you need it."

His reply was a drawn-out exhale.

We lay there a while, not daring to break the moment. Eventually, Will got up to wet a washcloth with warm water. He pressed it between my legs. I'd never allowed a lover to perform this intimate task, but he seemed to revel in every chance to touch me.

"I'm fine if you want to stay in my bed all day," he said with a grin. "In fact, you're welcome to crash here until you find a new place if you want."

"Bren might have some objections to that." I smiled back at him. Not to mention, I wouldn't be finding a new place. I'd be returning to Coleman Creek in less than two weeks. I promised myself I'd tell him later that day. Sometime when we weren't naked.

"Maybe you can talk to her. I can be a good boy and share."

"We'll see."

Will stood, tossing the washcloth into a laundry basket in the closet. "But if you're cool with getting up, I actually have something I'd like to do with you."

"Something more interesting than whatever we can get up to in this bed?"

He barked a laugh. "Not gonna lie. I could probably live in this bed with you for the next week if you'd let me. But I want to show you something before we go under the covers without coming up for air."

"What is it?"

"A surprise. Something Christmas-y."

"More Christmas-y than baking ten dozen gingerbread men?"

"Even better." His intense expression belied his light words.

"Um, okay. Why did your face just get all serious?"

He pulled on a fresh pair of boxer briefs. "Because. You told me less than two hours ago you didn't think I was truly ready to be with you. I know we talked through it, but I think I have another way to reassure you."

"Other than doling out mind-blowing orgasms?"

He chuckled. "Let's say it's complementary to that."

"Alright," I agreed, curious. "Let's do something Christmas-y."

An hour later, Will turned his car into an industrial neighborhood south of downtown. Warehouses and nondescript office buildings made up most of the area, lifeless other than a few lonely strands of holiday lights. He pulled up next to a three-story concrete building with steel letters in front that read "Custodial Solutions." I wondered what any of this had to do with Christmas, or Will for that matter, as he came around to open my door.

"It's over here," he said, pointing at a wall next to the neighboring parking lot.

Dried brown grass crunched beneath our shoes as we walked in that direction. Graffiti and square blocks of gray paint covered most of the wall's surface, although there were several worn attempts at actual art.

Will gestured to an extremely faded section. "Can you make out what this one is?" he asked.

I studied the piece he'd indicated. A few chunks of concrete had chipped off along the top, yet it remained relatively intact, the tags nearby touching but not overlapping or distorting it.

"I guess it looks like the Grinch," I said, hovering my hand above my brow to block out the wintery sunlight. "Or, actually, three Grinches. Making some, um, interesting hand gestures."

"It's mine," Will spoke matter-of-factly. "I was working on this the night of my accident."

He took out his phone and held it up. "I come every December and take a picture. I'm always a little shocked it's still here and that no one has painted over it." He gave a self-deprecating little chortle. "Maybe next year my luck will run out."

"I don't think it's too much of a mystery," I said, inspecting the wall. "This is a work of art, done by an obviously talented artist. Sometimes people just respect that. Like they would if it was a commissioned work."

He huffed playfully. "Can you imagine the city commissioning a painting of the Grinch flipping the bird?"

"You never know." I smiled. "And the ending piece is—that's 'I love you,' right? In sign language? Maybe it would be cool because you ended it on a hopeful note. Like, at first the Grinch is being a dick, but then he ends it with 'I love you.' And that's kind of what Christmas is about, isn't it? His story. Being inspired by the season to be the best version of yourself." I gestured to the final Grinch, less faded than the other two.

A strangled noise came from him. He looked as though he'd been struck.

"Will? Are you okay?"

"I'm good," he rasped out, shaking away his expression. "It's just... I'm always amazed at how thoroughly you get me. I guess I should stop being surprised by it at this point."

I grinned again. "You're saying I correctly interpreted your artistic intention?"

"Nail on the head."

I pointed at the phone he still held. "Why do you take the picture?"

He paused, tracing the first Grinch with two fingers. "Because I don't want to forget. It reminds me—even though that Christmas eleven years ago was total shit, I made it through, just like this painting."

I nodded in understanding. "In some ways, it's like we can track the stages of our lives by how we remember the holidays. And by the objects that remind us."

"This mural is always the Christmas I had my accident."

"It's the Christmas you *survived* your accident," I countered. "And I'm sure other things make you think of the good Christmases, too."

Will chuckled. "Sure. When I was six, I got this massive Ninja Turtle setup I totally wasn't expecting. My parents aren't much for pranks, but they had me believing I'd only be getting books that year. It's still in a box at their house."

"Marley is Christmas-crazy, so she puts up mountains of decorations and photos. They help me remember the good stuff—presents, matching pajamas, baking, letters to Santa, going to all the Coleman Creek events. Still, there's no getting away from thinking about the Christmas after my dad died or the first year my mom was too sick to come out of her bedroom and look at the tree."

Will exhaled quietly, eyeing the faded wall. "But even those Christmases that were a little sad, you wouldn't want to forget them, would you?"

"No."

The pieces started clicking together in my head.

"Will, why did you bring me here?"

He stuffed his fists in his pockets, staring at the Grinches. "Because five Christmases ago you got under my skin in ways I didn't fully comprehend. Every time I drove by Musicbox or ate at a Denny's or heard that Waitresses' song, I remembered. And it was painful, but I wouldn't have changed having those memories wash over me for anything."

His words lingered in the chill air, brushing through the last edges of my doubts.

Gathering myself, I reached a hand to his shoulder. "I feel the same way," I admitted. "Even when I hated you, I never wished I hadn't met you."

"And then last Christmas happened."

"When James made a fool of himself onstage in front of all our friends and neighbors?" I grinned.

He reached a hand up to place it over mine. "Last Christmas wasn't just James singing to declare his love for Marley. That's their story. To me, last year will always be the time I got to see you again, when I allowed myself to hope there might be another chance for us to be in each other's lives." His voice caught before he continued, "Second chances aren't always guaranteed."

I nodded, understanding that he thought about his friend Riley. "I know."

Will exhaled, smiling slightly. "I realize now we're not defined by our most painful memories, or our worst choices. We're not the sum of everything that's *wrong* with us." Using my belt loops, he pulled me into his arms. "Which brings us to this Christmas."

"This Christmas?" I leaned into his touch.

Hugging me tightly, Will pressed his cheek to mine as he spoke into my ear. "This is the Christmas you found out how much I love you." He bit the lobe gently.

"Will—" I breathed out huskily.

"I mean it, Maureen. I'm so in love with you. And I didn't want to wait another second to tell you, to risk having one more day where you didn't know how thoroughly you hold my heart." He placed a soft kiss on my lips. "This is our comeback, Maureen. The Christmas we claim our happiness, where we decide not to let it become another faded memory."

"Oh, Will." I wasn't ready to say it back—even though I felt it to the marrow of my bones—but the words felt inadequate in that moment. Instead, I crushed my mouth to his, putting all my pent-up fears and worries into it, knowing we could share those burdens.

Pulling back, he gazed at me and ran a thumb tenderly along my cheekbone. "You know what else I'll remember about this Christmas?" he asked.

"What?"

"It's the best one I've ever had."

Chapter Twenty-Eight

Will

Maureen and I held hands over the console and took the scenic route back to my apartment, singing along with the carols coming through the Audi's speakers. We grabbed hot chocolates from a coffee shop and checked out a few neighborhood light displays. Even though it was only late afternoon, the sky was already dark enough to see them.

Eventually, I pulled up to the automatic door for my building's underground garage. I heaved a giant sigh when I noticed a very unwelcome sight near the curb.

"Shit," I muttered.

"What's the matter?"

"That SUV over there is my father's."

"Oh."

After I swung my car into its designated space and killed the engine, I pulled my phone out of my back pocket to find I'd missed some texts from my parents. There were also a few unanswered calls. My parents weren't the type to harass me with texts every day. Sure, they worried and judged my choices, but they were also very busy people themselves. And since I didn't work for them anymore, it wasn't unusual to go weeks without seeing each other in person. I'd been able to conceal spending the last nine days in Coleman Creek with a few well-timed messages to make it seem like everything in my life was business as usual, although my mom had mentioned in her reply yesterday that I'd been "acting a little strange."

But my parents also had zero chill when it came to being left on read. When they texted or called, they expected an immediate reply.

That had been evident in today's texts.

MOTHER: Sweetheart, I just tried calling. We'll be in your neighborhood in an hour to meet with a client. We're going to stop by and see you. To say hello.
MOTHER: Are you at home? You're not answering your buzzer but one of your tenants just came out and said he saw you in the building an hour ago.

I recalled one of the ground floor neighbors waving to me as Maureen and I came down the stairs earlier.

MOTHER: We are going to get a bite to eat at the coffeehouse near your place. We'll stop by again before we leave.
MOTHER: We haven't seen you since Thanksgiving.
FATHER: Son, you need to answer your mother's calls. You know how she gets when you don't reply.

I rolled my eyes. All the missed calls and texts had come within the span of an hour. Couldn't they assume I was busy or away from my phone? So accustomed to a quick response, they felt completely justified to freak out when I didn't get back to them right away. Maureen was correct. It was past time to establish real boundaries.

ME: I'm just getting home now. I was driving.

My phone rang immediately.

"Sweetheart, I was so worried."

"Mother, you're being ridiculous. It's not like it's been days since I've contacted you. There are going to be hours in my life when I'm not able to text."

"Yes, yes. It's just that we are so near to your little apartment building. It would be a shame not to stop by. You've been so distant this past week."

Maureen and I got out of the car as I held the phone to my ear.

"I can go to Bren's place," Maureen mouthed.

Putting the device to my chest to muffle the sound, I spoke in a hushed voice. "No. Please stay." Her brows came together as I clarified, "I would love to introduce you to my parents, if you're okay with it."

"William?" My mother's voice came through. "Are you there?"

"Sorry, Mother. I'm here. How about you guys come over when you finish eating?"

"That sounds wonderful, sweetheart. We'll see you in ten minutes."

After I hung up, Maureen and I walked in silence up the side stairs from the parking garage into the lobby. Once we reached the third-floor landing, I turned to her.

"You can go to Bren's if you want, but I'd really love for my parents to meet you."

Her lips lifted into a wry smile. "I appreciate the offer. But there's no way I'm meeting your parents when I have sex hair and my makeup isn't done."

"Sex hair?"

"It's a thing." She kissed me swiftly. "How about you let me know when they leave?"

"Can I take you out tonight?"

"I'd love that. I'll shower and get ready. Text me when the coast is clear."

"I'm going to tell them about the concussion and being in Coleman Creek this past week."

"Good." She pulled away and walked to Bren and Chase's doorway. "Who knows? They might surprise you."

I doubted that. They would be hurt because I hadn't called them immediately, which was fair. But I didn't know how to make them understand why I kept them at a distance, that they weren't rational with anything reminding them of my accident. It triggered them into seeing me as that sullen eighteen-year-old kid who couldn't be trusted to make his own decisions.

We'd made a lot of progress over the past few years, with them giving me more space. Except that had largely been because I'd hidden things from them. Now I saw that to continue moving forward, there needed to be truth between us.

I loved my parents. They loved me. But if we were going to have a mutually respectful relationship, they needed to see me.

Not go off the rails if I didn't answer a text within an hour.

A few minutes later, I opened my door to find my parents in their typical weekday attire of dark navy suits. I admired their equal partnership in both the business and their relationship. That might have been the reason they'd invested so thoroughly in my relationship with Rosalyn—they saw it as a mirror of their own, and they were happy.

"Son, it's good to see you." The concern in my father's deep voice belied his mundane words.

"Um, it's nice to see you, too, but I'm confused by the barrage of texts. What's with all the urgency just to stop by and say hello?" I took my mother's purse and set it on the kitchen island.

"What do you mean?" she asked. "Is there a reason you don't want us to visit you?"

Her voice held the same note of unease as my father's.

"No, of course not. But you're acting like we don't live in the same city. Or that it's somehow unreasonable I would be away from my apartment. You didn't need to wait me out at the coffee place until I came home."

"But we're not in your neighborhood very often," my mother replied. "And today, we were, just by chance."

Her last words came out so stilted, I knew immediately they were untrue.

"Rosalyn," I stated flatly.

My father met my eyes as my parents sat down on the couch. "Yes, Rosalyn. She came storming into the office after lunch, very animated about how you refused to help with Wicklein."

My mother pursed her lips as she added, "I believe her exact words were, 'Your son is being a real dick.'"

I tried not to, but I couldn't hold back a small chuckle. It was difficult to imagine Rosalyn speaking like that to my parents. She must have been extremely upset to be anything less than deferential.

"You've been acting off for a while." My father remained stone-faced. "And now it seems it's affected Rosalyn. What the heck has gotten into you lately, son?"

I took a deep breath. "Look, it's exactly like I told you at Thanksgiving. And earlier in the year when I sold Yardhouse. And two years ago when I left Wallingford. And four years ago when I ended my engagement. I keep telling you, and you keep not hearing me. I'm going to make the choices I think are best for me. Not always the ones you want me to make."

"And one of your choices is to treat Rosalyn in such a way she comes unglued?" Mother asked.

I folded my arms, sitting down on the coffee table across from my parents. "Hurting Roz is not what I set out to do. She's upset because I said things she didn't want to hear. I told her I won't help with her accounts anymore. I needed to set firmer boundaries. She keeps acting like she's entitled to my time, like I owe her something. But I don't. I'm sorry our relationship ended sourly. I'll always be sorry for that. But she needs to let it go."

"Son, why can't you just help her on this one account? It's not like you to be so ungenerous."

"I disagree. It's not just about Wicklein's account, Father. Don't you see? It's confusing. I need to draw these lines. What we were doing before wasn't working."

My mother leaned back heavily against the cushions. "It seemed like it was working."

"Giving Roz my time and attention—I think subconsciously, it was my way of making it up to her for breaking off the engagement. But it hasn't done either of us any favors. It's just gotten us to where she feels free to call me or text me and hurl insults, like that's acceptable. Or this morning, when she showed up at my door without asking, and then got mad when I wouldn't do what she wanted. I don't even know how she got this address."

My mother's cheeks flushed, and I threw up my hands. "You gave it to her!?"

She ran her hands along her pantsuit. "It didn't seem like a big deal. I mean, she's your...your—"

"Nothing, Mother! She's my nothing. I've told you so many times. She's my ex-fiancée who also works for my parents. That's it."

My father held up his hands. "Okay, son. You need to relax. I won't deny we'd hoped you and Roz would find your way back to one another, but I see now that's not going to happen."

"Of course it's not going to happen! It's been years. This is exactly what I mean. You guys need to start listening!" My parents frowned at my raised voice. But before they could complain, I asked, "Is that what all this subterfuge was about? Did you really come here just to get me to change my mind about helping Rosalyn?"

My father sucked in a breath. "No. We told her we think it's a good idea for her to figure it out on her own. She's one of the smartest young women I've ever met. If Wicklein can't pull his head out of his ass long enough to see that, then he can take his business elsewhere. It'll sting, but I can't have him undercutting the woman who is the future of the company."

I nodded despite my upset. At the end of the day, my parents had their priorities straight. And I appreciated Rosalyn would always have a place at Wallingford.

"So, if you weren't trying to change my mind, why all the rush to come here? Waiting me out at the coffee shop?"

My mother folded her hands carefully in her lap. "Rosalyn made it sound like you might be in trouble. She said you were still in your pajamas close to noon."

I scoffed. "Pajamas in the morning is a cause for alarm? It's not like I have an office to go to."

My father coughed into his fist. "She also said your words were slightly slurred, and that you were walking strangely."

Interesting. Rosalyn hadn't mentioned anything when she'd been here, but it made sense she'd picked up on those things. The bruise on my hip ached after a long sleep, so I'd been limping a bit. And my speech was probably at about ninety-five percent of my usual fluency due to slight morning dizziness. Roz keying into that missing five percent would be very on-brand for her.

"What of it?" I shrugged. "She's pissed. That doesn't exactly make her a reliable witness."

My mother laid a cool palm on my arm. "William, you know how much we love you." She paused dramatically. "That's why we wanted to come here and speak with you directly."

"O-kay." I dragged out the word.

"We know it can be difficult when life sort of"—she waved her free hand in a circle—"gets away from you." My father gave her an encouraging nod. "And we realize self-medicating can seem like a very appealing option when things are a bit...chaotic."

Huh? A shock went through me as my brain caught up with my mother's words. I eyed her incredulously. She stared down, reluctant to meet my gaze.

Self-medicating.

Drugs.

They thought I was on drugs.

Holy shit.

I stood abruptly and balled my hands into fists, willing myself to stay calm, reminding myself that they loved me.

"Let me get this straight." I gritted out, releasing a long, audible breath. "I got mad at Rosalyn, and she said my words sounded strange, so therefore, I must be on drugs?"

My father's gaze narrowed. "Son, you must admit you've behaved out of character this past year. We didn't like it when you left Wallingford, but at least we could respect that you'd struck out on your own. But selling your business? Your condo? Buying this apartment complex? And we've noticed you've been dressing different lately—"

"Much less polished," Mother interjected.

My father continued, "When Rosalyn came into our office this morning and explained how you'd yelled at her and told her she wasn't welcome in your life anymore, it all fell into place."

I shook my head. "This can't be happening."

"We're here for you, William," my father went on as though I hadn't spoken. "And we'll help you with whatever you need. Rehab. Therapy. Anything."

My gut boiled. Part of me wanted to rage at my parents. But as they peered up at me earnestly from the couch, I couldn't hold on to my anger. Only my sadness.

They truly didn't know me at all.

"You're never going to stop seeing me as that kid who got into an accident, are you? The weird angsty teenager you didn't know what to do with. No matter how much I accomplish, it's never going to work, is it?"

"Son, we are proud of you. That's why we want you to know it's okay if you need to ask for our help—"

"No. *No.*" I threw up my hands. "You're only proud of the things I achieve on your terms. Your definition of success. I've been wasting so much time and energy when it was never going to happen. You're always going to be waiting for the other shoe to drop. That's why I'm focused on doing the things that make me happy now."

"Sweetheart, are you trying to tell us that drugs—marijuana or pills or whatever it is—make you happy?"

"Jesus Christ! No! I'm not on fucking drugs!"

My mother raised a hand to her chest as I glared at her. Both my parents looked skeptical, but I honestly didn't care. I couldn't control their perceptions, and if they were going to assume the worst, then I needed to stop trying to change their minds.

I exhaled forcefully and sat back down.

"The reason I was in my pajamas is because I've needed to sleep a lot lately."

"Sleep? Why? Are you ill?" My mother leaned forward to put a hand on my forehead, wincing when I jerked away from her touch.

"In a way," I began, pushing the coffee table back so there were a few more inches between us. "About a week ago, I got a concussion, not to mention some nasty bruising, and I've been recovering. I'm sure you recall naps are a big part of the process."

My mother shook her head rapidly, like a cartoon animal. "What? You got a concussion? How?"

"When I was in Coleman Creek last weekend. For James's engagement party. I slipped on some ice and hit my head, plus banged up my hip."

"And you're just telling us this now?" my father asked sharply.

"So you wouldn't worry. I got scans there, and I was in and out of the hospital in a day. I thought you might try to bring me back to Seattle or get really worked up."

"You're damn right we would have!" This time, he couldn't stop the explosion. "You're telling us you were in the hospital, and you didn't bother telling your mother and me? Of course we would want you to have the best care. You're our child!"

"I had great care in Coleman Creek—"

"There is no way you had the best care in that little town," my mother practically cried. "Did they even know about your accident? All the trauma you went through? Have you seen a specialist in Seattle since you got back?"

"For goodness' sakes, Mother, this is exactly what I was trying to avoid. The worst effects of the concussion only lasted a few days. And Seattle doesn't have the market on competent doctors. I'll check in with my regular MD this week. But I've had two scans and everything is fine. For the record, I was perfectly capable of giving the doctors there my medical history." I paused, resting my elbows on my knees. "It wasn't like eleven years ago."

She would not be easily placated. "And you're saying this happened last weekend? Who's been looking after you since then?"

"James and Marley, and their family. I stayed in Coleman Creek until yesterday. James's sister-in-law drove me back."

My mother dropped her head into her hands, and my father appeared equally stricken.

"Are you sure you're okay?" she whispered.

"I'm fine, Mother, I promise. But that's why Rosalyn noticed my words seemed off. And why I was limping."

"I can't believe you were in the hospital and didn't tell us."

I steepled my fingers beneath my chin. "Rosalyn told you my speech was off, and the first place your mind went was that I'm on drugs. That right there is why I didn't tell you."

They looked at one another in silent conversation. Finally, my father cleared his throat. "I'm sorry we assumed. I see now it was premature and presumptuous."

"You think?"

"And I know you want us to accept all these changes you're making." His knees bobbed beneath his hands. "Your mother and

I aren't as oblivious as you seem to believe. We realize Wallingford was never your dream."

I blanched at his unexpected admission. "Then why did you push it on me?"

He hesitated before replying. "We wanted to keep you safe."

I sat back on the table, gripping the edge. "And I'll be forever grateful for everything you did. But you need to stop over-correcting now. I'm good. I don't need you to protect me from myself. From every mistake I'm going to make."

His fingers dug into his legs, veins popping from the back of his hands. "I understand, son. But you need to realize, it's hard for us…to let go. And maybe we overdid it, but we don't want you to feel you can't tell us things."

I leaned back, looking him in the eye.

"Then we have some work to do," I replied carefully.

My father nodded resignedly. "It's…disconcerting…to imagine you're hiding things from us. We've only ever wanted what's best for you."

The expression on his face dissolved some of my anger.

"I know. But you need to let me decide what that is. Sometimes a parents' job is to sit on the sidelines, right?"

"We did that," my mother interjected, voice shaking. "When you were in high school. We knew those kids were being awful to you, and we pretended, watched from the edge, and worried and worried. And all that happened was we ended up next to your hospital bed praying."

I knew my parents also had scars from my accident. But for the first time, it didn't fill me with guilt. Watching my parents comfort one another, I discovered instead a sense of empathy.

My mother rose and began pacing behind the couch. "Did I ever tell you about Riley's funeral?"

I thought of all the things my parents had filled me in on that had happened after my accident, when I'd been in my coma, but I couldn't recall that story.

"No. I don't think so."

"Well, your father and I went to that poor boy's service. It seemed like the least we could do to pay our respects."

"That's surprising, honestly. I assumed you blamed him for my accident."

"A part of us did." My father took up the story. "But we also accepted the fact that you were officially an adult by then, and spending time with Riley had been your choice. And, of course, it would have been difficult to be upset with someone who died so tragically."

"The funeral was packed," my mother continued, sitting back down on the couch. "It sounded like Riley had minimal direction in life—" She glanced at me. "But it also seemed like he was a sweet kid. His parents were proud he'd finished high school and was working at that restaurant. Obviously devastated by his loss.

"When we arrived at the church, we told them who we were, and they had the compassion to ask how you were doing. They wished you well, and it was genuine. But all your father and I could think of was how easily we could have been the ones offering stories and memories. Afterward, I made you a firm promise I'd do better. Not just sit on the sidelines again. That you wouldn't end up like Riley."

"Oh, Mother," I shifted to sit next to her, hugging her slight frame to my side as my father squeezed her shoulders from the opposite end. "I'm okay. I can't promise I'll never make a mistake or have another slip on the ice, but I'm okay."

"Logically, I see that. I do." She gripped my hand. "And I want to work on doing better, giving you what you need... It's just hard."

I volleyed my gaze between my parents. "I'll do my best to keep that in mind. But I need you guys to step back a little. Even if it's hard. You don't always have to help me in order to love me. Sometimes, you can just be there, watching."

My father placed a hand on my shoulder. "I hear you, son. And I promise we'll try. I hope you can be patient with us."

"Yes, sweetheart," my mother agreed. "We can learn to be on the sidelines sometimes. Just don't kick us out of the game completely, okay?"

"Okay."

AFTER WE MADE A PLAN TO PICK UP our conversation in a few days—giving the heavy words a chance to settle—I said goodbye to my parents.

They'd get better, and I would too. It would take time to change our dynamic, but I felt optimistic it would happen. I couldn't wait to tell Maureen and texted her immediately after my parents left.

Her knock came a few minutes later. I opened the door and pulled her into my arms, breathing into her neck.

"I just had the most insane talk with my mother and father."

She kept her arms around my waist but leaned back. "By your tone, I'm assuming you mean that in a good way?"

"Uh-huh. It didn't start out very promising. They basically came over to yell at me for being mean to Rosalyn and then accused me of being on drugs."

Maureen blinked. "Um, what?"

"No. It's good. We opened some of our baggage, and in the end, it was cathartic. You were right I'd been putting it off too long."

"That's great, Will. I'm happy for you." She smiled and my insides flipped.

"And now I want to take you out to celebrate. Dinner? Anywhere you like."

"Thai food?"

"You got it."

She had showered and touched up her makeup, dressed in jeans and a silk top. With her heels on, she had about two inches on me, something I found incredibly appealing.

As I leaned in to capture her mouth, her eyes caught on the counter. "Will, whose purse is that?"

Suddenly, the door—which I stupidly hadn't closed all the way—swung open.

"Sorry, William. I left my purse. I'll just grab it, and then your father and I will be out of your ha—"

I froze.

Maureen's forehead dropped to my shoulder.

My mother stood in the doorway, gaping as my father came up behind her. "Oh," he said.

"Am I okay to introduce you?" I whispered to Maureen.

"Hard to see another option." I felt her nervous laughter against my jacket.

Though we'd spoken in hushed voices, I'd have given even odds my parents heard our conversation since they stood less than ten feet away. To their credit, they waited patiently for me to say something.

"Mother, Father, I have someone I'd like you to meet."

Maureen pulled away from my shoulder and turned around gamely with her hand outstretched. "Hello."

My mother gawked at her with a confused expression. Then her face broke into a grin, and she uttered the last word I expected. "Francesca?"

Chapter Twenty-Nine

Maureen

I smiled at the elegant woman in the impeccably tailored pantsuit who reached forward to take my hand.

From behind me, I heard the shock in Will's voice.

"Mother, you know Francesca?"

"Of course I know Francesca." She dropped her hand, but the enthusiasm on her face remained. "I love her videos, and especially how she isn't afraid to focus on fashion for women of a certain age."

I fidgeted, running my hands over my hair. "Thank you for the compliment. It's rare for me to run into a fan in the wild."

Will stepped forward. "Maureen, let me introduce you to my parents, Iris and Andrew."

"Pleasure to meet you." I reached to shake Andrew's hand. He looked like a silver-haired version of his son, only with a straitlaced accountant aesthetic as opposed to Will's trendier vibe.

He gripped my palm and pumped his arm up and down a few times, but his expression remained blank. "We didn't realize William was...dating someone. He never mentioned anything."

"It's new." I bit my lip. Hopefully, this surprise didn't affect the progress Will made today with his parents.

"Ah," Iris hummed, leading her husband farther into the room.

"So, you two are seeing each other?" Andrew's question, directed at Will, came across as an accusation. "We're so far apart you hid *a girlfriend* from us?"

"Yes, we are dating. But I wasn't *hiding* it. I absolutely want you both to get to know my...girlfriend." Will smiled slyly at me. "Like Maureen said, it's just early days. And to be clear, this falls under the category of things you trust me on."

Andrew nodded at his son's response, his shoulders relaxing. Will wore a subtly triumphant expression, which I interpreted as: *Wow. I effectively communicated with my father.*

Iris clapped her hands together in front of her chest. "Well, of course we trust you when we see this lovely young woman in front of us. This is the best news I've heard all week. I can't believe you're dating Francesca."

"Remember—it's Maureen. Francesca is a stage name," Will said, wrapping an arm around my waist and pulling me to him.

"Maureen." His mom spoke airily. "That's pretty."

"Thank you. Francesca is my middle name, after my late father, Frank."

Andrew cleared his throat. "How did the two of you meet?"

"Maureen is James's future sister-in-law," Will said. "We've known each other for a while."

Not a lie, although nowhere near the whole truth. I knew without asking that Will's parents would never learn the full story of how I met their son. It was enough that Marley, James, Bren, and Chase knew. That would be the extent of the circle.

"You're Marley's sister?" Iris asked. "Was it you who took care of William last week, after his fall?"

"I helped. Along with my sister and James. I also drove Will's car back to the city to spare him the long drive."

"Oh, that's right. You're local. Francesca's videos are in Seattle."

"It sounds like this relationship is serious." Will's dad interjected, more in summation than as a question.

"We just made it offi—" I started.

"Very serious," Will asserted. "Newly official, like we said, but very, very serious."

"Well, Maureen—forgive me if I accidentally call you Francesca—I am happy to meet you, and to find out William is dating someone." Iris turned to her husband. "I don't know if you've ever seen any of those videos I've watched, but this young lady does some wonderful man-on-the-street type interviews."

Andrew looked at me. "I can't say I ever watch the YouTube like my wife does, but if she says you're good, then I know you are."

"Father, it's not 'the YouTube,' it's just YouTube."

As Andrew opened his mouth to reply, a sharp knock came at the door. Will answered, finding Bren.

"Hey, Will! Is Maureen here?"

Uh-oh. Bren had that excited puppy energy. Something was either very right or very wrong.

"Yeah. My parents are here too. What's up?"

Bren barreled into the living room, sparing a few quick hellos for Will's parents before thrusting her phone in my face.

"You hit a million views!"

"What!?" I pulled the phone out of her hands.

"Almost 1.1 million so far! It helps that Stone Caseman shared it first, but now other people are too. It's just one of those weird things that's going viral for the holidays. Like cats destroying ornaments or toddlers only being interested in the boxes. Not only that, but the video of your divorced friend is also getting a lot of hits. People like her attitude, and it doesn't hurt that she's a knockout."

I smiled, thinking about how Katy would have appreciated Bren's assessment.

I'd made a point to stay off my page all day. If comments were negative, or if the weirdos had come out to play, I didn't want to know about it while I was busy dealing with Will. I'd barely had time to process that he loved me. That I was his girlfriend. Now I was meeting his parents and my YouTube channel—which had been flying under the radar for years—was suddenly blowing up. Talk about a Christmas to remember.

"I watched that video this morning." Iris came forward and eyed the numbers on Bren's screen. "A lovely little slice of holiday Americana."

I pulled out my phone. There were hundreds of thousands of interactions with the video, and I'd received a flood of messages.

"Oh my goodness," I said, after reading through the first few dozen. "A lot of these are from people asking me to do styling sessions with them. There are even some from other countries."

"Makes sense," Bren reasoned. "If they looked at your other stuff on the channel after getting lured in by your small-town, *aw-shucks* schtick, they'd see how awesome and positive you are. Country in the city, but not a total hick."

I side-eyed my best friend. "Watch it."

Bren pinched her index finger and thumb together, leaving a half inch of space between them. "Just this much of a hick. Mostly cool."

I snorted. "Seriously. People are offering me money to look at their outfits and their closets."

"Of course they are," Will said proudly. "You're amazing."

I scrolled through more of the messages. But my initial enthusiasm faded as memories from Kolya's flooded me. The store had offered a styling service. Most of the clientele had been wealthy people who wanted help choosing designer labels and pricey vintage pieces.

Will's warm hand landed on my shoulder as he read my face. "I meant it when I said I'd help you with a business plan. You don't have to do anything you don't want to do. Or work with anyone you don't want to."

"Yes. Listen to William. Because if anyone knows about turning down lucrative business in favor of following the whims of one's heart, it's him." Andrew's tone was dry, but his eyes danced.

I'd worried that Will's parents might be too set in their ways to change. Obviously, the opposite was true. They were clearly trying to meet him on his level.

I surprised myself by realizing I wanted to get to know them better.

Everything between Will and me was moving fast, and while it felt good, I couldn't risk another misunderstanding. It was comically past time to tell him about my decision to move to Coleman Creek. I needed to get him alone.

"Hey, Bren, thanks so much for letting me know about the video, but Will and I actually had plans to go out tonight."

"Oh, sorry! I just got excited and wanted to tell you. I'm on my meal break anyway and need to get back to the bar."

"No worries." She headed toward the door.

Iris picked up her bag from the counter. "I've never been happier to have forgotten my purse." She slipped it over her shoulder and turned to me. "I'm so glad my son had you to help him this week." Eyes teary, she added, "I appreciate knowing someone else is in his corner. I didn't realize how much I needed that until today." She gave my arm a gentle squeeze.

"We'll get out of your hair so you can enjoy your night," Andrew said, briefly clasping Will on the back before the couple retreated into the hallway. "But we'd love to have you two for dinner soon."

"If Maureen's okay with it, I'd like that," Will responded.

"Definitely," I agreed.

After they left, Will shut the door and rested his forehead against it. "This has been a surreal day. In a good way."

I circled my arms around his waist, resting my chin between his shoulder blades. "It has."

"I'm feeling like I want to push my luck."

"Huh?"

Will shifted to face me before leading us both over to sit on the couch. "I have a present for you. I was saving it for when you went back to Coleman Creek for Christmas, but that was before I realized this would be the day we made love for the first time, the day I told you I loved you, the day I made strides with my parents, the day they met you, the day your vlog took off."

My mouth turned down. "But I don't have anything for you. I haven't had a chance yet."

He hmphed. "Maureen, nothing you could give me could top today and everything you've already given me."

Will reached into the small drawer built into the side table. He pulled out a rectangle wrapped in shiny green paper, about eight by ten inches, and handed it to me.

"I drew a picture of us," he said, pulling me onto his lap.

I ran my finger underneath the tape. As I unfolded the edges, I expected to find a portrait-style drawing.

Instead, as the frame revealed itself, I found a picture of our hands. Only our hands. His scarred palm held softly in mine. The background was a kaleidoscope of grays, but the hands themselves appeared bathed in light. Even in the two-dimensional rendering, the features were so detailed, I could envision my thumb moving along his skin, as it had done so many times in real life. The drawing perfectly captured the roughness of his knuckles, the small hairs there, along with my fingers and nude manicure.

"This is us?" I asked.

"This captures how I feel when I'm with you."

"It's beautiful."

"No one has ever made me feel as okay as you do. Five years ago, and especially now."

I kept my eyes on the glass in my hands. "I love it."

He sat up straighter and brushed my hair behind my neck, causing a shiver. "In high school, I drew a lot of my favorite characters from movies and books. It helped me escape the bullying, like a fantasy world I could retreat to. After my accident, I started drawing places from my childhood that meant something. I think that was my way of finding a bit of the old me in all the numbness. Last week, I felt inspired in a way I haven't in a long time. I drew everything around me—Bambi, Oscar, James grading papers, Marley laughing, the Christmas trees. You. Art has always been a sort of therapy for me, not just a creative outlet."

"I feel that way about Francesca."

"I've always been compelled to draw things that feel like home, that make me feel safe."

My breath hitched as I glanced down again at our hands in the frame. "Thank you," I whispered.

"Look at the way you hold my scarred hand, Maureen. Look at the way you make me want to bring it into the light."

He lifted his right hand and ran the three fingers across my cheek, underneath my jaw, resting the remains of his pinky and ring finger under my chin. I closed my eyes and leaned into the touch, tipping my cheek into his palm.

"Having you in my life is a gift," he said quietly. "I won't fuck it up again."

I flicked my eyes upward as he leaned in to press his mouth to mine. His lips were soft and reverent as they worked against mine unhurriedly. He didn't deepen the kiss. Instead, he pulled back, pressing his cheek against mine. He then added a kiss to the shell of my ear. "Merry Christmas."

It had been an incredible day. The most perfect one I could have ever imagined.

I just hoped I wasn't about to ruin it all.

Chapter Thirty

Will

Maureen met my gaze as I pulled back from our kiss. Her expression looked...concerned.

I blinked. "Everything okay?"

"I'm not going to stay in Seattle," she blurted, wiggling off my lap to sit beside me.

"What?"

"I'm moving back to Coleman Creek." She put another few inches of distance between us. "I've been thinking about it for a while, and now I'm sure I want to go back. I'll never regret my years in Seattle, but it's time. And this present is the best one I've ever gotten. It's the most beautiful picture anyone ever drew. I'm so blown away by everything you just said and by what you told me earlier at the Grinch mural. I couldn't go one more second without letting you know."

"Oh." I registered her words, waiting for some insurmountable shoe to drop. But she seemed finished. "Um, okay."

"Okay?"

I nodded. "Yeah. Okay. After everything you've told me, it makes sense. I think I was almost expecting it." I tapped my fingers against my knee. "The Audi gets excellent mileage, so it shouldn't be too difficult until we figure out a better solution."

Maureen leaned back against the armrest. "That's it?"

My brows drew together. "What's it?"

"I tell you I'm moving five hours away, and you act like I just told you the weather." Her expression devolved into a puzzled frown. "You don't think it's a big deal?"

"I mean, of course it's a big deal. It would be easier to date if you lived next door. But I totally understand why you want to move home. I've seen you in Coleman Creek, remember?"

She still appeared flummoxed, pinching the bridge of her nose. "The past few days I've been thinking this was some sort of enormous obstacle, stressing about telling you—"

Laughing lightly, I reassured her, "I meant what I said, Maureen. I'm all in. Five hours is nothing. Not when we've been through so much. Real distance, not just miles. There are options here, but whatever we decide, we're together. You're home to me now. Even if we have to be apart sometimes, we'll figure it out."

She shook her head as her cheeks finally ticked up. "I guess that's what works for us. Having things be a little difficult."

"It's never been easy, but it's always been worth it. You're worth it, Maureen. You're worth everything."

The lava-hot look she gave me in reply went straight to my insides. And my dick had apparently decided a few hours was plenty of recovery time. It perked right up as her warm palm traveled up my inner thigh. Her mouth moved to land on my neck, and I practically flew off the cushion as she latched on and sucked at the delicate skin. I doubted there'd be a mark the next day, but damn if it wasn't sexy as hell to feel the sensation in the moment.

Her tongue lashed out to soothe the spot before she kissed her way up my jaw and cheek.

When her mouth finally reached mine, she threw her leg over to straddle me. She kissed me deeply, confidently exploring my mouth.

"This feels...*familiar*," she rasped, and I grinned as I recalled being in a similar position on the couch in Coleman Creek.

"Except this time, I'm not under doctor's orders to take it easy."

"Good thing."

A minute later, she had me in only my boxer briefs, and she'd stripped down to her bra and panties, still with her knees on either side of mine. I reached out and ran a finger over her center, feeling her sleek heat.

"What do you want?" I asked.

She pulled her panties off and shook them down her leg. Then her thumbs dug into the waistband of my boxers before she tugged those off in one swift move. "Condom?"

I groaned at the delay as I pointed at our discarded clothing on the floor. "Jeans. Wallet."

She leaned back to grab my pants, handing them to me. I got frustrated trying to fish my wallet out of the side pocket, which had suddenly grown ten feet deep, as Maureen drove me wild, sliding back and forth over my erection. I looked down to see the head of it peeking up at me from between her thighs. Finally rescuing the foil packet from my jeans, I sheathed myself quickly.

I debated whether to pick Maureen up and plop her down on my cock, or if it would be better for her to take control and saddle herself. Maddeningly, she continued simply rocking herself on top of me.

"You asked me what I wanted," she whispered, looking like a goddess as she sat atop my thighs. This afternoon, I'd made love to her, slowly and deliberately. Now, Maureen had me at her mercy. She arched back, squeezing her breasts.

"Mmm." Raising my arm to snap her bra open, I leaned forward to take one perfect nipple into my mouth.

"I want..." She continued rolling her hips, killing me with the ache to be inside her.

"Yeah?" I panted, barely containing myself as my body begged to surge upward.

Bowing her head, she intoned directly in my ear, "I want it hard and fast."

Without giving me a second to digest her breathy plea, she raised herself and then pushed back down onto my erection, filling herself to the hilt while triggering in me a pleasure so intense the room spun.

She was spectacular. Looping her hands around my neck. Riding me with purpose. I gnashed my teeth as I struggled not to blow immediately.

"Pull my hair, Will. Make me come."

Instinctively, I reached one hand behind her head to grip her ponytail by its base, just enough for her to remember I was there. My other hand found her clit. I massaged the small nub rapidly as she moved above me in a circular motion, whimpering and moaning as she squeezed my cock. The look of ecstasy on her face took my breath away. My fingers continued working as I felt her inner muscles clench.

"I'm close," she panted, sandwiching her body against mine, pinning my hand between us. "I want you on top of me when I come."

She jerked us back onto the couch, her head on the armrest and me above. I removed my hand and pushed my groin against her—fast and hard, as she'd requested.

"Make me feel you, Will."

Feverishly, I pounded myself against her center until she came with a groan before I released into the condom.

The couch wasn't the most comfortable place for an encounter. It wasn't deep, so one of Maureen's legs hung over the edge, her foot flat on the floor. I brought myself to a standing position, quickly going into the bathroom to tie off the condom. When I came back, she was still lying there naked, recovering, and I thought again about how I would do anything for this woman. To see her like this. Often.

I grabbed her hand and helped her to her feet, walking with her back to my bedroom, where we both fell back on the mattress and drifted in and out of slumber for a few hours.

At eleven p.m., we were still in bed. I ran my fingers lazily between Maureen's breasts. They truly were a photo-perfect set, with small dusky nipples that peaked immediately at my touch.

"Too sensitive," Maureen said sleepily. "Always, after sex."

I pulled my hand back and brushed my fingers slowly down her sides, a move that made her tremble and sigh in pleasure. "I'll learn," I said. "I want to know everything about your body. All the little touches that drive you crazy."

"This is a good start." Her breath hitched as my hand slid down her side and over her naked thigh.

"Interested in another round?" I asked softly, running my tongue across her collarbone. At that, her stomach gave a rude and noisy rumble. We both cracked up as she threw a pillow over her face. "Or maybe I should feed you? We never did get that date."

"Great idea," she said. "And I know just the place."

Less than an hour later, we were seated in a booth at the same Denny's we'd gone to five years ago.

"I don't know if this will be a fresh start or if it will curse us again," I half joked.

"I have no idea what you're talking about. My memories of this place and you are fantastic. It's the five years in between that are mostly a miss."

I laughed. "Well, that's an understatement."

We ordered nachos, french fries, and a strawberry shake to share, along with coffees. "I think it sends a message to the universe to order the same thing we had that night," she said. "Tempting fate, or whatever."

"We're gonna make it this time, Maureen."

"I know. I'm glad it's now."

We spent the next hour talking about what our relationship might look like. I wasn't stuck on the idea of renovating apartment buildings or even staying in Seattle. And she wasn't opposed to spending significant time in the city, especially since I lived in the same building as Bren. Her plan was to rent a house in Coleman Creek until she could get her business off the ground.

"I've been thinking about the messages and comments I received. I like the idea of styling people, or at least helping them hone their wardrobes. But not rich people. Just, like, regular people."

"Like Katy?"

"Exactly. But I'm not counting on making a living at that. It won't be in high demand, and one viral video doesn't prove anything."

"So you see it as more of a side project?"

"Right. Same with Francesca. I want to keep doing the videos, but the chances of making real money off them are slim. I'm realistic about that." She leaned back into the booth, pensively taking a french fry into her mouth. "I would like you to help me with the business side of things."

My heart leaped at her casual words, but I forced my voice to stay neutral. "What kind of help?"

"I want to open a shop in Coleman Creek, part consignment, part reasonably-priced boutique. The thing I miss most about Kolya's is interacting with customers. And I know I'd enjoy it even more if the folks coming into the store were my friends and neighbors."

"So, your plan for your career is to do three jobs?" I raised my eyebrows, even as I smiled encouragingly.

"I'm a hard worker, Will. And I'm good at setting my mind to things. And I'm not too proud to do multiple jobs at once. I've done that before when I had to do it. To make ends meet. This time, it would be my choice."

"I'm teasing you. Of course you can make it work. And it's not like you don't have options if you need to adapt, if the styling takes off, or if you're able to monetize Francesca. Careers evolve, just like people. Normally, I wouldn't be sold on a retail venture, but what you're proposing might work in a town like Coleman Creek, and you probably have enough of a following with your videos now to lure some curiosity seekers to the store if you wanted your viewers to know about it."

Her face lit up with excitement. "That's exactly what I was thinking! If I let people know about the store on my channel, I might find some that want to come for in-person styling."

I pulled out my phone and began taking notes as she spoke enthusiastically about her ideas. Getting those thoughts into a more concise plan would take a few weeks, but the bones were there.

Plus, she had me. She'd always have me.

A few hours later, we stood by the side of my car in the Denny's parking lot. Just like five years ago. Except this time, there'd be no broken promises. I'd be holding her all night. I'd be waking up next to her tomorrow morning, and if she'd let me, I'd be going home with her for Christmas.

All that terrible history between us, but here we were, starting over. Choosing hope. Our relationship still held a minefield of obstacles. It was complicated and uncertain. Marked with healed-over scars from the past.

It doesn't look very nice, but it's okay.

"Hey, Will." Maureen joined our hands, bringing me out of my musing. "I never said it today. But just so there's no confusion. I love you too."

It doesn't look very nice, but it's perfect.

Epilogue

Maureen

Will squished himself next to me. Even though we were in the bedroom I'd grown up in, my old twin bed was long gone, replaced by a queen-sized model years ago. As much as I enjoyed waking up in my boyfriend's arms, he was shoving my face into the pillow.

"Will," I whisper-hissed. "There's plenty of room in this bed. We can cuddle without you suffocating me."

"Mmph," he mumbled.

I reached over to push him back, realizing he was penning me in because Oscar and Bambi pressed against his other side. The dogs had developed a deep attachment to Will when he'd done his recovery week in the house. They'd been at his side nonstop since we'd returned to town two days ago, on the twenty-third.

Heaving myself out of bed, I shooed the dogs into the hallway, closing the door behind them. I crawled back over to give Will a peck on the cheek. "Wake up, sleepyhead. It's Christmas."

"Uh-uh. Come back to bed." He flipped over with lightning speed to grab me and pull me on top of him.

I kissed him, grimacing at our shared morning breath, before tapping him on the forehead. "C'mon, bud." I knew exactly why he was moving at the speed of a tortoise on wet sand. "Time to do our good deed. This means a lot to Marley and James. Remember, I'm in this with you."

He made a half-hearted growly sound, which was about as intimidating as a kitten, forcing me to stifle a giggle.

"Fine," he relented, smiling.

Ten minutes later, teeth brushed, we strode into the living room in matching green holly leaf footie pajamas.

Marley squealed when she saw us. "Oh my god, you guys look even better than I imagined when I bought those. So cute!"

"Absolutely adorable," Miranda deadpanned from her seat on the couch, sipping coffee in her tan gingerbread men onesie. She lifted her mug at us in a mock salute.

I gave her the middle finger and Marley made a horrified gasp. "Maureen! Not on Christmas."

"Sorry," I murmured. *Not sorry.*

James came out of the kitchen laughing. "I bet I can guess what Maureen just did."

"All I did was give my sister a Merry Christmas gesture," I said, going over to kiss him on the cheek. "And a very Merry Christmas to you too, future brother-in-law."

"Thanks." James stood next to Marley in their matching candy cane pajamas. "Breakfast is ready."

By the time we'd sat down at the table, Leo had arrived along with his and James's parents, Deanna and Chris. The older couple had on blue snowflake footie pajamas, while Leo matched Miranda's gingerbread men.

As they walked in, I leaned over and said to Marley, "You're lucky everyone loves you so much."

"Shush. Don't be a Negative Nelly. Everyone looks awesome. The pictures will be amazing."

I had to admit, it was pretty cute to have eight grown-ass adults dressed like toddlers in celebration of the day.

"Hey!" Miranda said to Leo. "Cool. Ours are the same."

"I think Marley wanted even pairs," Leo said.

"That's right," Marley chimed in. "There were only four different patterns, and you guys are good friends, right? Good friends can be a pair."

"Of course!" Miranda answered brightly, but Leo had an odd look on his face.

Twenty minutes later, I found myself alone with Miranda while James and Marley showed everyone else some updates they'd made to the backyard.

"Did you and Leo have a fight?" I asked.

"Not a fight, exactly," she hedged. "There's just been something recently...that we've disagreed on."

The slider opened. Leo and James came back into the room, ending our conversation.

AFTER PRESENTS—I'D GIVEN WILL one of my father's watches, rendering him speechless—we all sat in the living room enjoying hot chocolate while Bambi and Oscar shredded the wrapping paper.

I told everyone about my career plans.

Will had helped me draft a business plan and found a local lawyer and freelance bookkeeper I could work with as needed.

The building that had burned next to The Landslide would be a perfect location to house my retail establishment. The owners were amenable to me renting the space, and the repairs they needed to make on the building allowed me to craft a timeline for getting everything in order for sourcing merchandise. I hoped to be open by summer.

James proudly told his parents the story of going out on his first volunteer fire call. "I like to think the guys and I saved the building just so Maureen could open her business there."

While I established the store, I planned to keep doing Francesca videos and some virtual styling sessions with folks who had reached out through my channel. I probably wouldn't start until around Valentine's Day, since Will needed to help me do a market analysis and figure out what to charge and how viable and competitive a low to mid-level styling service could be. Even though that piece could end up being a flop, just trying felt exhilarating.

My whole life, I'd been reluctant to have any kind of partner because I'd been worried about feeling beholden to someone or getting lost in their life and dreams. Who knew that—with the right person—the opposite was true? Having Will in my corner while I worked made me feel freer to take risks than I ever had.

"I need to tell my current gig employer that I'm out, though." I laughed. "Hopefully, they won't feel bad when I inform them that processing insurance claims isn't my dream."

Deanna patted my hand. "Once, we needed to replace the water heater, the furnace, and the garage door opener all in the same two-month span. I took a second job selling cemetery plots...on commission."

She shivered, and everyone took turns telling hilarious stories about their worst jobs. Even Will got in on the action, talking about busing tables at the restaurant he'd worked at before his accident.

"I once had a customer offer me three hundred dollars to dig through the trash and find her son's retainer that he'd left on his plate."

"Did you do it?" James asked.

"Sure did. Jumped right in there. When I got home, my parents said I smelled like I'd been dumpster diving. Little did they know how accurate they were."

"I've watched a few of your Francesca videos, dear," Deanna said to me, changing the subject. "They're quite lovely."

"Thank you."

"It's still wild how your video about Coleman Creek blew up," Marley said. Turning to her future father-in-law, she said, "Almost two million views."

"It's dying down now," I said. "Hopefully, I can keep people interested."

Since then, I had only posted one other Francesca video—of Mrs. Allen, my former teacher. I did some styling and discussed her many decades of teaching and her impressions of how the profession has changed over time. It hadn't reached the level of popularity of the Coleman Creek video, but it had gotten more views than my earlier clips.

"It's not so crazy the Christmas video blew up." Will brought the subject back. "Stone Caseman has a ton of followers, so once he got on board, there was nowhere to go but up."

"It's such a massive stroke of luck someone like Stone even noticed it, considering Maureen's channel has nothing to do with the usual type of content he provides," James agreed.

"It surely is a mystery how that happened," Leo muttered under his breath. No one else seemed to hear, but I glanced sideways at him. From the corner of my eye, I saw him peer at Miranda. "I guess we'll never know."

After a delicious Christmas dinner of ham and Deanna's famous tater tot casserole, James's family returned to their hotel, and the rest of us went to bed.

Will and I lay down on the blankets together after kicking out the dogs. He flicked on the twinkle lights wrapped around the bedposts and the little tree on the dresser.

"This is so good," he said, leaning back against the gold pillow he'd brought. "Being here with you."

I agreed but didn't say the words out loud. I would never be the type to say everything I was thinking, and Will knew that. Reaching across his chest, I twined our fingers over his heart, rubbing my thumb along his scars the way he liked.

"When are you driving back?" I asked. "Still tomorrow?"

"Yeah. Second Christmas with my parents."

"I kind of like that they insisted. That they're clearly trying."

"True. You still don't want to come with me?"

"I need to stay here and get started on my plans. And you should have this time with them."

"You're giving me a chance to prove I'll come back to you."

I smiled in the dark. "I know you'll be back in three weeks, or maybe four, or five, or six. And I know we'll talk in the meantime. I think we need to get past this first separation to show ourselves it will work."

"It's going to work, Maureen. I understand you need to be here right now. Just like I have some things that need attending to in Seattle. I'm going to get the other units rented and hire a property management company. Spend some time with my parents. Then I'll be back."

What he left unsaid was the obvious—he would eventually need to move to Coleman Creek if we were going to make a real go of things. I imagined he'd keep the Seattle apartment—it was his building, after all—and we'd visit there often. The scenario seemed workable, if unusual. But nothing between us had ever been easy.

Except for this moment, cuddled together on the bed. This was easy.

And the next day, when I kissed him goodbye, it was easier than I'd imagined it would be.

And the texts and video chats that came every day, sometimes several times a day, for the next five weeks, were actually fun.

And then just before Valentine's Day, when he showed up on the doorstep of the house I'd started renting the week before, with his gold pillow in one hand and flowers in the other, the easiest thing I'd ever done was open the door.

And let him in.

Acknowledgements

It became clear to me while writing the first Coleman Creek book that the general theme of the series would be the holidays as a time of healing, emotional stories where imperfect characters get their happy endings. Trying to be true to that ethos, while still writing a fun and cozy Christmas book, requires a lot of patience, and frankly, a lot of editing.

That's why I want to thank all the folks who provided support and encouragement through the editing process.

To my author friends and groups—thank you! The camaraderie is a lifesaver, and the laughs are priceless.

To B for the sensitivity reading. You're my hero. That's all.

To the Monday Nighters, Alexander, Alicia, Judy, Marc, and Veronica—those alpha reads and early critiques were gold. Your careful attention to the story's foundation and excellent advice made the roadmap so much easier.

To the GLA, Aviva, Chun, Erin, LeAnn, Madison and Woody—swooping in for that final beta read like superheroes wielding red pens and word choice options. Thanks for making the story even better, and for making sure characters didn't have more than two hands at a time.

To Jenny at Editing 4 Indies—I can't thank you enough for your work. (Even if I wanted to cry a little the first time I opened the document).

To Melissa and Stephanie at Alt 19 Creative for the beautiful cover. I know we picked a lot of nits to get to the finished product. Thank you!

To Adam, Eric and Sara, for being the best author cheerleaders, and for providing the cabal of sanity I need to make it from Monday to Friday.

To my readers and friends on Instagram—when I set out to be an author, I never realized how much those comments and DMs of support would come to mean. There's a lot of negativity out there, and being part of a dedicated and positive book community truly helps combat it.

Last but not least, to my two best guys. I still can't believe this is my life.

About the Author

Rory London is a writer of contemporary romance who lives in the delightfully gray Pacific Northwest. Rory would spend a lot more time writing if there weren't so many books to read. When not engaged in something book-related, Rory is likely drinking large quantities of coffee or diet soda, watching football, or using music and podcasts to make it through a gnarly commute.

Rory lives with two other humans who bring laughter, joy, and sarcastic commentary into each day, as well as the world's most lovable dog, and three cats who are secretly plotting their revenge.

Connect with Me:
Email: rorylondonauthor@gmail.com
Website: www.rorylondonauthor.com
Instagram: @rory_london_author
Facebook: Rory London, Author
Goodreads: Rory London
Bookbub: Rory London
Book Playlists: Rory London on Apple Music

Also by Rory London

Standalones
The Outline

Coleman Creek Christmas
Christmas Chemistry
Christmas Comeback
Christmas Crisis (Fall 2025)

Made in United States
Troutdale, OR
11/08/2024

24584229R00212